DARK EMPIRE

Shadow Squadron #2

By David Black

Dark Empire

© Copyright David Black 2012

ISBN: 13-978-1480176539
ISBN: 10-1480176532
Paperback Edition published by David Black Books 2012

This book is a work of fiction. Names, characters and incidents either are the product of the author's imagination or are used fictitiously. Any resemblance to actual persons living or dead or actual events are entirely coincidental.

All rights reserved, including the right to reproduce this book or portions thereof, in any form. No part of this text may be reproduced, transmitted, downloaded, decompiled, reverse engineered, or stored in or introduced into any information or retrieval system, in any form by any means, whether electronic or mechanical without the express written permission of the author. The scanning, uploading and distribution of this book via the Internet, or any other means is illegal and punishable by law. Please purchase only authorized electronic or paperback editions, and do not participate in or encourage electronic piracy of copyrighted materials.

Cover design: David Black Books

Dedication:

'To our nation's soldiers, who gladly place their
own lives in danger, so that we may be free.

* * * * * *

With grateful thanks to Trevor Hall for his kind
assistance in the proof-reading stage before publication

Other great books by David Black:

Eagles of the Damned
(Roman Legion Series #1)

The Great Satan
(Shadow Squadron #1)

Playing for England

Siege of Faith
Chronicles of Sir Richard Starkey #1

Inca Sun
Chronicles of Sir Richard Starkey #2

For more information on these and future books see:

http://www.davidblackbooks.com

February 26th – 2008.

* * Classified * *

From: GCHQ – Government Electronic Monitoring Station – Cheltenham.

Route to: MI6 Headquarters, Vauxhall – 4th floor, African Desk (Congo).

Level Five (Commercial) Encryption.
Encryption broken: 23rd February 2008
Message ref: CU:4563357ZA6
GCHQ Outward Transmission Priority: - Routine

* * * * *

'Intercepted commercial telex decrypt - extracted from a 55 page intelligence review/analysis, reporting Pan Global Corporation's possible involvement in geo-political events, with regard to national economic and mineral assets of the African Congo.

Message begins:

Eyes only - Sir Hugo Maxton
C.E.O. - Pan Global Corporation.

'...Since the Belgium Government relinquished its iron grip on their former African colony on 1st August 1964, the Congo has been constantly torn by savage inter-tribal fighting; particularly, between the Tutsi and Hutu. Long standing feuds and widespread tribal slaughter escalated quickly into bloody regional insurrection shortly after independence, eventually culminating into the first of two bitter civil wars. For more than thirty years, due to constant political turmoil, and in no small part due to the unending conflicts within its borders, there has been only minimal investment and training of the national police service and military forces. As a result, little or more often, no tangible law and order exists within vast tracts of its considerable land mass, as security forces remain weak, underfunded, ineffectual, and corrupt. The Government of the Congo fails on an almost daily basis to exert sufficient and/or cohesive political control over its citizens, within its huge land mass of over one million square miles, comprising a diverse topological mixture of equatorial jungle, swamps, volcanic mountain ranges and endless open savannah.'

* * * * *

'...With almost incalculable reserves of so far unexploited mineral wealth, the Congo is endowed with huge deposits of cadmium, coal, columbium, copper and tantalum, diamonds, germanium, gold,

lime, manganese, petroleum, silver, tin, tungsten, uranium, and zinc. The Congo should easily have surpassed even South Africa after independence, and become the most prosperous nation in Africa. It remains, however, one of the poorest, corrupt and underdeveloped countries within the continent... '

'...its fertile soil; which incidentally, if managed efficiently, could easily have the capacity to feed the entire African continent. Due to a lack of strategic agricultural planning, incompetence, a general lack of resources and ever-present corruption, the Congolese Government struggles, and often fails, to adequately feed its own population of approx. 55 million people.'

* * * * *

'...A huge majority of the Congo's population remains illiterate and highly superstitious, living in abject poverty and constant fear of witchcraft and black magic, where witch doctors dominate entire regions, and wield enormous power and influence within their tribal areas.'

Conclusion:

Since Independence, like so many other African nations, endemic corruption has flowed through every level of Congolese society. From the Presidential palace, corruption and graft percolate down to the lowliest and poorest paid bureaucrat and police officer.

We believe this to be a distinct advantage to Pan Global's future ambitions within the country's political and economic structure, as it offers a backdoor to impending exploitation and dominance, within the Congo's central governmental structure.

'...vast region of the Congo still remains Africa's greatest and darkest paradox. Although certainly a third-world country, given an injection of sufficient funds and military resources passed into the right hands, this department believes, Pan Global could achieve economic control in the future, albeit in the background, of this huge and largely untapped reservoir of rich mineral resources.'.

'...It is therefore this department's conclusion that while the Congo remains a highly dangerous, wild and virtually undeveloped economic backwater, it should be seriously considered as an unripened plum, waiting for the imposition of firm government, and the resulting ripening, picking and exploitation of its almost incalculably rich mineral wealth....

* * * * *

Signed Dr F. W. De Keizer:
Head of Economic Intelligence Department
Pan Global Corporation - 22nd February 2008

Chapter One

Congo: Northern Katinga Province

Present day

As if drawn by an invisible magnet, the sickly-sweet smell of death attracted patrolling vultures from miles away. Soaring high above the remains of the smoking village, they effortlessly circled on powerful updrafts through a blue and cloudless sky.

Gliding across the soundless heavens on broad black wings, the ugly carrion eaters wheeled and spiralled, arcing slowly across the heavens as they looked down with hungry eyes, waiting patiently for the living to depart; for the moment, when they could descend and make their ungainly landings. Soon enough, they would hop and squabble over the tastiest morsels, and then begin gorging on the rich bounty of the dead, who lay scattered and silent, far below.

But for now, flying under the blazing African sun, the vultures must be patient; they would remain circling the smoking glade of the dead, and wait for the living to depart.

A tall rebel gazed through the acrid smoke, which drifted in a haze across the smouldering clearing. Bald and heavy set, he was dressed in military-style khaki uniform. Gold stars on his epaulettes displayed the insignia of high rank; he was the General, who led the dreaded Congo Freedom Party. There was so much more to the man, however; when he regarded his reflection; he saw a man meant for greatness, whatever the cost in death and misery. It was the high price of destiny, which others must pay. In his reflection, something lurked dark and terrible in his eyes, that reinforced his absolute authority, over the sinister legion that followed him, and gladly did his bidding.

Tutsi tribal scars stood out, in stark relief on his sweat-stained cheeks, as his eyes swept the destruction around him. A cruel smile of satisfaction spread slowly across the coal-black jowls of his glistening face. Before him, lay concrete evidence of his power and purpose.

The general paused. He stood alone for a few seconds breathing deeply, savouring the wafting aroma emanating from the smoking Hutu settlement. The scent floated invisible across the clearing; to him, an exquisite bouquet of burnt flesh, blood and best of all, cold lingering fear. Filling his flaring nostrils, the cocktail enthralled him, setting his chest heaving, and the blood racing through his veins.

Around him, huts burnt fiercely; each enveloped in dancing flame, as they crackled with intense heat. Close to the general, the charred remains of a mud and wattle wall suddenly collapsed, falling heavily onto a bed of smouldering thatch with a crash and shower of dancing sparks. Glowing embers swirled upwards through the smoke in the hot afternoon air, then slowly spiralled to earth like smoking autumn leaves. Beyond the destruction, hidden in the surrounding jungle, a dog shivered and howled forlornly for its missing master.

The carnage his men brought to the defenceless village excited the general more than any of them could possibly imagine, or begin to comprehend. Lost in his contemplation, suddenly, with a rapturous shudder, he smiled. To the victor, he thought ecstatically; the spoils...

The remains of the Hutu villagers lay everywhere, sprawled haphazardly on the sun-baked ground, wherever they were mercilessly cut down. Many bodies were riddled with bullets; most died instantly. The less fortunate were savagely hacked to death with razor-sharp machetes, carried by many of his rag-tag army of Tutsi Mai-Mai guerrillas. They charged like a pack of rabid animals through the village; their black faces contorted, snarling in their drug crazed frenzy, as they howled and thirsted for Hutu blood.

Already, fat bloated flies crawled across the mutilated corpses, which reposed in widening pools of black congealing blood. Dripping from the slaughtered victims, it leeched slowly into the parched earth, drying quickly under the burning African sun. The intense heat was changing the sticky pools into tragic shadows of the extinguished lives, which lay scattered and silent across the remote Congo killing field.

With a satisfied nod, the Mai-Mai General cleared his nose with his fingers, then hawked and spat. As his dark eyes savoured the butchery around him, he reached slowly into his breast pocket and removed a pair of sunglasses. They would shade him from the sun's intense glare, but add yet more to his sinister bearing, in the fearful, downcast eyes of his feral guerrillas, who obeyed his every word, as if they were the word of God.

With an occasional and casual flick of his hand, the General talked with some of his men, who stood around him excitedly boasting and laughing to each other; smoking cigarettes and drinking looted beer. These men were General Ojukwu's captains and lieutenants. Some bore the cruel native brands of criminals. In their tribal lands, these men were outcasts, but now, as officers loyal only to their general; they enjoyed privilege and power beyond their wildest dreams.

General Ojukwu's officers had exercised one of their many privileges, which came with rank. They had already claimed their position at the head of the long queue of his militia, who stood excitedly vying for a position around four naked village women. The females lay spread-eagled on their backs, pegged down on the iron-hard Congo earth.

The wretched women had survived the initial massacre, but had been found hysterical and cowering in different parts of the village, as the guerrillas swept through the settlement for a second time, in search of booty and sport. The youngest woman saw her crying baby's brains dashed against a wall by the Generals laughing men. Each of the terrified females had pled and screamed as their clothes were brutally ripped away by the savage Mai-Mai. Now, none screamed any more. They lay helpless; stripped and naked upon the ground. With eyes unfocused and rolling, they moaned softly as each sweating, grunting guerrilla claimed his prize, and took his turn to brutally enter them.

There had been no warning before the Mai-Mai appeared from the green wall of the surrounding jungle. Moments before, the Hutu village had basked in peace and tranquillity; only the usual noises broke the silence, which made it sound and feel like Joshua M'pani's ancestral home. Between crude huts, chickens clucked reassuringly to each other, scratching and pecking hopefully at the dirt. Here and there, babies cried; dogs barked and children laughed happily, as they played football in the open centre of the village, beneath the cooling shade of the great fig tree.

Suddenly, the serenity was shattered, as a long ragged line of men appeared from two sides of the jungle. On a curt signal from their leader, they levelled their weapons and swept the village with a lethal barrage of rifle and automatic fire.

The noise was deafening, as the guns boomed their deadly message across the isolated hamlet. Terrified screams were abruptly cut short by the first wild volley, as bullets ripped into victims caught in the open. Everywhere, villagers scattered in blind terror. Men, women and children dashed screaming for cover, abruptly toppling like rag dolls; their blood erupting when the crossfire caught them. All around the village, high-velocity bullets cracked, kicking up red earth and dust as a second wave of men appeared from the jungle waving machetes; a few carried heavy axes; their blades glinting menacingly in the sun. With a sweep of his hand, their leader signalled them to advance. Howling with excitement, swinging blades through the air, they rushed past the gunmen towards the huts, and the surviving villagers.

Some guerrillas were little more than half naked; others were dressed in a shabby and uncoordinated mixture of dirty sweat-stained tee-shirts and ill-fitting shorts. As the second wave stormed the village, the grinning Tutsi gunmen reloaded their hot smoking weapons from ammunition bandoliers, they wore about their chests. One of them, wearing a torn and faded football shirt, cursed as he struggled to clear a jammed cartridge from his Russian-made assault-rifle.

Advancing slowly in a ragged line, the Tutsi gunmen continued to fire haphazardly at any chance target that broke cover. Overcome with terror, a few survivors desperately sought the sanctuary of the lush green jungle, which surrounded the village. Above the din, snarling gangs of men armed with heavy blades kicked in crude doors and searched each hut in turn. In a frenzy of blood, they hacked and slashed without mercy, whenever they discovered a cowering and terrified villager hiding inside.

Crippled and unable to run from his attackers, the oldest village elder's shoulders were gripped tightly. He was forced forward by two laughing Mai-Mai and decapitated by a third, as he knelt beneath the great fig tree. His hands were still clasped together in supplication, pleading even in death to be spared, as his headless body fell to the ground. Another villager dragged screaming from his hut, tried in vain to parry a deadly blow with his raised forearm, but paid with his hand in a spray of gore, as it fell to the ground with a dull thud beside him. Nothing stopped the next frenzied blow, which cleaved the screaming man's skull in two.

Driven on by their lust for Hutu blood, whooping and dancing with excitement, the drugged, blood-splattered Tutsi killers moved on, hunting for more victims to add to their murderous tally.

As abruptly as it began, the screaming and killing stopped. Silence became deafening…the Tutsi gunmen and their machete wielding brothers simply ran out of defenceless civilians to slaughter.

General Gabriel Ojukwu, their tall broad-shouldered leader, stood at the edge of the jungle watching his deadly attack unfold, but now, he laughed as he swaggered forward into the eerily silent village. With a sweeping, imperious wave of his hand, he ordered the huts to be fired, but only after they had been thoroughly searched and cleared of loot and foodstuffs his men could carry away.

'Leave the Headman's hut alone!' he barked, pointing at the village's largest hut, to stop his excited men from burning it in error. He watched with satisfaction, as several surviving women were dragged into the centre of the village and stripped. General Ojukwu looked on with amusement; he smiled at their frantic attempts to save themselves from the inevitable consequences of being taken alive by his feral Mai-Mai warriors.

When its dark shadow was cast across the land, rape, pillage and burn were the ways of war in the Congo.

Joshua M'pani risked everything to come to the village that day. He worked diligently as the nightshift foreman at the Mpolo facility, a small exploratory mine owned by the Pan Global Corporation. The diamond mine was located less than a kilometre outside the township of Birundi, which for now, lay peacefully far to the south of the burning village.

Blind to the fate which awaited him, he had begged his manager for release from his supervision duties for 24 hours. He had pleaded for dispensation to drive Pan Global's newly arrived representative to his distant family village, where the white man was due to hold an urgent and secret meeting. Working far away, almost two hundred kilometres from home, M'pani began to hear worrying rumours from fleeing refugees. Frightened people drifted into the nearby township in small family groups, their women burdened with hastily gathered possessions crammed into wicker baskets balanced on their heads, seeking safety from General Ojukwu's invasion. The drums told that the general was moving an army of many times many Mai-Mai militiamen towards Birundi, from his own Tutsi homelands, which lay far away, to the distant northeast. The Mai-Mai General seemed intent on sweeping through the Hutu tribal territories; the route he was taking terrified M'pani. It was directly in the path of his home village, where his own young wife and children still lived.

Fearing for their lives, with the manager's grudging permission, he had set off as the sun rose over the distant mountains that morning, with the white man sitting beside him in the mine's ancient Land Rover. He calmed himself with the knowledge that the rains were not due for several days yet. If he was lucky enough not to wreck the vehicle during the journey, or meet a forward patrol of the invading Mai-Mai, he should be back to the safety of the Mpolo mine complex, complete with his company representative and his own family, well within his 24-hour window of special leave.

Given the poor condition of the dirt roads, which occasionally criss-crossed Katinga province, it took the two men almost seven bone-rattling hours to complete the journey on the potholed track, which cut arrow-straight through the dense virgin jungle.

A rich man by local standards, M'pani was considered something of a celebrity by his villagers. Alerted by the Land Rovers blaring horn, the whole village had turned out to greet him, ululating and waving as he arrived in a cloud of choking red dust.

Having made his introductions, he excused himself for a moment. Brushing aside the excited welcome, M'pani strode quickly through the village to his own family hut. He ordered his surprised wife to gather their few possessions, and quietly load them into the back of the company's vehicle when darkness fell. Speaking softly to avoid being overheard by his neighbours, he decreed that his wife and children must be ready for the return journey to Birundi at daybreak, the following day. His wife had heard the echo of the drums' days earlier, and with fearful eyes, respectfully acknowledged her husband's orders. Although she did not show it, she felt a huge surge of relief flood through her, as she nodded her understanding that all would soon be well.

Satisfied that everything was in order, M'pani quickly returned and settled comfortably under the shade of the great fig tree, holding a locally brewed beer while he translated for the white man who sat beside him. To the background babble of the children playing nearby, the visitor spent the hot afternoon discussing news of General Ojukwu's movements with the village elders; as he waited patiently for the Hutu military Commanders' arrival, and their all-important meeting, due to begin shortly before night fell.

A Mai-Mai guerrilla shouted to the general and his officers, as he and several others dragged the dazed foreman, and, to their amazement, a white man from their hiding place, behind an old water cistern which nestled on the edge of the village. Like a drunken prize fighter, holding up a newly won champion's belt, another of the general's men cavorted around the terrified pair, jabbering excitedly and holding aloft a brown leather briefcase.

Because he was dressed differently from the villagers in bush jacket and shorts, the Mai-Mai thugs had wisely spared Joshua M'pani for the general's sport. In their eyes, the white man was a prize beyond measure, but the Mai-Mai foot soldiers knew better than to harm a European captive, without the express permission of their leader. The general's cruelty was legend, and to earn his displeasure meant only one thing, a slow and painful death.

Not a single guerrilla had heard of the Geneva Convention, or its civilised protocols concerning decent treatment of military prisoners and unarmed civilians. Since its sinister history begun, the Congo had its own cruel tradition of dealing with captives, unfortunate enough to be taken alive.

'Put them in the Headman's hut, and guard them well,' boomed the general, 'I will deal with them shortly.'

Turning his attention back to the captured briefcase, he snapped his fingers at the guerrilla carrying it.

'Bring that here!'

Ojukwu was momentarily intrigued by its weight. Impatiently, he snatched a blood-stained machete from another of his men and kneeing down, used its blade to lever the locked lid. Both catches snapped open with the sound of pistol shots, beneath the pressure of the blade. Licking his lips with anticipation, he carefully raised the lid. His dark eyes glittered for a moment, before he quickly slammed the lid shut. Running his tongue over his lips again, he turned to one of his lieutenants.

'Soon we will show the white man how we deal with prisoners....' he growled. His eyes flashed triumphantly, 'I will use my magic to extract all the answers I require.'

Unlike most local children, years earlier, Gabriel Ojukwu learnt to read and write at a small school, which lay some three miles from his father's village. A bright and eager student, he made the hot perilous walk with his younger brother, along the narrow animal trail every morning, eventually gaining what passed for a good education in the uncivilised heart of Africa. Having survived the daily rigours of the wild and dangerous

African bush, and the animals and endemic diseases which always lurked unseen and waiting, he reached puberty unscathed. Unflinching, Gabriel Ojukwu received his facial tribal scars during the painful rituals which heralded his profound journey into manhood.

Now considered by the tribal elders as a young man, who must begin a lifetime of work, Gabriel Ojukwu showed no interest in farming. It was poorly paid, drudging employment and anyway; he was consumed with burning ambition, which set his future far beyond the edge of his own crude village. He had become intrigued and deeply interested during his lessons on government and politics, in his last year beneath the rusted tin roof of the hot, ramshackle bush school. At the time, his future was uncertain; meaningful work outside the village was scarce. Invariably in the dark Congo, prized employment went only to young men who had the right connections. Gabriel Ojukwu was lucky; after graduating top of his class, he adroitly used his family's reputation as feared tribal witch doctors, and the threat of their all-pervading black magic. He utilized his family name and the invisible levers of power and fear, which it's terrifying witchcraft represented. Pressure was exerted, and intimidation whispered darkly in the right ears. He was quickly offered employment as a trainee manager on the Congo's dilapidated railway network, at the line's distant terminus station at Kabbali.

As the murderous civil war dragged on, Assistant Stationmaster Ojukwu's loyalty to the railway waned; he had not been paid for months. One day he decided it was time to leave the railway's service and move on. By way of resignation, he used a machete on his elderly superior. Content and smiling that his employment contract's termination was accepted; Ojukwu stepped over the stationmaster's bloody corpse, and emptied the company safe. He left the office, locking the door firmly behind him. Carrying the station's takings in a bag slung over his broad shoulder, he calmly walked past the unsuspecting and fearful crowd of waiting passengers. Ignoring them, he climbed into the manager's car and drove off on one of the broader tracks, which disappeared into the surrounding bush, heading back towards his own tribal homelands.

In the turbulent war-ravaged months that followed, Ojukwu gave close regard to the general power vacuum which pervaded the lawless region. The Government and United Nations eventually sent in troops to observe the feuds and inter-tribal slaughter, but their worth as peacekeepers was strictly limited. The national army was hamstrung by corruption and indifference towards the plight of the northern tribes, and the U.N. forces were powerless; more observers than saviours. Judging his moment, Ojukwu took his opportunity to seize control. Recruiting men from the local Tutsi dregs, and surrounding himself with loyal members of his own family and tribe, he formed the Congo Freedom Party.

In the eyes of the Tutsi, black magic spells cast by feared witch doctors would, and certainly did, kill. Such was the native belief; a man duly cursed knew he was doomed. Hollow eyed and damned, the unfortunate victim simply curled up and died within days. Ojukwu's father and uncles were themselves formidable tribal witch doctors, adding to the ex-trainee stationmaster's reputation. When Gabriel Ojukwu called on all able-bodied male members of his tribe to join the military wing of the C.F.P., superstitious and poorly educated, they were too frightened of the Ojukwu family's sinister reputation to refuse his call to arms. They knew of the dark magic which surrounded him, and the ranks of his new Mai-Mai army quickly swelled.

Ambushing isolated army and police encampments in overwhelming numbers, weapons and ammunition were easily captured by his fledgling army. There were never enough guns, but those Mai-Mai warriors bereft of firearms, wielded razor-sharp machetes and axes, with horrific and devastating results.

Promoting himself General, Ojukwu embarked on a barbaric campaign of raids and terror. He quickly made a name for himself across the whole of Katinga province, leaving a trail of bloody destruction in his wake.

After several years of campaigning, fighting a savage bush war against inept government forces and weaker rival tribes, Ojukwu became his region's dominant warlord. His string of victories reinforced his reputation as a potent master of the darkest spirits, and the people of the vast jungle expanse of Katinga disobeyed or defied him at their peril.

By nature, General Gabriel Ojukwu was a cruel man, hungry for power over men. In a more civilised land, a psychiatrist would have easily diagnosed him as a pure psychopath, bereft of conscience and totally unaffected by others' pain and suffering. Without restraint, Gabriel Ojukwu became Katinga's all-powerful master.

His boundless cruelty made him feared in the remote Katinga region of the Northern Congo. Even the whispered mention of his name sent shivers of terror through those who lived and scratched a meagre living, on lonely farms around the isolated villages which were scattered here and there between the tracts of the wild and primordial jungle. When he needed more soldiers, or lost men to sickness or battle, General Ojukwu simply replaced them by kidnapping terrified boys and young men in the night; forcing them into service with his dreaded Mai-Mai army. Plied with cocaine and marijuana, initiation and their ultimate tests of loyalty and obedience were combined, by making them shoot down helpless members of their own hamlet, in a drug crazed pool of cold blood.

In the smouldering village, Ojukwu's men continued to satisfy themselves, with their torn and bleeding female captives.

Becoming bored and in need of distraction, the general remembered the white man and his briefcase. He ordered some of his satiated warriors to erect stout wooden posts in the cleared centre of the village. His men's sweat streaked faces grinned to each other. Their blood still hot from killing and raping, they knew what was coming next, and set to work in the blistering heat with looted shovel and pick. The post bases must be firmly buried, to keep them rigid and strong for the task to which their general would shortly have them put.

Satisfied that all was ready, General Ojukwu barked at his men in his deep baritone voice.

'Bring out the prisoners!'

With broad grins of anticipation spreading across their shining black faces, his men threw open the crude wooden door of the headsman's hut. Terrified, the captives were dragged outside, surrounded by a crowd of excited and whooping Mai-Mai. The prisoners cringed and writhed against the iron grip of their captors. One begged for mercy. Joshua M'pani knew only too well what the Mai-Mai would do to him, and wished with all his heart that he had been killed with his family and the other villagers when the rebel attack had begun. New to the Congo, the tall European beside him could not begin to comprehend what was about to happen, but was, nonetheless, consumed with a terrible knot of fear in the pit of his stomach.

In the centre of the village, still firmly held by their laughing captures, Joshua M'pani and the white man were pushed roughly against the crude wooden stakes, and securely tied to them. Freshly cut lianas were brought from the jungle, and wound around their waists by grinning guards, who knotted them tightly. One guerrilla thrust his face just inches from each of his captives, screaming and jabbering incomprehensible threats and insults at the terrified men. M'pani's arms and legs were left unbound for the coming ritual. He hugged himself and moaned softly. Keeping his eyes downcast, he tried desperately to close his mind to the pain and horror, which he knew would shortly befall him.

Under the eager gaze of his guerrillas, still carrying the blood-stained machete and briefcase, the general walked slowly up to his prisoners. Placing the briefcase at his feet, he folded his arms as he stood in front of them, savouring the rank smell of fear and despair, which surrounded them both. The general held up his arms. His men fell silent.

'Strip that one,' the general suddenly barked, pointing towards M'pani.

Rebels sprang forward and ripped M'pani's clothes from him. In moments, he stood trembling and naked before his captures. Turning his attention to the other prisoner, General Ojukwu raised the blond European's chin with the machete, until the terrified white man was forced to look into the obsidian depths of the general's cruel eyes. Ojukwu smiled, and without warning, smacked the flat of the heavy machete blade hard against M'pani's naked elbow. Under the burning sun, the terrified site foreman screamed with pain and fright, emptying his bowels onto the hard-baked earth beneath him. Grinning with satisfaction, the general turned back to the European.

'Now tell me, my friend,' he rumbled silkily, 'Who exactly are you, and why have you come here, with a briefcase full of American dollars?'

Chapter Two

Kilimanjaro

Kenya

His shirt soaked with sweat, territorial SAS Sgt Pat Farrell winced as he lent forward to ease the weight of his heavy bergan, giving momentary relief to stiff and aching shoulders.

His men appeared fine in the rarefied atmosphere; there had been no signs of altitude sickness in any of them, since they left base camp days earlier. Many symptoms of high-altitude sickness were similar to hyperthermia, which Pat had seen only too frequently on the bleak Welsh mountains of south Wales. High altitudes of more than five thousand metres invited potentially deadly cases of hypoxia, but so far, his men showed no signs of dizziness, vomiting or the headaches which were early markers of an impending attack. Severe cases, Pat knew, could lead to a built up of fluid in the lungs, and without prompt treatment, the patient would quickly die. Pat was mindful of the risks of High Mountain trekking, and had deliberately kept the pace of the climb to a sensible rate, to allow his men to gradually acclimatise, as they slowly ascended the mighty African mountain.

As he rested, Pat's attention switched from the main body of his Troop, to one trooper lagging behind, who was giving him cause for concern. Taking a long pull from his water bottle, Pat called down to one of his two snipers.

'Come on Frankie. Pull your finger out. We haven't got all day.'

More than thirty metres lower down the track, he watched the limping man with growing apprehension. Pat's time with the SAS Regiment's Training Wing taught him to recognise someone doing his best to conceal an injury. Turning back to his men, he called out to them.

'Take a short breather fellas, but do not get too comfortable. We have still got a good way to push, if we are going to make the last R.V. before dark.'

Grins and light hearted groans went up from the rest of the territorial SAS Troop, as they thankfully slipped off their bulky bergan backpacks and sat down on them. The break was welcome; it had been another punishing day of hard marching up the narrow rock strewn path, which would eventually lead his troop to the mountain's snow-capped mantle. The glistening white snow line a few hundred feet above them spread across the permanently frozen summit of Mt. Kilimanjaro. As the Dark Continent's highest volcanic mountain, it was Africa's greatest challenge at over nineteen thousand feet, even for the superbly fit, mountain trained SAS reservists. Pat turned and watched in silence as Frankie Lane limped slowly up the track towards him.

When he made his initial map study at the troop's base camp, down at the regional Kenyan army base at Talinga, Pat began crafting his plans for the troop's assault on the summit. He had chosen this particular route because it was considered by the Kenyan garrison commander as the hardest way up the extinct volcano, and he had decided that it would keep them well clear of the soft tourist safaris, which used the easier five-day climb routes as the highlight of a civilian trip into the immense, dormant volcanic region, situated squarely in the middle of the vast Kilimanjaro national park. As the territorial SAS soldiers had gained altitude, weighed down with their bergans and weapons, each of them had noticed breathing was becoming more and more difficult. The air was definitely getting colder and thinner. Now at over sixteen thousand feet above sea level, despite the blazing sun, there was a distinct and penetrating chill to the air which surrounded them.

As an active member of the SAS territorial reserve, Frankie Lane, along with the other members of Two

Troop, had been recently seconded into the newly formed, and highly secret Shadow Squadron. When the need arose, the phantom Squadron was charged with an immediate response to any terrorist threats to London.

Having completed their initial three-month tour of duty, and after been relieved by B Squadron's crack Seven Troop, Pat's men were now reaping the benefits of an unofficial reward for a job well done.

As one of its two highly trained snipers, Frankie Lane managed to secure a much sought-after place on the overseas adventure training exercise, set in the desolate volcanic mountain range, on the borders of the African Commonwealth counties of Kenya and Tanzania. The exercise had been quietly and unofficially sanctioned, by the head of the SAS brigade, as due reward for the troop's very successful involvement in Operation Windmill, where the new Shadow Squadron members had been blooded for the first time. Using the intense counter revolutionary warfare techniques learnt at the regular SAS base in Hereford, they had recently neutralised a deadly Al Qaeda terrorist cell, intent on detonating a stolen Iraqi nuclear weapon in the very heart of London. The battle had been short and bloody, but as always, the SAS was invincible.

Before Pat's Troop had left their territorial Special Air Service base in London's fashionable Chelsea, the Regiment's Medical Officer had reluctantly given Trooper Lane the green light to make the trip, despite Frankie having injured his leg during training on a night-time parachute decent some weeks earlier. Lacking well defined reference points on a dark moonless night, due in no small part to a sudden rogue gust of wind, Frankie misjudged his drift in the darkness, hanging suspended under the parachute's canopy, during the very last moments of his descent. He took the full heavy impact of landing awkwardly on his left leg, when he had hit the frozen ground of the Welsh Sennybridge dropping zone. Frankie was carried off the drop zone on a stretcher by some of his friends in Two Troop. Assessing nothing was broken; the medic suspected a damaged ankle ligament or tendon, as putting weight on the injured limb was impossible for Frankie at the time. Later X-rays and further detailed examination had proven inconclusive, and after several weeks, not wishing to miss the trip, and quietly dosed up with painkillers Frankie swore blind that he was fully recovered, and was feeling absolutely fine.

As the young trooper limped painfully up the track towards him, Pat watched his movements closely. The

Troop still had several thousand feet to climb, before they reached the frozen snow-capped summit. They had spent the last three days climbing the uninhabited mountainside, following the rough boulder strewn track. The lush vegetation which had surrounded them when they began the climb was now just a memory. Little plant life other then scattered mosses and hardy lichen clung grimly to life on the otherwise barren rock strewn terrain at this high altitude.

Pat's plan required the 16-man troop to make the concluding dawn assault after a good night's sleep, from their final encampment 1,000 feet from the summit. He waited patiently until the limping, sweating trooper arrived beside him.

Pat shook his head. 'Not looking too good, is it Frankie?'

Frankie Lane looked up at his troop sergeant and grinned to hide his discomfort.

'I'm fine Pat. The ankle feels sore, and it's slowing me down a bit, but I'm OK, really.'

Pat knew his man would not admit how he was really feeling; it simply was not done in the Regiment, to cry off anything with an injury that wasn't obviously life threatening. Tradition dictated that he would have to be ordered off the mountain, but that, Pat thought ruefully, was what Troop Sergeants were for.

Pat's initial reaction was to send him back, but to be fair to the young trooper; Pat decided to examine the damaged ankle closely, before reaching a final decision.

'Right then, drop your bergan. Boot off, and let's take a look.'

Frankie winced slightly as he transferred his weight onto his injured leg, and released the shoulder straps of his heavy bergan. Easing it to the ground, he did his best to stifle a sigh of relief. He sat down on the pack and began untying his bootlace.

When both boot and sock were removed, Pat knelt down and examined the ankle. It was badly flared and swollen. Pat stared up at Lane.

'Hmm, doesn't appear too good Frankie. We have still got a couple of thousand feet to climb. That ankle just doesn't look like it is going to support you all the way to the top.'

Frankie opened his mouth to disagree, but Pat silenced him with a wave of his hand. Seeing the disappointment on the young trooper's face, his sergeant thought for a moment.

'Tell you what Frankie; before I decide, I'll get a second opinion.'

Pat grinned, turned away and called out to trooper Mickey Green, who had recently passed the SAS Regiment's intense battle medicine Para-medic course.

'Mickey, get over here! I have got a patient for you.'

Mickey was sitting on his bergan twenty feet further up the track, chatting casually to one of the other members of the troop. This mountain phase of the training exercise lacked an enemy, and was what the big army referred to as non-tactical. Such periods were considered by its special force's participants, as little more than a few fun days out in the African outback, with a decent stretch of the legs thrown in for good measure. Everyone in the troop was relaxed, simply enjoying the tough walk up the mountain path, and the fantastic views of the other surrounding extinct volcanoes, and the wide sprawling savannahs beneath Mt. Kilimanjaro, which stretched dancing in the heat-haze below them far off to the distant horizon. Mickey Green ambled over to Pat and his friend. He crouched down beside Frankie and began his examination by gently rotating his patient's foot. Frankie yelped suddenly with pain.

'Sorry mate,' Mickey said, as he continued pulling, pushing and slowly twisting the injured ankle. As Frankie took a long swig of water from his canteen, Mickey stood up, shaking his head. There was a look of genuine concern on his face.

'So what's your diagnosis then, Doc?' said Pat with a grin.

Mickey thought for a moment as he rubbed his hand over his chin.

'Looks like the Achilles tendon, Pat. It's not snapped or anything, but the area around it is badly inflamed and swollen,' he glanced at his mate and grinned, 'and it is clearly bloody painful.'

Frankie let out a long sigh, but remained silent. His sergeant nodded; Mickey's careful examination confirmed his own findings.

'So carry on, or off the mountain?'

Mickey looked down at his friend. With an apologetic smile, he said.

'Sorry Frankie, but I reckon you're off mate, before you do some serious, and possibly permanent damage.'

Pat nodded.

'Yep, that is what I thought.' He looked down at Frankie again. 'Get your boot back on as best you can.' He held up his hand to show the injured trooper his decision was final. 'No arguments now laddie, you are off the mountain, I'm afraid,' Pat turned to his medic, 'You go down with him, Mickey; give him a couple of painkillers, take your time, with plenty of rest stops, and get him to the base camp at Talinga. The Kenyan's have their own military hospital there. They will fix Frankie up. I'll tell Spike to set up the radio and send a signal down to our guys at base, and let them know you are on your way.' With a grin, Pat added. 'Might even manage a vehicle to meet you, if you're lucky... but don't hold your breath.'

Standing up, he stared down at his crestfallen sniper. Frankie's face betrayed his disappointment, but he knew both Pat and Mickey's diagnosis were exactly right. He did not bother to mention to either of them that he stumbled badly, earlier that morning under the weight of his bergan, and twisted his already aggravated ankle. He genuinely believed he could tough it out and make the summit with the rest of the boys, but as the hours wore on, and the sun climbed higher in the sky; his ankle burned, and he simply could not maintain the pace with the rest of the troop.

'Never mind Frankie, we'll see you in a couple of days, after we have pushed on and nailed the summit.'

Chapter Three

Hack

Birundi Township – Katinga Province

Hours after sunset, bathed in pale, gentle moonlight, the sleeping township of Birundi nestled quietly cocooned, within the Congo's vast jungle region of Katinga province. Crickets chirruped their nightly chorus across the untidy sprawl of houses, shops and workplaces, which made up the heart of the ramshackle African township.

Bright light spilled into Birundi's main square from three buildings which were permitted to draw power from the town's ancient electrical supply system, after 10'clock at night. A few haphazardly parked cars and lorries cast long silent shadows, which criss-crossed the deserted, rubbish strewn square. An asthmatic diesel generator chugged slowly, muffled down to a soft rhythmic purr inside the hut which housed it, as it grudgingly supplied electricity to the local police station, and the small medical clinic. Both buildings served the township's steadily growing population. Outlying farmers, and their families, in fear of the advancing Mai-Mai, had made the long walk into the supposed safety of Birundi.

The last building blessed with the luxury of electrical power, was the Hotel Armond. In more prosperous times, it was a smart and popular watering hole for the province's Belgian administrators, and affluent white colonial farmers. However, the building's tired facade and peeling paintwork betrayed years of post-colonial neglect, and displayed no more than a seedy air of long forgotten splendour.

Barney Morris belched loudly, wiping the sweat from his forehead with the back of his chubby hand, as he swayed unsteadily at the bar in Birundi's only hotel.

'Manners!' he said loudly, to no-one, in particular, as except for himself and the hotel's bartender, the grubby room was empty. The only working ceiling fan squeaked as it turned above them, fighting in vain to circulate the hot night air. The other fans were suspended still and silent above the two men. They had long since fallen victim to lack of maintenance. The barman slowly polished a glass with his stained apron, and grinned broadly at his only customer of the evening,

'Want another beer Boss?'

Barney Morris turned his head and slapped at a mosquito, which was busily trying to bite him on the back of his neck. Looking with distaste at the squashed insect plastered to the palm of his sweaty hand, he sighed miserably,

'Why not, you smooth talking black bugger; there's nothing else to do in this stinking shithole,' sighing deeply again, he flared his cheeks and belched once more. There was resignation in his voice, as he announced to the otherwise empty bar,

'As a long-serving member of the press, here I am on overseas assignment. I'm writing a piece on dedicated British doctors and nurses, working in darkest Africa,' he paused, sniffed loudly and gazed sadly around the empty bar. 'You would think I could find something better to do with my time off, but sadly, I cannot,' he wiped the mess from his hand onto the broad rump of his trousers, then lent heavily onto the stained counter of the bar.

'Better make it a whiskey my boy, or whatever you heathen's drink in its place?' he slurred. Barney Morris was well on the way to doing what he did every night, whenever the opportunity presented itself; he was lining his ample stomach with alcohol, in preparation for getting, as he liked to put it, industrial-grade falling-down drunk. He knew his booze habit was behind his editor's decision; to send him out to this God-forsaken spot, deep in the African wilderness.

Recently, he had crossed the line, and gone way beyond being a simple embarrassment to his newspaper in the UK, after a late night drunken brawl with a young, junior Royal outside a chic nightclub in London's West end, several weeks earlier. This was his last chance to make good, in his editor's eyes, before he joined the self-employed ranks of the gossip hungry paparazzi, chasing bimbo small c celebrities across town, in the hope of selling worthless journalistic nonsense to some equally worthless tabloid newspaper.

To add to his misery, he was saddled with the onerous task of wet nursing his editor's niece; fresh out of University, and just commissioned by her uncle's paper, for her first overseas photographic assignment.

'Christ!' he exclaimed with a gasp, as he took a sip from the brimming spirit glass, which the barman had passed across the counter to him. His eyes watered as he coughed.

'Sweet Jesus boy, that tastes like someone's pissed in the petrol,' he pulled a face, which betrayed his disgust, as Morris regarded its clear liquid contents for several moments. He quickly lifted the glass to his lips again and drained it.

'What the hell is this stuff, Henry?'

The barman's face split into a huge grin, revealing two near rows of white teeth.

'It is called Cavalla Boss. It's a Congo drink for real men; for warriors! It makes you hard like iron, and strong, like lion.'

Henry slapped his thigh, and laughed at his rhyme. With mock seriousness, he added,

'That's if the first one don't kill you, Boss.'

Barney Morris held up a hand and shuddered.

'Yeah, yeah,' he blew out his ruddy cheeks, 'I get the picture'.

He exhaled loudly again, and thought for a moment. His mind made up, he said,

'Better give me another one,' he nodded with a sly wink towards the bartender. Puffing out his cheeks again he said, 'It's OK Henry; I think I'm going to make it. It is starting to feel like that first one inoculated me against the rest of the bottle.'

While Barney Morris explored the alcoholic delights of the hotel's bar, outside in the darkness, the harmony of the peaceful African night was suddenly shattered by a loud and violent commotion. Its engine revving insanely, a vehicle screeched to a halt outside the hotel. A wild fusillade of automatic fire rent the peaceful atmosphere of the township. As the deafening gunfire stopped, one of the vehicle's doors banged shut and the driver screamed something into the square. He stamped down hard on the clutch. With a grinding of gears, the ancient Land Rover suddenly lurched forward and sped away from the village square. It disappeared in the glare of its headlights into the surrounding streets, in a cloud of dust, as more bullets were fired into the star-studded sky, by the vehicles two other laughing occupants.

Barney Morris and the barman rushed outside. In front of the hotel's steps, something lay on the hard red earth of Burundi's main square. From the building opposite, they heard harsh orders being issued, and saw shadowy figures running towards them, from the police station opposite.

Morris checked himself and stopped suddenly, as he realised what the pale bundle lying upon the ground, actually was.

'Jesus! It's a body!' he said. Realisation overcame his initial shock. His confidence grew by the moment, and he moved forward again, down the concrete steps onto the dusty street. Bathed in the moonlight, the naked body groaned, and tried to sit up. Morris saw in the gloom; a heavily stained sack lay on the ground beside him.

Henry stood still, transfixed with fear. He stared unblinking at the injured man's bleeding face.

'Move yourself, you lazy bastard!' screamed Barney. 'Get some help!'

Startled by Morris' shouts, Henry shook himself from his daze, and sped off towards the clinic. Native gendarmes arrived from the police station, and started pointing and jabbering excitedly between themselves. Their sergeant appeared moments later. Shouldering past his men, he crouched down beside the injured man. Looking up at the journalist, he enquired,

'What happened here, Monsieur?'

Barney looked down at the tall black policeman, his face betraying his bewilderment, before he stuttered his reply.

'I'm... I'm not sure. I was having a quiet drink at the hotel bar, and suddenly I heard a vehicle stop outside, some gunfire, then the vehicle took off at speed. I came outside....' He pointed to the groaning man, 'and found him lying here on the ground.'

The policeman nodded, and turned his attention from the shaken journalist, to the sack lying on the ground in front of him.

'And this, Monsieur?'

Barney shrugged his shoulders. 'I don't know. It was just there when I came outside.'

The policeman nodded. He lent forward and untied the liana which held the burlap sack closed, and immediately recoiled with horror, as a severed human head rolled from it.

'*Merde!*' gasped one of the other gendarmes, as he and the others leapt backwards. Barney also backed away, feeling vomit rise into his throat. He turned and retched noisily as he puked up the beer and Cavalla. The Gendarme sergeant ignored him; he had a stronger stomach than the white man, and he'd seen this sort of thing before.

Educated as a boy by nuns at a Catholic school, Congolese police Sergeant Pierre Labella crossed himself before lifting open the sack. He stared at the contents inside, already knowing what he would find. Releasing the sack with distaste, he stood up. In French, he spoke rapidly to his men.

'It is the hands and feet of some poor bastard,' he looked back towards Barney Morris, who was standing a few feet behind him, looking pale and shaken. Slipping into heavily accented English, the Gendarme sergeant said,

'It is very bad, Monsieur.'

His mind still trying to comprehend the horror before him, Barney remained ashen faced and silent.

The police sergeant shook his head, and looked down again at the blood-stained sack.

'This is the work of an evil and unholy beast ...I have seen the same thing once before, up in the north.'

Fear overcame the apprehension which had filled his voice moments earlier, as his mind fully digested what lay before him.

'This is the work of a dark and powerful Witchdoctor,' Sergeant Labella tongue flicked nervously across his dry lips. There was genuine fear in his deep voice. 'It is him Monsieur... The beast Ojukwu is coming.'

'Any problems getting through, Spike?'

'Nah, piece of cake, Pat,' Spike was busy rolling up one of the long wire dipole aerials, which were fitted snugly into the powerful Tribesman radio transmitter, 'Talinga got the message OK, and said they would send a vehicle as far up the mountain as they could, to link up with Frank and Mickey.'

Pat nodded. 'Fair enough, how was comms?'

'Yeah, booming through Pat. I'm getting fives all the way. We are so high up here, that it is pretty much line of sight,' Spike pulled a face and shrugged. 'There's nothing much in the way of the signal, so no background clutter and hardly any interference.'

Satisfied, Pat stood up.

'Right, hurry up and get the rest of your gear packed up and stowed away. We have still got some serious walking to do; at least, another two hours before we reach that last point below the summit where we're going to get our heads down tonight.'

Spike nodded and called over to his friend.

'Hey, Danny! Give us a hand and roll up the other aerial, will you mate?'

Chapter Four

White's Club

Central London

Since 1778, Whites Gentlemen's Club has quietly nestled, private and comfortable, on the east side of St. James. It's door is discreetly hidden between Piccadilly Circus and Trafalgar Square; setting it apart from the vibrant pulsing heart of London's busy West End. Throughout its long and distinguished history, as a result of old feudal ties, exclusive membership had often been passed down from father to son. Newly elected members were invariably drawn from the highest strata of London's privileged political and financial elite. Whites richly panelled dining room not only bestowed relaxation and good food on its members and guests, but it also endowed them with comfortable and discrete surroundings, where senior Civil Servants and Politicians could wheedle and deal with each other, and the heads of immensely wealthy corporations could discuss delicate matters, which were best arranged without the glare of publicity, or knowledge of their shareholders. Within such comfortable surroundings, they could privately plan hostile takeovers, surprise dawn raids, or explore exciting new opportunities, which would dramatically enhance their corporate balance sheets.

Whites Club was the perfect oasis where things were quietly arranged between powerful Mandarins, between visits from the attendant white coated waiters, without any need to preside over formal meetings of the Board of directors.

Sir Hugo Maxton Q.C. pursed his lips as he slowly savoured the rich full flavour of his expensive brandy. Sitting in a private corner of the dining room, at a small table laid for three, he looked up from swirling the dark aromatic contents of his brandy balloon. He spoke softly to his two companions. They were Archie Campbell, his Director of Operations in Africa, and Dr. Franz De Keizer, Head of Pan Global's Economic Intelligence Department.

'Personally, I think South African Klipdrift Brandy is far superior to the average French Cognac,' Sir Hugo smiled, 'White's import it especially for me, you know?'

His Director of African Operations nodded and said quietly, 'It is amazing what a generous donation to their Death Watch beetle problem will do.' He allowed himself the luxury of a faint smile. Sir Hugo shook his head slowly.

'You are becoming a true cynic Archie. When did you stop believing in the purity of mankind, and the nobility of the human spirit?'

Archie Campbell thought for a moment and shrugged his shoulders.

'Hmm, I believe it happened just after I started working for Pan Global, Sir Hugo.' It was Sir Hugo's turn to smile.

As refugees from Hitler's Germany, Sir Hugo's family had fled to Britain in 1936, soon after open and widespread attacks on the Jewish community, by state sanctioned, black-shirted Nazi thugs had begun. Rumours spread quickly that German Jews had been forcibly evicted from their homes, and 'resettled' in the new concentration camps, which were still being built, and expanded, in east Prussia and other parts of eastern Germany. His Grandfather was a shrewd merchant banker, and had successfully managed to, not only extract his family from the Nazi's grasp, but also save a substantial portion of their family fortune.

Born in Golders Green in 1950, Hugo Maxton had benefited from a first class education at Haileybury Imperial College, adjacent to the picturesque Hertfordshire village of Hertford Heath. He went on to gain a first class honours degree in Criminal law at Oxford University.

Hugo Maxton joined the renowned barristers' chambers of Tanville, Walsh and Coombes, in the legal enclave of London's Temple, just off the Strand, where he quickly earned the respect of the senior members of his firm. He proved himself to be a formidable tactician and advocate, in the Law courts of the Old Bailey. He took silk after only seven short years, but reluctantly left his law firm soon afterwards, when his father died suddenly after a massive stroke. As the oldest son, it fell upon him to take control of the family's small merchant banking business. The loss of his father allowed him the financial resources to spend the next fifteen years quietly expanding his other interest; buying up ailing mining and mineral processing companies, which he believed still had connections and potential, invariably turning their fortunes around, and substantially increasing the turnover and profits of his new Pan Global Mining Corporation. Those few companies that did fail despite his best efforts were ruthlessly asset stripped, without any compassion or consideration to the human dimension. He believed above all things in the business creed, that profits must flow. Hugo Maxwell let nothing stand in his way of making new acquisitions, when his shadowy business intelligence department advised him that the moment was right to begin negotiations with the Receivers, over some broken company, which still showed a glimmer of promise and profit, despite an uncertain future.

International demand for raw materials had never been greater. World consumption of natural resources was the bedrock on which his worldwide corporation now stood. Pan Global's latest markets in India and China were proving particularly well placed conduits for sell vast quantities of raw materials into their hungry, burgeoning economies. Supplying them with raw materials was the key to the future; Sir Hugo was convinced of it. However, always in the back of his mind was his concern that economically extractible mineral reserves, wherever they were to be found, were finite. As demand grew, viable, profitable and extractable deposits were steadily diminishing around the globe.

Sir Hugo's knighthood had come in last year's birthday honours, from a grateful government, who appreciated his corporation's efforts in the export market, which definitely helped the nation's ailing Budget deficit, and the heavily manipulated statistics which had been made public, by the Ministry concerned. They also quietly appreciated the generous donations he made to their Party coffers.

Having refilled their coffee cups, the elderly waiter discreetly withdrew. Sir Hugo's face took on a more serious look as he leant forward and quietly spoke to his two closest and most trusted employees.

'Within the next two years gentlemen, we will begin to struggle to meet our customer's current levels of consumption of natural resources. Given that demand has increased globally by more than 7% in the last two years, we are in serious danger of simply running out of raw materials to sell. This will become a crisis, which if left unchecked, will ruin the corporation, unless we ramp up our operations in Africa, and implement the final stage of Condor soon.'

He inclined his head towards his chief intelligence officer. His face was grave.

'Tell us please Franz, what is the latest news from our operation in the Congo?'

It was De Keizer's turn to look grave.

'Well Sir Hugo, the good news is that our latest reports indicate that the country remains in its usual state of political and economic turmoil. The truth of the matter is that due to our covert intervention and support of various rebel factions, the current government cannot manage their own interior. The northern half of the Congo has slipped completely out of their control. The bad news, however, is that General Ojukwu's Mai-Mai militia has begun a new putsch, sweeping south across their neighbouring Hutu tribal homelands, killing everyone in their path, and looting anything of value.'

Sir Hugo nodded.

'Ojukwu certainly seems to have maintained a firm grip on his territory over the years, and now he is clearly beginning to expand his own little empire. He appears to be the man we should seriously think about doing business with. Perhaps, it is time to switch sides, as it were, and back him instead, as time is beginning to run short? Sir Hugo stared intently at De Keizer, 'Can we stop our representative out there, or has he already contacted the opposing Hutu?'

De Keizer face remained grave. He cleared his throat. 'Well, yes Sir Hugo, in a manner of speaking, he did make contact.'

Confused by his director's tone, Sir Hugo looked quizzically at his intelligence chief.

'What exactly do you mean, in a manner of speaking, Franz?'

His aide's face began to pale as he contemplated the fold in his serviette for a moment.

'Well Sir Hugo. I received a report four hours ago that our man was taken during a Mai-Mai militia raid on a small village, deep inside Hutu territory. The mine manager's report says that they butchered our man's driver in cold blood. Apparently, it is well-known in the Congo, that the Mai-Mai has a tradition of incredible cruelty towards their captives. The report says that Ojukwu personally hacked off the driver's arms and legs, skinned him, and then ripped out his heart, while it was still beating.'

Suppressing a shudder, De Keizer paused for a moment, and took a sip of water from the nearest glass on the table.

'Apparently, it is the trademark of a really powerful witch doctor, to be able to remove the beating heart, while the victim is still alive.'

De Keizer paused again, and drained his glass.

'Then they cooked and ate parts of the poor bastard, to increase their prowess as warriors, or some such filthy mumbo-jumbo.'

Sir Hugo's turned away for a moment, appalled at what he had just heard.

'Dear God!' he muttered. Quickly composing himself, he looked back at his intelligence chief and said, 'What about the $100,000 dollars, our man was carrying?'

De Keizer nodded wistfully,

'I'm afraid; the money you were um...donating to the Hutu fighting fund is missing. Apparently, Ojukwu has seized it.'

'Damn and blast!' whispered Sir Hugo indignantly, as De Keizer continued his report.

'Our representative was deeply traumatised, and in a dreadful state of course, but was returned alive, and otherwise unharmed, yesterday. He was dumped back in the township of Birundi, which is close to our exploratory mine out there'. De Keizer reached for his water glass once again, 'His name is James Wright, by the way.' Seeing it empty, he refilled it from the carafe again, before he continued. 'I'm afraid it gets worse Sir Hugo. Under threat of similar treatment to his driver, Wright admitted to the mine's manager about telling Ojukwu of the fortune in red diamonds, locked up in the safe at the Birundi mine, and that Pan Global is backing Ojukwu's main opposition in Katinga province.'

Sir Hugo closed his eyes for a moment, hunching forward as he suppressed the growing anger and panic which were in real danger of overwhelming him. His two senior directors sat nervously waiting for his response to the dreadful news, which threatened at a single stroke, to destroy operation Condor, and seven years of meticulous planning, manoeuvring and huge amounts of his money, paid to the Hutu in Katinga province. A fortune in bribes, weapons and equipment provided to the tribe they currently were backing, was hanging by a thread. Sir Hugo remained still, as he sought to calm himself, as he desperately sought a solution to his fast unravelling plan to salvage the fortunes of Pan Global. From his hunched, subdued position, his eyes suddenly flicked open, and he sat bolt upright, startling his two companions.

'Those diamonds are absolutely critical to our last push towards civil war in the Congo, and the subsequent installation of a government of our choosing in the region. If we do change our support over to General Ojukwu, and that looks increasingly likely, I want to use a small part of the money to supply him with just enough arms, ammunition and equipment to consolidate his position, and hold the entire region, until he declares independence. I already have the tacit agreement from the Foreign Office, that they will recognise whoever we install in power, when the time comes.'

Both directors looked genuinely surprised.

'You have secured government backing Sir Hugo?' whispered De Keizer in amazement.

Sir Hugo looked down at his hand, as his fingers tapped on the table top.

'Of course, that is, as soon as we have arranged our future monopoly on extracting the mineral wealth of the entire area of Katinga, and perhaps one day even the whole Congo.' Sir Hugo's eyes closed to slits, 'government support rests on discretion and success gentlemen. I do not want this fellow Ojukwu to grab the diamonds for himself, leaving us out in the cold,' his voice dropped to a bare whisper, 'we must recover the diamonds at all costs, before he takes possession of them gentlemen, or government support, Operation Condor and the Pan Global Corporation, for that matter... are finished.'

He caught the eye of the waiter, and signalled for the bill. Dinner was at an end.

'Our collective futures balance on the next few hours' gentlemen... I want a recovery plan on my desk at nine o'clock sharp, tomorrow morning'. He stared intently at the two men. 'Do I make myself clear?'

De Keizer and Archie Campbell climbed out of the taxi and walked quickly through the cold night air towards the glass and chromium entrance of their corporation's head office. The building stood imposing and silent off Leadenhall Street, in the business heart of the nation's capital. The journey from Whites took only a few minutes. The black cab made its way quickly across Trafalgar Square, through the nearly deserted Strand, around the Aldwych and on past the old, closed and shuttered offices of the national newspapers of Fleet Street. The commissionaire on night duty looked up from his paper with surprise, when Archie Campbell rapped smartly on the thick plate-glass door. The uniformed commissionaire stood up quickly from behind the large wooden reception console, and having instantly recognised both men, unlocked the door. Straightening his tunic, he saluted smartly as they rushed past him and the tall sentinel potted palms, and on through the deserted marble clad atrium towards one of the lifts.

'Working late gentlemen?' he enquired as the lift's door opened.

'I'm afraid so Mullins, duty calls,' said Archie Campbell. The elevator's doors closed behind the two worried directors, with a loud pneumatic hiss.

'We need to get some people to Birundi quickly Franz,' said Campbell as he took off his overcoat, and hung it on the stand beside the door, inside his plush sixth-floor office.

'Why can't we just get the mine's manager to get the diamonds out, Archie?' said De Keizer, frowning deeply.

'No, you do not understand the geography Franz. I visited the mine last year, and there are only two viable ways in or out of Birundi; by plane via the local airstrip, or using a boat along the river. There is a road of sorts, but it is in a terrible state of repair, and runs through the centre of the war zone, were the natives are to say the least, unfriendly. The nearest proper settlement is almost a hundred miles downstream, at the rail head of Kabbali, and it would take days to arrange transport, using a boat capable of making the journey up the Mpana River, from Kabbali to Birundi. We simply cannot expect him to make the journey alone in a native canoe. It is just too far and dangerous. There are native tribes all along the river, who might well kill him, and probably eat him, if they catch him trespassing on their stretch of the riverbank.'

Campbell raised an eyebrow as he thought for a moment, trying to comprehend the almost primordial society which existed in parts of the Congo.

'He can't just bury the diamonds in the bush either. If he's killed, we'll lose them forever, and if they catch him, bearing in mind, he would have nowhere to run to, he will get the same treatment as Wright's driver, and he would certainly talk before he died,' Campbell sighed deeply, 'No, Franz, there's only one way to be absolutely sure. He needs a proper armed escort, and a plane to lift him and the diamonds, safely out of the region.'

Franz De Keizer nodded.

'What sort of value has been placed on the diamonds, mined so far, Archie?'

Campbell raised his eyebrows, and chewed his bottom lip for a moment.

'Well, we are looking at uncut red diamonds, which are flawless and very rare. When we ship them over to our facility in India, where our labour costs are low; they will have been properly sorted, cut and polished. They should fetch between two hundred and eighty to three hundred million pounds on the international gemstone market. The Argyle mine in Kimberley, Western Australia, by the way, is the only other known source of red diamonds, which helps considerably to boost their value, although in carat weight, they are relatively small stones.' he shrugged, ' total weight should be about, say, twenty-five to thirty kilos.'

De Keizer nodded thoughtfully. 'Not a trifling sum. Little wonder Sir Hugo wants to keep hold of them,' Campbell agreed.

'Yes indeed, but something else has just occurred to me. We will need to seal the mine before Ojukwu, and his men arrive, or they will turn it into a conflict mine, and clean it out before we get it back in there.'

It was De Keizer's turn to agree. Conflict mines, all over Africa, were being systematically stripped and looted by guerrilla forces, which happened to be in control of them, at any particular moment during their own internal conflicts.

'So we'll need men willing to go in, seal the mine, recover the diamonds and then get out again under Ojukwu's nose, within what, a week at most?'

Campbell thought for a moment,

'Probably less. Nearer four days, to be sure, I think

Campbell walked to the window, and with hands clasped behind his back, looked out into the darkness, at the sprawl of London's silently twinkling lights.

'There are, if I remember correctly, at least seven or eight local policemen, or gendarmes as they prefer to be called, in residence at the police station at Birundi, near to the charity clinic in the centre of the township. The clinic is run by a small volunteer British Medical team, by the way. The policemen are lightly armed, but if they don't simply bolt into the bush when Ojukwu gets there, they will only fight to save their own skins. The odds are hopeless, so let's not put any faith in them staying. The question is though Franz; should we warn the medical staff?'

De Keizer looked at the African Operations Director, and slowly shook his head.

'What is the point Archie? You heard what Sir Hugo said. They must already know the General is coming.' He shrugged his shoulders, 'and where the hell would they run to, anyway?

Archie Campbell nodded sadly. 'Poor devils...Perhaps we can still save them though?'

De Keizer looked doubtful. 'Maybe we can Archie? It is probably best to run that aspect by Sir Hugo.'

At nine o'clock the following morning, the two exhausted directors finished their plan, and the subsequent list of international telephone calls. They had begun to brief Sir Hugo on the proposal they had hastily put together, to remove the diamonds from Birundi.

'In essence, Sir Hugo, the plan is a simple one. We fly in a low-key security team, aboard a chartered cargo plane, to the airfield just outside Birundi; seal the mine with explosives, and recover the diamonds from the manager's safe. The plane has to be relatively small, or it will not make a safe landing on the local airstrip. It can be refuelled on the ground while it is waiting. Having collected the diamonds and sealed the mine, once the team is safely on board, the plane takes off, and flies straight back to our mining operation on the Skeleton Coast in Angola. It is a long round trip, and the distances are tight, but we calculate we can have our people on the ground at Birundi within 12-14 hours from now.'

Sir Hugo looked up from contemplating his blotter, while he carefully listened and digested the plan's outline.

'Once they are safe, we can then send the diamonds on to India for processing, using our usual security protocols and couriers...I presume we are clear to lift out the white medical team, and our men Wright at the same time.'

Sir Hugo laced his fingers together, deep in thought.

'But extra weight increases fuel consumption, and your margins are already tight, are they not?' he enquired slowly. Sir Hugo shook his head. 'I want those diamond's, gentlemen. They are absolutely crucial to Pan Global's future survival, and I'm sorry to say are therefore, of paramount importance.' Grimly, Sir Hugo shook his head, 'I cannot risk failure by sanctioning a humanitarian rescue. Time is too short, and by your own definition, the resources are simply unavailable. I think we will leave the issue of the medical staff to fortune and providence. I want it made abundantly obvious to our team leader over there, exactly where his priorities lay.' he stared coldly at each director in turn. 'Is that absolutely clear, gentlemen?'

With heads bowed, both directors nodded.

'Perfectly clear Sir Hugo,' said Archie Campbell. Sir Hugo turned his head, and looked at his intelligence chief.

'Who exactly do you plan to use, Doctor?'

de Keizer smiled.

'We have a small, highly trained, and very professional security team currently guarding our diamond mining operation on the Skeleton Coast. They are a mixed international bunch; tough, experienced and ex-military to a man. Before foreign professional soldiers were banned from working inside Africa by the United Nations, these men would have been considered mercenaries. We have them working for us as...ah, security advisors. They are an existing armed force down there anyway, so weapons will not be a problem, and explosives, and detonators are readily available from our mine complex on the Skeleton Coast.'

Sir Hugo allowed himself a smile for the first time since the previous evening.

'Good Franz, it is starting to look very promising. How soon can you have your goon squad underway?'

Archie Campbell stood up, smiled, and placed his hand on the telephone on Sir Hugo's desk.

'We stood the team ready during the night, and the flight plan has already been lodged as a mining supply run. No-one will notice, as we do it routinely every few months anyway. It just needs one phone call to get them into the air.'

Satisfied that all was in order, Sir Hugo exhaled deeply.

'Make the call, Archie,' he said smiling broadly at his African Operations Director. 'If this works successfully, Operation Condor is back on track, Pan Global's future will be secure…and no-one outside this room need ever be any the wiser.'

Chapter Five

Birundi Township

Katinga Province

Having covered his semi-conscious body with a blanket; escorted by the young English doctor and his nurse, the four gendarmes carried Pan Global's man across the square on a stretcher to the medical clinic. Barney Morris returned to the bar and with a shaking hand, fortified himself with several shots of fiery Cavalla, as his mind whirled, thinking through the whole ghastly incident.

With the instincts of a professional journalist, who had spent most of his working life sniffing out a good story wherever it was to be found, he knew this was his ticket back to mainstream journalism in the UK, rather than the next stinking God-forsaken foreign hole, or the dole. It was also his chance to reinstate himself in the eyes of his editor, and the newspaper's publishers. If he got this right, all would be well; he would be top man again, and life could slip back to a boozy, comfortable routine at home.

He reviewed the facts. There was everything he could wish for here. It would take all his skill to stretch journalistic credibility and describe Birundi as an exotic backdrop, but he would work on that as a matter of detail. There was potentially intense human drama, and overwhelmingly savage, bloodcurdling background material. He had a small British Medical team that was under threat of a horrible death, surrounded as they were by countless miles of sinister and impenetrable African jungle. Barney Morris searched for an angle, with which to slant the story. The medics were cut off and in a hopeless position, with thousands of screaming savages baying for their blood. He would have to interview the surviving victim and the mine's manager, and use what he already had, concerning the medical team. With a little adjustment and manipulation, and perhaps a short update with the medics, he could easily invent a cry for help from them, directed the British Government, by asking in banner headlines, why the Prime Minister and the Foreign Office were not aware of the situation, and busy arranging help to the beleaguered medical 'Angels?'

The Cavalla was starting to take effect, calming him. Now that his heart had stopped hammering, and his hands were no longer shaking, Barney Morris licked his lips and took out his notebook and pen.

'Henry, go and wake up that silly little cow of a photographer, then bring me another one of those fire waters, I have got some serious writing to do.'

It may have been the Cavalla flooding into his empty stomach, or the excitement of such a ripe opportunity falling into his lap, but it was only when he started to write initial notes, that he suddenly realised that he was in the same invidious position as the others. He was also trapped inside Birundi Township, waiting on the arrival of the diabolical Mai-Mai, and their brutal leader.

'Oh sweet Jesus!' he muttered to himself, as Henry arrived with his next drink. Morris' hand shook again as he lifted the glass to his lips. If he was to save his career, and more importantly, his own skin, this would have to be the greatest piece of writing he had ever done. It must be hard hitting, filled with heart-rending pathos and just the right amount of pressure, subtle or otherwise, to get the British Government to send in the cavalry before it was too late, and they were all chopped into pieces.

The police station's telephone connection to the Congo's capital Kinshasa crackled and buzzed infuriatingly, as Barney Morris tried to re-establish his international connection. He stood with the receiver pressed tightly against one ear, and the index finger of his sweaty left hand jabbed firmly into the other.

'No operator, London – England!' he yelled into the handset, trying desperately to overcome the constant background electronic chirrups and whistles, which were making his crackling conversation so difficult. It was the second time the connection had been lost, as he frantically read out his story to his paper's copy editor, who was thoroughly enjoying Barney's discomfort, as he sat comfortably in the London newspaper's fortress-like Wapping Offices. Barney shouted his paper's telephone number down the line again, much to the amusement of Sergeant Pierre Labella, and the other grinning Congolese policemen on duty, who stood together on the other side of the counter. Barney turned his back on the gendarmes to hide his frustration, as Sergeant Labella shook his head and whispered with a smirk to his men in French.

'He's already managed to connect with Kinshasa three times; he does not know how lucky he is!'

Eventually, the connection was re-established, and Barney finished sending his copy. Just before he hung up, Morris promised that he would fax some pictures, providing the bloody machine would work in this God awful country, he thought to himself morosely.

Nodding his thanks to the tall police sergeant, Barney Morris slipped the sergeant a wad of local banknotes, and walked out of the police station, into the bright early-morning sunshine. Satisfied with his efforts, he felt in his pocket, and took out a crumpled pack of cigarettes. Lighting one, he drew the smoke deep into his lungs, and exhaled slowly. Somewhere above him, he heard the faint drone of aircraft engines. Looking up, shielding his eyes with his hand, he scanned the cloudless sky as he searched for the plane. He spotted the fat silver dot on the horizon, far to the Southeast. The ancient twin-engine DC3 Dakota was slowly descending, as its pilot lined up to make his final approach, and land at Birundi's outlying grass airstrip. Rubbing his hand over the stubble on his chin, Barney Morris continued to stare at the Dakota, and wondered absently how much it would cost him, if they had a spare seat on its outward journey.

When the right honourable David Benchley MP, Minister for Foreign Affairs took the call, he was feeling relaxed and smug; in fact, rather flattered and pleased with himself that an editor from one of the National newspapers wanted to speak to him personally on his first day in his new Ministry. Recently promoted from the backwater Ministry of Agriculture and Fisheries, after a highly publicised scandal concerning leaked documents, and the subsequent Cabinet reshuffle, it was going to be a good opportunity to immediately heighten his new profile. He wrongly assumed it was just a formality call, to discuss the forthcoming meeting of the Commonwealth's Heads of State, scheduled for a weeks' time in Pretoria.

When the paper's editor had finished reading out Barney Morris's piece to him, the colour had drained entirely from the Rt. Honourable David Benchley's face. As he listened, his mood quickly changed from one of self-congratulation, to abject horror, when the editor added that his niece Patti was on overseas assignment for his newspaper, and among the Britons trapped in the Congo. The Minister had tried to calm the irate editor, who minute by minute was becoming more and more agitated, by the ineffectual efforts of the Minister to plicate him.

'I want my niece out of there, before those bloody murdering Mai-Mai arrive. My paper's readers will want to know exactly what the hell you intend to do about it?'

David Benchley's instincts for political survival had always served him well, and did not let him down now,

'Dominic... please, calm yourself. I will seek advice and call an urgent meeting within the Foreign Office, to see exactly what can be done to bring your niece and the others out... Don't worry; I mean of course, long before anything unpleasant happens.'

As a very junior reporter for the Daily Telegraph, Dominic Chandler had cut his teeth on the political scandal of the John Profumo and Christine Keeler affair many years earlier, and had never trusted or believed a politician since. He was not convinced by the Foreign Secretary's spin, knowing full well that time was of the essence. Ignoring the Minister, he pressed his point home,

'My paper will publish Morris's story tomorrow morning. I'm not going to bury this Minister; I'm going to give it the full treatment. I'm contacting other editors and leaking the story to them too. I'm putting it on our own front page, along with your picture under full banner headlines.'

David Benchley sat bolt upright. His voice was pleading.

'But Dominic, we can sort this out, I promise you. At least give me a chance to say what the Governments solution will be.'

There was silence at the other end of the line for a moment. At last, the reply came.

'All right then. I will put in the Government's response by publishing your press release on exactly what you plan to do.' The editor glanced at his watch. He was in no mood for further negotiation.

'I want the press release on my desk within the next hour!'

As he sat cocooned in his quiet, beautifully panelled new office, overlooking Whitehall and the entrance to Horse Guards, there was a hollow click on his telephone handset, as the editor hung up. The newly incumbent Minister stared at the silent receiver for several moments, before slowly replacing it onto its cradle. He knew this situation would cause him deep personal embarrassment and even political ruin if it turned really nasty. It would not only be a national story, but would go international within hours. As the new Foreign Office minister, his credibility at the Commonwealth Heads of State meeting would be shot to bits, even before his aircraft touched down on South African soil. God alone knows, he thought glumly, what the Americans would make of it, if he bungled things, and the trapped doctors got the chop. There would undoubtedly be questions asked in the House, perhaps even a vote of no confidence, launched he suspected, not by the opposition, but by his own enemies within the Party.

The Minister sat with his head in his hands for several long moments, the stillness of his plush office broken only by the soft ticking of the ornate antique clock which faced him, and the soft burr of the Whitehall traffic outside. Lurid images of frenzied black guerrillas hacking unarmed British citizens to death flashed vividly through his mind. When the paper appeared on the streets tomorrow morning, and the general public got wind of this story, worse still, the voters in his own constituency heard of it, there would be hell to pay if he hadn't come up with something, and fast. The media, voting public and the P.M. would collectively have his balls for breakfast, if anything happened to that blasted girl, or the doctors and nurses in Birundi. Tearing himself away from further thoughts of imminent political ruin, he lent forward and buzzed through to his Press Secretary.

'Would you step into my office please? Something awkward has happened, and we have a rather nasty situation brewing in the Congo.'

With a final roar of its ageing engines, the ancient DC 3 Dakota rolled to a stop beside the equally ancient and rusty maintenance hangar, besides the rough Birundi airstrip. The white South African pilot immediately cut the engines, removed his headset and hurried through the small cockpit door into the belly of the aircraft. As the cargo plane's side door swung open, and his tough-looking passengers prepared to disembark, he blocked the exit as he spoke to their leader.

'Look man, I'm telling you, we have got a problem. My port engine is badly overheating.'

Otto Krutz, retired veteran officer of South Africa's crack 32 battalion, and 1st Reconnaissance Commando, their elite Special Forces Regiment, was now employed as head of Pan Global security operations on Namibia's Skeleton Coast. He stared at the pilot coldly. Cooped up in the narrow confines of the hold of the uncomfortable aircraft for over six hours, he was in no mood for bad news. He betrayed his ancestry when he spoke in his broad Boer accent.

'So fix it...man!' he growled coldly, pushing the pilot's arm away and climbing down the metal steps. Carrying their bulging backpacks, his seven-man security team followed him out of the aircraft, smirking at the pilot as one by one, they gratefully climbed onto the hard dry earth, and ambled towards the mine's battered lorry, which stood silently waiting for them at the side of the ageing hanger.

The pilot jumped down from his empty aircraft and ran after Krutz.

'For God's sake, you do not understand! This isn't bloody 'Joburg International airport. I have got to find out what is wrong with the engine first. It might be nothing more than a blocked oil line, or it could be something really serious. Maybe it's a bird strike or even a cracked cylinder head, for all I know.' He looked forlornly across the deserted airstrip, and the dense jungle which surrounded it.

'As I came in for my final approach, the temperature gauge suddenly went off the scale. I only just managed to land that crate, before the bloody engine caught fire,' he shook his head miserably, 'I doubt there is a spare part for a DC 3 within five hundred miles!'

Resisting his growing urge to shake the whining pilot, Krutz struggled to control his fiery temper.

'Then you'd better get on with it, and find out what's wrong, hadn't you?' he hissed angrily. He turned and spoke to one of his men. 'Jan, you know a bit about engines. Stay here and do what you can to help, while the rest of us go up to the mine.'

The big Swede nodded. Ignoring further conversation, Otto Krutz turned on his heel and climbed in beside the lorry's African driver, while his men transferred their grips and a heavy wooden crate containing the dynamite, into the open back of the lorry. Staring through the insect splattered windscreen at the expanse of flat deserted airstrip beyond him, Krutz growled.

'Right then Kaffir, get this pile of filthy scrap moving. Take us straight up to the mine office.'

Having left the grey Ministry of Defence building on the Thames side of the busy thoroughfare of Whitehall, Brigadier Lethbridge and the Under Secretary for defence, Sir Julian Armstrong walked briskly through the throng of pedestrians and gawping tourist parties, past the Cenotaph and then changing direction, plunged into the traffic as they crossed Whitehall. They dodged speeding buses and taxis, which growled past them in clouds of acrid diesel fumes towards Parliament Square at one end, or Trafalgar Square at the other end of Whitehall. The leaden skies above threatened rain, but to the Under Secretary's relief, having forgotten his umbrella, it stayed dry during their short journey. A few hundred yards away, Big Ben boomed out, and chimed nine o'clock. Turning into King Charles Street, and arriving at their destination, they both nodded curtly to the uniformed commissionaire, as they climbed the steps and entered the non-descript entrance to the Foreign and Commonwealth Office. The Royal Crown emblem and small polished brass plate mounted on the wall outside were the only clues to the true identity of the otherwise drab government building. Like his companion, Brigadier Lethbridge - Director of the SAS, he was dressed in civilian suit and tie. His visit to the Ministry of Defence building that morning began with a dull meeting, with a collection of equally dull civil servants from the Treasury, and some home-grown bean counters from the Defence Ministry. They had gathered together to discuss matters concerning long term Special Forces weapons and equipment procurement policy. In Lethbridge's eyes, the meeting suddenly took an unexpected, and the most welcome turn. It had become considerably more interesting, when someone had interrupted their discussion, who was obviously flustered by something. The man requested an immediate audience with the Brigadier, in private, outside.

Standing in the empty panelled corridor, the Under Secretary introduced himself and then quietly said. 'I'm sorry to interrupt your meeting Brigadier, but a problem has occurred over at the Foreign Office. I'm afraid my Minister is in a frightful state. He ordered me to come and find you myself, and politely request your attendance at his office...Um, he said....without delay!'

The Brigadier regarded the man coolly. Although he kept his opinions quietly to himself concerning politicians and civil servants in general, the paunchy bespectacled little man wearing an ill-fitting pinstripe suit standing before him, reminded Britain's most senior and distinguished Special Forces soldier, more of a down at heel door-to-door insurance salesman, rather than a knighted senior bureaucrat, working at the very heart of government.

'Very well, Sir Julian,' he said calmly... 'We'd better go and see him straight away then, hadn't we?'

Chapter Six

Foreign and Commonwealth Office
Whitehall - London

David Benchley's briefing was at an end. He sighed deeply,

'So there, in a nutshell, we have it Brigadier.'

Brigadier Lethbridge sighed quietly, and enquired,

'So why not just ask the Congolese Government for assistance. Surely, it is their responsibility for foreign national's safety on their soil. Isn't it down to them to lift our people out?'

The Minister frowned. 'We cannot rely on the Congolese authorities to affect a rescue. I spoke to their Ambassador earlier this morning over the telephone. He was surprisingly candid. He admitted that his military forces were not in control over the area surrounding the township of Birundi. Frankly, they are not even close. He described the entire province as a lawless wilderness, filled with jungle and bandits. He was full of apologies, but said with such short notice; it was an impossible task for the Congolese military to mount such an operation.'

Lethbridge nodded, 'Yes, I understand the problem Minister, but what do you want me to do about it...exactly?'

Showing obvious disappointment that he was not already listening to some bold, imaginative and daring rescue plan spilling from the Brigadier's lips, the Minister sighed deeply, clicked his tongue softly and said, 'Well, I thought it was self-evident Brigadier. We need a trained military group, to escort our people out of danger. I simply want your people to lift the trapped British citizens, and spirit them away to a place of safety. Your SAS chaps are highly trained specialists in these matters, after all. God knows; we spend enough money on them.'

Heads nodded around the table in support of the Minister. Not one of them could claim a day's service with the Colours, thought Lethbridge ruefully, and nothing was simple when it came to operations in Africa. The Brigadiers face remained impassive at the Minister's sideswipe. Nothing leaked out, or showed, of the thoughts which flashed into the SAS officer's mind. He wondered in that instant what would happen to his career prospects, if he launched himself across the table and smashed his fist into the jaw of the snide, mealy-mouthed little shit sitting in front of him. Instantly suppressing the urge, and the smile that came with it, the Brigadier remained impassive and outwardly calm. Keeping his steely grey eyes fixed firmly on the Minister, he said,

'Our Brits are trapped in a very remote and dangerous region of the Congo's interior Minister. With Afghanistan and our numerous other worldwide commitments, the SAS are already stretched pretty thinly around the globe. Time seems to be against us. At best, disengaging from current operations, then transporting my men will take days, depending of course, it being feasible in the first place. If you want me to arrange and mount an extract and mission, I will first have to see who we might have available, to achieve it.'

'Damn this bloody man,' thought Benchley scowling. He clearly had no appreciation of the political whirlwind, which was waiting to erupt and descend on him as head of the Foreign Office, and the UK government's credibility, after the coming mornings trumpeting headlines. Should any harm come to the medical team, or the niece of that damned newspaper editor, there would be incalculable embarrassment to the government, both at home and abroad...

'This is a top-priority Brigadier. I have No. 10's full support in the matter.'

Brigadier Lethbridge nodded slowly. He could imagine the tabloid headlines, No. 10 would like to see:
'*GOVERNMENT SENDS IN SAS TO SAVE OUR ANGELS!*'

Good for their ratings on the 6 O'clock news, but they were not, the Brigadier thought ruefully, much help for the men who were about to be ordered into harm's way.

'Do we have clearance from the Government of the Congo to cross their borders, or is this mission to be planned as clandestine, Minister?'

Beside him, The Minister's Under Secretary shook his head, and fielded the question,

'We are working on that Brigadier. A formal request has been made to the London Embassy of the Democratic Republic of Congo, for permission to cross their borders, and affect a rescue. We are currently waiting for their government's reply.'

The Brigadier nodded. He had played these games before. He knew they must expect deliberate delays on a formal answer, while some senior Congolese official worked out a demand of one sort or another which, given the endemic corruption thriving across Africa in general, would ultimately benefit the official concerned, personally.

Probably better to plan for both options, he thought to himself.

There was a pregnant lull in the conversation, and the Brigadier correctly assumed his part at the meeting was over. The Minister's cards were face up on the table. Brigadier Lethbridge nodded and stood up.

'Very well Minister, as time is of the essence, I'd better get cracking, but in the first instance, I will have to get my own people over at the M.O.D. in Operations Planning, to see if this mission is feasible at all.'

David Benchley had heard enough. Shaking his head, he said,

'Perhaps I have not explained things properly to you Brigadier, or made the Governments position crystal clear. No. 10 has decreed that our citizens must be saved, whatever the cost, so you *will* make it feasible.' The Foreign Office minister jumped to his feet. 'Do you understand, Brigadier? That is a damned order, straight from the Prime Minister himself!'

The ancient lorry chugged and ground its way in low gear, surrounded in a cloud of red swirling dust, as it toiled its way along the deserted track towards the Mpolo mine. Krutz absently looked back through the smeared driver's cabin window. His men had discarded their own packs, which now lay at their feet on the lorry's metal floor. Although braced on the rear benches at the back of the lorry, they bounced and jarred as the lorry hit each new rut in the pitted, uneven track. One of his men had a wooden box resting across his knees, and was intent on cushioning it from the punishing journey up the mountain to the mine. The box was emblazoned with large red letters, which gave all the warning needed – 'Danger Explosives!'

Unlike military-grade plastic explosives, commercial dynamite was notoriously unstable, especially when subjected to high temperatures over long periods. Safety protocols demanded that its detonators must always be kept apart and separate from explosives, to avoid premature detonation. Under the right circumstances, dynamite had a nasty habit of sweating pure, highly sensitive nitro-glycerine. A sharp blow could cause the extremely susceptible nitro to explode, with all the devastating results associated with high-yield explosives. Krutz turned his attention back to the driver beside him.

'For Christ's sake, take it easy, Kaffir!'

The African driver turned his shinning, sweat-stained face towards the tough South African. He missed the double declutch, and the gearbox let out another scream of grinding metal in protest. With a broad grin, he said, 'OK Boss, sure - no problem.'

Finally reaching the otherwise deserted chain-link gate on the mine complex's outer perimeter, the driver slowed and stopped. Wrenching on the handbrake, he reached into his pocket. Removing a fat brass key, he showed it to his passenger and said, 'No problem Boss.' Without waiting for a reply, the driver opened his door, climbed down onto the dusty track and walked towards the gate.

Having unlocked the padlock and swung the squealing gate open, the driver walked casually back and climbed into the lorry's cab. On a nod from their leader, two of Otto Krutz's security team jumped down from the back of the lorry, to begin their duties as sentries. Without sufficient men to establish a proper security perimeter, Krutz thought ruefully that Terry and Carl would have to do their best, while the rest of his team were busy up at the mine. As the two men knelt down and busied themselves with the contents of their backpacks, with another grinding of gears, the lorry lurched forward and drove slowly into the heart of Pan Global's Mpolo mining complex.

On either side of the track leading to the small cluster of ramshackle buildings and the mine's main office, great piles of rock spoil lay bleached and silent under the burning sun. A bulldozer and other heavy earthmoving vehicles were parked haphazardly. Here and there, African miners wearing dirty orange coveralls and dented hard hats sauntered nonchalantly from the mine's canteen, towards the central lift shaft. The grinning driver called out to one of his friends who was ambling by, then with a wave of his hand, continued to the mineshaft's entrance, after stopping to drop off Krutz, who wanted to report directly to the mine's manager.

The security men knew that Ojukwu was coming soon, and to them, the incident outside the Almond Hotel was old news. The team had worked together for a long time, and were full of confidence that the mission would be quick and clinical. One of them ordered a messenger into the mine to clear the miners labouring deep inside. As an incentive for them to move quickly, the message ended with a warning that the entrance would come down in thirty minutes. Anyone remaining inside after that would be sealed in and buried alive by the blast, so they had better get a move on, and get out...or else!

Dressed in civilian T-shirts and shorts, three of the four security advisors began to unpack their holdalls, while they waited at the mine's mouth for the tunnels inside to empty. The other security man carefully carried the box full of explosives from the lorry and gently placed it in the shade, just inside the mine's entrance. Otto Krutz's second-in-command, ex-US Navy SEAL, Buzz Holman took out his folding stock FAL assault-rifle. He hefted its reassuring weight. Inside the holdall, five fully loaded magazines lay ready. He cocked the weapon and glanced into the breach, to check the chamber was empty. He said,

'We'll start laying the charges in twenty minutes, guys. Get your weapons out and get 'em loaded, just in case those Mai-Mai bastards pay us a visit before we are set up and ready.'

He lifted a magazine from the holdall and snapped it, with a loud metallic click, firmly into the FAL. With an exaggerated flourish, he pulled back the cocking lever, and snapped a 7.62 round into the assault-rifle's breach. Making sure the safety catch was firmly set at the *on* position, Buzz grinned at the other three men.

'Cos guys, you just never know, do you?'

Standing in the wooden hut which passed as the mine's office, Otto Krutz waited impatiently for the manager to open the safe and remove the diamonds. Krutz was uncomfortable with the situation. His group were badly exposed up here. No perimeter to speak of, precious little firepower in support, and because of the geography, only one way in and out of the complex. Krutz did not like it one bit. His past battle hardening experiences in Angola set alarm bells ringing, as he stood waiting in the office. The hit-and-run tactics of lightly armed UNITA guerrillas were well-known, and during the Angolan conflict, led by their Cuban mentors, had proven damned difficult to defend against, even with a full company of his tough, heavily armed Reconnaissance Commando. Nothing felt good about this operation. Bad enough, he thought, to be suddenly ordered here in the first place, without any prior warning or proper preparation. They'd been cooped up in an aircraft, for hours, which in Krutz's opinion should have been nothing more than an exhibit at a flight museum. Now, to cap it all, he was left sweltering in a dilapidated tin hut in the middle of the arse end of God knows where.

The South African snorted to himself. It was hot as hell inside this bloody poke hole, with no sign of an electric fan or air conditioning. Despite the open windows, the room was airless, small and sparsely furnished. A wooden desk scattered with papers, two chairs and a metal filing cabinet was all the furniture the room boasted, save for the heavy Chubb safe which sat upon the floor in one corner. A large map of the area was pinned on one wall, and an old, out of date Pirelli calendar hung lopsided on the opposite wall, with a smiling Miss August 2008, doing her very best to display her ample charms, and brighten their day.

Noting the security man's obvious discomfort, the chief mining engineer, who also doubled as mine manager; a ruddy faced greying Scot named Angus McGhee said,

'Aye, you've noticed. It is pretty basic up here I'm afraid. The Corporation will not spend the money on luxuries like replacing the air con, and my only electric fan died on me yesterday,' he shrugged apologetically, 'we do not get many visitors... Drink?'

Without waiting for an answer, McGhee turned away and shuffled over to the safe. Putting on his reading glasses, which until then had hung from a string around his neck, he crouched down and swiftly turned the tumbler left and right until he was rewarded with a loud click from the safes locking mechanism. The mine manager grasped the metal handle, and yanked it down hard. The heavy safe door swung open, and with a satisfied sigh, McGhee lifted out a half-empty bottle of whiskey and two glasses. Krutz regarded the stocky Scotsman for a moment in silence, as a fat bluebottle buzzed noisily around the office's ceiling.

'I have to keep my whiskey under lock and key.' He shook his head sadly. Jerking his thumb at the African workers chatting outside, he said, 'they will steal the pennies off a dead man's eyes.' Looking lovingly at the malt, he continued, 'nothing is sacred in this God-forsaken wilderness, and this is the last of it until I go on leave in a fortnight.' He stared at his guest once again. 'Now do you want a wee dram, or not?'

Krutz snorted. 'Hell, why not?' he grinned as he glanced at his watch. 'We will not blow the mine for another twenty minutes or so, and I could do with something to wash out the taste of that damned old crate we flew in on.' He stared at the safe. 'It is probably just as well to leave the diamonds safe in there until the last minute anyhow.'

The mine manager appeared confused for a moment, as he looked from the tough South African towards the ancient safe. There was a faint smile upon his face when he said,

'Good God, that old thing's fine for hiding the Scotch, but I would not trust leaving a fortune in diamonds locked up in it. Since the rumours started about Ojukwu moving south, I have had them locked up securely in Birundi's only bank...you understand, for proper safe keeping?'

Clicking his tongue with irritation, Kurtz growled, 'Well, let's go and get them out then. I want to seal the mine and be away from here within the hour.'

McGhee looked at his watch, and then back at his guest. Shaking his head apologetically he said.

'I'm sorry Colonel, but you are out of luck I'm afraid. It's Sunday, and the bank is shut at weekends. The diamonds are safe where they are though. The bank and its vault are a left over from the old colonial days. It is about the only thing that still works properly in this God awful place. I chose it because it is the most secure spot in the province. Before putting my trust in it though, I got the bank's manager to let me inspect it. The actual vault is a big impressive bastard made from hardened steel, and its floor is reinforced with pre-stressed concrete. It's set to work on a time-lock. It will not open again until nine o'clock, tomorrow morning, when the bank opens for business...' He shrugged apologetically, 'Sorry.'

Kurtz fumed silently. Clearly, his bosses in London knew nothing of the mine manager's security concerns, or his diligence in securing the diamonds. Kurtz was trapped by circumstance. There was nothing he could do but wait, and he knew it.

McGhee splashed a generous measure of the fiery single malt into both tumblers. He handed one to Krutz, then lifted his glass in salute.

'Here is to the best-laid plans, eh?'

Before the South African could lift the glass to his lips, McGhee had drained his with a single gulp, 'another?'

Krutz was about to reply, when the quiet outside was shattered by sudden and deafening exchange of gunfire, which crackled from the direction of the mine's main gate. Both men ducked involuntarily as more shots were fired. Incoming and outgoing high-velocity rounds cracked and whizzed around the mine's office building.

'Jesus!'

Shaking with fright, McGhee stared anxiously towards his visitor. The Scotsman's ruddy complexion was gone; his face blanched with shock. Dropping his glass, Krutz ran to the door. Wrenching it open, he yelled desperately back into the room.

'For God's sake, get down and stay there!'

McGhee obeyed and threw himself to the floor. Krutz disappeared into the deafening maelstrom of the gun battle raging outside. As McGhee muttered a silent prayer, the small office was suddenly rocked by a cataclysmic explosion. The massive blast came from the direction of the mine's entrance.

Chapter Seven

Operations Planning – Special Forces
Ministry of Defence

When Brigadier Lethbridge strode into his high-security SAS Operations Planning and Support complex, in the basement of the Ministry of Defence, its main hall was filled with the usual shambolic arrangement of desks and tables. Each was covered in the clutter of maps, high-altitude aerial reconnaissance photographs and close-up pictures of foreign buildings and suspects from around the world, which were currently of interest to British Intelligence and Special Forces. To an outsider, the apparent clutter looked chaotic, but not to the team of tough-looking men who were intently studying them. Valuable intelligence could be gleaned from each of the documents and photos, and this in turn would be passed by ultra-secure, super-fast burst radio messages to the SAS and SBS soldiers on the ground, in their distant theatres of secret operations around the globe.

A large-scale map of Columbia was pinned to one wall, showing elevated southern and central regions, where huge quantities of coca leaves were currently being grown and processed into cocaine and its derivative crack, in crude laboratories carved out deep within isolated jungle hideaways. Makeshift airstrips and winding tracks were hacked from the primal jungle. They had been clearly marked and photographed by surveillance satellites, and the Regiment's own covert ground patrols. Several points dotted on the map were ringed in red marker, where a successful operation had been recently recorded by the Regiment; the laboratory attacked and permanently destroyed with the assistance of Colombian Special Forces drug enforcement soldiers, and their Narcotics police.

Covering a section of another whitewashed wall, was a rogue's gallery of swarthy men dressed in unkempt black turbans and stained flowing robes. At first glance, the men in the photos might have been mistakenly considered nothing more dangerous than local Afghan mountain farmers, or simple shepherds. A closer look revealed the truth to a casual observer however, as each man's cruel face had been clandestinely photographed; each picture betrayed a slight blurring around its edges, the sure sign that they had all been snapped at a very long range, using extremely powerful telephoto lenses.

Closer examination still, would reveal that each of the men was armed with an AK47 assault-rifle or RPG rocket launcher. One Afghan was standing in a mountain village, talking with another man wearing a crude suicide vest, packed with explosives and studded with nails. Another wore a string of fragmentation grenades across his chest and the scars of numerous battles across his dark hook-nosed face.

The Afghanistan desk of MI6, Gt. Britain's overseas intelligence service, flagged each of these men as most wanted. From thousands of miles away, the Afghan's fate already was sealed in the eyes of British Intelligence and the SAS. As senior captains of the Taliban in the war-ravaged Helmand province, once identified, their individual details had been sent back to London and lodged into red folders in the bowels of the MI6's headquarters in Vauxhall. As a result, each of the men had been officially sanctioned...The red folder placed their lives on a knife edge. Orders had been issued that they were to be captured alive if possible, or shot on sight by concealed SAS sniper teams, if taking them prisoner for later interrogation by the intelligence services, proved impracticable.

In the bustling headquarters, several men dressed in civilian clothes looked up and acknowledged the Brigadier, with nothing more than a casual nod. Not a hint of a smart salute anywhere, and no-one snapped to attention when the Brigadier entered the planning office. Normally, senior line officers would have bridled at the apparent lack of deferment to their rank, by the men under his command. Brigadier Lethbridge did not mind in the slightest, however; spit and polish were not their way in the secret world of Special Forces. If he wanted salutes, he thought to himself ruefully, he would have bloody well joined the brigade of Guards.

'Where has Rocky Blain got to, Taff?' He asked one of the men who was passing him, carrying an armful of rolled maps. The man stopped; a quizzical look clouded his face. He thought for a moment, and then in a soft Welsh accent, he grinned back at the Brigadier, and replied,

'Oh...I think he's gone for a dump, Boss.'

Irritated not by the comment, but rather by the fact his acting head of Ops Planning was not immediately available; Lethbridge was caught off-guard by the honesty and lack of political correctness of the answer, and despite his mild irritation, returned the grin.

'Well, go and dig him out for me, will you?'

The stocky SAS sergeant major dropped his bundle of maps onto a table, scratched his mop of curly black hair, and still grinning replied, 'Sure thing Boss... I think I know where he will be.'

Outside, the lunchtime traffic continued to rumble down Whitehall, oblivious to the mercy mission which was in the initial planning stage by the Regiment. Deep beneath the Ministry of Defence building, Brigadier Lethbridge finished briefing his temporary head of Ops. Planning, on his earlier meeting with the Foreign Office minister. Normally, he would have liaised with Colonel Mike Hanna, but he was currently representing the SAS at a high profile Nato Special Forces meeting in Washington DC. Until he returned, RSM Rocky Blain was covering for him. With almost twenty years of dedicated active service within the regular SAS Regiment, Rocky had earned the respect of everyone; the Brigadier included.

'So there it is Rocky; our masters have decreed that we mount this damned rescue with immediate effect. I know it's a fast ball, but what is your initial take on this...tell me, what do you think?'

Regimental Sergeant Major 'Rocky' Blain scratched his chin,

'Well boss, on the face of it, it is a simple in and out job, but I'm concerned that we have not had time to do even a preliminary Intel workup on the opposition forces, or find out exactly where they are in Katinga province. There's no time to get an RAF high-altitude reconnaissance drone over the area, so we are going in almost blind. The Foreign Office and Embassy in Kinshasa might be able to help, and I will call their Military Attaché for any updates they might have, shortly. We do not have much time, so it seems the best course of action is for the team to fly in, gather up the doctors and nurses and fly straight out gain, before the opposition realises what we are up to. As far as I can see, it should be straightforward...' Rocky's weather-beaten face creased as his brow furrowed, 'maybe...?'

Brigadier Lethbridge nodded. 'Go on.'

'Some questions do occur immediately though. First on the list of course, is whom we send in to make the rescue. We'll need to have a close look at that one. We'll also need to plan exactly where they will take the medics, when our guys have got them safely in tow.'

The Brigadier raised an eyebrow. 'Anything else?'

'Yes Boss. Will the Congolese Government give us permission to enter their airspace fully armed, in the first place?'

Lethbridge nodded. 'That is down the Foreign Office. I'm assured they are working hard on that point right now.'

Rocky Blain snorted. 'I'll bet. I suspect if they thought it would be easy to get permission, they would have just sent in a rep. from the British Embassy in Kinshasa, and grabbed the headlines for themselves?'

Brigadier Lethbridge smiled sardonically,

'I suspect you are right, Rocky. I think we had better plan on getting a team in under the Congolese radar for now. If it turns out that permission is granted, in the meantime, we can adjust our plans accordingly. Now, most importantly, who do we have available to mount the rescue?'

Both men turned to the large-scale world map, which covered an entire wall in Rocky's private office. There were a number of small coloured pins dotted around the globe, showing current SAS deployment. Rocky stared at the map for a few moments, while he rubbed his chin and silently considered his options.

He pointed at the map and said. 'Well now, we currently have the whole of 'A' Squadron out on Ops in Afghanistan. Half of 'B' Squadron are on anti-narcotic Ops. in Columbia, and the other half are out on that big joint exercise with the Sultan's Gurkhas, in the Brunei jungle. 'D' Squadron is currently in Hereford working up to replace 'A' Squadron, when their tour finishes in the 'Stan next month. 'G' Squadron are currently providing anti-terrorist cover in the UK, with some of their blokes out in Iraq, still working with the yank's Delta force, against the Al Qaeda bombers and the militia death squads.'

The Brigadier shook his head. 'With our chaps embedded on active operations in Afghanistan, or deep in the South American and Brunei jungles, getting them out and re-briefed, then deployed will take too long. The UK anti-terror cover must stay in place, and the Americans will have a screaming fit if we suddenly ship out our entire team from Iraq. Surely, we must have someone already in central Africa?'

Both men stared at the map. The vast African continent was almost devoid of coloured pins. Rocky Blain's face showed his discomfort. He shook his head.

'It's no good Boss; we have none of our guys there at the moment; they are all fully committed elsewhere.'

The Brigade Commander raised an eyebrow. 'Then why prey, is there a blue pin just there Rocky?' He pointed towards the middle of the continent.

RSM Blain let out a sigh and shook his head. 'Oh that; it's nothing... A territorial SAS Troop on exercise in Kenya.' He shrugged, 'they are just out on a jolly, training on Mt. Kilimanjaro.'

Brigadier Lethbridge snapped his fingers as memories flooded back. 'Why yes, of course! Now I remember... That's Pat Farrell's Two Troop from 21, isn't it? I signed off on their exercise a couple of months ago.'

Rocky Blain's discomfort was self-evident. His face darkened, as his craggy features betrayed his regular soldier reservations.

'Surely you don't want me to send in a bunch of part-time reservists on a job like this Boss? What if things went wrong?'

Pursing his lips, the Brigadier said slowly, 'They performed brilliantly during Operation Windmill, Rocky.' He held up his hand, 'I know all about the doubts in Hereford towards our territorial counterparts, but remember this: it was men of the Territorial SAS who saved London a few months ago...Not the regulars from Hereford. Circumstances dictated then that there was no other choice but to put them in harm's way at the time...they were on the ground, in the right place, at the right moment and unfortunately, it appears current circumstances dictate that history is about to repeat itsself.'

Rocky knew the Brigadier was right. When the shit hit the fan, only the men of the newly formed territorial SAS Shadow Squadron were immediately available, to stop London being turned into a glowing radioactive cinder. Although keeping his opinions to himself, Rocky did not like the current situation one little bit. Like so many other hard-bitten senior NCOs from the super élite regular SAS based in Hereford, he had scant regard for his part-time territorial counterparts. He knew Pat Farrell well enough though; they had shared plenty of adventures, when Pat had been regular SAS. He was also aware that the men in Two Troop were already cleared by the Government for immediate active service, as members of the recently formed, and top secret reserve Shadow Squadron. Grudgingly, he had to admit that they had done well enough, when the Al Qaeda terrorist cell had got within a whisker of detonating their stolen Iraqi nuclear bomb in London's densely populated heart.

The acting head of SAS Operations Planning and Support puffed out his cheeks and exhaled slowly. Circumstances had overwhelmed and outflanked Rocky's misgivings, and he well knew it.

'OK Boss, if there's no other way,' he shrugged, 'fair enough. I'll go and get a signal off to their base camp at Talinga, and tell them to get Pat Farrell and his men off the mountain ASAP. In the meantime, I will liaise via the secure satellite link with our Defence Attaché at the British High Commission in Nairobi. I will request he flies up there in person to brief Pat on the mission. As the Attaché is our local man on the ground, I will instruct him to arrange their transport into the Congo as well.'

Rocky Blain turned away; his face creased into the sour look he habitually wore when details of a mission remained uncertain. He had been left feeling dissatisfied with the plan as it stood. Next to Afghanistan, the northern Congo was one of the most dangerous places on earth, but he had been given no choice, and had no alternatives to offer. Pat and his part-time troop had to go in, and go in quickly. When planning a covert mission for the boys down in Hereford, Rocky always liked to allow for the 'sod's law' factor. What worried him now was that there were just too many variables; there was any number of loose ends that might go catastrophically wrong. No backup force was available; they were a long way from home, and there would be no-one to help them if they got into trouble. Irritated, Rocky clicked his tongue. This might turn out to be a challenging op, even for the superbly trained regular SAS from Hereford, but territorial part-timers? With a resigned shrug he arrived at the communications wing filled with growing unease. As he swiped his security pass through the electronic locking system and pulled the heavy steel door open, he was still muttering under his breath. This whole thing was a disaster waiting to happen.

'Poor bastards... could be worse though, I suppose. At least, the bloody weekend warriors are being led by an ex-Hereford man.'

'Pardon?'

Rocky Blain stopped at the entrance to the room, which hummed with powerful electronic transmitters and television screens. He turned toward the man behind him.

'Oh, hallo Cornelius.'

Cornelius Wilde, Shadow Squadron's MI6 Intelligence liaison officer's face was quizzical. 'What is that about my boys, Rocky?'

Chapter Eight

Pat Farrell and the rest of Two Troop sat relaxing on their bergan backpacks, surrounded by clouds of pungent hexamine fumes wafting up from their small individual cookers, as they chatted to each other in the cold rarefied atmosphere, on the snow-covered summit of Kilimanjaro. They were casually enjoying the blue skies and magnificent view, as they prepared a well-earned hot brew. It had been a difficult last stage, and all of them had felt the extra physical effort needed, as straining lungs struggled to draw in the scant air available at such high altitude. Resting for a short while had quickly eased the burning in their oxygen starved thighs and calves. Here and there, his men were beginning to stand up and rummage through their bergans, extracting the inevitable Mars bars. Some were putting on extra layers of clothing, to combat the creeping cold which was quickly cooling their overheated bodies, now they were high above Kilimanjaro's snow line, after the tortuous punishment of the last few hundred metres, climbing up the treacherously icy track leading to the vast and deserted rim of the extinct volcano.

Pat stood up and stretched stiff muscles. He glanced at his men until he spotted who he was looking for.

Frozen snow crunched beneath his boots as he casually sauntered over to his young radio operator.

'Get your brew down your neck, Spike. I want you to set up the radio and send a message off to base camp. Tell them that we've nailed the summit. Once that's done, pack up, and we can start the descent phase.'

Spike stopped stirring his steaming tea. He looked up with a grin.

'Sure thing Pat, no problem.'

His brew finished; Spike set up the radio and re-established comms with Talinga. He passed on Pat's message, but was surprised when the base camp operator had acknowledged their arrival, then ordered him to dial in a new frequency, and stand by for a coded message on the secure burst channel, via the British military SkyNet 5 network.

High above them, in the cold vacuum of space, the SkyNet chain of satellites, locked in their respective geostationary orbits, some 35,800 kilometres above the earth's surface, provided excellent and highly secure communications with any British forces on deployment anywhere in the world. London could issue real-time orders and intelligence briefings to any of their forces, night and day, irrespective of location, or local weather conditions.

After Spike had reset the frequency dials and undone the side pocket of his bergan, he pulled out the code book and one-time pad, to decode and decipher the message he would receive shortly. Quizzically, he looked over to his friend and said,

'That is a bit odd Danny, why is London sending us a fully coded message, during a non-tactical training exercise?'

As Danny looked up from his half-finished brew, a quizzical look also spread across his sunburnt face. 'Stuffed if I know mate,' he shook his head, 'doesn't make any sense?' He raised an eyebrow, 'it must be something serious though.... Better give Pat a shout, and let him know something's up.'

Franz De Keizer sat white faced, staring mutely at the telephone, which now lay silently cradled on his desk. Moments earlier, before the call had ended, his face had mirrored both growing concern and shock. As he absorbed the detail, his face quickly changed into a look of horror, as he listened intently against a background of chirrups and whistles, which continuously threatened to overwhelm Otto Krutz's devastating report from the police station, in the ramshackle township of Birundi, buried deep within the Congo's violent hinterland.

'Christ!' he whispered softly to himself. Otto Krutz' report meant only one thing. The hastily arranged recovery plan, which would have quietly saved Pan Global's future, was fast unravelling and turning into a debacle. Krutz had told him that four of their men had been blown to bits, and another two badly wounded in what he described as a huge slice of bad luck, shortly after their arrival at the mine, during nothing more than a probing attack by the Tutsi militia's advance guard. To make matters worse, the security team's aircraft was currently crippled by mechanical failure. The diamonds were safe for now, but for how much longer? de Keizer had no idea.

Pan Global's economic intelligence director pushed his chair back slowly, and stood up. Straightening his tie, he sighed deeply. He must seek an audience immediately, and pass the bad news to Sir Hugo.

Having decrypted and decoded the message, Spike stared at its contents with utter disbelief. He'd never received a signal quite like it. The message had been transmitted from the Ministry of Defence as a Flash Signal

– Its security clearance was - SAS eyes only. Those two categories meant it carried the absolutely highest priority, and must be acted on immediately.

Grasping the message pad firmly in his fist, Spike jumped up and ran over to Pat, who was lying on his waterproof thermal mat, with his battered bush hat pulled down over his eyes.

'Hey Pat...Wake up. You are not going to believe what I've just decoded!'

Pat lifted his hat from his face and held out his hand, 'Show me.'

Pat saw the priority first, then read the message. His face registered his surprise. 'Bloody hell!' was all he said.

Minutes later, the troop was packed up and ready to move. Ingrained patrol doctrine ensured every man had checked his own space for forgotten equipment or even the tiniest piece of litter. Swept clear, there would be no trace left behind, of their short stopover. The troop stood ready and silently waiting for Pat's orders.

Pat felt the old adrenaline rush. His heart was beginning to beat faster. This is what he came back into the reserve SAS for. Something was in the wind, and judging by the urgent tone of the signal he and his men were going to be at its very heart.

'Right lads, we have received a priority one message from SAS Group in London. Something's happened, and we have been ordered back to base camp at Talinga asp. We have got to get down to the plateau four thousand feet below us in,' he glanced at his watch 'in just over one hour. We'll be picked up by a Kenyan Air force chopper, and flown the rest of the way back to base.' Pat looked at the faces around him. He had seen the look before. There was eager anticipation written all over each of them. 'I don't know yet what it is all about, but I've been ordered to attend a full briefing when we land. I'll brief you guys when I know more.' Pat paused for a moment, and then changed the subject to a matter which was of more immediate importance to all of them. 'Now you have all used this technique plenty of times coming down off the Fan in Brecon, so we are moving off in a minute at a nice steady pace down to the plateau. I do not want anyone losing it and breaking his neck, so I will set the pace on this run, and you will follow me. Clear?'

All around the troop heads nodded. Pat was right; they had all had to learn the fast descent technique, the Regiment used to lose height quickly on a mountain during their selection phase, before ultimately joining the ranks of the few successful candidates badged into the territorial SAS. Running down a steep mountain like Brecon's pen y fan (Penny Fan) with a weapon in their hands and a heavy pack strapped to their backs, made balance extremely precarious; running down a treacherous icy path was no laughing matter. It was dangerous and exhausting work, but to make the almost impossible qualification times set by the regular SAS attached to the reserve Regiment's Training Wing, during gruelling individual selection marches by day and night across the high mountains of south Wales; speed was always of the essence. Climbing mountains is a slow and exhausting process, and precious time had to be made up at any opportunity, particularly on the rare areas of flat ground, or when the going was at its easiest during a descent. To ensure proper balance and to restrict a headlong uncontrolled scamper, which inevitably led to disaster, each man knew that he had to lean back and run from the knees down. Thighs had to be kept almost locked together; it saved energy and stopped the individual's downward rush from quickly and literally running out of control. Alone and always under the cosh of the clock, fatalities in the past, during the Regiment's uncompromising selection process on the mountain wilderness of Brecon, bore silent witness to the dangers to those who ignored their instructors and failed to use the technique properly.

Nodding to his men, his face set grim Pat said, 'Right boys, remember this will be three or four times as far, compared to coming down from the trig point at the top of the Fan, so stay behind me and go at my pace.' Pat turned away from his men, and stared in the direction of the dangerous route he was about to lead his men. Swivelling his head, he called back over his shoulder. An intense grin of anticipation was spreading across his face.

'Right then ... Let's do it!'

Sir Hugo Maxton listened in silence as his intelligence chief spelt out the disaster which had unfolded in Birundi. The silence continued for several awkward moments after the director's report ended. Franz De Keizer nervously shifted his weight from one leg to the other, while his chairman stared at him stone faced, digesting the full depth of the unwelcome and tragic news.

De Keizer was first to break the silence. His voice was almost pleading. 'Men in our employ are dead. What in God's name are we going to do now, Sir Hugo?'

Ignoring the question, Pan Global's chairman stood up and walked toward the window. When he stopped, he gazed in silent contemplation at the spectacular panorama of the Thames below, and the grey spires of south London across the grey water. With his hands clasped behind his back, he half turned and spoke softly,

'We have done what we can to take care of things Franz, but these latest developments have raised the stakes. Circumstances now dictate that we must look beyond our own resources...' Sir Hugo pursed his lips and said, 'it is time to call in a favour from a friend in high places.' Sir Hugo turned away from the window and walked slowly back to his desk. Despite the grave news from Birundi, there was a hint of relief on his face. He lent forward, depressed a button and spoke calmly into the intercom.

'Margery, please telephone David Benchley on his private number at the Foreign Office. Convey my compliments to the Minister, and tell him I must see him... immediately.'

Pat raised his arm to slow and then finally stop the troops' forced march, as they came to the end of their rapid descent. Pat's steady, controlled pace allowed all fourteen men to arrive safely, in one piece, on the barren deserted plateau. Pat glanced at his watch. He nodded to himself with satisfaction. They were seven minutes early for the rendezvous with the helicopter.

Sweating profusely despite the cold, he slipped off his bergan and called out to his men. 'OK guys, take a short breather and get some water inside you.'

Shading his eyes from the sun's glare, Pat stared through the crystal clear air towards the southern horizon, where he hoped, the chopper would appear. It was a matter of training and policy to always be at an R.V. at least five minutes early, but that, thought Pat ruefully, was when they were working with their own British Special Forces pilots. They were some of the best in the world, and he hoped the Kenyan pilot was on the ball, and would arrive on time.

Spike's sharp eyes were first to spot the tiny black dot on the horizon. 'There Pat!' he called, pointing down the mountain. 'It's there about half-way down the slope. Look slightly right of that big brown patch with that bushy topped tree.' Spike pointed in the direction he was looking. The rest of the troop craned their necks to catch a glimpse of the aircraft, which was ordered to take them back to base camp.

'Yeah, got it! Nice one Spike.' Pat looked away from the rapidly growing smudge. 'Right boys, hats off and get your bergans across one shoulder.' He pointed to his left. 'Shake out into line there...you all know the drill.' As the troop quickly deployed, Pat removed a metal cased smoke grenade from the side pocket of his bergan. With a last glance at his men, who had now crouched down into a tight line, Pat grasped the signal grenade tightly, and pulled the pin. With his arm straight, he lobbed it well ahead of the troop. The fizzing grenade bounced on the hard dry earth. With a loud hiss, it suddenly erupted into a cloud of swirling purple smoke. In the distance, the big helicopters straining engine began to overcome the silence of the barren plateau, where the SAS men patiently crouched in silence.

Far to the west, only twenty miles north of the Birundi Township, General Ojukwu listened with growing fury to the wounded guerrilla, as the man knelt before him and recounted the attack on the mine, and the vicious firefight with the white men who had defended it. Behind the man, the bullet ridden Land Rover stood silent. It bore stark witness to the accurate fire, which had come from the mine entrance before the explosion. Some of Ojukwu's men were respectfully lifting the bloodied bodies of their dead comrades from it.

'Where is my brother?' demanded the general.

The man before him moaned softly to himself. It was not his fault. With eyes still downcast, and his voice trembling, he said reluctantly. 'He is dead Excellence. The white men's magic was too powerful. We shot at them, but they killed him with their enchanted bullets.'

With a primordial snarl, Ojukwu kicked the man in the face. Already wounded, the man screamed and rolled in the red dust. Ignoring the blood which stained the guerrilla's ragged shirt, and still oozed from a bullet wound in his arm, Ojukwu hissed,

'Then why do you still live you cowardly scum?' Shaking with anger, he turned to his second-in-command who stood close beside him. Pointing to the machete hanging on the man's belt, he held out his hand expectantly.

High above, a great eagle cried out to the heavens.

With a sly and knowing grin, the guerrilla officer silently slid the heavy blade clear of its battered scabbard, and handed it to his general.

With the contemptuous look still lingering on his sweat streaked face, in a sudden and explosive blur, using every ounce of his considerable strength, Ojukwu hacked down at the cowering guerrilla at his feet. With a dull thud, the hissing blade cut into the man's unprotected neck, instantly slicing through his spinal column and severing his head completely. As dark arterial blood spurted from the headless torso onto the sun-baked ground, Ojukwu casually handed the machete back to his startled subordinate. Kicking the head away like a football, and ignoring the still twitching body sprawled on the ground, Ojukwu burned with blinding rage at his brother's death. The general spat out the words which would seal the fate of the distant mining township.

'I will take half my men and continue the drive towards Birundi. I want you to make a sweep further south with the rest of my warriors, while I make an example of the township's people. The whole of Katinga province must feel my power, and the wrath of the Mai-Mai... You know where I want you to go. Kill all in your path, I want them **all** dead!' Glaring at his brother-in-law, shaking with rage he snarled savagely, 'No exceptions...Do you understand me?.. *Kill them all!*'

Awed by the sudden execution, and Birundi's death warrant, the startled C F P officer nodded obediently. Despite his strong family ties, it did not do to show hesitation or reluctance when dealing with his leader. General Ojukwu turned and began to walk away, but abruptly he stopped. Spinning around he fixed the man with a stare filled with malevolence. He hissed softly. 'When I arrive, I have something special in mind for the white foreigners we find in Birundi... I want any whites taken alive!'

With an imperious wave of his hand, the general spoke again as he dismissed his subordinate.

'We are close to Birundi now, no more than a day's walk. I will take my men and attack on foot. Collect your own men, issue your orders and move south immediately. Take all the vehicles we have...and go.'

Chapter Nine

Talinga Garrison

'Battalion...*HALT!*'

The wide dusty parade ground was busy. A full battalion of smartly dressed Kenyan light infantrymen were being drilled by one of their Sergeant Majors beneath the burning sun, under the watchful eyes of a member of the small British Army Training Team contingent, which were currently on secondment to the L.I.

The Kenyan President and his Minister for defence were due to make a morale boosting visit to the Talinga border garrison in a week's time. Under the orders of the Garrison commander, he was determined to display his soldier's prowess, and rehearsals for a full military parade were well under way.

Immaculate in his starched uniform, Grenadier Guards Sgt Major Bob Bartle was serving on attachment to the British military mission's training team in Kenya. He winced as the marching column came to a ragged and untidy stop. He was generally impressed with the professional standards of field craft and tactics when the lads he was engaged in training were out in the untamed bush on exercise, but even with the help of the off-key bugles and rapid beat of the Light Infantry's regimental band, the Kenyan soldiers' coordination still required days of intense work before it came remotely close to the high standards of rifle drill he was used to instilling into green new recruits at the Guards depot at Pirbright in Surrey.

'Better that time Bob?' enquired the stern faced Light Infantry NCO to his mentor. At six feet six, Bob Bartle towered over his Kenyan counterpart. Looking down, he said quietly.

'We are certainly getting there Joshua,' he glanced at his watch. 'But I think you'd better let them have some water, then keep marching them around the parade square for at least another hour, until they get the basics right.'

Pat Farrell watched the efforts of the sweating African infantrymen on the shimmering square, from the cool shade of the veranda outside the briefing room close by. He had come straight over from the heli-pad, as time was clearly of the essence. Helping himself from the cooler, he sipped at the iced glass of water. Memories of his own basic training came rampaging back and brought a fond smile to his face. He remembered being an awkward kid of seventeen, and the teenage images of his old training platoon's infantry Corporals, as they bellowed and ranted in frustration at his young squad's hopelessly uncoordinated initial efforts at rifle drill, on the parade square. It was a tough eighteen-week introduction to army life at his infantry training depot at Bassingbourne, close to the ancient city of Cambridge. His quest for adventure began only days earlier, when he cut his final ties with home, waved good-bye to his parents and began a long contract with the British army.

The years of infantry soldiering had come and gone. Promotion came quickly and easily. At just 19, Pat was the youngest NCO in his battalion, but after tours of Northern Island and five years of basic soldiering, Pat felt that he was heading into a black hole of utter boredom. Doubts on his future began to invade his mind, but things happen sometimes, which change lives forever.

Always looking for fresh material, a team from the secretive SAS Regiment visited his battalion on a recruiting drive. Pat's battalion had by then moved back from Germany, and were now stationed in the tedious garrison town of Colchester. The Special Forces team's slick presentation on life and service with the SAS lit a spark in Pat's imagination, and having considered his options carefully, he applied next morning for permission to try their rigorous selection course on the Welsh mountains.

His Colonel reluctantly agreed, and Pat was given his chance.

The SAS selection process was long and gruelling; the toughest Pat ever experienced. For 18-20 hours, by day and night the SAS hopefuls marched alone and navigated across the wild Black Mountains and Brecon Beacons of south Wales, fighting through the most atrocious weather conditions carrying ever heavier packs and weapons; always mindful and fretting with regards to their times on each leg of the course. Distances and pressure increased daily. If a recruit failed to make the cut-out time set for each long march over towering mountains and through deep windswept valleys, they were summarily returned to their parent unit without even the offer of a second chance. It did not help that the ever vigilant SAS instructors kept each route under observation. The times set for each leg were a closely guarded secret. Stone faced; the hard-bitten instructors simply recorded each candidate's performance daily, when they arrived exhausted at the final R.V..

Years earlier, during Pat's initial infantry training, his instructors would give the recruits boundless support, yelling encouragement and forcing them to learn the hard way what they could achieve if they plumbed their own depths to succeed. It was a good system for unworldly and inexperienced teenagers, but during SAS selection, the instructors silently watched their more mature charges and assessed their every action in minute detail. There was absolutely no encouragement whatsoever from the selection staff. Every ounce of motivation came from each individual on the course. Simply put, the candidates dug deep and came up to scratch, or they did not. The whole course was designed to see exactly what the men were capable of, through their individual resources and their own determination to pass or fail. This added a heavy psychological dimension to the remorseless physical demands loaded onto each man's exhausted shoulders. Pat Farrell watched other candidates broken by the course; they had succumbed to its many rigours, or convinced themselves in their few quiet moments that they did not belong in Hereford. The difference between Pat and most of the others was that he knew something they did not; he had found his place in the universe; his future, and his soul belonged to the SAS.

Pat prepared himself well for the challenge, both physically and mentally. Avoiding injury, he got on with the selection process without complaint. He knew only too well that the whole point was to root out the unworthy, so he gritted his teeth and took everything they threw at him.

During his selection course, through voluntary withdrawal or physical injuries, the initial intake dropped from fifty-eight men to just six, who had pushed themselves beyond even their own expectations and passed the testing mountain stage of selection. To earn their coveted sandy beret and winged dagger cap badge however, there was yet more arduous training to endure. Of the remaining six, another man lost it, and was cut during weeks of hot, claustrophobic jungle training in Brunei. The many individual qualities the Regiment were looking for in their new recruits were rigorously tested time and again, from the icy grip of frigid mountains, to the sweltering heat of steaming jungles during the different stages of selection. The SAS selectors knew their job, and maintained their standards accordingly. They chose whom they wanted Pat remembered, and simply binned the rest without the slightest hint of sympathy or one whit of mercy.

'*You there!* Are you Farrell?' demanded a curt, cultured voice behind him.

Pat's reverie collapsed like a burst balloon. He turned his gaze from the parade square and the sweating Kenyan infantrymen and stared at the man standing in the doorway behind him.

'Yes, I'm Pat Farrell, what can I do for you?'

The dapper white-haired European before him was smartly dressed in a lightweight grey suit. His ruddy complexion, bearing, and clipped moustache screamed army background thought Pat, but his accent screamed of Eaton, and the gin and tonic brigade of the old-boy network.

Out of step, and still dressed in their sweat-stained lightweight jungle combat uniforms, Spike and Danny ambled over to the veranda. Seeing that Pat had a visitor both young men waited, and remained silent.

'I am Major William Forde, formally of the Household cavalry, and presently serving as HMG's Military Attaché at the High Commission in Nairobi.' He said importantly. The tone of his voice and general look of disapproval registered instantly with Pat and his two scruffy young troopers.

'Why aren't you and your men wearing proper headdress, Farrell?'

Spike turned away from the doorway and winced at his friend, who grinned back at him. Danny winked; this should be fun.

Pat sighed to himself. He'd come up against these types occasionally during his military career. Most officers were OK, but he knew instantly that this guy was old-school, and would be a serious grade A pain in the arse. He might be ex-army thought Pat, but right now, he was just another bloody civil servant.

'Because we're on foreign soil; our standard operating procedures say we don't have to...Oh, and it's *Sergeant* Farrell, by the way.'

Danny did a poor job of stifling a smirk. Pat glared at him for a moment. Spike saw the look, took the warning and both troopers turned away.

Major Forde, late of the Household cavalry bridled. He well knew he could not pull his old rank on these insolent men any more. It was a courtesy to use his redundant army rank nowadays, rather than be simply addressed as Mister Forde. His hackles had risen in Nairobi when he first saw the signal ordering him up to the Talinga garrison. He carried an instinctive aversion and dislike of the piratical activities of the SAS. Their unconventional approach, lack of smart military bearing, and general disrespect towards officers left him ice cold. To make matters even worse, this impudent fellow and his 'gang' were mere part-time territorials.

'When I was a Company Commander with the Blues and Royals, we dealt harshly with insubordination....*Sergeant* Farrell.'

'Yeah, I'll bet you did' thought Pat. He had had enough of this pompous, passed over ex-cavalry major. The conversation was going nowhere, and Pat was eager to know why they had been pulled off the mountain with such urgency. 'What exactly can I do for you...*Major* Forde?'

Pursing his lips, Forde cleared his throat and said,

'I received a high-priority signal this morning from the Foreign Office in London...instructing me to come up here to brief you on a situation, where your...ah, abilities might somehow prove useful.' The sour look lingered, 'I suggest you step inside, and I'll brief you on what I know. 'He stared at Spike and Danny for a moment, and then returned his cool gaze to Pat. His irritation was unmistakable. 'And we can get this over and done with...as quickly as possible.'

Word of General Ojukwu's invasion spread like wildfire through the frightened population of Birundi. Fears for their families were well-founded. Across Africa, genocide was a deadly serious business, as the carnage in Rwanda had so recently and graphically demonstrated. The U.N. estimated 800,000 deaths after the bloodletting was eventually brought under control. None of the frightened Hutus living in and around Birundi had any doubt as to their fate, if they stayed behind and were caught by the Tutsi killers. Word had spread from upcountry that the guerrillas has been seen moving towards them and given the Mai-Mai's current rate of advance, they would arrive on the outskirts of the township in a matter of days. The news terrified the population, sparking a rushed evacuation. Fleeing the overcrowded township, some took to their heels and fled into the bush, where they would hide until the Mai- Mai was gone, but still fresh rumours grew like spreading ripples on a pond; stories of even more barbaric rape and slaughter began to circulate. Most people had contented themselves by packing up and leaving their homes, with what possessions they could carry balanced precariously on their heads. Long lines of terrified people were herding their children the short distance on the red earth road leading down to the old ferry crossing, which was their only other avenue of escape.

Along one edge of Birundi, the wide muddy waters of the Mpana River flowed serenely past the township, meandering slowly through the parched savannah towards the Kabali railhead, some eighty miles downstream.

Since ancient times, men braved the dangers of collision with submerged hippo or crocodile. They spent long hot days drifting in the current, bobbing silently on the sparkling waters of the slowly flowing Mpana waterway in crude canoes, fishing with spear and net to feed their hungry children. What surplus remained was sold fresh on the riverbank or from stalls in the towns thriving market. Sometimes, the fish were simply bartered for life's basic necessities like salt and grain.

Now spears were idle, and the fishermen's nets lay abandoned; they were busily involved in a new and highly lucrative business, haggling and shouting in rapid high-pitched tones, charging extortionate fees to ferry men, women and their crying babies across the dark river to the safety of the other side. Locals seethed with anger. The only alternative was to swim; huge Nile crocodiles waited hungrily for those foolish enough to try.

It was the end of the dry season, and the river remained sluggish, but the Monsoon was due any day. Torrential rain would fall in the mountains to the north when the wet season began to rampage across the continent. With frightening speed, the Mpana River would swell and become a raging, foaming torrent of immense roaring power. It would thunder inexorably past the township towards the falls beyond the distant settlement of Kabali Junction. When the rains came the river would become impassable; it would be suicide to even attempt a crossing. The unfortunates unable to escape would be trapped on the wrong side of the river; they would be too late to flee the guns and hissing machete blades of the dreaded Mai-Mai.

Less than half a mile upstream, the Captain of the Queen Victoria raged with fury as he cursed his young engineer for the umpteenth time that morning. The Queen was an ancient American flat-bottomed tank landing craft, which had been bought as surplus and hauled up to this stretch of the Mpana in pieces, a decade after the end of WW2. It was then reassembled on the very banks of the river where it was currently moored. Several welded steel plates bore witness with occasional collisions with partly submerged rocks over the long years it had plied its trade up and down the Mpana River. A mosaic of reddish-brown rust patches threatened to overcome its faded, peeling paintwork. Hanging limply in the hot African morning, the faded tarpaulin strung fore and aft, which had been erected to protect passengers from the worst ravages of the sun, appeared more patches than original material.

The Queen usually chugged up and down the river weekly, between Birundi and Kabali Junction, ferrying fare paying passengers, livestock and farmer's harvests when the dry season permitted. It was the only flat-bottomed vessel of any commercial size, which could handle the treacherous sandbanks which changed location and depth depending on the whim of the wide and capricious river. Her unshaven, white-haired Captain stamped his foot on the termite ridden wooden jetty where his vessel was currently tied. The old Queen's engines were cold and silent.

'I don't care what it takes, you lazy bugger, find that bloody spanner and get the engine working properly again....or never mind Ojukwu ...I will cut your bollocks off myself!'

Crouching in the narrow confines of the crafts filthy oil soaked engine room, the young black engineer cringed under his Captain's tirade. His boss man was a bad-tempered devil when he was sober, but now he stood swaying on the jetty with a half-empty bottle of locally distilled Cavalla in his hand. The engineer kept his head bowed and remained silent. He didn't mean to drop the spanner down the starboard engine intake manifold; it was a genuine accident. He would probably have hidden his clumsiness and left it were it was until the next maintenance overhaul, but the Captain happened to be in the cramped engine room at the time, and had heard it clank all the way down to the bottom of the shaft, when it slipped from his greasy fingers. The old Queen's master suspected it was lying wedged somewhere inside one of the massive rocker boxes, and wouldn't risk taking to open water while it stayed embedded in the heart of the ancient engine.

'You have got to treat these diesels with respect Julius, if you want to keep your job aboard the Queen... Jesus Christ, the starboard engine is only a couple of years younger than me! God alone knows how old the port engine is?' He wiped the back of his free hand across his sweat covered brow before taking another swig from the bottle, and limping off the jetty.

Like the locals, Captain Horatio O'Rourke had heard the whispers concerning the impending arrival of Ojukwu, and his black-hearted cut-throats. He had no desire to lose his beloved boat, or any of the more essential parts of his body, to a bunch of murdering, blood thirsty heathens.

Before he reached the end of the jetty, he turned and snarled, 'For God's sake, get it fixed!'

Chapter Ten

When the Military Attaché at last strode from the briefing room, Pat stared silently for a moment at the empty doorway, then down at his notebook. There were not many lines, he hadn't much to go on as current intelligence on enemy forces was sketchy; the mission's logistics looked poor, and time was, as always, going to be against him. Major Forde had treated the whole episode as little more than an amusing errand, but then he did not have to go into harm's way and do the job. Pat was not too sure, on what Forde had described as a mere jaunt.

Pat had an uneasy feeling in the pit of his stomach about this job. Warning bells were ringing, and nothing felt right. He had no backup available except the rest of his Troop, most of whom he must leave behind in Talinga. He was flying a thousand miles into a dangerous hostile territory virtually blind, in a hired civilian aircraft which Forde had assured him was capable of flying the distance, but at best, was only capable of carrying a maximum of twenty people, including the pilot. Apparently, the major informed him, there was a problem with the length of the runway in Birundi. Evacuation by a bigger aircraft was out of the question. The plane, a Short Skyvan, was specifically designed for short take-off and landing, but what concerned Pat was that it was too small for the job. Anyway, thought Pat, that meant he had to keep his escort team to an absolute minimum, as his primary objective was to lift the medics and a couple of British journalists who had also become trapped. His secondary brief was to extract every European he could cram into the aircraft when it was time to go.

Pat rubbed his chin, deep in thought as he studied his maps. The aircraft was scheduled to arrive at the garrison's airstrip just after dark. Pat knew it had been hired in for the op by the British High Commissioner in Nairobi. It was not a bad aircraft; some years earlier, during his advanced parachute training at Hereford, he had made numerous free-fall jumps from a Skyvan, temporally borrowed from the Red Devils; the Parachute Regiment's free-fall display team. The Sky Van was a slow and cumbersome beast, but he expected, depending on the weather conditions during the dangerous low level night flight, that barring problems, they should arrive in Birundi by dawn at the latest. Pat rubbed his chin, as he reviewed his very limited options. He should allow at least two hours for refuelling the aircraft, and searching out and gathering up his passengers. With luck, they should all be back safely on the apron at the Talinga garrison's airstrip before nightfall tomorrow. Pat snorted to himself and shook his head; one thing he had learnt the hard way long ago, was *never* to plan a new mission relying on no more than a huge slice of luck.

Something else had concerned Pat before Major Forde had finished his briefing. The Military Attaché had made it quite clear that in his opinion to save weight, Pat and his men should not even consider taking anything more than personal side-arms with them. It was after all, the Major had casually emphasised, nothing more than a simple, straightforward mercy mission.

'It certainly shouldn't be considered an armed incursion onto foreign soil, old boy,' Major Forde said, a little too pompously for Pat's liking. 'If you must take a couple of pistols with you, for God's sake keep them out of sight when you arrive. The last thing the High Commissioner wants is a wild west shootout on foreign soil.'

Pat kept silent and nodded. There was no mileage in rising to the man's constant sniping, and getting himself embroiled in a pointless argument. He had already decided to ignore the Attachés tactical appreciation anyway, and most of the man's other advice, for that matter. In Pat's years of experience in the dangerous world of special force's operations, he'd soon learnt that it was always advisable to have plenty of firepower available.

When Pat finished making his own initial appreciation of the task, it would soon be time to brief the others, who would accompany him on the mission. He knew two of them were already waiting outside.

'You two...*get in here!*'

Spike and Danny appeared in the doorway. There was eager anticipation written all over both their grinning faces. Pat looked up from his notes. Sternly, he issued his orders.

'Get your butts over to the accommodation block and stand the boys ready for a full troop briefing in thirty minutes. Then go and find Duggen. I want the three of you in front of me in five minutes...clear?'

With a curt nod, both young troopers disappeared in silence through the doorway into the sweltering blast of the afternoon's heat outside. Pat tapped his pen on the table before him. He sighed to himself. He had serious reservations about this mission. It didn't feel right somehow. Despite the Attaché's optimism, things had a habit of getting tricky during a job like this, when important questions remained unanswered and pre-op intelligence was thin. What concerned Pat most was that there was precious little hard Intel on the potential threat of the enemy forces he might be facing. True, he thought to himself, there seemed to be plenty of pretty solid rumours folded into the major's briefing, but very little hard evidence or cast iron fact. When he had enquired on Mai-Mai numbers, the major was vague and dismissive.

'Oh, it is probably just a rag-tag force made up of nothing more than old men, and young boys co-opted into Ojukwu's militia.' Major Forde shrugged. 'That is the normal pattern of rebel recruitment in Africa nowadays.' Almost as an afterthought he added, 'One of my colleagues in Nairobi, this morning suggested there might be as many as a thousand Mai-Mai moving towards Birundi, but personally, I think that is utter nonsense.'

Pat decided not to press the point concerning enemy numbers. Clearly, the Attaché did not have a clue as to the actual figure of enemy boots on the ground. It seemed pointless to pursue the question. Pat decided to work on the highest figure currently available.

It occurred to Pat that the easiest way to get an update on the situation in Birundi was to make a telephone call to the township's police station. When he mentioned the idea, Major Forde tapped the side of his head and looked condescendingly at the SAS soldier in front of him.

'Yes, already thought of that, old boy. Nairobi says the local Birundi telephone line is down at the moment,' he held up his hand to admonish Pat, who had not moved a muscle. 'Before you jump to any conclusions on the lack of communications, apparently that is nothing unusual for the Congo in general, I'm afraid. It could be absolutely anything causing the problem. Poor maintenance is most likely, or the weather might have washed out the line,' he shrugged. 'Mechanical and electrical things do not tend to do too well in Africa, you know.'

'Or the lines might have been cut by the guerrillas?'

The Attaché shrugged. 'Who knows Sergeant? Let's move on, shall we?'

The next critical issue to the operation was exactly how close were the rebels to the township? Were the guerrillas ten, twenty or even a hundred miles away, Pat asked.

'Latest reports say that General Ojukwu and his Mai-Mai are in the region, but no specific information is available as to their exact location, relative to Birundi.

Pat nodded. Clearly, the Attaché didn't have any recently updated information at all concerning Ojukwu's exact whereabouts.

'What sort of the transport does the Mai-Mai have, and how quickly could they move on Birundi, if that's part of their game plan?

The Attaché shrugged again.

'They are probably using mostly captured or stolen vehicles. Toyota land cruisers and pickups are pretty popular with these sorts, if they can get their grubby little hands on them. Given the state of the local roads, off-road vehicles are the only reliable way to move anywhere reasonably quickly. The rainy season is due to start any day now, and roads will deteriorate into mud filled tracks. Without enough four-wheeled drive vehicles, they would be reduced to moving on foot, and realistically, probably would not manage I should think, more than a few miles per day.'

Pat nodded. That might be an advantage. He was not so sure that off-road vehicles would be much help to the guerrillas once the rains began. Years earlier, he had read several of Major Mike Hoare's books, written after the rogue British Major had served as a mercenary officer in the Congo, back in the '60s. During the rainy season,

Hoare once attempted to relieve a besieged township during the Congo's first post-colonial civil war, by leading a 'flying' column of Government vehicles to their rescue. It rained constantly, and had taken more than ten days to cover just ninety miles. Many of the vehicles Pat remembered, had repeatedly sunk up to their axles in thick clinging mud, snapping half-shafts or slewed off the waterlogged tracks, becoming firmly wedged in flooded drainage ditches. When what was left of the column finally arrived, they were too late. The beleaguered township had been overrun, and the unfortunate inhabitants slaughtered by the rebel Simba's.

Major Forde's answer belied another question. Did Pat have just hours to complete the mission, or days to play with when their plane touched down on Birundi's airstrip? The Military Attaché answered with yet another frustrating shrug.

What sort of weapons did the enemy have Pat wondered, and what was the state of their field training? The chances were that many Mai-Mai would be armed with the ubiquitous Russian-made AK47 assault-rifle, which the Soviets had flooded the African continent with, years earlier.

The Soviet plan was to covertly equip communist rebels; destabilising newly independent African countries, making the fledgling and politically unstable republics ripe for communist led insurrection. Providing huge quantities of weapons fermented the Soviet Politburo's global plan to arm the world's disgruntled workers, ultimately creating a global communist revolution.

Pat assumed the Congo had followed the pattern of Angola years earlier. With the fall of the Iron Curtain, the Soviet trained Cuban advisors swiftly took their leave. Huge quantities of Russian-built weapons were abandoned to the mercy of any would-be rebel leader, who grasped the opportunity to seize them.

Mechanically simple, the reliable and iconic AK was an ideal weapon for illiterate and poorly trained militias. The assault-rifle would fire on single or fully auto, with very little care, even in the hands of untrained and untested recruits.

The more Pat thought about the glaring gaps in his intelligence briefing, the greater difficulty he had making his own tactical appreciation. He wondered if the Mai-Mai had any heavier support weapons, captured or stolen from Government forces. Machine guns, mortars and RPG rocket launchers could well be in the guerrillas inventory; it was certainly a distinct possibility. Pat knew it might prove fatal to ignore the threat. Not only had the departing Russians left enormous amounts of military hardware lying around, but captured government weapons could also be part of their armoury; he had to assume the rebels had at least some heavy weapons available, whatever their source. Planning was going to be difficult. His transport was severely limited, and apart from his own distant troop resources, there were no other friendly forces available if things turned ugly.

Bloody typical, Pat thought to himself. He scratched his head. There was just so little information to work with. Still, he mused, there was nothing to be achieved by bitching about it. Some bright spark in the Foreign Office had thought this one up. The prospect of going in almost blind was not appealing, but Pat had his orders, and he had to get on with it. A bumper sticker he had spotted from his taxi while driving along the Strand months earlier had summed his current situation up succinctly.

'The impossible I do at once; miracles me take longer.'

Pat smiled. Although he had to hope for the best, he knew he must plan for the worst. This sort of op. came up from time to time, with the SAS called in, to make the impossible happen. The Regiment's reputation was well justified; their free booting ethos worked miracles daily during operational deployment, but things did not always go right. Pat winced to himself as he thought of the recent embarrassing cock-up in Libya. As he went back to his notes and began his mission planning in earnest, Pat sighed. 'Just take a couple of pistols' the Attaché had said. In the quiet of the briefing room, Pat shook his head. Somehow, he didn't think so.

Chapter Eleven

The young doctor slowly removed the stethoscope, which until moments before had been clamped firmly to his ears. There was no detectable heartbeat, no sign of life. He gently pulled the blood-stained sheet up over the pale figure. Covering the dead man's face was final confirmation that his dying patient had ebbed away. It always hurt to lose a patient, but even with two years of bush medicine behind him, and the limited operating facilities available in Birundi's ramshackle hospital, there was still nothing he could do. The man's gunshot wounds and massive blood loss proved fatal. Life slipped away somewhere on the dusty road between the mine and the clinic. Sadly, Dr Frasier turned to the tall figure standing at the end of the chipped hospital bed. In his soft Scottish burr, he said,

'I'm sorry Colonel; there was too much trauma...he's dead, I'm afraid.'

Otto Krutz seethed inside with confusion and anger. Reality and loss overwhelmed him suddenly. This had been one of his best men, a friend who he had worked with for three years. They had been joking with each other just an hour previously.

'But I told you, Carl had a pulse...'

Dr Frasier sighed and shook his head gently. 'No Colonel...I'm sorry, he's gone.'

When the firing stopped, with pistol drawn, Krutz had raced first to the mine's entrance, and then to the mine's main gate. Surrounded by spent cartridge cases, he found Terry lying dead, and Carl unconscious on the dry ground beside him, in a pool of rapidly spreading blood. Carl had taken three hits between his chest and abdomen. Krutz had seen similar wounds too many times before. He knew instantly that any one of them might prove fatal.

The damage left by high-velocity bullets was always hideous. Massive gaping wounds the size of dinner plates ripped out of Carl's back, as bullets tumbled and tore through his body. Each smashed bone and ripped muscle, leaving a dark and bloody mess. Even plunging a clenched fist into the wound was not usually enough to stem the flow of life-giving blood. Thrusting his fingers to Carl's neck, Otto Krutz had detected the faintest pulse. It was just a flutter of his still beating heart. Sweeping Carl's limp body up in a single motion, he desperately ran towards the nearest vehicle.

Losing one man was bad enough, but the explosion at the mine's mouth had ripped the others to atoms. He would have to go back and bury them. He snorted to himself at the reality of war, and the pain it left behind. From what he had seen, when he first rushed toward the explosion, there didn't appear to be enough left of any of them, to fill a single coffin.

In one blinding moment, he and Jan were all that was left of the security detail that had flown in so confidently from the Skeleton Coast. In a few savage minutes, in this miserable back end of nowhere hole, the others were dead. Slipping into his native Afrikaans he snarled at the world in general.

'Vok! Wat die donder, jou klein etter!'

Fighting to regain his composure, he quickly slipped back into English.

'I need a drink!' Angrily, he turned and strode through the doorway, glad to be free of the stink of blood and death, which mixed so easily with the heat and stillness of the small hospital anteroom.

Trooper Charlie Duggen had joined the Regiment more than three years before Pat arrived in Chelsea. He was a popular member of the troop, despite the stick he occasionally received because of his civilian job. In Civvy Street, Charlie made his living as a scientist. He worked for the Home Office over on the other side of the River Thames in Lambeth. Charlie investigated blood samples for those unfortunate drivers arrested on drink driving charges by the Metropolitan Police. Wearing a Home Office white coat in the South Bank laboratory, he analysed blood-alcohol levels, which paid his rent, but Charlie's real two loves were the Regiment, and explosives...

He caused quite a stir when the truth came out, after assisting on a recent 'A' Squadron homemade explosive's weekend, on a M.O.D. training area outside Farnborough. No-one noticed anything strange when Trooper Duggen lifted his heavy bergan into the back of the lorry before they left Chelsea. He heaved it a little more carefully than the rest of the troop, as they got ready to leave their London base. Charlie developed a mild stutter when he got excited or nervous. When one of his friends dropped his own pack onto the pile of begans in the back of the lorry, Charlie had shouted:

'Rory! For f..f..f..fuck sake be careful!'

Knowing how much Charlie loved playing with explosives, everyone wrongly assumed he was just excited at the prospect of spending the weekend blowing things to smithereens; as a result, the guys around him paid it little mind. He firmly regained their attention several hours later however, when the convoy arrived at the Hampshire based military demolition range. When the vehicles had parked up and their engines went silent, the troop disembarked and busied themselves unloading stores and equipment. Charlie identified his own bergan and crouching down, produced from its depths two plain litre bottles filled with clear oily liquid. Both were missing labels, which might betray their purpose. Grinning, he gingerly handed one to Pat, for his troop sergeant's inspection. Pat was busy checking a manifest and clicked his tongue with irritation at the distraction. Absently turning the bottle over in his hands, Pat frowned as he looked down at it for a moment. He was clearly unimpressed and slightly confused by Charlie's strange offering. His face betrayed his lack of interest. Pat was about to sling it back to his trooper when wide-eyed, Charlie threw up his hands. Suddenly ashen faced he cried out.

'S..s..stop! Don't throw it Pat. It's f...f...full of my homemade n...n...nitro glycerine!'

Pat had finished outlining the mission in his mind when the three panting troopers arrived in the briefing room's doorway.

'Right you three, come in and sit down. Questions at the end'

The young troopers arranged their chairs in front of Pat. Each man had a pen and notepad open and ready. Details could be jotted down as necessary, memorised after the brief and the paper destroyed.

Having pinned it to the wall while waiting for Spike and the others to arrive, Pat opened the briefing by referring to the large-scale map of the Congo which the Attaché had left him. Using his pen as a pointer, he circled a small area within the Congo's northern border area.

'At first light tomorrow morning, the four of us are flying into a small airstrip just outside the township of Birundi, here in the Congo.' Pat tapped his pen on the map, 'We have been tasked to remove four British nationals who are trapped there. Two are doctors and nurses working for some charity at the local clinic, and the other two are journalists. We have to lift them before the regional warlord; General Ojukwu sweeps through and sacks the place. He is a vicious bastard by all accounts, and heads up his own private army of about a thousand Tutsi

Mai-Mai guerrillas. Intelligence reports say he crossed the tribal border into Hutu territory about a month ago, and has spent the last four weeks sweeping south, burning every Hutu village in his path,' Pat added grimly, 'These animals don't do mercy, so I will leave it to your imagination what's happened to the locals.'

Glancing at the wall-mounted map, Pat widened the imaginary circle on the map. He looked back at his men and continued, 'As far as we are concerned, the whole province is bad bush. It's a mixture of open savannah and primary jungle, but we'll treat all of it as bandit country. There's no real law enforcement in the area, and to make matters worse, our High Commission in Nairobi says after Ojukwu's invasion, there is the beginnings of a civil war kicking off. As far as we know, there will not be any friendly forces to back us up if things get hot.'

The three troopers looked quizzically at each other. Danny made a face clouded with mock horror, which made the other two grin broadly. Pat waited for a moment; he understood the flood of adrenaline, which was suddenly coursing through his trooper's veins. This was another chance for some real action; it focused the reality of spending tortuous months training on the mountains of

Brecon. It was why they had worked so hard to pass SAS selection.

'Why us, Pat?'

Pat shrugged, 'I expect Hereford is getting pretty stretched at the moment, and we happen to be closest, Danny. Ojukwu is getting too close to Birundi and there is not enough time for local Government forces to launch a full-scale rescue, so we've pulled the job.'

Danny nodded. 'OK, Fair enough.'

'All right boys, settle down...'

Pat spent the next few minutes adding detail to his briefing and passing on what he knew of the operation and a general outline, of how they would complete the mission. In conclusion, he gave each man individual administration tasks to complete before they took off, and the mission's initial timings. Part of the more detailed instructions concerned weapons.

'We are going in with 9mm pistols as side-arms, but I've decided that we're going to take AK47's with us as well. The Kenyans use them as standard personal weapons and I have arranged with the BATT training team that we can use some of theirs. That way, if we do get into a heavy contact, the opposition will be using the same ammunition as us. We can't take much spare ammo with us, so if the chance presents we can always resupply ourselves with identical ammunition, if we need to, from captured stock.'

Spike and the others nodded. Their basic training included using the rugged AKs. Working deep in very dangerous territory and being familiar with the universally used weapon, they could see the sense of Pat's decision.

'We'll take an RPG rocket launcher and half a dozen rockets,' Pat grinned and winked, 'Might be overkill, but I reckon better safe than sorry.'

The briefing was drawing towards a conclusion as Pat added, 'I'm treating this as at most a two-day mission, so Spike, I want you to draw a couple of 24-hour ration packs for each of us from our troop store.

Spike nodded.

'Danny. I want you to bring your radio. If we do run into trouble, I want comms available to get us out of the shit, pronto.' Pat turned his attention to his last trooper, 'Charlie; I want you to draw detonators, two pounds of PE4 plastic explosive, and a couple of claymore mines. You'd better bring the rest of your nasty little bag of tricks with you, as well.'

Charlie Duggen grinned as his pulse quickened, 'Can do, Pat.'

The British army's equivalent to reddish-brown Czech Semtex or off-white American C4, PE4 remains one of the most powerful military-grade plastic explosives in the world. Packed in 8oz sticks, its white putty-like consistency can be moulded to any shape and be pressed into gaps and cracks in buildings, bridges, equipment or machinery. It also has the advantage over commercial explosives like dynamite, because it is extremely stable. A hammer blow would not detonate it, and in moderation, it can be burnt without fear of an explosion. Placed correctly, even small amounts of the explosive cut tempered steel girders and railway lines as if they were made of tissue paper. In the hands of an expert, PE4 is a formidable weapon in its own right, and Charlie was in his element using it.

'I have been advised that we will not need much in the way of weapons,' Pat's face betrayed his doubts, 'but as far as I'm concerned, I would rather have 'em and not need them, than need them, and not have them.'

'Damn right!' snorted Spike. All four had fought the terrorist cell in Ealing months before, and they knew firepower was king during a battle. The others nodded. To seasoned veterans, there was no need for further explanation of the point.

In conclusion, their troop sergeant summed up the mission. 'We are keeping this op. simple. We fly into Birundi, find our Brits, get them aboard the aircraft then ex-filtrate straight back here....Questions?'

No-one spoke. Pat checked his watch. 'It will be dark soon. We'll draw weapons and ammunition in thirty minutes, and I want you all back here, in civvies, with your bergans packed and ready to go in forty. We'll double check everything then and I will run a final Intel update if anything else surfaces. We'll move over to the airfield in exactly one hour from now. Clear?'

'We're going in civvies Pat?'

Pat nodded. 'Yeah, Spike. The trip hasn't been officially sanctioned by the Congolese Government yet, so as far as anyone is concerned, we are just civilian minders in a non-military aircraft...right?'

Heads nodded. Pat said, 'Right, get away and get it done, while I go and brief the rest of the Troop, and break the news that they are not going.'

As they left the briefing room, Danny whispered to his two friends.

'Into the valley of death, then?'

Spike looked serious. Suddenly, the op. was all too real.

'Yeah man...something like that, but I bloody hope not!'

Chapter Twelve

Above the rhythmic drone of the engines, the Sky Van's Australian pilot stared at the huge cumulonimbus cloud which hung dark and foreboding in the skies ahead of his aircraft. The massive cloud's distinctive anvil shape was an ominous warning of the deadly peril within the thunderhead. He'd seen too many before, and they always spelt trouble.

Clearly outlined by the seeping glow of the dim horizon, flares of brilliant lightning flashed earthwards from the heart of the electrical storm hidden deep inside its black heart. The lightning and rolling peals of thunder were the storm's spectacular fanfare; vivid warnings of the danger which lurked ahead. The pilot stared up at clouds for a few seconds then reached for his throat mike. Anxiously, he depressed the intercom button.

'Thought you would like to know; looks like we are in for some seriously bad weather ahead.' Releasing the button for a moment the pilot stared at the huge thunderstorm again. It had to be at least ten miles wide and towered over them, rising to perhaps 50,000 feet. He reached for the send button again,

'Hey Pat, we need to talk, mate.'

Surprised by the sudden crackle in his headphones, surrounded by a jumble of stowed equipment, weapons and sleeping troopers Pat looked up from the Katinga map he had been studying. Removing the pencil torch from his mouth, he looked towards the pilot's cramped cockpit. The cockpit door was missing and despite the gloom, he could clearly see the pilot's outline looking back towards him. The pilot repeatedly stabbed the air as he pointed beyond his cabin's windscreen, into the darkness ahead.

Pat nodded and unbuckled his harness; he guessed he'd better move forward and see what the problem was. Standing up, Pat stretched his cramped muscles as he glanced at the luminous dial on his watch. They had been in the air for over three hours now and must be well over half-way to Birundi. Shuffling forward, Pat moved into the cockpit and eased himself into the empty co-pilot's seat. Staring quizzically at the aircraft's driver he said,

'What's up?'

The pilot looked away from his passenger and nodded beyond the reinforced windshield.

'We have got a problem with the storm up ahead; we are currently flying into. My service ceiling is only 22,000 feet. There's no way I can climb over that beast ahead of us.'

Pat nodded and looked in awe at the flashing wrath of tropical storm in front of the aircraft.

He whistled softly, 'It's a big bastard. Can't we go around it?'

The pilot shook his head, 'No. We've been flying in a natural depression with mountains on either side. Visibility is not exactly great at the moment sport...can't see a bloody thing outside. I'm flying on instalments as it is, and I've got no on-board radar. We try to fly off the bearing, and the first time we'll know we are too close to a mountain, is when we hit one.'

Pat sighed to himself. Typical he thought. 'So what do you suggest we do?'

The Aussie grimaced but there was no hint of fear in his face, 'Well, if this was a normal flight, common sense says we'd turn back.'

Pat's face darkened. His mind flashed back to his unknown mission timescale. He did not have the luxury of a reschedule. He shook his head rapidly.

'No way, forget that! Every second counts mate. We have to be on the Birundi airstrip by first light. You know what will happen if the Mai-Mai gets there before us?'

The pilot nodded. With more than twenty years of hard-won experience flying over Africa's untamed wilderness, he had seen it all before. There was always bad blood below; one tribe was chopping up their enemies somewhere on the continent. He had witnessed first-hand the horrific results only months earlier during an U.N. charter into Southern Darfur in the Sudan and worse still several years before when he had been hired to fly a Danish team of doctors into Rwanda, after hundreds of thousands of defenceless civilians had been slaughtered during the vile bloodletting of their savage war of genocide.

The Pommie High Commission had paid in full, in advance, the ridiculous fee he had demanded to make this dangerous return flight. These 'no questions asked' jobs came up from time to time for a few bush pilots who could keep their mouths shut, and knew better than to ask too many questions. He had been well paid and had his future reputation to think of among certain military attaches who contacted him when the need arose. Sensitive and highly lucrative flights like this occasionally relieved the boredom he carried as extra baggage, when hauling cargo for cheapskate mining companies that always quibbled over their bill and invariably paid him late.

As usual, on a job like this there was no recorded flight plan and no paperwork granting him permission to overfly at least half a dozen African states; any of which would be only too happy to throw him in some stinking jail if he had to make a forced landing carrying a group of heavily armed white men.

The pilot shrugged. Part of his generous fee included taking risks.

'What the hell?' he said. 'Better wake up your boys and get them strapped in tight,' He nodded towards the fast-approaching storm, 'this is going to get rough.'

Night fell softly across Birundi. Inside the township, a lone dog barked hungrily in a deserted street. Most of the frightened population had already fled to the bush or gone south of the river. Here and there, merchants and shop keepers paced nervously inside barricaded stores, determined to defend their valuable stock until the last moment against the looting which would surely come before the Mai-Mai arrived. They knew they must flee before the guerrillas, but could not afford to ignore gangs of thieves who still prowled the deserted streets in search of booty, before they also joined the exodus and fled.

Otto Krutz sat hushed and brooding in the Hotel Armond's bar. With his head bowed and broad hands resting on the table, he clutched the half-empty tumbler in cheerless silence. He remained perfectly still and stared unfocused at the clear fiery Cavalla it contained.

Barney Morris stood at the bar, still smarting from the angry rejection of his friendly overtures to the big South African visitor. He had offered a drink when the man had walked in several minutes earlier. Barney's instincts as a journalist suggested this man was something to do with the attack on the mine, but the dark scowl on the man's face, and the holstered pistol he wore on his belt warned Barney that this was not the moment to spark up a new drinking partner and grill the stranger with questions in the process.

Barney's thoughts were distracted when an equally large white man, also wearing a pistol on his hip burst into the bar. The man was panting...he'd clearly been running.

'Is it true Colonel...Are they all dead?'

Krutz looked up from the table before him. With a deep sigh, he said,

'Yes Jan. They're dead....all of them.'

The big Swede slumped down in a chair beside his leader,

'What happened, I heard a big explosion?'

Colonel Krutz snorted and shook his head,

'Just damned bad luck, Jan. Karl and Terry were hit defending the gate, when the rebels made a probing attack on the mine. By sheer dumb luck, a stray bullet must have hit the dynamite and killed the others,' He snatched up his glass and drained it. Shuddering as the Cavalla burned down his throat he added morosely, 'Poor bastards didn't know what hit them,' sadly he added, 'they didn't stand a chance.'

Without speaking Jan stood up and gathered up the Colonel's glass. He walked to the counter and ignoring Barney completely, addressed the barman,

'Two more of these. Bring them over, and keep them coming. Understand?'

Henry nodded as he wiped his palms on his apron,

'Sure Boss,' he said, reaching for another glass and the bottle. 'Right away.'

Satisfied, the blonde and powerfully built security man nodded. He turned away, and went back to his chair. He had new information concerning the plane. He did not want to add to the misery, but he needed to share news from the airfield.

'I'm sorry to bring this up now Colonel, but I'm afraid I have got some more bad news.'

Krutz closed his eyes for a moment, and then he growled,

'Spit it out man.'

Henry brought over two filled glasses. He placed them carefully on the table before his customers. Sensing the sudden silence his appearance had caused, he beat a hasty retreat back to the sanctuary of his bar.

Jan lifted his glass but did not drink, 'Sorry Colonel, I'm afraid the Dakota's port engine is completely shot.'

Krutz shoulders slumped even lower. He looked up and stared hard at the concerned face of the big Swede who sat opposite.

'Well?'

Jan sipped at the clear contents of his glass. Wincing, he said,

'When you went up to the mine, me and the pilot unbolted the engine's cowling. Soon as we could get into the engine properly we saw the problem. There's a bloody great crack in the number three cylinder head. That is where the oil went and caused the overheating.'

'Can't it be fixed?' growled Krutz.

Jan shook his head. 'No chance. Our pilot reckons the engine needs a complete rebuild before it runs again. He said without oil, it was a bloody miracle the piston didn't heat up and weld itself into the cylinder, before we landed.'

Krutz nodded. The engine was shot, there it was. There was fatal resignation in his voice; an old soldier used to dealing with catastrophe. 'How long will the repair take?'

Jan shook his head slowly. 'There might have been a slim chance to weld it and make a temporary repair, but we couldn't do it. There was half a bottle of oxygen in the hanger, but the acetylene tanks were all empty. We even searched the hanger and airfield for a replacement radial head for the damaged cylinder,' he shrugged.

'DC3s' are common out here, and I thought we might have hit gold when we found a rusty head under a pile of scrap.'

With a sigh Krutz uttered just one word,

'But?'

'Sorry Colonel. It was from an old Fokker radial and did not come even close to fitting the Dakota.'

The Colonel drained his glass. The big Swede took the moment, and followed suit.

Barnet Morris was leaning on the bar with his back towards the two tough-looking men, but for once, he ignored his drink. He was intent on eavesdropping on their conversation. He needed to get out too.

'The goods are locked up in the local banks safe, and we cannot get them out until nine o'clock, tomorrow morning. We'll escort the mine manager down first thing and get them then. When we're finished at the bank, we find a vehicle and bug out, or we'll be stuck here when the Mai-Mai arrives.'

Jan nodded and looked away towards the bar. Pointing to his empty glass, he called to Henry, who was busy polishing a glass.

'Hey you, barman, two more.' Seeing the dark scowl on the Colonel's face he thought for a moment then added, 'Fuck it, bring the bottle over and leave it here.'

Krutz nodded, 'We'll have a drink to our dead comrades Jan...Then we'll get some sleep.' With a knowing nod he said. 'We will finish up our business tomorrow morning then make for the border.' His faced suddenly scowled. He looked more serious to Jan than he had seen the Colonel for a long time, 'Then we get ourselves the hell out of this mess.'

Chapter Thirteen

'Jesus!'

Tightly strapped to his seat, Spike ducked involuntarily as another blinding flash lit the interior of the shuddering aircraft. Above the roar of the slipstream and the straining engines, the storm raged outside as he shouted to his two companions.

'Last time I fly bloody Kamikaze Airways.'

Danny and Charlie grinned but there was no mirth in their smiles. All three had a massive knot in their stomachs but were trying their best not to show it. None of them had experienced the ferocity of an African storm before, or felt the turbulents created by powerful up and downdrafts clashing together inside it.

Their apprehension began early, prior to take off from Kalingi's grass runway, even before they climbed aboard the ageing aircraft several hours earlier. Each of the young troopers had begun to feel uneasy when they noticed the aircraft's peeling paintwork and the faded markings of previous owners, which were now no more than poorly over painted shadows on the wings and fuselage. It had not helped when the pilot introduced himself to each of them, as they heaved bergans and weapons up into the cargo hold before scrambling aboard.

'Brogan,' said the ruddy faced pilot, 'Welcome aboard.' The man's broad Australian accent was not the problem; it was the vodka bottle he offered each of them a drink from. Pat was standing behind Brogan and sternly shook his head.

'No thanks,' said each of them in turn.

'Suit yourselves boys, but it is the only in-flight refreshment you will get on this trip.'

Lightning flashed, and deafening thunder echoed through the heavens. It boomed above the aircraft's straining engines as the pilot struggled to keep the Sky Van in the air. The plane suddenly dipped again, dropping a stomach-churning hundred feet through the black void. Rain lashed the aircraft as the sweating pilot regained control.

Pat sat beside him; knuckles white, his hands clamped to the control column. Both men were frantically wrestling with the dual controls as the aircraft violently juddered again, tossed like a cork by the storm.

Between blinding flashes outside, visibility beyond the cockpit was non-existent. Suddenly, the torrential rain was replaced by hail, which hammered against the cockpit's windscreen and rattled against the aircraft's metal skin. Brogan's eyes flicked down from the swirling void outside to the comforting glow of the instalment panel. Ignoring the ear-splitting tumult which filled the cockpit, he took another swig from the almost empty bottle and leant over. Pat took a full blast of vodka fumes as the pilot stashed the bottle between his thighs and yelled into his passenger's ear.

'This wind shear's going to bloody kill us if we don't gain height quickly, sport. The altimeter says that last drop forced us down to a couple of hundred feet off the deck.'

Glancing back at the raging storm outside, he yelled,

'There's only one thing we can try. When I say, keep your feet clear of the foot pedals and pull back on the stick, as hard as you can...understand?'

His shirt stained with sweat, heart pumping as if it would burst from his chest Pat nodded vigorously. His eyes were blazing as he shouted back,

'Yeah, understood. Just tell me when!'

Leaning forward Brogan let go of his column with one hand and grasped the fat throttle controls mounted just in front of him, between the two pilots' canvas seats.

Without warning the plane lurched and dropped again. Lightning flashed and for a split-second, Pat was sure he saw the skeletal outline of a huge acacia tree just beyond the port wing. Even as he drew breath to shout a warning, the pilot frantically yelled,

'Get ready!'

Pat braced himself as best he could. Suddenly, the aircraft reared up when it hit a powerful new updraft. For another split-second, it pinned the two men back into their seats. It was the moment the pilot was waiting for. Forcing himself towards the dashboard, he rammed the engines' throttle controls forward and was immediately rewarded with a new roar from the aircraft's turboprop engines.

'Now!'

Hearts pounding, both men frantically pulled back on their controls with every ounce of strength their adrenaline filled muscles could muster. In the shaking cockpit, above the appalling din of the storm raging outside, and the deafening roar of engines screaming at full power, the altimeter needle flickered slightly inside its glowing dial. To both men's horror it had been bottom lined and was registering zero feet.

'Keep pulling sport, it's now or never!' The pilot yelled desperately; his eyes were glued to the glow of the instrument panel.

With every muscle taut and aching, sweat dripped from both men's faces as they battled to raise the aircraft's nose. Pat groaned aloud with effort. The vibrations through his chipped control column made his teeth rattle. It felt as though the old aircraft's metal skin was about to shake apart. Despite the last twenty minutes of violent air turbulents and unpredictable battering, the riveted seams had somehow stayed together, and the wings had remained firmly attached to the airframe. It was a tribute to the Sky Van's manufacturers, and its rugged design that the airframe's welds held together at all.

The engines screamed as the aging aircraft's propeller blades fought to grip the turbulent air and respond to the pilot's desperate demand for more power. Both men sat hypnotised; their eyes stayed firmly fixed on the flickering needle. A mistake now and their bodies would be picked clean by the animals that lived in the wilderness below, once the fires from their lonely crash site had burnt out.

Imperceptibly at first, the altimeter's needle began to twitch. Agonising seconds ticked by before it began to swing slowly away from its lowest mark; reluctantly, the aircraft began to climb.

'Yes. It's working!' yelled the pilot in triumph. His eyes glittered with excitement as he stared at the altimeter and called the numbers. '200 feet...300...Do not let go...Keep pulling back!'

His face flushed with success but Brogan's eyes never left the dial until he suddenly shouted at Pat again.

'OK, relax. I'll level her out at one thousand feet.... that should be high enough.' Breathing a sigh of relief he added, 'Don't worry about radar; we are still well shielded by the mountains.'

His heart still pounding like a sledgehammer, Pat nodded. Without a tell-tale blip on some distant operator's monitor, the plane would remain invisible and avoid being picked up on either military or commercial radar systems. Under Pat's order, they maintained strict radio silence since leaving the airstrip. So far, without a transmission from the mercy flight, not a single inquisitive voice had crackled over the headphones, asking their purpose or destination.

Pat let out a deep sigh of relief. They were still in one piece, and the mission had not been compromised. Forcing himself to relax in his harness, Pat savoured the victory of the moment, as his heart rate began to slow. This was why Special Forces soldering was so addictive, and kept him inside the clan. Always lurking unseen on any operation, near-death experiences like this kept the rush of adrenaline coursing through his body. It's sudden and explosive release, was the drug which no money could buy. Somehow he thought; its powerful blast gave meaning to his life, when faced with the alternative realities of dreary part-time civilian life at home, in London.

Pat shook himself free from reflection and looked back into the gloom of the aircraft's hold. He saw three very ashen faces staring at him. There was no point in trying to make himself heard over the cacophony of noise, which still surrounded them all. Pat grinned and gave an inquisitive thumbs-up sign to his young troopers. For a moment, no-one in the darkened hold moved, but slowly each of his shaken young men returned the signal. Spike locked eyes with his Troop Commander and said something, which was instantly lost in the surrounding din. Pat wasn't sure that his lip-reading was up to scratch, but it looked very much to him that Spike had mouthed something, which spoke copious volumes for all three passengers, and how they were feeling in that moment.

'Fucking Hell!'

Pat grinned his understanding and nodded. He turned back towards the front of the cockpit and stared through the windshield. For a moment, he thought the rain had eased and the storm was abating slightly. Without warning, still under full power the aircraft suddenly zoomed clear of the black cloud, into a calm and peaceful sky. It was as if they had abruptly flown into another dimension; a world where peace and tranquillity reigned and the terrifying storm lived only in the dark worlds of memory and nightmare. Above, a shining lattice of stars twinkled serenely in the black heavens, and a broad silver ribbon sparkled beneath the aircraft. The river glittered in the reflected moonlight, meandering lazily across the wide valley floor, a mere thousand feet below.

'Christ, that had its moments!' the pilot grinned, as he exhaled loudly demonstrating his own overwhelming relief, tinged with triumph. 'We are through it sport. We're in the clear.'

Pat nodded. 'Yeah Brogan, pissed or sober mate, that was a really impressive piece of flying.'

Still grinning, Brogan replied, 'All part of the service mate. It's what I get paid the big bucks for...' The pilot belched, filling the cockpit with the acrid stench of vodka again, 'You did pretty well yourself. Ever thought of taking up a career in bush flying? '

Pat blew out his cheeks, which in the moonlight were only now beginning to regain their true colour.

'No chance of that mate. Flying an old crate like this is far too dangerous... even if I had a bloody parachute...which I bloody haven't!'

Brogan roared with laughter as he reached forward and gently eased back on the aircraft's throttles. The twin turboprops roar immediately dropped to a steady and comforting drone. Satisfied that all was in order, having scrutinised the dials of the instrument panel; Brogan felt under his seat, and lifted out a battered map. By the glow of his dials, he used his index finger to trace the course of the river below them. Looking up, he checked his bearing on the compass. Giving the fuel gauge an absent flick, he said,

'We are right on course. That is the tributary of the Mpana I have been looking for. We follow that for another seventy miles or so, then turn south and follow the main Mpana River straight into Birundi. Barring any more storms, we should be arriving at first light in about... two hours.' Nodding to himself, he added, 'Fuels getting a bit low, but we should be OK. I have arranged to refuel at the airfield.'

Replacing the map under his seat, he fished around for something else. With a look of triumph, he lifted out an almost full bottle of Irish Bushmill's whiskey. He passed it over to Pat.

'I keep the good stuff handy for emergencies...better take a good swig and pass it back to your boys.' He glanced into the hold then winked at his co-pilot. 'Tell you the truth sport; you all look like you could use a stiff drink...'

Chapter Fourteen

In the silence of his ministerial office, David Benchley was reading a memo from his red dispatch box, concerning details of the planned Commonwealth Meeting. It would make a fine high profile beginning to the newest member of the Cabinet. Suddenly, his telephone rang. Startled, the Foreign Secretary looked up from the paperwork spread before him and reached forward, lifting the receiver to his ear.

'David Benchley.'

His Permanent Secretary spoke to him from his own office, in the Foreign Office building.

'Minister, sorry to disturb you, but we have had a reply from the Congolese Ambassador on the Birundi affair...'

Irritated by losing his train of thought about the coming meeting, over something so trivial which he had already dealt with, Benchley snapped, 'Well, what did he say?'

There was a pause from the Permanent Secretary. Not long, but long enough for the Minister to know it was not good news.

'I'm afraid it is a no go Minister. The newspapers leaked the story about our military going into the Congo this morning. The Congolese Ambassador is furious, that we have ordered troops onto their soil without first securing his Governments' formal permission.'

David Benchley sighed. 'Is there anything else?'

His secretary's voice sounded grave. 'Yes, I'm sorry Minister, but I have been instructed by the Ambassador to inform you that the Congolese Government considers a violation of their borders by any foreign power as a hostile act, and unless our peoples' mission is stopped; it will be met with lethal force...'

The Foreign Secretary winced as a knot of panic flooded through him.

'Oh, Christ Almighty! You had better come up right away Julian. I think we need to start a damage control exercise, to smooth feathers before the whole damned situation gets out of hand.'

There was a hollow click from the receiver. The Foreign Secretary replaced the handset onto its cradle. Focusing at the Sovereign's portrait above the clock on the opposite wall for a moment, he cursed under his breath, and then dropped his head into his hands. As a keen student of political history, something suddenly dawned on

Foreign Secretary. The full potential of what could become a highly publicised and extremely embarrassing international disaster fully dawned on him. He snatched up the receiver once again. Unilateral action of this kind had led to the ruin of high-ranking politicians before. Sir Anthony Eden's long and eminent political career, and his ultimate premiership, had been ruined by the Suez fiasco years before. Since the end of the Second World War, in the post-colonial world, the international stage remained a dangerous graveyard, littered with political disasters. Eden had made a series of gross blunders in conjunction with the French and Israelis, when Egypt's Gamal Abdel Nasser had seized power and nationalised the Suez Canal in 1956. Eden's plan was to encourage the Israelis to invade Egypt, and then in conjunction with the French, would step in with combined Anglo French military muscle, act as peacekeepers and quietly remove Nasser from power. Unfortunately, evidence began to emerge of the three countries prior collusion, and following intense diplomatic pressure at the U.N.'s headquarters in New York, by the United States and the USSR; the French and British troops were ignominiously forced to withdraw. The affair finished Anthony Eden as Prime Minister. He resigned shortly afterwards, having lost the election he called, after losing a vote of confidence in the House of Commons.

The Foreign Secretary shuddered at the memory. To add to his woes, Dominic Chandler and most of Fleet Street would be on his back now. With the nations whistle blowing culture charging pell-mell through British society, if Chandler or one of his gutter press cronies got wind of the Ministry's involvement in Pan Global's attempts to destabilise the Congo, he, like Eden before him, would be publicly ruined.

In the privacy of his office, self-pity overwhelmed him. He had not been in office when Condor was first agreed at the highest and most secret level. His Party was not even in power then, for God's sake. This spiralling mess was not his fault; he had done his best. If things went public, he knew the P.M. would put up the umbrella, and hold him personally accountable; his ministerial head would roll if he did not act quickly. Pressing the intercom button, he spoke with his secretary. There was more than a hint of panic in his voice.

'Margery, get hold of Brigade Lethbridge at the Ministry of Defence...I want him in my office for an emergency meeting... get him over here, NOW!'

As the sun broke, the horizon flooded the silent township of Birundi with brilliant early-morning light, illuminating the activity inside the police station.

'I am sorry Monsieur; our radio has not worked for weeks, and the telephone line is still dead.' Sergeant Pierre Labella shook his head. 'Since the guerrillas came we have been cut off from the outside world.' With a resigned shrug he admitted, 'I think it must have been them that cut the line.'

Barney Morris stepped back from the police station's stained counter. Since the grisly incident outside the hotel, Morris had only one thing on his mind. He simply had to get out of Birundi.

'Well obviously it was them.' He snapped. Inside his ill-fitting and crumpled suit, his flabby shoulders slumped with frustration. These were not good old-fashioned English Bobbies he was dealing with, who could be relied on in an emergency. Morris could feel growing fear gnawing inside his ample belly.

'Then exactly what do you intend to do about getting us out of here? You know what will happen to any Europeans that bastard Ojukwu catches alive don't you?'

The policeman shrugged apologetically. 'I am sorry Monsieur. I have had no orders on the matter, and must look after the safety of my own men. I promise you; they will suffer much more if Ojukwu catches any of them. Perhaps you should make your own arrangements to leave?'

Grinding his teeth in frustration, the reporter turned on his heel and strode out of the police station into the growing heat of the morning. Clearly, he was going nowhere with the local authorities. The police obviously were not interested in his fate; they just wanted to save their own miserable skins. Reaching into his pocket for a cigarette, Barney Morris stared across the deserted square. The silence which filled it had an unsettling and eerie quality about it, as if the dilapidated shanty of Birundi Township knew what was soon to be unleashed upon it.

Snatching the unlit cigarette from his lips, he snarled '*Bastards*' to himself and angrily strode towards the peeling facade of the Hotel Armond's grand entrance. There was still one option of escape left open to him, and he was determined to talk to Krutz and make the most of it. If he could get an extra seat for his photographer so much the better, but if not, she would have to take her own chances. As he crossed the dusty square his heart suddenly leapt. Morris looked up as he detected the faint but unmistakable drone of an aircraft somewhere to the northwest. His heart leap inside his chest and his breathing quickened. The aircraft could have only one purpose, he thought with growing relief. The droning sound meant a real chance of salvation. It put a new spring into his step. As he climbed the steps outside the hotel, he reasoned with himself. Flying as it was across the back of beyond, surely it must be coming in order to land on Birundi's airstrip?

Having already flown over the township to announce his arrival, Brogan slowly lowered the Sky Van's wing flaps as he went through the routine of readying his aircraft, on its final approach toward the single strip of runway, less than three miles ahead.

Earlier, his tough-looking passenger had sat quietly beside him studying a map. Brogan had not quite made him or the others out. The young men in the hold were fit and tanned, and clearly deferred to the man who had sat beside him in the co-pilot's seat. Brogan stole a glance at his profile. Somewhere around his early to mid-thirties, lean and quite handsome in a rugged sort of way, he supposed. Brogan assumed they were all servicemen; probably Royal Marines, attached to the security staff of the High Commission in Nairobi, he supposed, seconded for the extraction of medical staff they had been sent to rescue.

Through the cockpit's toughened windshield, the Sky Van's pilot could see the narrow ribbon of the grass runway, hacked from the surrounding jungle, several miles ahead. The flat roofs of the sprawling township of Birundi nestled peacefully nearby. The hills across to his right were cut by a single winding track which disappeared beneath the canopy somewhere half-way up the tallest of them. Brogan guessed that must be the track leading to the local mine. To his left, besides the far edge of the township, the blue Mpana River shimmered in the sunlight and snaked lazily off towards the far horizon, its banks narrowing in the distance, shrouded on both sides by high walls of lush green jungle.

Parked inside the cleared perimeter of the airstrip, he could see the distinct shape of a faded yellow twin-engine aircraft. It was the unmistakable outline of an old Dakota, standing idle beside the airfields isolated hanger. In the closed world of the bush cargo business, absently, he wondered who the pilot was. The blurred markings on its wings and fuselage suggested it might be Johann Van de Merwe's plane out of Joburg. Absently, Brogan wondered what he was doing here, and why he had not already taken to the skies and made good his escape, from what was said to be sweeping towards Birundi from the northwest.

To Brogan's relief, as he stared across the chaotic patchwork of rusted corrugated roofs of the silent township, there appeared no sign of the savage urban devastation which was the universal trademark of all African inter-racial conflicts. As yet, the peaceful scene below gave no hint of scattered corpses, burning buildings and tell-tale smoke spiralling into the cloudless sky. Everything appeared quiet and calm; clearly, the Mai-Mai had not arrived yet. He failed to see any movement of the townships' population below, but that he mused, was hardly surprising, given the murderous guerrillas' imminent arrival. He guessed the township's people had all hopped it in the last 24 hours, and were hiding below, somewhere in the surrounding bush.

Satisfied that all was in order, and it was safe to land, he reduced the engines' power by gently easing back on the throttles. As the Sky Van continued to lose height, he reached for his throat mike and pressed the intercom button. With one eye on the approaching airstrip, with a sly grin, he made an announcement to his passengers sitting in the aircraft's hold.

'Ladies and gentlemen, we will shortly be landing at Birundi international airport. Please ensure all smoking materials are extinguished, and your seats are in the upright position. Thank you for flying Brogan airways.'

Danny, Spike and Charlie looked towards their sergeant. The troopers' colour and humour had returned after the recent battering they had endured during the storm. It was Danny who spoke first.

'Is he taking the piss, or what?'

Pat grinned. 'Yes, of course he is you idiot... but you'd better do as he says and strap in tight.'

Danny nodded and reached for his strap buckles.

His sergeant stood up and headed for the front of the plane. Before he disappeared into the cockpit he turned and said.

'I'm going to sit with the pilot; I've always wanted to have a go at landing something as big as this. Better stay here and hang on tight.'

As Pat disappeared into the cockpit, Spike looked horrified. Staring at both his friends he said, 'Oh my Gawd! Now who is taking the piss?'

'I'm afraid there is very little we can do Minister.' Brigadier Lethbridge glanced at his watch, 'my men are committed and should be touching down in Birundi anytime now.' Turning his attention back to the Minister he added, 'With luck, they should be refuelled and in the air within an hour or so, with the medics and any other Europeans they can find safely aboard.'

The Foreign Secretary exploded, 'No, no! I want this mission cancelled Brigadier! Your men must not land on Congolese soil. I absolutely forbid it!'

Brigadier Lethbridge's face remained impassive. The option to plant this odious little man, who seemed on the verge of hysteria, was still tempting, but his coming retirement and generous pension were enough to keep him in check. An uncomfortable silence filled the room as the clock ticked officiously behind his two visitors. Besides the Brigadier, Cornelius Wilde broke the stalemate suddenly when he said.

'Ah, if I may, Minister?'

David Benchley glared at the analyst.

'Yes?'

Cornelius cleared his throat.

'I have been doing some intelligence work on the current state of the mission. I've had GCHQ monitoring radio chatter across the Birundi area, and there's been no mention of an unregistered flight anywhere in the last 24 hours,' Cornelius always enjoyed playing the conspirator, 'We have been scanning all the high band frequencies used by the countries the flight has crossed. Military frequencies naturally, Oh, and civilian channels too of course, including Ham operators.'

'The Minister's face brightened slightly. 'You can do that?'

Cornelius smiled. 'Oh yes! Using the highly sophisticated facilities at Cheltenham, of course we can. We scan millions of frequencies worldwide as a matter of routine.' He shrugged. 'You would be amazed what interesting snippets of information we gather on behalf of Her Majesty's government from unguarded chatter on mobile phones, tele-printers, faxes and even the old telex machines.' The conspiratorial smile returned. 'Of course, some of the messages are coded or encrypted, but we have ways of dealing with them, too.'

'So nothing from the Congolese army or their air force?'

Cornelius shook his head. 'Not directly, no Minister. They have ordered reconnaissance flights into the area, but nothing specifically targeting our mercy flight.'

Relief flooded David Benchley's face. Before he could interrupt, Cornelius continued his briefing.

'The flight's mission commander has orders to stay low throughout the flight, and as a precaution, we have arranged to have our own radar net thrown over the area.'

Startled, the Foreign Secretary said. 'How on earth...?'

Cornelius looked triumphant. 'Bit of luck really. The Royal Navy's assault ship HMS Ocean has been stationed off the Liberian coast on anti-pirate patrols for the past couple of months. We contacted the Admiralty and asked them to signal the Ocean's Captain, and order him to put up one of their look-down radar enabled Sea King helicopters, to sweep inland and see if they could detect our flight...without, I'm delighted to say, any positive results.'

'So you mean no-one over there even knows of the flight's existence?'

'Well yes, that appears correct Minister.' Before Benchley could speak Cornelius held up his hand. 'There's something more to add while I think of it, which I believe has considerable bearing on this whole episode.'

David Benchley stared at the MI6 analyst. He desperately needed some good news.

'Yes, what is it?'

'The man leading this mission is the same SAS commander who led the assault team during the operation code named Windmill a few months ago, that saved London. He... Pat Farrell is his name, by the way, is an extremely tough and resourceful soldier....I know him personally, and I'm delighted to report Minister; he is one of the very best men we have working for us.'

Unimpressed, the Minister sighed. His political neck was on the block, and his future rested on some boneheaded grunt presently landing in the distant Congo, who he had never even heard of before. Nodding slowly he said.

'I sincerely hope you are right, Mr Wilde.'

Chapter Fifteen

Holes in the poorly maintained roof let shafts of brilliant sunlight cut into the gloom of the airstrip's empty hanger. A jumble of wooden cargo crates stood haphazardly along one side, against the corrugated iron wall. Opposite them, a long work bench scattered with a mixture of rusty tools lay silent. Besides the bench was a metal cage, containing several heavy gas bottles and an abandoned acetylene cutting torch. In his haste to escape, someone had left the cage door wide open. From the dim interior, Spike's voice echoed across the deserted hanger.

'There's no-one here, Pat; looks like they have all had it away on their toes.'

Pat stood at the doorway, outlined in the morning sunlight.

'Yeah, I'm really not surprised, Spike.'

Danny and Charlie walked up and stood beside their sergeant. Each of them carried a pistol concealed beneath their shirts. Clearing his throat, Danny made his report.

'No sign of anyone about Pat, and I'm afraid that old Dakota is not going anywhere soon.'

Pat turned and looked quizzically at Danny.

'What's up with it?'

Danny shook his head. 'One of the engines is in bits. My guess is that someone must have tried to fix it,' he shrugged, 'but couldn't.'

Pat nodded his understanding. Danny had a way with anything mechanical, particularly combustion engines. If he said something was bust, Pat trusted his judgement.

Spike stepped out into the sunlight and joined the others.

'Morning campers!'

Ignoring him, Pat stared across the deserted grass runway towards the flat roofs of the nearby township.

'Where's Brogan gone?'

Charlie pointed. 'He is over there by the refuelling point, Pat. He said the airfield's electric pump doesn't work, and it is going to take at least an hour to hand crank enough juice into the Sky Van tanks to get us home.'

Pat nodded. 'Did he say he needed any help?'

Charlie shook his head. 'No, he said he could handle it. The pilot of the Dakota is helping him.'

'Fair enough Charlie, I bet he's done this plenty of times before.' Pat glanced down at his watch. 'It is 07.20 hours, and we need to be away from here as soon as possible. We might as well go to the township now and round up the medics. Has a seen a vehicle we can use?'

All three troopers remained silent.

Pat cursed to himself.

'OK, we'll have to walk then. We'd better take our bergans. Strip your AKs down...' the surrounding silence was ominous, 'and pack 'em, just in case.'

'What about the RGP Pat?' Danny enquired.

Pat shook his head. 'Leave it in the plane for now. I'll...'

In the distance, a vehicle suddenly growled up through its gearbox, throwing up a cloud of swirling red dust, as it sped along the perimeter road leading up towards the mine.

'Well, someone's still here Pat,' said Spike.

The four men watched the vehicle until it disappeared behind a dense curtain of trees.

Turning his attention away from the settling dust in the distance, Pat said.

'Right then, over to the plane and get your kit sorted out. We are off in ten.'

Grimly holding onto the leather strap, which was anchored to the doorframe above his head, Otto Krutz shouted over the noise of the Toyota's straining engine.

'Come on Jan, keep your foot down. We need to pick up McGhee and get back to the bank before those bastard Mai-Mai arrive.'

Jan nodded. After the disaster yesterday, like his passenger, he had no desire to mix it with the guerrillas again. Stamping down on the clutch, Jan thrust the gear stick forward and dropped a gear. As he floored the accelerator again the Toyota shuddered and surged along the track, an eddying cloud of dust spewing and swirling from its spinning wheels.

After another bone-rattling twenty minutes, their vehicle neared the mine. Krutz remembered most of the route along the single track from the previous day. Since leaving the hotel, neither of the Toyota's occupants had seen another living soul. As they careered around a last tight corner, Jan was first to notice the ominous columns of smoke darkening the skies ahead.

'Christ Colonel. *Look!*'

In an instant, both men saw, clad in swirling twists of oily smoke, the mine buildings ahead were burning. It was too far to see the scene in detail, but hundreds of dark shapes were milling around what was left of the smoking mine complex. There were far too many to be mine employees. Scattered here and there between the silent earthmovers, offices and workshops were smudges of orange, which stood out clearly, in stark contrast with the dark earth where they lay.

The retired Colonel gasped, *'Die bliksemse!'*

Remembering that his driver did not speak Afrikaans, Krutz quickly slipped back into English.

'Shit Jan, it's the Mai-Mai. The bastards have beaten us to it.'

Heart pounding, Krutz glanced around the thick curtain of jungle, on either side of the track. Old habits die hard among veteran soldiers, as his eyes automatically flicked from tree to tree, in search of hidden ambush.

A moment later he snapped out of it.

'For Christ's sake, slow down and turn around!'

Without reply, Jan spun the wheel and pulled on the handbrake. He didn't need to be told twice, but in his haste to execute the handbrake turn, his foot slipped off the clutch, and the engine stalled, as the vehicle spun around in a cloud of dust. With a curse Jan reached for the starter. It fired immediately, and he gunned the engine. Krutz scowled at his driver, then looked back towards the pall of rising smoke. He shook his head, sighing and winced sadly at the awful truth. He knew that somewhere in the complex; the fate of the mine's manager was already sealed. Those had not been bundles of discarded orange rags they had seen, but the bodies of the local workforce employed by the Pan Global Corporation. With so many guerrillas swarming through the complex, there was absolutely no chance of just two of them mounting a rescue. Even if the manager was still alive, it would be suicide to try, and both men knew it.

'We are too late to help that poor bastard, McGhee.' Krutz drew the pistol from his holster. Pulling the slide back, he snapped a 9mm bullet into its breach. Keeping the pistol reassuringly in his big hand, he said,

'We can't do anything here Jan. The explosion yesterday must have sealed the mine. Let's get back to Birundi quickly.' He glanced at his watch and added, 'We've got to grab the diamonds and then get away across the river, before those murdering devils attack the township!'

Still smarting from his embarrassment of stalling the engine, eyes firmly fixed on the track in front of them, Jan nodded his agreement. He thought for a moment, and then said.

'Something I do not understand Colonel. Why didn't we hear any shots coming from the mine?'

As the vehicle surged back along the dusty track, the Boer Colonel shrugged.

'Perhaps we have underestimated Ojukwu and his cut-throats, Jan. It is logical to take the mine out silently just with machetes or whatever. Tactically, it makes complete sense to secure the mine first. Why alert the township unnecessarily, and lose the element of surprise?'

Although on foot, Pat and the others quickly reached the deserted town square. Apart from a few mangy looking mongrel dogs sniffing around piles of litter, they had seen no other sign of life in the rubbish strewn alleyways, off the main road which dissected Birundi. They had passed a deserted market. There were no ringing cries of street vendors eager to sell their colourful wares, no farmers offering their home-grown foodstuffs at knockdown prices. There was no sign of the usual traders, or the usual hustle and bustle of an open bazaar, which was the heart of every township, everywhere across rural Africa. The SAS men saw empty stalls and hastily abandoned trestle tables, but nothing else.

'I do not like this one bit. It is too bloody quiet.' Spike murmured under his breath.

A dog suddenly barked nearby.

Spike jumped.

'Wanker!' Grinned Danny, just a few yards behind his friend.

'All right, settle down,' growled Pat, 'you two, stay focused, and keep your eyes and ears open.'

Danny looked suitable chastened.

'Sorry Pat.'

Pat accepted the apology with a curt nod. Charlie kept silent, lest he too incurred his sergeant's displeasure.

'Take the other side of the street...both of you.'

Danny and Spike doubled across to the other side. Spreading out, the patrol assumed a standard 'brick' formation. Pat searched ahead, and then looked behind him. Clearly, the population had already fled, he thought. Not a sign of traffic or pedestrians anywhere, which could mean only one thing. The guerrillas must be a hell of a lot closer than his briefing before they left Kenya, had suggested.

An eerie silence had initially greeted them when they crossed the airfield and entered the outskirts of the township; now, under the rising sun, it surrounded them and had stayed bound to Pat and his men, like an unwelcome visitor, all the way to the main square.

As they rounded the final corner Pat held up his hand. Turning to his men he said. 'Right you lot, look into the square. That building opposite with Gendarmerie plastered all over it must be the local police station. Spike, I want you and Danny to go over and see if you can get an update on the guerrillas' whereabouts, and while you are at it, see if their phone is working. If they ask, tell them you are backpackers on holiday, and for God's sake, keep your guns hidden. Be polite, and don't take too long about it... Meet us over at the clinic when you are done. Clear?'

Spike and Danny nodded.

'Right, get away.'

Both troopers turned on their heel and began to walk quickly towards the police headquarters.

Pat turned to Trooper Duggen.

'Charlie, you and I will go and link up with the medics.' He glanced down at his watch, 'I don't think we have much time to play with, so come on, let's get it done.'

With a snarl of frustration, the Mai-Mai's general kicked the lifeless body of the mine manager. Moments earlier, one of his men had nervously knelt before his leader and reported that the entrance to the Mpolo mine was buried under hundreds of tons of rock.

Beside the body, the safe hung open and empty save for a bottle and a few worthless papers. Before he died, the terrified Scotsman had told Ojukwu where the diamonds were. The words had frantically spilled from the Scotsman's lips, as he eyed the machete in the Generals hand, with growing fear and horror.

Ojukwu glared at the messenger,

'We must take the township quickly. Gather my officers and bring them here to me.'

Looking up, he walked towards the map which was still pinned on the wall by the window. Ojukwu stared silently at it for several minutes, as his most trusted men began to assemble.

Even the last of the officers arrived quickly. They knew better than to keep the general waiting. Some were panting. General Ojukwu addressed them coldly.

'We will attack the township and drive its inhabitants towards the river.' Ojukwu pointed to one of his officers, 'Take your men and move to the other bank before we begin the attack.' The general turned and pointed to the map. His finger traced the blue ribbon printed on it. It stopped just to the west of the township. He indicated a point on the map.

'I want you to cross here. The bend in the river will hide you while you cross. When the attack begins, your men are to stop anyone trying to escape to the other bank. Do you understand Joshua?'

His cousin nodded.

'Good. Gather your men quickly, and go.'

As he turned towards the door Joshua stopped. The Mai-Mai major turned and hesitatingly asked.

'What will be the signal to begin the attack general?'

The general beamed. 'You will know it, when it comes.'

As the man hastened outside, the general switched his attention to another of his officers inside the sweltering room.

'Take your men and secure the airstrip. I do not want anyone to escape from there.'

Turning his attention back to the remaining officers, sweeping his hand slowly across the map, he said.

'The rest of you will take your men and cross the airstrip. You will attack south through the township, towards the river. Make sure you spread your men out, and show no mercy to anyone you find,' he pointed down at the headless corpse lying on the floor. His eyes narrowed;

there was a sinister menace in his voice as he spat the words that ended his council of war.

'Do not forget. I want any whites brought to me... alive!'

Chapter Sixteen

After the sapping heat outside, the clinic's deserted waiting room felt cool and inviting. As he entered the medical centre Pat's nose wrinkled; it was immediately assaulted by the pungent smell of carbolic disinfectant. It made a welcome change from the stink of the open sewers they had passed during their journey to the town centre.

The morning sunlight streamed through the slatted windows, creating a sharp lattice of light and shadow on the opposite whitewashed wall. Worn, chipped metal framed chairs were neatly arranged along the edge of the silent waiting room, but like the small reception desk in one corner, they were empty. A child's rag doll lay abandoned on the floor.

Charlie broke the silence. Quietly, he said,

'Maybe no-one's home Pat?'

Pat shrugged. There was irritation in his voice as he growled,

'It's a bloody long way to come, if they have buggered off already.'

He nodded towards the door opposite. It was marked with a large printed sign, which boldly declared, 'MEDICAL STAFF ONLY'. Sliding his heavy bergan off his shoulders, Pat rested it soundlessly on the floor. Charlie did the same.

Pat turned his head and glanced toward his companion. Keeping his voice low, he whispered,

'If they are still here, they must be out the back. Come on, let's go and find them.'

Crossing the waiting room, Pat listened for a moment as he reached forward and grasped the door handle. With his other hand, he slowly reached around to the back of his waistband and drew the pistol concealed under his shirt. Charlie took the hint and did the same.

Pulling the pistol's hammer back with his thumb, his voice still a whisper, Pat said,

'Keep your eyes open Charlie, we don't know what is on the other side...ready?'

Licking his lips and unconsciously tightening his grip on the 9mm pistol, Charlie cocked his own gun and nodded.

Satisfied that they were both ready for whatever awaited them beyond, Pat mouthed the numbers as he silently counted down,

'Three, two, one, *GO!*'

The door banged open. As they'd done countless times before in training; their guns levelled in a blur of practiced motion, both men burst into the shadow filled corridor beyond.

From inside the nearest open doorway, there was a shrill scream of surprise, and a crash of medical instruments falling with a loud clatter onto the stone floor.

Angrily, a women's voice cursed,

'Jesus, mother and Joseph... who?'

Both men instantly recognised the soft burr of her Irish accent. Whoever she was; she had clearly been startled by their sudden and dramatic entrance.

As her words faded, a flushed but lovely face appeared from the treatment room doorway. For a split-second, Pat was transfixed. He had known plenty of attractive women in his time, but to his eyes this one had a face to die for. Red haired and green eyed, she was dressed in the starched white uniform of a nursing Sister. The woman was in her early thirties; her beauty glared disdainfully at the two crouching figures either side of the open doorway.

Clearly unfazed by the two pistols pointing at her flat stomach, she stared at them coldly for a moment, before placing her empty hands on her hips. Surrounded by the fallen collection of kidney bowls, her face flushed. She tilted her head slightly to one side. With more than a hint of sarcasm, she said,

'If you are not going to shoot me with those things, will you please show the good manners to stop pointing them at me?'

Like a slap in the face, the nurse's question snapped Pat out of his momentary daze. With a surge of unaccustomed embarrassment, tight lipped, he nodded to Charlie. Colouring slightly, both men stood up as they lowered their pistols.

'Err, hallo. I'm Pat Farrell. We have been sent from the High Commission in Nairobi, to rescue you.'

Still standing with her hands on her hips, she straightened her head. Did Pat notice the faintest flash of amusement in those lovely emerald eyes?

'Well, it is about time!'

With a toss of her head, she turned and began to walk down the darkened corridor. Over her shoulder, she called back at them,

'You will wait here, the both of you, while I go and fetch Doctor Frasier.'

Both SAS men watched her disappear through the door at the end of the corridor. It was Charlie who broke the silence. He whistled softly,

'Blimey Pat...'

At that moment, there was the sound of movement behind them. Pat spun around, but just as quickly, he lowered his pistol and relaxed.

Spike bound into the waiting room, closely followed by Danny.

'The police station's completely empty Pat. We searched both floors; there's not a soul in there, even the cells in the basement are deserted. The place is totally empty. Looks like the local coppers have done a bunk like everyone else.'

Pat nodded; he had been expecting that. Without a population to police, given the circumstances, he would have been surprised if they had stuck around to be slaughtered, instead of following everyone else's example, and fleeing into the safety of the bush.

'What about the phone line?'

Danny shook his head.

'Nah, sorry Pat. It's dead as mutton.'

Pat nodded. He had one last question. He had spotted the lattice mast mounted on the roof of the police station, when they had first entered the square.

'What about the police radio?'

It was Spike's turn to shake his head.

'Tried it, but it's no good. It powered up OK, but nothing happened when I hit the transmit key. It might be something simple, and I could probably fix it if I had enough time...and the spares were handy,' he added as an afterthought. 'But I didn't see any lying around....Sorry."

Pat nodded.

'OK, fair enough. Both of you get over to the hotel and see if you can locate the journalists, I briefed you about before we left Talinga. Bring them straight here when you find them.'

As Danny and Spike nodded and turned to leave, still staring intently at the pair, Pat added,

'You'd better make this quick boys. I have got a gut feeling we are fast running out of time. I want out of here and back to the airfield asp.'

As the two men left, Pat and Charlie heard an engine revving outside, and then a loud squeal of brakes.

Pat strode back to the entrance of the medical centre, and cautiously peered outside. Across the deserted square, close to the police station, he saw two white men climb out of their vehicle and run towards the only bank they had seen since reaching the township. As he watched from the cover of the doorway, one of the men on the other side of the square grasped the handle and tried the door, but clearly, it remained firmly locked. He then tried to shoulder it open but without success. The other, older man held up his hand and said something. Rubbing his shoulder, his companion nodded. The man took a step back. Turning again, rearing back, he trust his leg violently forward and smashed the sole of his boot into the door, just below its brass handle. With a splintering crash, the door flew open. Without a word, one of the two men quickly disappeared inside, while the other returned to their vehicle.

Charlie had followed his sergeant, and had been watching over Pat's shoulder.

'Bloody hell Pat, this is a funny time to rob a bank.'

Pat shrugged. Whatever the two men were up to; it was none of his business. He had a job to do and a mission to complete. Dismissing the incident, he turned back to his trooper and said,

'Whatever they are up to; it has got nothing to do with us, Charlie. Come on, let's go and find out what is holding up the Doctor?'

Chapter Seventeen

Otto Krutz squinted into the cool gloom of the banks deserted interior. As his eyes adjusted to the semi-darkness, he felt along the wall for the light switch. Finding it, he flicked it on, but nothing happened. With a muttered curse, he strode towards the empty counter. Beyond it, he saw what his straining eyes had been searching for.

'There Jan, there it is!' he called out triumphantly. Kicking the low counter door aside he walked quickly behind it and stopped in front of the vault's massive steel door. Big enough for a man to walk through without stooping, it was clearly old and its outer paint was faded and peeling. A brass plaque announced it had been manufactured by the Chamois Corporation- Brussels - 1931. There was a small metal wheel in the middle of the vault's door, and a solid looking steel handle. Krutz grasped the handle and tugged at it, but it stubbornly remained in the vertical position. Whatever it's vintage, it remained firmly locked. Clearly, it would not easily give up the secrets it contained, until the moment when the time-lock tripped. Krutz ground his teeth in frustration. Accepting that it would not open yet, he decided to explore a little. Besides the steel facade of the vault, mounted securely on the wall was a toughened steel box. Krutz could hear a faint ticking inside the mechanism, which he assumed must be the all-important time-lock. He glanced up at the clock mounted high up on the concrete wall above it.

'It is almost 8.57, Jan. With luck, if McGhee was right, this bastard should automatically open in just a few minutes.'

Jan nodded. There was no sign of the bank's staff, and although he did not expect them to appear, he drew his pistol anyway. He walked back towards the bank's splintered front door and positioned himself behind it. His eyes swept the square but nothing moved, just the usual rubbish strewn here and there, a few old tyres and a stray dog. Wiping a speck of dust from his eye, he glanced outside again. His voice betrayed alarm, as he suddenly hissed back into the gloomy interior.

'I see movement outside, Colonel. Two men have just gone into the hotel.'

Krutz felt his stomach tighten. They were too close now to fail. He called anxiously to his companion keeping watch by the door.

'Were they Mai-Mai?'

Jan turned his head and shook it. The tone of his voice changed abruptly from alarm to confusion,

'No Colonel, I do not think so, they were both white.'

Krutz sighed. With the Mai-Mai close on their heels, he didn't need any more complications. Probably just the civilians he was warned about. Gruffly he said,

'OK Jan, keep an eye on the hotel and let me known if they come out again.' Krutz listened to the soft rhythmic tick inside the time mechanism for a moment as he pondered his options, then he said,

'Tell you what Jan, go over to the hotel and see if they are anything to do with that plane that arrived this morning. I would rather we hitch a lift with them, than chance our arm driving out of here.'

Jan nodded. The thought of driving several hundred kilometres through sun-baked, hostile territory did not appeal to him either.

'Will you be OK here on your own?'

Colonel Krutz nodded eagerly. He drew his pistol and cocked it. With a leer, he growled,

'Sure, it is not a problem. If a bloody Kaffir comes in here in the next few minutes, trust me man, I will blow his fucking head off!'

With a grin, Jan nodded.

'I'd better make sure you know it's me when I come back then,' he opened the door and stepped into the brilliant sunlight outside.

Standing alone in the empty bar, Barney Morris heard the hotel's main door bang open. Dropping the drink he had just helped himself to, he rushed into the foyer. Two young white men stood inside. Both he noted with a start, held pistols levelled at his ample stomach.

One of them barked at him.

'Stand still. Do not move!'

Frightened by the cold look in the young men's eyes, despite the warning Morris threw up his hands. As he surrendered, words tumbled from his suddenly dry mouth.

'No! Don't shoot. It's OK. I'm English. I'm a journalist… oh sweet Jesus, thank God you're here. Are you from the plane?'

Neither of the young men moved for several heartbeats. Suddenly, one of them barked again. His voice cut the journalist like a knife.

'Name?'

With an ear for accents, Morris new instantly this man was a Londoner, but there was a trained confidence and hardness of his tone that brooked no lies.

'M..M..Morris, Barney Morris,' he spluttered. With his hands still raised, he nervously added more when both men remained unmoving holding him captive with their guns and their dark hypnotic eyes.

'I've...I've got my press card in my pocket.'

One of the two nodded.

'Take it out and give it to me...very slowly.'

Sweat erupting from his brow, Barney Morris complied. With exaggerated care, he slowly lowered one hand and reached into the breast pocket of his crumpled suit. He produced the dog-eared card. Eagerly, he offered it for inspection.

While Spike kept his gun pointed at the middle of the sweating journalist's chest, Danny stepped forward and snatched the card from the journalists trembling hand.

After scrutinising the photograph it contained, then the other side of the plastic-coated card, he spoke to his companion.

'OK Spike, it's him all right.' He looked back at Morris, as he lowered his pistol and returned the card.

'All right, put your hands down mate. Where is the other one, the girl?'

His eyes followed the sweating journalist's finger, as Morris pointed towards the ceiling.

'She is up there. I expect she's snivelling and hiding under her bed.'

Angered by the sudden arrogance and contempt in Morris's voice, Danny snapped back.

'Well go upstairs and get her then! We have orders to lift you both out, and believe me; we don't have much time.'

Pat shook hands with Frasier.

'We have been sent from Nairobi to evacuate you and your staff. You know the Mai-Mai are getting close, don't you?'

The doctor nodded.

'Aye, we have been getting ready to leave for the last week.'

Pat glanced down the darkened corridor, and said,

'How many patients have you still got here, then?'

Frasier visibly relaxed a little and smiled.

'Thankfully it has been quiet recently; I have only got one left. We had a couple of locals in bed with malaria, and a few scattered cases of malnutrition among the refugees, but their families took them away once we'd loaded them up with medicine and high-energy biscuits. No-one, no matter how sick, wants to get caught by the Tutsis. The local Hutus are absolutely terrified of them...With just cause, from what I have seen and heard.'

Pat nodded grimly.

'What is the status of your remaining patient, can he walk?'

Dr Frasier pointed towards one of the rooms leading off the corridor.

'Physically, he is fine. A few cuts and bruises, but nothing serious.' The doctor nodded down the corridor, 'he is in there, poor chap. It's the guy from the company who owns the local mine, that the Mai-Mai caught a couple of days ago. They dumped him in the square with the remains of one of the mine's employees. He is still in deep shock, and since saying a few words to his mine manager yesterday, has mentally deteriorated into an almost catatonic state.'

Almost apologetically, the young doctor added with a sigh,

'I just do not have the facilities to treat him; I'm afraid. I don't know what they did to him, he's hardly uttered a word to my staff, or me, but it must have been something pretty awful. The physiological damage they inflicted is clearly immense; he needs intensive post-traumatic treatment... I had him scheduled to be evacuated out of here on the next flight in a few days' time, but that is not going to happen now, is it?'

Pat snorted, and shook his head.

'No, no chance of that. We'll have to take him with us. If you can grab him and whatever personal belongings you can carry, we need to get back to the airfield straight away.'

'You have a vehicle?' enquired the doctor.

Pat shook his head again.

'We haven't got one; there isn't anything serviceable left in the township, from what I've seen so far.'

Alan Frasier allowed himself a wry grin.

'Yes, of course. The locals have taken everything with wheels in the last few days. It got quite ugly out there before the final ones left. They were fighting each other for a place on the last few vehicles to leave. I suppose we can't blame them for wanting to get as far away from here as possible?'

Pat sniffed. With an ironic grin, he replied,

'Yeah, same as us, Doc.'

He turned to Charlie,

'Nip over to the bank and contact the blokes in the Rover. Tell them we are heading back to the airfield in a minute. Offer them a couple of seats on the plane, in return for a lift up there, OK?'

Colonel Krutz glanced towards the clock above the vault again. As the second and minute hands slowly swept around and reached the top of the hour, suddenly, there was a loud click inside the ancient time-lock mechanism. He heard securing bolts withdraw inside the heavy steel door with a dull metallic thud. With a grin of triumph, the Colonel holstered his pistol and strode over to it. He grasped the metal wheel again. This time, its well-oiled internal thread engaged and turned. When he had spun the wheel as far as it would go, Krutz released his grip and grasped the steel handle beside it. To his relief, it turned obediently under his hand. The ex-Colonel pulled at it hard, and the steel door swung open.

It was dark inside the narrow vault, but the light flooding in from outside gave just enough illumination to see by. Neat bundles of near worthless Congolese francs, and clear plastic bags filled with base metal centimes crowded the shelves. There were bundles of U.S. dollars in one section; a currency readily trusted by local merchants and inhabitants everywhere in the Congo. Ignoring the money, Krutz began to search. He found the pack he was looking for at the back of the vault, laying on the concrete floor. Krutz lifted the rucksack and checked the Pan Global label attached to it. He moved back to the vault's entrance where it was lighter. Krutz undid the buckles and loosened the draw string which secured the pack's outer flap. Inside was a red cloth sack. He quickly untied its drawstring.

A low whistle suddenly escaped from his lips. As he had hoped, the sack was filled with raw uncut diamonds. Despite the need for a swift exit, Krutz was mesmerised for a moment, and could not resist plunging his hand into them. He had never seen or felt such a fortune before on the Skeleton Coast. Everything there was transported in locked, sealed containers. Almost reverently, he lifted one of the biggest milky red/white stones up to the light.

The stone was roughly oblong in shape, about half of the size of a hen's egg. In its current state, the milky stone did not look too impressive, but Krutz knew that cut and polished, even on its own, it was worth a fortune. His mouth suddenly dry, he stared intently, in awe for a moment at the raw diamond. Then a single word slipped softly from his lips.

'Jesus!'

Suddenly, something tore Krutz from his reverie. He froze for a split-second. A footfall scuffed on the step outside.

Dropping the stone back into the sack, Krutz snatched out his pistol. If it was Jan, he knew the danger and would have called a warning. A shadow suddenly fell across the splintered doorway. In a reaction honed from years of fighting on countless African battlefields, Krutz's bulky frame came into a crouch as he lifted his pistol in a double handed grip. With a deafening roar, he fired a single shot through the open doorway....

Only the soft tick of the time-lock disturbed the silence inside the bank, as a thin swirl of smoke eddied from his pistol's muzzle. From beyond the shattered doorway, a shaken voice spluttered.

'For Christ's sake, hold your fire, you idiot...*I'm on your fucking side!*'

On the airfield, Brogan and the Dakota pilot both heard the echoing boom of the distant shot. They listened for another, but none came. Brogan was busy in his cockpit, running through his usual pre-flight checks. He'd guessed the Mai-Mai were close. He had no intention of waiting for a moment longer than absolutely necessary when his passengers returned from the township, but they were in for a long return flight. Right now, aircraft serviceability was critical.

Sitting on the starboard wing, the other pilot snapped the filler cap shut and called out,

'That's it; all the tanks are full…Did you hear that shot just now?'

Brogan looked up from his instruments and said,

'Yeah, I heard it. It's probably nothing…'

He stopped speaking abruptly. Over the Dakota pilot's shoulder, he spied movement on the edge of the jungle, less than three hundred yards away. A large group of men appeared, cavorting and waving glinting machetes. Like the waters bursting from a breached dam, they spilled out onto the open grassland beside the runway. As more emerged, they began to jog towards his parked plane.

'Oh, sweet Jesus!' he muttered in horror. There could be only one explanation. Leaning forward, abandoning the rigid protocols of his pre-flight checks, he frantically began flicking switches on the dashboard. Hitting the master switch, with a whine, then a sudden roar, the port engine coughed into life. Starting the starboard engine, above the deafening noise, he pointed frantically past the confused Dakota pilot and bellowed through the open cockpit window.

'For Christ's sake, get down off the wing and into the plane! Behind you man …the bloody guerrillas are here!'

Chapter Eighteen

'Sorry if I frightened the shit out of your man.'

Otto Krutz stared with cold eyes at the tough-looking leader of the rescue party. Then a hint of a smile played across his face as he shrugged and said,

'Sometimes in Africa, it is just safer to shoot first, and ask questions later.'

Pat nodded. He knew the truth of it. He'd used the same principle too often in the past to argue the point. It had kept him alive when things sometimes went bad, and the Congo was a dangerous place to be, at the best of times. This was no time for recrimination. Pat returned the half grin and said.

'All right, no real harm done. I reckon Charlie will get over it.' He held out his hand and introduced himself, 'Pat Farrell.'

The Boer ex-Colonel nodded. He grasped Pat's hand firmly. Keeping his eyes locked on the Englishman he said,

'Otto Krutz.' Abruptly he enquired, 'was it your plane that landed earlier?'

Pat nodded.

'Yeah! We flew in this morning to lift out the British Medical party. Who are you, and how many are there in your group?'

Before he could answer, both men's attention was drawn to one side. The medical team left the clinic and headed towards them. Spike and Danny steadied Dr Frasier's patient between them. The doctor and his senior nurse were both struggling under the weight of suitcases and backpacks. The reporter and his photographer followed close behind them, also struggling with their baggage.

Krutz looked back at Pat,

'There are just two of us now. We are from the security detail up at the mine.'

In Krutz's eyes, further detail was none of the Englishman's business. There was bitterness in his voice when, eyes downcast, he added.

'Apart from my driver, I lost the rest of my men in a rebel attack yesterday…You'd better known; we saw what looked like the main force of guerrillas taking the mine over, earlier this morning. '

Pat nodded. That changed things. The Mai-Mai was much closer now, too close. There was a new urgency in his voice when Pat said.

'Look, we're running out of time. I have got to get these civvies to the airfield quickly. There's room on the plane for both of you.' Nodding towards the mines battered hardtop Toyota, he enquired, 'Can give us a lift up there?'

Hefting his rucksack over his shoulder, Krutz calmly lit a cigarette and nodded,

'Sure Farrell, no problem. It will be my pleasure.'

Pleased to have solved their immediate transport problem, with a curt nod of acknowledgement Pat turned and waved the rapidly approaching civilians forward. It was going to be tight inside the Toyota, but his passengers' comfort on the short trip was not an issue worth consideration.

'Right everyone, get aboard and make it quick...I've just heard the guerrillas are almost on our doorstep!'

Charlie appeared, dragging all four of the SAS men's Burgan backpacks behind him.

'Sling those on the roof rack with the other luggage Charlie. There won't be room inside.'

Danny and Spike heard Pat's instructions too. Danny climbed up the steel ladder welded onto the back of the vehicle, then onto the Toyota's roof. The two other troopers passed suitcases and bergans up to Danny, as the civilians assembled at the vehicle's rear door. Barney Morris didn't wait to be invited in. Hitching up the belt which surrounded his ample stomach, he barged past the others and climbed aboard.

'Well now. Isn't that just charming!' snapped the redheaded nurse angrily. Her face flushed as she helped her patient aboard. Glaring at the two grinning SAS men as she climbed inside herself, she snapped at them both. *'Men!'*

When the Toyota was fully loaded, Pat took a last look around the deserted town square. His eyes stopped on the shattered bank door. For a second, he wondered what the two security men had been doing in there, but further thoughts on the subject were torn from him when, standing beside him, Spike announced,

'We are ready to go, Pat.'

Pat nodded. Peering into the back of the tightly packed Toyota, he said, 'Looks like we get to ride outside. With a reassuring nod, he added, 'don't worry, even going economy class, it's not far, and definitely better than walking.'

Spike nodded as both men climbed onto the vehicle's rear steel bumper, and took a firm grip of the handles welded to the Toyota's back end. Pat banged on the thin metal side and shouted,

'Let's go!'

Jan heard the call, and the Toyota's engine growled into life. He selected first gear. As the overloaded vehicle began to roll forward, Pat called to Spike, 'Hang on tight mate, this could get a bit bumpy!'

To the relief of the passengers, the short journey through the deserted township was proving as uneventful as the four SAS men's walk in. There was a palpable air of relief among the civilians inside the vehicle. Spirits were high; they felt safe, and were going home.

Both Pat and Spike were keeping their eyes open, watching for movement in any of the untidy side streets, but spotted nothing which might cause alarm. Suddenly, above the noise of their vehicle's engine, Pat saw something, which instantly made his blood run cold. He yelled a warning to Spike. Before Spike could reply, still low at only two hundred feet, with a roar, the Skyvan zoomed through the heavens above them.

His face betraying his shock, Spike yelled desperately at his sergeant,

'Christ Pat, the bloody things taken off without us!'

Krutz and his driver saw the aircraft too. Still several hundred yards short of the edge of the township, abruptly, the four-wheel drive Toyota squealed to a halt in a cloud of dust. Krutz threw open his door and leapt from the front. He ran to the vehicle's rear.

'*Die bliksemse* - What the hell?'

His eyes still wide with surprise, Pat stepped down and shook his head,

'I don't know; I have no idea?'

As both men stared at each other in search of an answer, there was a sudden scream and whoosh above, quickly followed by the dull crump of an explosion somewhere behind them, in the middle of the township. Almost immediately, it was followed by another. Both Pat and Krutz ducked involuntarily. They had both heard the sound before, at different times, on different continents. Only one thing made that same unique noise and flat muffled explosion. Krutz yelled what Pat already knew,

'Jesus! The bastards have got mortars!'

Heart racing, Pat nodded. There was no point in heading towards the airstrip anymore. With their plane's sudden exit, it was clear the Mai-Mai had already overrun it. Above the scream of another bomb arcing high above them, urgently Pat shouted,

'The airfield must have gone. We'll have to head back towards the river!'

Krutz nodded, 'You're right.' The ex-commando Colonel knew this was no time for debate. Looking up at the sky, as if searching for the missing plane, or another projectile, he yelled,

'Let's go!'

Pat jumped back onto the rear of the Toyota, and Krutz raced forward to his seat. As his door banged shut, the vehicle surged and began to turn, almost shaking Spike free of his handholds.

His face mirroring surprise and confusion, Spike yelled,

'Bloody hell, Pat, what's happening!'

Pat's face was grim. 'Not good Spike, looks like we're in a bit of trouble, son!'

High on an adjacent hill, close to the airfield, with a collective whoop of glee the sweating Mai-Mai mortar crew loosed off another bomb towards the township. They waited as the bomb arced over the airfield, and cheered loudly when it exploded inside the township.

With his fingers in his ears, their commander watched them closely. He had been with the Mai-Mai only a short time. A deserter from the national army, he was well trained by the Government's forces in the weapon's use. Distantly related by marriage to his new general, sensing opportunity for advancement, he answered Ojukwu's call to arms. A rapturous welcome awaited him, when he suddenly arrived, horn blaring, in a stolen army lorry at the rebel's headquarters, deep in Tutsi territory months earlier, complete with the mortar and several dozen boxes of high-explosive ammunition.

Realising the benefit of such a weapon, the general had instantly promoted his latest recruit to Captain of artillery in the military wing of the C.F.P., and ordered him to begin training a crew, ready to serve the mortar, when Ojukwu's invasion southwards began.

Ordering his crew to cease fire, Able Ngoa swept the airfield with his binoculars. They were an extra trophy; loot he had snatched from the dead body of the officer he had shot, before stealing both mortar and truck, and making his dash north to his tribal homeland.

Below, he could see several hundred of his Mai-Mai brothers running across the grass airstrip, past the hanger, towards the closest buildings of the township. He was glad he was not responsible for the aircraft's escape. The officer in charge of attacking the airfield would pay dearly for his failure to capture the plane. Able Ngoa lowered his binoculars for a moment and smiled to himself. He would make no mistake; his orders were simple. He was to fire a few rounds into the township, then wait to see if a target presented itself. The fin-stabilised ammunition was precious; he must not waste a single bomb. Lifting his binoculars back to his eyes, he refocused slightly, and swept the township, searching for the slightest sign of movement.

On his third sweep, he spotted something. A swirling cloud of dust wafted slowly above the buildings. It seemed fairly close to the airfield, but was moving away towards the broad river, which flowed on the far side of the township. Ngoa smiled again. Whatever was causing the cloud was hidden from view by the low tin roofs, but must be a vehicle of some sort, he decided, flushed out by his barrage.

Scampering down to the mortar, he shouldered the crew aside. Lacking an optical sight, he would have to aim manually. Lifting the bipod legs, Ngoa lined up the narrow white line painted along the length of the hot barrel, with the distant target. Stepping back, he checked the alignment, and satisfied, grasped the elevation wheel. He cranked it quickly until the barrel leant sufficiently forward.

Stepping back, he ordered a single ranging shot. One of his crew ran several yards behind the mortar, and snapped open the second steel ammunition box. Carrying the 82mm Russian mortar bomb back to the weapon, he knelt down and set the fuse, as Ngoa had taught him. He passed the live bomb to another crewman, who slipped out the safety pin, and offered up the heavy bomb to the mouth of the mortar's tube. Turning his head towards Ngoa, the loader waited for his Captain's order to let the bomb slide down the tube, strike the firing pin at the bottom, and launch itself with a deafening bang towards its target.

Ngoa licked his lips with anticipation. Placing his index fingers firmly back in his ears, he glanced from the young crewman towards his distant target, then again, at the waiting loader. Satisfied that all was ready, he drew a deep breath and shouted,

'Fire!'

Having turned around safely, with Jan's foot to the floor, the battered Toyota sped through the deserted streets as he retraced their original route back towards the centre of Birundi. To Pat's relief, there was no sign of pursuit as they entered the main square, but suddenly, a new mortar bomb shrieked overhead, this time, louder than before.

Pat yelled a warning to Spike, and the others inside, 'Watch it; this one's going to be close!'

With a blinding flash, the bomb exploded on the police station roof, in a deafening maelstrom of fire and smoke. Suddenly, a hysterical, piercing scream erupted from inside the packed Toyota, as pieces of razor-sharp shrapnel and masonry hit the top and side of the vehicle, with the speed of rifle bullets.

The tall latticed radio aerial toppled down from the flat roof, and landed with a crash just in front of the speeding vehicle. In a billowing cloud of dust, Jan frantically spun the wheel, swerving the Toyota. He missed the crashing tangle of jagged steel by mere inches. Both Spike and Pat had crouched down, making themselves as small as possible, when the mortar bomb arrived in the square. By a miracle, although Spike felt something fizz past his ear, neither he nor Pat was hit.

Spike's knuckles were white, as he gripped the hand holds. Taking his lead from his sergeant, desperately exposed, he pressed himself as close as he could to the rear of the vehicle. Knowing his life depended on it, Spike hung on grimly as the Toyota cleared the dust and pile of mangled metal, and careered on towards the river.

Inside, Patti Chandler's screaming stopped abruptly, when the red-headed nurse lent forward, and slapped her hard across her exposed cheek. Shocked into silence for a moment, Patti burst into tears. The cause of her distress was instantly obvious to all the cramped passengers. Beside her, the Pan Global man had slumped forward. Hit by flying shrapnel, there was a hole in the back of his head, big enough to conceal an orange. Sprayed with blood and brains, Barney Morris whimpered with horror and revulsion at the gory lifeless corpse, collapsed beside him.

Danny and Charlie were both momentarily engulfed in the same horror within the blood-splattered interior, but then, experience and training kicked in. Charlie snatched out a blanket he had been sitting on, and threw it silently to Danny. Danny did not hesitate; he quickly launched the blanket over the corpse, hiding it from further view.

Relieved that the gory spectacle was gone, savagely, Barney Morris snarled at the crying photographer,

'He's dead girl, so deal with it!'

Danny glared at the reporter. He had already bridled once that morning at Morris' callus attitude towards her. Somehow though, in that moment, it seemed like a lot longer than just an hour earlier. Danny came to her defence, and returned the snarl,

'One more comment like that sunshine, and trust me, you will be walking home!'

It was Morris' turn to bridle, but seeing to murderous look in the young man's blazing eyes, and remembering he was carrying a concealed pistol, Morris, in that brutal moment, thought better than to challenge him. The reporter broke the stare and looked down at his feet, as he awkwardly fished out a hipflask, and took a deep pull from its contents.

Danny ignored the humbled hack. In a voice he hoped would reassure the other civilians, he shouted above the roar of the straining engine,

'Anyone else hit?'

Ashen faces looked towards him. Heads shook in silence. Danny nodded. Raising his voice even louder, he shouted forward,

'You both OK in the front?'

With his feet resting firmly on the pack he had lifted from the bank, Krutz turned and gave a thumbs-up.

To the whoops of his young crew, Captain Ngoa watched the explosion with satisfaction. The bomb landed just ahead of the dust cloud, on the roof of one of the buildings, somewhere in the centre of the township. He quickly ordered four more bombs to be prepared, as he crouched down and spun the adjustment wheel, decreasing the angle of the mortar tube by several degrees. Checking the alignment once again, he snapped his fingers and barked orders to the loader, and the other two excited young boys holding live fused bombs,

'Quickly now, we have them. Michael, I want all four bombs in the air, as fast as you can fire them.'

Michael, an illiterate thirteen-year-old abductee, recruited by force into the Mai-Mai, nodded with a broad, ingratiating grin. Like the others, he had already received several painful cuffs from the Captain, as they set up the mortar. His Captain was cruel, and the boy did not want another stinging blow. He removed the safety pin, and heaved the heavy bomb up to the mouth of the mortar's tube and immediately released it, letting it slide smoothly down the inside of the barrel. Ducking down, he and the other teenaged crewmen waited for the round to fire. With a deafening crash, the bomb hit the firing pin and launched itself from the tube. Snatching the next bomb from his friend, he quickly stood up, whipped out the safety pin and dropped the round into the barrel…

With a familiar whoosh, the first bomb screamed into the centre of Birundi. It exploded a hundred yards in front of the speeding Toyota, down a side street, in a cloud of fire and dust. Moments later, the second bomb landed closer than the first; it exploded ahead, on the other side of the main street. It threw a shower of rubble and thick cloud of black acrid smoke in all directions.

The third mortar round screamed in and exploded, only fifty yards in front of the fugitives. Something shattered the windscreen, and the vehicle juddered, as red-hot shrapnel peppered the front of the Toyota. Inside, it felt like Jan had driven into a swarm of giant angry bees.

Clouds of steam began to spew from the Toyota's radiator. Colonel Krutz, bleeding from a fresh cut to his forehead, held up his hand to ward off the hot stinging water vapour, which poured in clouds through the shattered windscreen. Frantically trying to see his way ahead, he screamed at his driver,

'Vok!... Keep going Jan, do not stop for anything!'

Jan needed no urging. He grasped the stick, dropped a gear and stamped down again on the accelerator. As the wounded Toyota burst through the drifting cloud of dust and burnt explosive, something flashed from the sky and smashed into the left-hand side of the vehicle's bonnet. It all happened so fast; a split-second, but felt to all the shaken occupants of the Toyota, like the impact of a giant's sledgehammer...

Captain Ngoa laughed and clapped at each explosion. Michael had done well. There would be no need to beat him further today for his usual laziness. The boy had successfully managed to launch all four rounds into the air, before the first detonated on the far side of Birundi. With unconfined glee, Ngoa counted each explosion aloud when he saw the vivid flash, and seconds later, heard the distant crump, as the bombs exploded.

'One!...Two!...Three!...'

Then, there was a very pregnant silence. He searched in vain for the tell-tale cloud of black smoke and listened intently for the flat thud from number four, but saw, and heard nothing from the direction of Birundi. Torn from his excitement, Ngoa frowned. Although it had launched successfully, why hadn't the fourth bomb exploded? He knew duds were to be expected occasionally, especially from these old Russian rounds, which bore the legend *'1945'* among the unintelligible Cyrillic characters embossed into the nosecone of each bomb. As he searched in vain for the fourth explosion, he failed to notice Michael slipping three safety pins out of sight, and hiding them under a discarded ammunition box.

Although Ngoa did not realise Michael's mistake, Michael had. Equal measures of fear of punishment, and the overwhelming excitement of the moment, caused his error. Determined to obey his commander's orders, avoid a beating, and get all four bombs in the air, he forgot to remove the last safety pin. He launched the fourth bomb, with the pin still securely holding the bomb's sensitive percussion fuse, in the *safe* position.

Chapter Nineteen

The bombardment suddenly stopped, and no more mortar bombs rained down on the fleeing vehicle. Despite their tension, each rapid heartbeat of the frightened passengers brought them closer to the salvation of the river, as Jan did his best to nurse the damaged Toyota towards it. The vehicle's temperature gauge was fast edging towards the red line. Both Jan and Krutz constantly glanced down at it. Looking up at the deserted road ahead, through the steam which still spewed from the punctured radiator, Jan spoke to his South African boss,

'Shall I stop and try to get some more water into the radiator, Colonel?'

Krutz thought for a moment then, his face grim, he shook his head,

'No Jan. We dare not stop. The Mai-Mai must have entered the township behind us by now. We need to put as much distance as we can between them and us. It is only about half a kilometre to the river, so keep going. Our one chance is to try to ford it. That should cool the engine for a while. We can pick up plenty of spare water then, and make repairs over on the far side, after we've limped a few more kilometres.'

Jan nodded with relief. It made sense. If the Colonel had ordered him to stop, the engine might stall. If the starter motor was damaged, the Toyota would never run again. Absently, he dropped one hand from the steering wheel. It rested momentarily on the hard and reassuring mass of the pistol tucked in his waistband. He had no intention of being taken by the guerrillas; his friends were dead, and he would put a bullet in his own brain before he'd let the Mai-Mai capture him alive.

Spying Jan's inadvertent gesture from the corner of his eye, Krutz knew the civilians must be sharing the same cold fear he felt emanating from the man beside him. Jan was a good man, and had every right to be scared in the present circumstances. It would keep him sharp, for the trouble which surely, Krutz knew, awaited them. Krutz turned his head to reassure the passengers. He shouted into the cramped rear compartment,

'We'll be at the river in a couple of minutes. Hang on until then; we'll be in the clear and safe once we reach the other bank.'

Danny glanced at Charlie with a raised eyebrow. Charlie's slight shrug spoke volumes. Somehow, after the violent events of the last few minutes, neither man felt too sure that the Colonel's optimism was in the least bit justified.

It was quiet on the banks of the Mpana River. The flat water sparkled in the morning sunlight, as it flowed serenely past the abandoned township. The Toyota rolled to a stop, still hissing steam, two hundred yards from its nearest bank. There were a few scattered huts on either side of the vehicle, and a narrow, rubbish strewn side street running parallel to the river, away to their left. They had reached the southern edge of Birundi without further incident. Pat and Spike gratefully stepped from the rear of the vehicle, glad for a quick opportunity to relax aching hands. Drawing their pistols, they walked to the front of the vehicle, intently scanning the open stretch ahead, which would lead them down to the river, and the safety of the far bank.

Through the open passenger window, Colonel Krutz growled,

'We have got to go straight across Farrell. It looks clear, and we've no other choice.'

Pat sniffed. The security man was right of course, but looks could be deceiving. Suddenly, something glinted in the bush beyond the far bank.

'Have you got a pair of binos in the vehicle?' the SAS man enquired.

Krutz nodded, reached forward, and opened the glove compartment in front of him. He passed out the binoculars. Pat nodded his thanks and began a sweep of the tree line and dense bush on the other side of the river.

Keeping the binos to his eyes, Pat abruptly muttered a curse, then, with a sigh he said calmly,

'Spike, get back on the vehicle, and don't let anyone get off. Move slowly laddie, don't run.' Casually lowering the binos, Pat turned to Krutz and shook his head. Softly, he said,

'There's no chance of getting out this way. Their field craft is dreadful; I spotted at least a dozen armed men moving around over there. In my book, that still makes an effective ambush; they are just waiting for us to try to cross.'

Pat passed the binoculars back to Krutz and added,

'Here, check it for yourself.'

The Colonel swept the distant tree line. He could clearly see undisciplined movement. Angrily, the Boer snapped,

'*Die bliksemse!* You are right.' Sighing deeply he added, 'the other bank is crawling with Mai-Mai.'

Pat nodded. 'I think we'll bug out and disappear down that side road. The Mai-Mai over the river are bound to have seen us, but can't make up their minds what to do.'

Irritated he had not been consulted this time; Krutz nodded, turned to Jan and snapped, '*Do it!*'

Pat stepped onto the running board beside the ex-Colonel. They were less than ten yards from the side road when the Mai-Mai realised their quarry was trying to escape, and opened fire.

A ragged fusillade of shots cracked around the Toyota, but it was too late. The vehicle disappeared moments later, when the Toyota's driver floored the accelerator once again. As Jan weaved through the shanty, past miserable hovels and crude shacks made from scavenged sheets of corrugated iron and decaying plywood, they entered the heart of the ramshackle slum area, which had grown up over the years and become home to several hundred fishermen and their families. It was the very poorest quarter of the remote township.

Pat shouted a conversation with Krutz, over the noise of the revving engine, and the hiss of escaping coolant,

'Just as well we moved out from back there, when we did. If we'd stayed much longer, the Mai-Mai sweeping down from the airfield would have trapped us. They would have caught us cold...' When he received a nod of agreement, he asked, 'Know where this track will lead us?'

Krutz shrugged and shook his head,

'No idea!'

Pat thought for a moment, then said,

'The doctor in the back should know this area; he must have visited it from time to time to tend the sick...see if he knows where we are going.'

Krutz nodded his understanding and turned to address the passengers in the back. After several moments, he turned back to Pat. To the SAS man's surprise, the strained look had gone from his lined face; he was smiling...

'There!...there it is. That must be it!'

The excitement in Jan's voice was infectious. All the passengers crammed inside the Toyota craned their necks to see what the driver was shouting about. Dr Frasier quietly nodded his confirmation to Krutz and Pat.

Three kilometres outside Birundi, the Toyota had reached the turnoff they were desperately seeking. The Toyota's temperature gauge had swung far into the red now, and the flow of steam from the holed radiator had all but stopped. It would not be long, before the super-heated engine's core reached critical, and the pistons welded themselves to the block, as the engine gave up its battle, and seized.

As Jan spun the wheel and skidded off the main track, the vehicle quickly disappeared just a few yards inside the shade of the dense tree line. Pat immediately shouted for him to stop. Jan reacted quickly and stamped on the brakes. The Toyota shuddered to a halt. As Pat jumped down, he called to Spike,

'With me!'

As Danny, Charlie and Krutz climbed out to establish a defensive perimeter of sorts, Pat ripped down a low-hung branch from a nearby tree. Spike scooped up a handful of earth and quickly rubbed it into the livid white scar left on the trunk, to hide the damage from casual sight. Satisfied with his efforts, Spike followed Pat and ran back to the point where the Toyota had left the main track. Handing the bushy branch to Spike, Pat said,

'Here, take this and brush out those fresh tyre tracks, as quickly as you can, from the main track to well inside the tree line. Make sure you back into the trees as you do it, and scrub out your own footprints at the same time.'

Spike nodded,

'Sure Pat.'

Spike had done this plenty of times before, on exercise with the regular Paras when he served with them as a teenager, but now, he wasn't just going through the motions. This time it was for real, and he knew their lives may very well depend on it.

From the shaded cover of the treeline, Pat lifted the binoculars once again, and searched along the deserted track, which led back to the fallen township of Birundi. All seemed quiet. Through the dancing heat-haze, there was no sign of movement yet, but he was convinced that pursuit was inevitable. Wiping away a bead of sweat which had trickled into his eye, Pat considered their immediate future. He knew he must plan for the worst, and assume there would be a follow-up by the Mai-Mai, once they had combed every part of the township, and realised that their quarry was not hiding, but instead, had made a successful escape.

There was a low whistle behind him. Pat turned. He saw Spike pointing to the track. The trooper gave him a thumbs-up signal. Pat looked towards the short spur of dusty track leading into the trees. The recent imprint of fresh tyre tracks was gone. Taking a last look towards

Birundi, Pat jogged the short distance to his companion. Nodding towards the track, he said,

'Good job Spike. Now come on, let's get back to the others.'

Balling his big hands into fists, General Gabriel Ojukwu stood silently in the cool gloom of the bank vault. He had known something was wrong when he entered the deserted bank with his posse of heavily armed bodyguards. He discovered the vault's heavy steel door was wide open. With a snarled curse, the general had been first to enter the vault. Ordering his curious men to wait outside, he had searched it thoroughly for the knapsack, filled with Pan Global's diamonds. Finding nothing, he snarled angrily at his men, and ordered them to enter and gather up the piles of banknotes. He was too late; the whites and a fortune in diamonds had slipped through his hands.

Still smarting from losing the aircraft, and the fortune it contained, he stamped angrily from the bank. One of his captains' arrived, panting after the exertion of his long run from the other side of the airfield. Ojukwu vaguely recognised the sweating man kneeling before him.

'Your Excellency,' said the Captain between gasps, 'I thought you should know that I fired my mortar at a vehicle, which left the township as you attacked it. It was the only sign I saw of anyone still here.'

Now, the general remembered the man. Staring thoughtfully down at the deserter, Ojukwu rumbled,

'Tell me, what exactly did you see?'

Ngoa's reply came immediately.

'A dust cloud Excellence, hidden by the buildings. It was too big and moved too fast to be men on foot. It had to be a vehicle.'

The general stood on the shaded veranda outside the bank in silence for a moment, staring at the facade of the abandoned clinic. He considered the news. His heart began to quicken as something occurred to him. Urgently, he demanded,

'Was this before… or after, the aeroplane took off?'

Licking his dry lips, Ngoa replied,

'It was after the plane took off, Excellency.'

Ojukwu pounded a fist into his other open palm, as realisation dawned. No white man, he thought, would stay behind and face his warriors when there was a chance to escape in the plane. Clearly, he thought, his men had cut them off, before they could escape with his fortune.

As a cruel smile played across his mouth, he snapped his fingers at one of his captains,

'Send word to the ambush party at the river. I heard shots. Find out if they saw a vehicle.' He turned to another of his officers. 'I want the township searched. If there are white men still here and hiding from us, I want them found, and brought to me.' Suddenly, his eyes glittered dangerously. It was as if they stared straight through the man before him. Feeling the fear he always felt when the general addressed him, the officer turned to organise the search. He froze for a moment, when the Ojukwu rumbled.

'And mark me well... I want them brought before me, Captain...*alive!*'

Chapter Twenty

Danny met Pat and Spike, as they returned from the tree line. His face was masked with shock; it screamed the gravest concern.

'Sorry Pat, but we have got a new problem.'

A faint sigh; with a frown, Pat enquired,

'Well, what's up now?'

Danny half turned, and pointed towards the idling Toyota,

'Probably best, if you just come and take a look.'

Intrigued, but also worried by Danny's reluctance to explain further, Pat followed him to front of the vehicle. Danny stopped, and pointed to a round hole punched neatly through the front edge of Toyota's bonnet.

Wiping the sweat from his brow, Danny said,

'There Pat, there's the problem.'

Pat lent forward, and peered into the hole. What he saw made him step back. With a sharp intake of breath, he muttered,

'Jesus!'

Embedded inside the hole, lodged to one side between the empty radiator and the hot engine block, was the finned tail of an unexploded mortar bomb.

Pat stared at it, open-mouthed for a moment. Recovering his surprise, he remembered the bone-rattling crash that had shaken the vehicle just after the last bomb had exploded, when they made their frantic dash from the centre in Birundi. Eyes wide, two more words escaped from his lips,

'Bloody hell!'

Krutz and Charlie joined them,

'Looks like we got lucky today, Farrell…eh?' Krutz growled.

Struggling to overcome his surprise, with some difficulty, Pat tore his eyes away from the bomb. He looked instead at Charlie.

'What do you think?' he enquired.

Charlie blew out his cheeks. Nodding towards the bonnet, he said,

'These things fully arm themselves in flight Pat, after they leave the barrel of the mortar. I don't think it's wise to lift the bonnet, to take a closer look. I doubt it is a delayed-action fuse.' He rubbed his chin, deep in thought for a moment, then, his decision made, he added, 'No, on balance, I think it's a dud, but I have no real idea what state it is in, or for that matter, why it didn't just blow us to bits when it hit.'

Remembering, with a cold knot in his stomach, the shaking it must have received as they fled Birundi, Pat said,

'So do you reckon it could still go off?'

Charlie shrugged and shook his head,

'Beats me Pat, but personally,' he raised an eyebrow, 'I would rather walk, than risk it again.'

Pat nodded. He could not agree more.

'Right, Danny, get the civvies out. Spike, you nip up on top, and pass everything down to Charlie.' As his troopers turned to comply, Pat added with a half grin, 'and fellas…make sure you do it gently!'

Fearing a general panic, Danny did not mention the unexploded bomb when he ordered the civilians from the Toyota. He didn't trust Morris, and half-expected him to rock the vehicle if he lost it and tried to fight his way past the others, and be the first one out. Leading them all to one side, only then, as his two mates carefully unloaded the Toyota's roof rack, did he calmly explain why they had to abandon the vehicle where it stood.

Danny was caught off-guard, when Dr Frasier's nurse angrily turned on him and said,

'What about the man who is dead? We have got to bury him; it is our Christian duty to give him a proper burial!'

Barney Morris snorted with derision, but before an argument could break out, stern faced, Danny held his hand up for silence. He stared at the redhead for a moment. Not wanting disagreement in the highly charged atmosphere which surrounded them all; lacking both an answer and suitable response, he said,

'Look, I'll go and ask Pat, OK?' There was a new urgency in his voice when he added, 'but please folks, no-one approach the vehicle anymore. If that thing goes off, believe me, it could easily kill us all!'

Well?

Sitting imperiously in his new headquarters in the Hotel Armond, General Ojukwu polished his sunglasses and glared at the Captain who had just entered the foyer, to deliver his preliminary search report.

'Nothing has been found so far, Excellency. The men you ordered to the far bank of the river did see a vehicle on this side, but it escaped before they could capture it. I ordered them to cross over, and join in the search.'

The general nodded,

'Have all the exits out of the town been blocked, as I ordered?'

'Yes, Excellence. I ordered roadblocks to be set up immediately, when the search began. There are men guarding every exit from Birundi.'

'Very good Captain; you have done well.' Ojukwu rubbed his chin, and thought for a moment. 'Tell me, where exactly did the vehicle go?'

'It went into the slum district, Excellence, along the upstream bank of the river.'

The general stood up, clasped his hand behind his back and walked thoughtfully to one of the banquet room's large bay windows. Drawing the curtain aside, he looked into the deserted square. Silently, he regretted the necessity of his decision to temporarily strip his command of vehicles. But what other choices did he have at the time? He must secure his exposed flank hurriedly, and the Kabali Junction railhead was vital to protect his sweep further south. He had had to act quickly, and send every man he could spare, in case the Government forces used the railway line to bring up troops, and perhaps even armour, to launch a counter-attack against his invasion. The vehicles would return soon to take his men on to Kabbali. The trouble now, however, was things had moved rapidly in Birundi, and chasing a vehicle on foot, put his men at a huge disadvantage. Clicking his tongue with frustration, he turned back towards his waiting officer,

'Concentrate your search in the slum district, Captain. Tell my warriors to look carefully; there will be a generous reward for those who capture the white men I believe are still here...' he shrugged, 'somewhere? To increase our chances, we must widen the search area. I order you, while daylight remains, to send out patrols to scour the surrounding countryside...' The general's eyes glittered dangerously, 'and find them!'

*'Boss!...*Boss, wake up!'

Julius stepped back from the Captain's bed, in the dingy riverside shack Horatio O'Rourke called home. The morning's sunlight battled to illuminate the shack's gloomy interior, and sparkled here and there on the empty beer bottles which surrounded the unmade bed. Much of the light was deflected by the grime and dust which coated the window, but to Julius' relief, cloaked in semi-darkness, something groaned and stirred beneath the untidy blankets. Muffled by the bedding, and still a little slurred by last night's binge, O'Rourke growled at his crewman,

'What...what do you want, damn you?!'

Pleased, for once, it had taken so little time to wake his employer, Julius said urgently,

'Boss...There's people outside. They want you to take them to Kabbali...they said the Mai-Mai is in Birundi, and coming here, real soon!'

There was a sudden eruption of bedding at the mention of the Mai-Mai. His untidy covering of blankets fell away as O'Rourke sat up, revealing his unshaven face, bloodshot eyes and a very crumpled shirt collar.

'What are you talking about?...What people?...Where?'

Julius was almost frantic. He was Hutu, and unlike the inhabitants of the township, had reluctantly stayed behind out of loyalty to his boss, with the expectations that he would keep his prized job, and they would sail down the river and escape in plenty of time, long before the arrival of the dreaded Mai-Mai butchers. The two men should have gone the previous night, but the boss man was too drunk, and had fallen into a deep, drunken sleep shortly after the sun had gone down.

Julius had spent the night alone aboard the Queen Victoria. By the light of a paraffin lamp, he eventually found, and extracted the spanner which had caused him so much trouble. Dawn was breaking when he finally finished reassembling the engine's exhaust casing, and lay down to snatch some sleep.

'Boss, they woke me up and said we must go, quickly.'

Trying to fend off a king-sized hangover, with his head pounding, O'Rourke swung his legs over the edge of the bed. His first attempt to stand proved a dismal failure. With his brain feeling like it was about to explode, he sat down again heavily, with his head in his hands for several moments, before trying once more. With a groan, his second attempt was more successful. Casting about, he found a small amount of Cavalla in one of the discarded bottles. Swilling the bottle's contents up to the light for a moment, he said, before draining it in a single gulp,

'Alright, Julius, go and tell them I'm coming for Christ's sake.' With a sly grin he added, 'that is, just as soon as I've had a quick hair of the dog.'

Julius grinned. He had never seen this mysterious hair from the invisible dog, but it was powerful magic, and always seemed, almost instantly, to make his Captain feel better.

'Sure Boss, I will go and tell them, straight away.'

Pat and the others stood impatiently outside the ramshackle hut, waiting for the owner and Captain of the old landing craft, moored to the jetty close by, to appear. Earlier, when Krutz had explained about the craft's existence, Pat knew it was their only chance. Now he looked at the peeling paint, patched hull and the boat's ragged awning; somehow, he was not quite so sure any more. It was Spike who suddenly chirped up and put the whole party's deflated thoughts into words,

'Hell fire! What an old pile of junk. It's a bloody museum piece!'

As they all gazed rather forlornly at the rusting landing craft, a voice from the doorway of the shack behind them snapped,

'I would be careful what you say, boy. Do not insult the old Queen, or she just might not let you on board!'

The fugitives spun around. Standing in the doorway of the shack, O'Rourke was holding on to the doorframe for support. Squinting into the bright sunlight, he coldly returned their stares.

The man, if he was the Captain, looked as wrecked as his vessel, Pat thought. He could be anywhere between fifty-five and seventy. White stubble covered his unshaven, ruddy cheeks and chin. His clothes were creased, oil-stained and dirty, and he did not look too steady on his feet. Clearly, his shock of white hair had not seen a comb for weeks. Pat stepped forward; there was not time for the usual pleasantries. Jerking his thumb over his shoulder, he simply enquired,

'Are you the owner of this boat?'

Still holding onto the door jam, the man gave a nod of acknowledgement towards Dr Frasier, then, with a sweep of his hand, bowed theatrically,

'Captain Horatio O'Rourke, master of the Queen Victoria, and owner of the Mpana Shipping Company, at your service. Now then… what do you want?'

Pat replied, 'The Mai-Mai has taken Birundi. We have just escaped from there.' Pat half turned and nodded towards the others, 'I need to get these people to Kabbali.'

Sensing a chance to make a profit on a trip he must make anyway, with his head clearing quickly, O'Rourke rubbed his hand over his chin. He looked at the pile of suitcases and backpacks beside them,

'You will be wanting to take those too, I suppose?'

Pat nodded.

'OK, but they count as freight, and will cost you extra.'

Pat grinned. He'd been expecting this, and had a solution.

'Fair enough.'

Satisfied that they understood they were paying passengers, not freeloading refugees, O'Rourke sniffed,

'How are you going to pay? It is strictly payment in advance out here.' He shrugged, and waited for a reply, before adding, 'in cash.'

Pat turned away, and walked to the pile of luggage. Opening a side pocket of his bergan, Pat extracted a narrow cloth roll, which the Attaché had made him sign for in triplicate at Talinga, the previous evening. Pat walked casually back, wondering if he was going to be filling in paperwork for the rest of his life, to explain giving away the contents of the precious bundle.

Pat stopped at the shack's doorway, in front of O'Rourke. Unrolling the cloth bandoleer, he handed it to the Victoria's owner.

'Will these do?' he enquired.

O'Rourke took the bandoleer and stared at it for a moment. It had a dozen small compartments stitched into the material, and felt surprisingly heavy. O'Rourke picked at the stitching, to open one of the compartments, and see what each of them concealed. To his surprise and delight, a gold sovereign slipped out. Deftly catching it, he turned the heavy coin in his hand; it glinted in the morning sunlight. Lifting it to his mouth, he bit into it. With the price of gold at an all-time high on the international market, he knew he was holding a small fortune in his hands. Gold was universal; he could spend it anywhere. Today was getting better by the minute. Leaving the other compartments for later inspection, a satisfied grin spread over his unshaven face as he sniffed again and nodded towards his moored vessel.

'Better get your people and their luggage on board quickly,' he said, 'before those heathen, murdering bastards catch us.'

Chapter Twenty-One

It was cramped in the narrow cockpit at the back of the landing craft. Pat was standing beside the Victoria's Captain, as Julius untied the last securing rope and pushed off against the wooden jetty. Beneath the patched awning, the civilians sat on their suitcases in silence, watching as Danny, Spike and Charlie removed the stripped-down components of their Russian-made assault-rifles from their bergans, and began to reassemble them. As Julius scrambled aboard, Pat turned towards O'Rourke and said,

'Can we go upstream until nightfall, and find a place to hide out?'

O'Rourke shrugged and nodded,

'Sure, no problem. We can't go too far though, maybe, ten kilometres or so, at the most.'

Pat nodded, that should be far enough for what he had in mind. He asked,

'We can't go upstream any further?'

O'Rourke shook his head. He opened the landing craft's throttles and rapidly spun the Victoria's wheel. Raising his voice almost to a shout, above the sudden growl of the ancient diesel engines, he replied,

'No, there are waterfalls further upstream, and the river narrows considerably before we would reach them, with tall cliffs on either side.'

Pat nodded again. He was not going to lead his people into an ambush, and was happy to defer to the Captain's local knowledge,

'What about somewhere to hide for the rest of the day?' he enquired.

The Queen Victoria's master pulled a face. Clearly, Pat thought; he had somewhere in mind.

'After the cliffs peter out, there's about a kilometre of flat swamp on either side of the Mpana. It is a foul, stinking place, full of mosquitoes and crocodiles.'

Pat's face became grim at the news. To fit into the plan, and keep them alive, he needed one last piece of the jigsaw to fit,

'Is the swamp an easy area to approach from dry land?'

O'Rourke shook his head,

'No chance; if the quicksand doesn't get you, the crocs and bull leaches will.'

Pat grinned. With a glint in his eye, he said,

'Perfect!'

O'Rourke shrugged. His face betrayed his foreboding. He spun the Victoria's wheel again, now they were in mid-channel. As the prow swung upstream, he grunted,

'OK, on your head be it.' Staring down at the civilians in the flat-bottomed hold, he added 'They are not going to like it, one little bit; but it is your charter!'

As the Victoria chugged slowly up the Mpana, away from Birundi, Pat left the cockpit. He jumped down into the large open hold. Spike caught his eye,

'Quick word, Pat?'

Pat nodded and walked to the corner were his men had gathered.

'What's up?'

'More bad news I'm afraid, Pat. When I'd finished putting the AK together, I thought I'd better check the radio.' A sigh escaped from the young trooper, 'when I took it out, I found a hole punched through it,' he shrugged, 'bit of shrapnel or a bullet; I'm not sure which, but either way; it's wasted.'

Pat nodded in silence, then said,

'Can you fix it?'

Spike shook his head.

'Nah, no chance. The transmitter modules got a hole the size of a hen's egg going straight through it. I doubt it, but there's a slim chance it might still receive, but there's absolutely no way we're 'gonna send anything.'

Pat exhaled hard at the news. Quickly recovering, he said,

'Well, never mind. We'll just have to find another way to let base know we are OK.'

Pat turned, and gathered the civilians around him in the landing craft's iron hold. The morning sun was rising higher in the sky, and the patchwork awning, despite its ragged condition, provided the passengers with welcome shade from the sun's intense glare, and the growing heat.

As his troopers kept watch, Pat explained his plan to his civilian charges, and the two Pan Global security men. Using a metal rod he'd found, he began by scratching a line in the dust, which covered the inside of the Victoria's flat hull.

'OK, folks,' he said, 'we have got to get far away from here, and make it to the Kabbali railhead, about fifty kilometres south. From there, we should be able to get a train out of the province, and away from the fighting. Now, this line represents the Mpana River,' Pat marked an oblong on one side of the scratch line. 'This box is

Birundi, where we were, and where the Mai-Mai is now presently concentrated.' He looked up, to see that they understood. Satisfied, Pat looked down at his map in the dust again, and marked a small area, several feet past the oblong box, also beside the line of the Mpana. 'We can't go south yet, as it would mean passing Birundi in daylight. We are currently heading away from Birundi, about eight or nine kilometres away, that is, towards this area here.' He rested the end of the rod on the new area he had just marked. 'This little box represents our hiding place for the rest of the day. It is a swamp on both sides of the river. Now it's not going to be pleasant in there, but if we want to stay alive, we must keep out of sight, stay quiet and hide until dark. We'll be hidden in there until past midnight, and then we'll swing back onto the Mpana, and head south.' Once again, he looked up. Every eye was fixed on him, or the map. Pat pointed his rod towards the horizon, where a dark line of clouds was gathering. 'With luck folks, those clouds will be here by nightfall. They will help shade the moon, and make it darker on the river, when we slip past the Mai-Mai in Birundi,' he shrugged, wishing to instil confidence into the civilians, 'it should be plain sailing, all the way to the railhead at Kabbali….Questions?'

Nervously, Barney Morris blurted out,

'What happens if the Mai-Mai does find us before tonight? Can't we call for help?'

Pat nodded. He knew they all wanted an answer to the same questions. He quickly replied,

'Yep, good question. Well, the radio has a bullet hole through it, so we couldn't call for help, even if there was anyone out there on our side, which there is not.' Pat grinned reassuringly, 'Don't worry though. When we reach the swamp, we'll get the Victoria in as far as we can, break up her outline with local foliage, and camouflage her so that she is hidden from the river. Once that is done, my men and I will keep watch. We'll stand guard throughout the day while you all get some rest. As you have seen, we now have additional firepower available. If we get bumped…trust me, we'll take care of it.' Heads nodded, 'The Captain says it is impossible to get at us from the dry ground beyond the swamp, because the area is full of quicksand, so don't worry; we will be well hidden, and perfectly safe until it gets dark.'

Satisfied with Pat's answer, Barney Morris nodded, but almost immediately; another question came tumbling from his lips. 'That is all very well, but what if the Mai-Mai sees us, when we try to get away tonight?'

It was another good question, which certainly deserved an honest answer. Pat shrugged,

'Well, with luck, they won't detect us. If they do, as long as you keep down, nice and low, you will all be fine. Remember, this boat was originally designed for beach landings under heavy fire,' he hammered the steel side of the craft with his fist, 'this is armour-plate, and will stop all types of small-arms fire.'

Although he was not too sure about the crafts armour-plated manufacture, Pat knew he must instil confidence in the civilians. The last thing he needed from now on, within the relatively cramped confines of the Victoria, was an outbreak of panic among the frightened civilians.

Morris was clearly on the edge. Pat had met his sort before. The man had self-preservation, at any cost to the others, written all over him. Pat made a mental note to brief his men to keep a special watch on the journalist. His photographer seemed to be living on the edge of nervous collapse. Pat had not heard her utter a word since they'd come on board. Her body language sounded a warning. As she had listened to his short briefing, she had hugged herself tightly, and rocked back and forth as she listened. Pat was worried she would lose it at the wrong moment, and snap completely. She was another one to watch, he thought, especially as they had to keep very quiet when they reached the swamp. The doctor seemed calm enough, but strangely, his nurse was not showing the obvious signs of fear which the journalists certainly were. Instead, she looked flushed and unhappy about something. Pat could see clearly that something was bothering her, so gently, he enquired, 'Is everything all right, Miss?'

Born into a devout Catholic family, something certainly was troubling her. Her eyes flashed. She flared at him...

'Yes! Something is bothering me!' She snapped, pointing at Danny, who was keeping watch from the vessel's prow, 'Your man there promised to talk to you, and there was plenty of time to bury that poor soul before we left, but you just ignored him.' She flushed as she added, 'he died in this Godless wilderness, and it was our duty to see him safely interred in a proper Christian fashion.'

Given the terrible fate which could await any of them, Pat stared at her open-mouthed for a moment. He hadn't much time for religion. He'd seen too much violence and death, supposedly in the name of religious conviction, to hold serious belief in any particular deity.

From what Pat had seen during his service in the regular SAS, particularly in the Middle East and Balkans, too many warlords, under the guise of one faith or another, had corrupted their followers' beliefs in their ruthless pursuit of power and ethnic cleansing, to carry much weight with Pat. At this moment in time, as far as Pat was concerned, their survival trumped all religious niceties. It was time for the brutal truth. Reluctantly, he said,

'No miss; I'm sorry, but I'm afraid you are wrong. There wasn't a moment to lose when we left that jetty. The Mai-Mai could have arrived at any moment. We have to get as far from the guerrillas' as we can, as quickly as we can... My boys and I were sent here to save as many of you as we could. The man was dead, and past caring. I have a duty to the living, and believe me... I intend to fulfil it.'

Listening closely to the exchange, Charlie winked at Spike with a veiled grin. The girl did not seem to understand they were in deadly peril, in the middle of a war zone. More to the point, she certainly would not have understood Pat's earlier whispered order to him and Spike.

Led by Danny, and weighed down with their personal luggage, the civilians had left the Toyota and begun their walk to the riverside jetty. Still covered with the blood-stained blanket, the dead man's body was left inside the abandoned vehicle.

Signalling both to hang back, moments after the civilians had disappeared around a bend in the track, Pat had nodded towards the abandoned vehicle. His face impassive, he said simply,

'*Booby-trap it!*'

Almost two hours after leaving O'Rourke's jetty, the Queen Victoria reached the swamp. There had been no sign of pursuit or movement on either bank, except when several large crocodiles, disturbed by the chug of the vessels muffled engines, had slithered down into the river, in a splash and spray of foam, from their solitary basking positions on the Mpana's muddy banks.

They had also passed several herds of partly submerged hippos, which, from the safety of the deep water, grunted angrily at the Victoria.

Danny was watching them, when Spike whispered,

'Strewth! This is like being at the zoo.'

Danny sniffed. 'Yeah, but we are inside the bloody cage, living with the animals, mate.'

O'Rourke was watching the hippos too. Pat had joined him again in the narrow open cockpit, at the stern of the landing craft. The Victoria's master nodded towards the bobbing grey heads, floating in the sparkling water, close to one side of the bank. He spat towards them,

'Bad-tempered, dangerous buggers they are... Did you know they kill more people in Africa every year than crocodiles or lions?'

Holding up his hand to shade his eyes from the sun's glare, Pat stared at the animals. Judging by the size of their heads, and the huge ivory tusks in their mouths, which gaped at their passing, he could well believe it. He grinned,

'Better keep well away from them then. There are already enough things out there trying to kill us at the moment.'

O'Rourke returned the grin. He throttled back on the engines, 'Up ahead.' He said suddenly, 'There...that's the start of the swamp.'

Pat turned his head away from the snorting hippos. On the banks ahead, there were tall stands of papyrus growing from where he guessed the river bank should be. The river's current had slowed to a lazy crawl during the last kilometre, and now the air around them had become even hotter and more oppressive.

O'Rourke stared at the tangled green wall ahead and the distant blue mountains beyond. He said,

'After the falls, the river sort of pans out, and spreads into a wide shallow lake. It is almost completely covered in papyrus. I'm not sure if there is a main current running through it at all; I have only bothered coming up here once before, when I was chartered by a party of scientists, who were doing some research on the area, about ten years ago. I know the lake drains back into the Mpana, but really, I'm as blind as you on what lays beyond the reeds we can see.'

Pat stared at the solid reed wall for a few moments, and then he said,

'Best we don't go too far in then. If we can find a narrow channel somewhere up ahead, we'll hide the Queen inside it. I'm not sure the guerrillas' will bother looking for us, especially this far up the river, but we can't risk it, just in case they do.'

O'Rourke nodded. 'Agreed. With the lake being so shallow in places, I don't want to foul the propellers in the mat of papyrus roots, or ground her in the mud...'

It was getting late in the afternoon when the guerrillas found the Toyota.

There were six of them. They had been searching fruitlessly since morning. Hungry and thirsty, none were really interested in finding the missing white men anymore.

Their leader had spied the vehicle first, after ordering his patrol down the narrow track. It would be their last sweep before he called off the search, and they made their way back to Birundi. Every one of them had sauntered in single file, their weapons carried casually, held by the barrel, balanced on their shoulders. They were more concerned in not missing out on the looting of the township, and wanted to get back before the best had been taken.

Taking cover in the surrounding bush, they watched the vehicle for several minutes. There was something inside it, but they were too far to see exactly what.

Deciding it was safe to move forward, their leader cautiously waved them towards the silent Toyota. Alert now, with fingers on triggers and crouching low, the Mai-Mai patrol crept closer towards the forsaken vehicle.

Among the guerrillas, over-confidence grew at the lack of apparent movement, or ambush, around it. The leader called out to his men. They stood up, and lacking any caution now, confidently swaggered forward for a closer look. They crowded around the battered Toyota, all grinning and loudly expressing their opinion at the same time, on what should be done next. They could see what must be a body inside, covered with a blood-stained blanket.

Their leader was the first to notice the expensive wristwatch at the end of the dead man's uncovered arm. Standing at the side of the vehicle, all five Mai-Mai looked over the shoulders of their leader, jabbering loud and excitedly to each other when he announced officiously that the wristwatch was his.

He marched to the rear of the Toyota, grasped the rear passenger door, and tugged it open. It was his last action on earth. In the shaded gloom of the track, he failed to notice the near invisible wire, attached to the inside of the door handle. It led into the Toyota's driver compartment, and then disappeared somewhere beyond it, into the engine compartment.

Hours earlier, Charlie carefully packed four ounces of plastic explosive against the body of the unexploded mortar bomb. Once he deftly connected a simple pull switch to the detonator, which he had already embedded deep inside the white ball of plastic putty, the deadly booby-trap was armed.

The combined explosive blast of the plastic charge and 82mm mortar bomb tore through the vehicle, in a single devastating instant. Shrapnel ripped into the men crowded only feet away, shredding each of them as the powerful explosion hurled their torn bodies, like broken rag dolls, through the air. All but one died instantly in the ferocious blast of smoke and flame. The last, who had laughed so gleefully as he beheaded the wizened Hutu elder just days earlier, quickly bled out from massive wounds to his legs and stomach. As he lay dying, he jerked and moaned among the smoking debris, which lay scattered and jumbled around the burning shell of the Toyota.

Chapter Twenty-Two

Fires were still burning brightly in Birundi, as darkness fell. General Ojukwu angrily called off the search for the vehicle which had eluded his men, before walking out into the night with his bodyguards, in search of food and diversion. His warriors were hungry, and must be fed. He had released most of them from their duties. Now, apart from a few who patrolled the outskirts, they were engaged in ransacking the commercial centre of the township, in search of food, booty and entertainment.

Ripping down their steel shutters, shops were raided, and quickly picked clean of anything edible or valuable by feral gangs of Mai-Mai. Alcohol was also taken, along with several unfortunate shopkeepers who had stayed too long in a futile attempt to protect their livelihood and valuable stock.

Ojukwu settled in with a band of his men. For his amusement, the Mai-Mai had nailed one luckless storekeeper to a tree, and were taking turns, amid uproarious drunken laughter, to see who could shoot closest, without hitting him anywhere vital. The flames consuming the nearest building threw dancing light into the small square, where the gruesome scene was unfolding.

The flickering flames glittered in the general's eyes, as he licked his lips and savoured the prisoner's pain and anguish.

Hit in both arms and legs, the Asian merchant groaned and begged his tormentors for mercy, but his desperate pleas only added to the amusement of the gang, who waited impatiently for their turn to shoot.

Beckoning over one of his officers, the General whispered something to him, and pointed to their captive. The Mai-Mai Captain nodded, laughed and slapped his thigh. He staggered over to the front of the line. Swigging the last from a looted bottle of whiskey, he snatched up a discarded rifle and waved away the man who was next to shoot, snarling a drunken curse at him. Staggering over to the storekeeper, he patted the man's blood-splattered cheek, and then placed the empty bottle on the man's head. It brought a grin of anticipation from General Ojukwu, and delighted cries and torrents of laughter from his men. Struggling to focus, swaying just inches from his bleeding prisoner, hiccupping, the Captain leered,

'If you want to live, you dog, do not move!'

Terrified, the agonised shopkeeper froze. The Captain turned, and swaggered drunkenly back thirty feet, to the other side of the square. Already, between shouts of encouragement, his men were laughing and noisily betting with each other on the outcome.

The Mai-Mai officer faced his target, cocked the weapon and tried in vain to focus on the bottle sitting on the man's head. Licking his thumb, with an exaggerated flourish, the Captain rubbed the foresight of the AK47 he held, which brought even greater peals of laughter from the drunken, howling mob which surrounded him. Pulling the weapon into his shoulder, the Mai-Mai officer took aim and pulled the trigger... but nothing happened. Swaying and looking unfocused and inquisitively at the rifle, he noticed the safety catch was still set at safe. He pushed the change lever down to its third setting; in his stupor, mistakenly setting it to fully automatic. Taking aim again, he fired at the bottle. The entire target disappeared in a ferocious whirlwind of tree bark and dust, as a full magazine of bullets hit target, shopkeeper and the dry wall behind the tree. The recoil of the weapon knocked the Captain backwards. He fell heavily, gazing up at the blurred, star-studded sky in momentary confusion. The general laughed and nodded his approval. His men were howling their applause. When the drunken Mai-Mai Captain looked at his former target, he saw why his men were happily clapping his efforts and cheering loudly. Only the top half of the prisoner remained. The Captain had cut the hapless merchant in half, with a roaring blizzard of thirty, close range, high-velocity 7.62 bullets…

Surrounded by darkness, serenaded by the whistles and chirrups of unseen legions of nocturnal frogs, Pat kept watch, while the others rested, sitting and lying on the open steel floor of the camouflaged Queen Victoria. None of them managed to sleep in the uncomfortable, oppressive heat, concealed within the tall papyrus. Only O'Rourke, who seemed impervious to the heat and insects, snored softly in the cockpit.

Pat's men and their civilian charges had spent a miserable afternoon and evening, fanning themselves, and slapping at clouds of biting mosquitoes, which constantly whined around them. The insects' attacks were relentless, but to add to the passengers' misery; the mosquitoes were hidden now; still attacking, but enveloped by the darkness of the night.

Angry clouds had drifted over the silent vessel as the sun dipped below the horizon, as the long, dull hours of darkness dragged by. The clouds and distant flashes of lightning were harbingers, threatening the onset of the first heavy rains, which were due to deluge from the heavens at any time.

After dark, Pat had forbidden any naked lights, and ordered them all to keep absolutely quiet. He had patiently explained to them that sound was dangerous. It carried a long way over still water, and any unusual or unnatural noise might prove to be their downfall.

As the clouds enveloped the full moon, the darkness became almost absolute in the swamp. Pat could see only a few yards beyond the boat into the swaying reeds, and was relying on his ears to give warning of compromise. Suddenly, someone gently tapped his calf. Pat tensed, but it was only Spike. He crawled up beside his sergeant, and whispered,

'Times up, Pat. It's my turn to stand watch.'

Pat nodded into the darkness. He flipped open the leather cover of his wristwatch, and checked its luminous dial. It was almost midnight. He whispered back,

'OK Spike. We'll be off soon, but keep your eyes open till we move. I'll go and rouse the others, and wake O'Rourke. I need to brief the civvies for actions on contact… if we get bumped,' he sniffed, 'so as soon as everything is set; we're off.'

Spike nodded in the darkness. Like the others, he could not wait to put the stinking swamp, the stifling heat, and the irritating hell of buzzing mosquitoes behind him.

As Pat slithered quietly down the craft's unloading ramp, he sensed someone behind him. A faint whiff of carbolic assailed his nose. He said,

'Everything all right, Miss?'

There was a silence between them for a moment, and then, almost apologetically, Dr Frasier's nurse whispered softly,

'Siobhán.... my name is Siobhán Whelan.'

Pat heard the smile, in the soft Irish burr of her voice.

'Whelan means wolf in the Gaelic,' she purred softly, 'but don't worry, I don't bite...much.' With that, she giggled, and faded back into the darkness of the hold.

Pat stood still for a moment, and then scratched his head as he wondered what the hell that had been about. His tough, logical mind did not understand women. There had been plenty of women in his life, but to him, they remained a complete mystery. Pat sighed softly and shook his head in the darkness. Given their current circumstances, the last few moments did absolutely nothing to bring even a glimmer of enlightenment. Mildly irritated, but secretly intrigued, he cast further consideration aside. There simply was not time to ponder the mysteries of the pretty Irish nurse. He had a mission to complete, and people's lives were in his hands. Growling softly to himself, he whispered for the others to join him…

As the Queen Victoria chugged softly through the darkness towards Birundi, Pat stood in the cockpit with the craft's Captain. Like his men, Pat's face and hands were blackened, smeared with stripes of soot from the Victoria's exhaust, to hide their white faces from the night.

It was a relief to be clear of the heat and stink of the marshes. Pat ordered the rushes left attached to the outside of the landing craft. He hoped it would help to break up their outline, when the Victoria passed the township. His troopers and the two security men arranged themselves around the vessel; their guns would provide suppressive fire on the riverbanks, if the Mai-Mai detected the Queen. Pat had briefed them not to open fire, unless he gave the order. The civilians were huddled together at the bottom of the craft, with orders to lie down on the inside of the flat-bottomed steel hull, if they came under fire. O'Rourke's crewman sat in the narrow engine compartment, oiling and tending his two ancient charges. Pat was deeply concerned about the noise from the diesel engines. Above the rhythmic chug of the engines, he turned to the ship's master and said,

'Can we cut the engines when we get close, and drift past Birundi?'

His eyes fixed on the darkness ahead, O'Rourke rubbed his hand across his stubble,

'No. No way. If I cut the engines, we'll drift with the current OK, but we'll lose steerage. This old girl is hard to handle at the best of times. We need to be going just faster than the current, or we could end up running aground on the bank.'

Pat cursed silently to himself. The Mai-Mai would need to be deaf not to hear the Victoria's engines, even from the far side of the river. Pat didn't know if the ambush party was still on the other bank, so he would have to stay somewhere in the middle of the river, as they coasted down the Mpana past the township. Ideally, before they made their dash, he would like to have carried out a recce on foot, to find exactly where the enemy were, but there was simply no time. If they were to put Birundi far behind them, and escape well before the coming dawn made them an easy target, they had to go now. A memory surfaced as idea came to him suddenly. He needed an edge. Grimly, Pat said,

'Fair enough, we can't risk grounding on either side, so we'll have to take the middle channel, with the engines throttled back to an absolute minimum, well before we reach Birundi. We'll go as slowly as we dare, but if they open fire on us, I want you to give me everything your engines have got, understand?'

O'Rourke nodded. He was not happy, but knew the plan was as good as they'd get. He wished for a moment he'd asked for more money for this trip, but if they got through, his beloved Victoria wouldn't fall into the hands of the guerrillas. He could buy enough fuel for a year, and stay drunk for a month on what he'd already been paid. Tapping back on the throttles, O'Rourke patted the consul in front of him and said,

'Don't worry about the old girl, Farrell. She'll not let you down, when the time comes.'

Pat stared at the Captain for a moment,

'Good...Now, before we reach Birundi, there's something else I need to do...'

Behind the Victoria, lightning flashed, and thunder rumbled across the clouded heavens. Pat turned, and watched the approaching storm through the darkness. Without warning, it began to rain. Not a gentle shower, but a sudden roaring deluge. Great drops of rain suddenly bounced and splattered on the boat's awning, and ran in torrents from its ragged edges. Pat grinned to himself; the raging downpour might make the difference; everything helped, and it could only improve their chances.

Ignoring the storm, as O'Rourke guided the landing craft around a lazy bend in the river, less than a kilometre away, Pat saw the cherry glow from scattered burning buildings, fired by the Mai-Mai when they sacked Birundi earlier.

Pat hissed softly to his nearest trooper,

'Pass the word Danny. That's Birundi up ahead. We're going straight in. Tell everybody to get ready…'

Chapter Twenty-Three

He was just sixteen.

Robbed of childhood innocence, the hollowed depths of his dark eyes betrayed the Tutsi teenager as the ruthless, stone killer he had become. The darkness which surrounded him, was mirrored by dark thoughts he concealed, hidden behind the vivid scars of a gravely damaged mind.

Hefting his rifle over his shoulder, which had long replaced the boyhood slingshot, the teenager continued his search, using the powerful torch he had looted earlier from one of Birundi's hardware stores. As long as the batteries lasted, he would continue to hunt for fresh victims.

Berningi had been with the Mai-Mai for more than two chaotic years. The boy, who once sang innocently in the choir, and served at the Christian alter of his village chapel, was ripped away one terrifying night from his clay brick home and loving family, by men with guns. Like most boys of Ojukwu's army, he had become lost to the kaleidoscopic months of brainwashing, beatings and the brutality which followed.

Since he was taken, his father's gentle teachings long forgotten, murder and rape became a way of life; his new family became his whole world, as he spiralled downwards into the depths of depravity. Death and cruelty were the ways of the Mai-Mai; they stalked his soul and eventually consumed the lost boy completely. In the last year, lacking conscience or restraint, he had done terrible things, which would turn the stomach of outsiders; however, within the ranks of Ojukwu's killers, he was held up as an example to all.

His growing savagery was recognised by those who mattered, and now, he had become a leader of savage men. Even the older Mai-Mai feared Berningi, for his unpredictable temper, and the bestial things he did to his captives; particularly, the special attention he gave to his favourite prey, that of new-born, defenceless babies.

Before the storm broke above Birundi, the nightmares which plagued his dreams had woken the savage teenager once again. Berningi could not control or stop the dark terrors which haunted his sleep. He accepted them as the price he must pay for the new and glorious life, given to him by his beloved general, whom now, he adored.

Further sleep having eluded him, he rose quietly, and had stepped into the night.

Ignoring the rain, Captain Berningi swept his torch back and forth in a wide arc as he sauntered through the township, down towards the river. The brilliant beam illuminated the destruction his men had brought to Birundi. It pleased him to stroll in the flickering shadows among the carnage and smouldering ruins. It felt almost like he was an avenging angel, blessed with the power of life-and-death over all those, whose path he crossed.

Despite the fruitless search for the white men during the day, perhaps he would be lucky, and find a sentry asleep on guard. Berningi enjoyed making examples of bad soldiers, if no helpless, terrified prisoner was available. It filled him with an overwhelming sense of power to mercilessly beat errant soldiers in front of the others at his command. Sometimes, on a whim, he would shoot one for their dereliction, as they lay bleeding and semi-conscience on the ground. That always made the best example, he thought, but sloppiness was too commonplace to kill them all.

As Berningi walked in the darkness, he shrugged to himself and smiled. It felt good to be a Captain in the feared Mai-Mai; and despite the storm beating down around him, it was wonderful to be alive…

The rain continued to hammer the Victoria. With her navigation lights blacked out, and engines throttled back to a minimum; she chugged softly downstream in the main channel of the Mpana, drifting with the current towards the nearest edge of Birundi. Pat and the others were tensed; weapons held tightly, ready for the fire-fight which must surely come. Despite the heat during the night, the civilians in the hold shivered fearfully. Like Pat, his men searched the darkness; they were ready.

In the middle of the river, the rain fell so heavily, that both riverbanks were nothing but a smudged blur; almost hidden from view by the awesome power of the raging, torrential torrent from above. The noise of the wind and pounding rain were effectively muffling the sound of the Victoria's engines, to virtually nothing beyond its steel hull.

O'Rourke was ignoring the others. He was engrossed in watching his position, and the river's capricious current; carefully, and constantly adjusting his wheel and the vessel's throttles, he maintained their headway using the absolute minimum of power.

Standing close beside the cockpit, Pat caught the Captain's eye for the briefest of moments. Pat nodded reassuringly... Perhaps, despite the odds, they would make it past Birundi, and survive the night. Pat constantly wracked his brains. Had he thought of everything, and done enough?

Captain Berningi walked idly towards the main concrete jetty, which in more peaceful times, served the commercial boats that plied the river, bringing valuable waterborne trade up from distant Kabbali.

Berningi stopped. He switched off his torch, hoping to conceal his arrival, and perhaps, if he was lucky, catch an unwary sentry sleeping. Instead, to his disappointment, he found both sentries awake and talking softly, as they sheltered from the driving rain under an old tarpaulin. Deferring to both his rank, and his fearful reputation, one of the sentries nervously stubbed out his cigarette and reported that all was quiet; they had seen and heard nothing unusual or suspicious.

Berningi scowled at them, and then he hissed,

'Keep your eyes awake, both of you; or I will make you wish you had died at birth.'

Knowing it was no idle threat, his sentries nodded eagerly.

Angry that he had found neither man sleeping, Berningi half turned to continue prowling the shattered township, when something beyond the jetty caught his eye as he began to turn. Taking a step forward, he said,

'What is that, out there on the river?'

The two sentries left the cover of the tarpaulin, with their rifles half raised. Despite the rain in their eyes, both could see a dark shape out in the murk, some fifty yards beyond the jetty. Wary of the spirits they knew dwelt in the Mpana; reluctant to approach their watery realm in the darkness, one said,

'It is just a big tree in the river, Sir.'

The other added,

'Yes, it must have been washed away in the storm.'

Berningi nodded. Both the sentries were just stupid foot soldiers, but they were probably right. The rivers always filled with floating debris when the rains came, and the levels began to rise. He was about to reply, when he remembered the torch in his pocket. Rain dripping from his hand, he brought it out, and almost absently, switched it on...

The beam cut through the darkness and rain like a knife. The teenaged Mai-Mai Captain stared for a moment, as his tired brain overcame the surprise which flooded through it. Caught in the brilliant light, was a big flat sided boat, strangely covered in vegetation and reeds. Both sentries stood beside him open-mouthed, until, as realisation dawned, Berningi suddenly screamed at them,

'It is the missing white men!...Quickly you two, shoot! Shoot at them, damn you!'

Still shocked by what they saw, the sentries cocked their rifles and aimed towards the boat, floating silently past them on the river. In the sudden excitement, both snatched at their triggers, making their first volley fly harmlessly over the Victoria.

As green tracer rounds cracked above them, Pat shouted at O'Rourke,

'NOW! for Christ's sake. Give it all you've got...*everything!*'

The Victoria's master didn't need to be told twice. His hand slammed both throttles forward in a blur of movement, and, in a cloud of black exhaust, the Victoria's ancient engines roared. As more bullets cracked overhead, two great gouts of white foam erupted behind the landing craft, as its spinning propellers bit faster into the murky water, and the craft surged ahead.

There was pandemonium on the jetty and riverbank. Alerted by the shouting, and the sentries deafening shots, groggy, half-asleep Mai-Mai stumbled pell-mell from wherever they had been sheltering. Men shouted and jabbered with excitement, running along the riverbank in the pouring rain, to try and see what the others were shooting at.

Aboard the Victoria, crouched down beside O'Rourke in the cockpit, Pat ordered his men to hold their fire and take cover. Bullets and tracer ricocheted off the vessel's flat side panels, splashed into the water and cracked overhead. The noise was deafening, but Pat judged the fire ineffective. It sounded awful, a cacophony straight from hell, but the thick steel panels were deflecting the growing number of rounds coming from the riverbank. Pat did not want to fire back yet. In the limited visibility, their gun flashes would give the Mai-Mai something definite to shoot at.

In the tiny engine compartment, Julius sat in a hot puddle of his own urine, with his fingers in his ears; eyes shut tight. Tears ran down his burning cheeks. In the maelstrom of deafening noise, he was shaking and crying with pure, uncontrollable terror.

A flare arced into the sky, and burst high above them. As the cold white light bathed the Victoria in its ghostly luminescence, the rate of fire from the bank increased, as more and more whooping Mai-Mai saw the target, and opened fire on the fleeing vessel. Suddenly, mixed in with the sparkling lines of tracer, a rocket-propelled grenade, fired from the concrete jetty, whooshed in front of the Victoria. Leaving a trail of sparks behind it, the rocket exploded with a thunderous bang in the trees on the opposite bank. Debris splashed into the water's edge. The girl screamed shrilly from within the hold. Ignoring her anguish, Pat knew instantly what had narrowly missed them. Now was the moment. He leaned forward and roared at his men,

'RPG! Return fire. Pour it on, and shoot that bloody light out... *NOW!*'

Spike was closest to him, and first to respond. He sprang up, yelling,

'I'll nail the light!'

The young trooper shouldered his rifle and took careful aim, lining his sights up somewhere over a foot above the far end of the dazzling torch beam. Controlling his breathing, Spike squeezed the trigger and fired five rapid shots. With an instant growl of triumph, he watched the shining torch suddenly spin in the air and go out.

On the jetty, Captain Berningi, the swaggering baby killer coughed and looked down with surprise and confusion, at the two small bullet holes in his chest. He could not see or feel the massive damage left by both bullets as they ripped through him, or what was left of his shredded back. Blood trickled from his mouth as he struggled to focus on the spreading stains covering his tee-shirt. His last breath came in a ragged gasp. Light faded from his eyes. Legs buckling suddenly, Berningi pitched forward off the edge of the jetty, and disappeared with a mighty splash into the deep water beneath it.

Only a second behind Spike, Pat's other troopers, and the two security men jumped up; their short controlled AK bursts, and well-aimed pistol shots swept along the crowded riverbank. Tracer hissed back and forth across the dark waters, as the fire-fight began in earnest.

With heart pounding and a massive overdose of adrenaline pumping through his veins, Pat reached into a corner of the cockpit, and grasped the handle of the old bucket he had secreted there earlier.

He did not have time to notice the scattering of the Mai-Mai, silhouetted against the dying glow of Birundi, or those who dropped their precious weapons and flopped face-down into the mud on the riverbank. In that one moment, not even the guerrillas, who screamed or bolted back into cover caught his attention, as small-arms fire erupted from the vessel on the river.

As they dived for cover, the sudden lull in the guerrillas' firing gave Pat the moment he was waiting for. Bracing himself, he stood up in full view. Heaving the sloshing bucket over his head, he emptied its contents down the nearest exhaust pipe opening. Dropping the empty bucket, with ragged shots ricocheting from the ironwork around him, it clattered on the decking. Pat launched himself headlong back into cover.

The raw diesel oil flooded down the pipe onto the hot cylinder block of the Victoria's starboard engine. Less combustible or volatile than petrol, it vaporised immediately to airborne gas, which expanded instantly, surging back up the exhaust pipe and throwing out dense clouds of billowing white smoke. Within seconds, mixed with the rain, and surrounded by the murky darkness, the Victoria disappeared from view in the impenetrable smokescreen. More bullets cracked angrily over and around the vessel, and another RPG rocket hissed from the jetty, but because of the swirling smoke, fired blind, it exploded harmlessly in the fading wake, well behind the Victoria in a huge spray of smoke and water. A heavy machine gun opened up from the bank. It chattered and raked the water around the landing craft. More flares crisscrossed the skies, and burst in the stormy heavens above, but the wind quickly blew them back towards the smouldering township.

Grinning savagely, Pat called into the hold,

'Anyone hit?'

Silence confirmed that all were safe and well. With a smirk, Danny called out,

'Everyone's Ok Pat, but I think Spike's just shit himself.'

Laughter erupted among the men, as Spike angrily denied his grinning mate's accusation. Pat welcomed the momentary distraction. Black humour under fire was strange medicine, to those who had not experienced it; but better than the most advanced counselling, it instantly released the tension, of the men holding smoking guns aboard the Victoria.

With her engines still roaring at maximum revs, the Queen Victoria was now five hundred yards beyond the last huddle of crude buildings, built on the extreme edge of the township.

The firing had all but stopped from the riverbank. Just the odd, haphazard shot was fired in temper by the raging Mai-Mai, when they saw the bloody bodies of their own dead lying haphazardly scattered along the riverbank, and floating slowly downstream, face-down in the water.

In their frustration and anger, some Mai-Mai cleaved the empty air around them with machetes, vowing terrible revenge on the hated white men, who had escaped them in the darkness, hidden in the swirling depths of Pat's improvised smokescreen.

With nothing to shoot at, the men aboard the Victoria stopped firing. Hammering hearts began to slow. They were beginning to relax a little, when Pat gave the formal order to cease fire. As a precaution, he added,

'Reload, then watch and shoot... but only on my order!'

Pat's caution was well-founded, but unnecessary. After several agonising minutes, as the last of the smoke began to fade, the dying glow of Birundi was behind them. With a sigh of relief, Pat shouted down into the hold,

'OK folks, you can relax now. We are through... we've made it!

Chapter Twenty-Four

While Jan and Krutz kept watch, Pat's troopers were chatting and taking the opportunity to clean their weapons.

'That was a neat trick with the smokescreen,' said Danny, as he sat on the floor, in the dark hold, cleaning his AK.

Charlie and Spike both grinned. Charlie stopped wiping the fouling on his own AK's stripped-down receiver, and said,

'Yeah, I asked him about that once we were clear of Birundi. Pat reckons he read about it somewhere, years ago. Apparently, Russian tanks have used the same trick since the second world war.'

Spike chipped in.

'Well, whoever thought of it first, I reckon it saved our bacon a couple of hours ago…'

Pat ordered the Victoria kept at full power after they made their escape, until, several hours later; O'Rourke tapped one of the dirty gauges on the basic control panel in front of him. Making up his mind, as Captain, he suddenly throttled his tired engines back.

Pat had been curled up in a ball asleep beside him. The change in the vibrations and the reduction in noise woke him. Instantly alert, he demanded,

'What's up, why have we slowed down?'

Standing in the cockpit with his hands firmly on the Victoria's wheel, O'Rourke looked down and said,

'If we stay at this speed any longer, we are going to run out of fuel, long before we reach Kabbali.'

Pat struggled to sit up. To his relief, he realised it had stopped raining. His muscles were cramped and stiff. Shrugging off his discomfort, he stood up and stretched. He said,

'How far have we got from Birundi?'

O'Rourke shrugged.

'We have been sailing for about three hours since they stopped shooting at us. At full power, the old Queen will make about ten knots with the current, so I reckon that puts us…Hmm, allowing for all the twists and turns, as the crow flies, we are maybe thirteen or fourteen miles from Birundi.'

Pat winced. It wasn't anywhere near far enough; not to be sure they were clear of the long reach of the Mai-Mai. The meandering Mpana River brooked no argument, however, and Pat knew it. Reluctantly, he nodded his acceptance,

'No sign of pursuit?'

The Victoria's Captain shook his head.

'No, nothing at all. Nothing on the water behind us, and there's no track they could follow along the river by vehicle. If there was, we would have seen their lights.' O'Rourke slowly rotated tired neck muscles. 'It is pretty much solid bush for the next thirty miles or so, before we reach open country.' He grinned, 'I reckon we caught them cold. They're probably still running around trying to get organised.'

It was Pat's turn to shrug,

'I hope you're right.' Swatting at a mosquito that was buzzing around his head, Pat stared at the faint glow on the eastern horizon. He enquired,

'How long before dawn?'

O'Rourke sniffed and rubbed his chin. Looking across to the faint blue ribbon of light behind distant hills, he replied,

'About forty minutes… give or take.'

Pat checked his watch, as O'Rourke yarned.

'Fair enough. I'm going to check on our passengers… Have you had any sleep yet?'

O'Rourke shook his head,

'Not yet. I wouldn't trust Julius to steer the old Queen at night, and no-one else is qualified. I'll get him up here when it's light. He can take over then, while I grab some sleep. He patted the hipflask in his pocket, 'After I've had a decent nightcap or two that is.'

In his cramped flat on the edge of London's busy Bayswater, Cornelius Wilde was dreaming when the telephone beside his bed jangled angrily and woke him. His wife Jennifer stirred beneath the blankets and groaned something unintelligible, as he slipped on his reading glasses, and reached momentarily towards the off button of his bedside alarm clock. When it did not stop the noise, he realised it must be the telephone. Lifting the receiver, he sleepily answered it.

'Hallo?' The voice at the other end of the line was clipped, and urgent.

'Cornelius? It's Lethbridge here. We have lost contact with Pat Farrell in the Congo. Something's gone drastically wrong, by the sound of it.'

The MI6 analyst was instantly wide awake. Matching the urgency of the caller, he replied,

'My God, what has happened?

Cornelius didn't recognise several people sitting around the table, at the hastily arranged crisis meeting, in one of the many briefing rooms inside the Foreign Office building beside Whitehall. He glanced at his watch; it was still only 6.40 in the morning. Given the gravity of the situation, he had been picked up from home by police car, and under flashing blue lights, had made the fastest journey through London's almost deserted streets, that he could ever remember.

A secretary smiled, as she placed a steaming cup of coffee in front of him. The chairman cleared his throat, rapped lightly on the table and called the meeting to order.

'Gentlemen, now we are all here, thank you for coming in at such short notice. Before I begin, I believe introductions are in order.'

Cornelius knew all but the two men dressed in dark suits, sitting to the left of the Minister. He noticed the dark circles under the men's eyes.

'These two gentlemen, Dr De Keizer and Mr Campbell, are both Directors of the Pan Global Corporation. It has now come to my attention that Pan Global have personnel involved in this mess, and I thought it wise to invite them to this meeting, so that we could swap information, and, of course, fresh ideas.'

David Benchley MP, Minister for Foreign Affairs, sat back comfortably in his chair. That would do for introductions between the Corporates and the military. The Government's covert involvement with Pan Global and their attempts to topple the current government of the Congo had nothing to do with Lethbridge, or his own small entourage. Some highly secret operations run by Benchley's Ministry were strictly 'eyes only', and required the very highest political clearance, and authorisation from the P.M.'s private office, before such briefings could take place. No authority had been forthcoming, so Benchley said nothing more by way of introduction. Clearing his throat once again, after sipping at his coffee, the Minister continued,

'At 011.34 UK time last night, the aeroplane chartered by our people in Nairobi, returned empty. When the Military Attaché questioned the pilot, it appears the airfield in northern Congo was overrun by guerrillas. Unfortunately, according to the pilot, they attacked while Brigadier Lethbridge's men were in the township of Burundi, collecting the civilian medical team, you are all aware of. Apparently, the pilot escaped by the skin of his teeth, and was unable to make contact with the SAS chaps before he got away.

Brigadier Lethbridge interrupted, at the mention of his men,

'Did the pilot see any sign of them?'

Irked by the interruption, Benchley glared at the head of the SAS.

'Ah...If I may be permitted to finish... as the pilot over flew Birundi, under fire incidentally, he saw a vehicle driving through the township, at speed, heading away from the airfield. Given that our last report indicated that the civilian population had already fled, I think it fair to assume that the SAS men and civilians were inside it.

It was De Keizer's turn to halt the Minister's flow,

'What about our people, Minister?'

There was an awkward silence for a moment, before the Minister answered,

'Well, it is possible that they were the only occupants of the vehicle of course, or perhaps, all parties were altogether?'

Stern faced and frustrated by the lack of accurate intelligence, both directors nodded.

The Minister noted their silence and continued.

'We cannot expect any help from the Congolese Government at present. As some of you are already aware, they have forbidden access, and threatened to use deadly force to stop entry. My Ministry is currently working at a political level on the problem, but as yet, they have proven to be very difficult, and refused point-blank to co-operate.'

The silence returned, as each man around the table digested the news. It was Cornelius who broke the silence.

'If I may please, Minister?' Turning his attention to the two Pan Global directors, he said, 'What exactly were your employees doing at Birundi, Dr De Keizer?'

Caught off-guard, De Keizer blustered for a second.

'Ah.., just making routine safety checks on our mining operation. Standard procedure you see, we do it every six months.' He smiled weakly at Cornelius.

Cornelius nodded in silence. After a lifetime of working within the secretive world of intelligence gathering, the analyst could read body language like an open book. He knew instantly when he was being lied to. He felt the Brigadier's steely grey eyes boring into him, but said nothing more.

Regaining his position as Chairman, the Minister turned his attention to the Brigadier,

'What are your thoughts, Brigadier, why haven't your men been in contact?'

Brigadier Lethbridge cleared his throat,

'Well Minister, assuming they are still alive, it could be lack of opportunity to set up their signalling equipment, or perhaps, a technical problem. Our standard operating procedures demand a situation report from our men on the ground,' he shrugged, 'so whatever the current situation, I'm in no doubt Sergeant Farrell will phone home when he can.'

The Minister nodded. He said,

'Clearly, without contact, we remain in the dark. I have instructed our Embassy in Kinshasa to quietly send someone up to the north, to try to find out exactly what is happening in the region, and also see if they can find what's happened to our people. We are also, of course, continuing to monitor the situation, via GCHQ.'

As the emergency meeting broke up without resolution, Cornelius and the Brigadier walked back together briskly, crossing Whitehall towards the Ministry of Defence.

'What did you make of that?' The Brigadier suddenly enquired. Cornelius did not look happy.

'Well Brigadier, that Pan Global man, De Keizer, was clearly hiding something.' The two men walked into the Ministry's main entrance, before Cornelius added,

'Their involvement goes deeper than just a routine safety check. I think I will talk to my colleagues over the water in Vauxhall, and spend the morning doing some digging.'

Chapter Twenty-Five

Worried by growing reports of the Mai-Mai's sweep south, the Congolese Government placed the national army on alert. As they were blind to the rebels' intentions, following an emergency Cabinet meeting, their defence minister urgently ordered more reconnaissance flights into the war-torn Katinga region.

As the sun lifted over the horizon, the ancient piston-engined T-6 two-seater Harvard banked steeply through the clear air, at an altitude of three thousand feet, as it approached the outskirts of Birundi. Using the old map resting across his lap, the observer sitting behind the pilot was following the terrain and guiding the pilot towards their destination. Their flight plan brought them in from the west, but the observer needn't have bothered navigating for the last fifteen miles. Both Congolese airmen could clearly see the spirals of dark smoke rising high into the sky, above the shattered township, which was now apparently in rebel hands.

The pilot's pre-dawn flight briefing had been simple. Without friendly government troops yet operating in the area, all hostile movements were to be observed, numbers and enemy concentrations recorded, and directions of advance noted. If necessary, at the pilot's discretion, he was cleared to attack targets of opportunity, engaging them with the aircraft's machine guns and five-inch rockets, which hung strapped beneath each of the aircraft's wings.

There was an extra part in the briefing. A warning had been issued, direct from government, that foreign mercenaries, possibly British, might be operating in the province. The pilot's orders concerning them were as brutal as they were simple: They should be shown no mercy, and were to be attacked on sight.

When their general was in a rage, his men and officers feared him more than ever.

They had seen him angry many times before, but now, as he surveyed the bodies of his dead foot soldiers lying along the riverbank, he was incandescent with rage.

They had slipped through his fingers once again, defied his magic, and killed his men.

Shaking with fury, he spun around and snarled at the small group of officers, whose duty was to attend him,

Pointing downstream, with flecks of spittle spraying from his mouth, Ojukwu raged,

'*I curse these white men!...* My magic will trap them until I will have them before me, where they will spend their last miserable hours feeling the true meaning of my wrath.' He turned, and began stamping back towards the crude buildings which lined the riverbank. Still seething, he stopped abruptly, and returned his burning gaze to his officers. With downcast eyes, they listened to the pure malice behind the words of his deep, rumbling voice. The words chilled their very blood, when he said,

'They are to be captured quickly, or *you* will take their place.'

Pat's men and the two security guards were sleeping as the sun rose higher in the sky. Apart from the rhythmic chug of the engines, everything seemed quiet, so Pat stood them all down. He wanted the men sharp when the time came, as tired men's reactions are slowed by fatigue, and they make mistakes. The civilians were also lying huddled together sleeping, as Julius stood behind the wheel, keeping the Victoria in mid-stream, well away from the rapidly thinning jungle which still adorned both banks. Besides the grinning helmsman, O'Rourke lay on the steel floor plate, snoring contentedly, exhausted after guiding his vessel down the treacherous waters of the Mpana, throughout the long, and adrenaline filled night.

A nesting flock of white birds lifted suddenly and noisily into the air at their passing. Silver fish jumped and splashed on the sparkling surface of the river, as they hunted the iridescent insects which buzzed lazily across the shimmering water. Pat breathed the warm, clean air deeply into his lungs. The irony was not lost on the tough SAS sergeant. After the intense action of last night, he thought, was there ever a more peaceful spot around the world, than where they were now?

Pat's forehead suddenly furrowed. He was concerned about the lack of communications. Their plane must surely have returned to Nairobi by now. There was probably a massive flap on because his entire party was missing. He shrugged to himself. There was nothing he could do about it for now. Perhaps, he wondered; they could simply make an international telephone call from Kabbali when they arrived? Pat sniffed and put it to the back of his mind; he would have to sort that one out later.

As the Victoria continued to float serenely on the sparkling waters, Pat's mind wandered to the pretty redhead lying huddled and asleep close by. What was her name? Pat remembered; Siobhán, he thought, that was it.

Pretty name; he grinned to himself. Perhaps she did have the hots for him after all? Well, he thought; the Irish connection was always dodgy, but there wasn't any particular woman right now, so what the hell? Since Candy had flitted from his life, there had been too many lonely nights, at home, in his flat in Paddington. Maybe when they got back to the UK, he would link up with her for a drink sometime? She was certainly pretty and bright enough to be worthy. Given their current situation though, that was definitely something else for the back-burner; he thought with a mischievous grin.

As Pat lay on the narrow prow of the Victoria, basking in the bright sunshine, he relaxed as best he could, but deep inside, a part of him remained alert to any potential hazard. Suddenly, adrift in the tranquillity which surrounded him, his mind whirled as an alarm went off deep inside his head. He sat bolt upright. For a moment, he searched his senses. Something felt wrong; something had changed. Pat couldn't quite put his finger on it, whatever it might be, but then, he realised. The visual sweep showed nothing. It was not anything around him that he could see. It was something he could hear, at the very edge of his registry. Above the Victoria's engines, Pat detected what had put him into alert mode... He recognised the new sound… it was the growl of a low-flying aircraft.

The pilot took in his wide panoramic view from two thousand feet. Only a few miles ahead of his aircraft, the lush green ocean, which had covered the ground below in all directions until now, gradually surrendered and changed to a seemingly unending tract of brown savannah. The dry grassland, dotted with an occasional acacia tree, disappeared only as it melded with the distant horizon.

It was his observer sitting behind him, who suddenly yelled excitedly that there was a disturbance below them, on the river.

The pilot of the vintage T-6 ground-attack aircraft dipped his starboard wing, as he and his crewman stared down at the winding ribbon of the Mpana. His eyes flicked back momentarily, to the line of fresh bullet holes in the leading edge of the wing, which had suddenly appeared in a flash of tracer and a series of juddering thumps, as they had flown over Birundi, only minutes earlier. Before their aircraft was hit, both airmen had seen the dots of many Mai-Mai moving below in the township, but they were scattered and did not present sufficient concentration, that he could make out anyway, to offer a decent target for his guns. Having realised his aircraft had been hit by ground fire; the Congolese air force Flight Lieutenant decided that today, discretion was the better part of valour. They had completed their primary mission, and found the rebels. Satisfied that his sortie was successful; he turned the aircraft south, before one of the Mai-Mai's bullets hit something vital.

The pilot identified for himself what his observer had seen. In the middle of the Mpana, the long white scar of a boat's wake stood out clearly, in stark contrast against the sparkling water.

Levelling off, the pilot looked ahead, through the blur of his propeller. Reaching up, he depressed the send button on his throat mike,

'What do you think?' he enquired.

'Well, it is a boat of some kind coming downstream from Birundi,' replied his observer, 'perhaps they are a Mai-Mai reconnaissance party, spying out the river route to Kabbali?'

The pilot turned his head, and nodded his agreement,

'Yes, that is what I think too. We'd better go down for a closer look…'

The pilot pulled down his flying goggles, and applied slight pressure to one side of his rudder pedals. Pushing the stick slowly forward, and easing it gently to the right, he banked the aircraft into a lazy 180-degree turn. He only levelled out when he was satisfied that he was properly lined up, and ready to make a close fly past, and a more detailed visual inspection of the mystery boat ahead.

Below, Pat's unease grew as he watched the small aircraft fly past them, then suddenly bank and lose height, arcing slowly back towards the prow of the Victoria. Realising they had been spotted by an aircraft which might be military, and quite possibly a threat, he yelled down into the hold,

'Hey, you guys! Wake up down there... *Trouble!*'

Unable to see the reason behind Pat's shout, Spike shook his two friends urgently,

'Come on, wakey, wakey you two! Pat says something happening!'

As the troopers scrambled to their feet, the civilians stirred.

'What's going on?' demanded Barney Morris angrily, irked at being woken from his first sleep in over thirty-five long and terrifying hours. Picking up his rifle, Charlie looked down, and grinned at him,

'Dunno mate, I'll give you a shout when I find out.'

The T-6 pilot lost altitude, until he levelled out at just over three hundred feet above the jungle canopy. Beyond the large engine cowling, in front of his armoured windshield, he could clearly see the angular box-like shape of the boat ahead, and the broad bow wave foaming in front of it. As the aircraft commenced its flyby, the airspeed indicator showed it was fast approaching at the plane's maximum airspeed of 208 knots. He depressed the switch on his throat mike again,

'I will make one high-speed pass only. Take a good long look with your binoculars, and tell me what you see, as we climb out.'

There was a faint click in his headphones. His observer replied tensely,

'*Roger.*'

Listening to the increase in the growling drone of the aircraft, Pat was doing his best to organise and protect his passengers. He pointed, and called out to Julius, who was staring up at the quickly approaching aircraft.

'Put us closer to the bank. Try to get under the trees!' he turned to the frightened passengers, 'OK folks, probably nothing, but it is time to take cover. Get down flat, all of you, and quickly!'

In seconds, its engine a deafening roar, the aircraft zoomed past them and began to climb away. Its markings and camouflage paintwork were plain to see, and so were the rockets slung under each wing. Lying face-down on the deck, Morris suddenly looked up,

'Are they going away? Is it all right now?'

Pat kept his eyes glued on the aircraft, as it slowly began to gain height. He said,

'Dunno yet mate, keep your fingers crossed.'

Morris groaned and replaced his forehead on the cold steel plate of the hull. Shivering with fright, he put his hands over his head. Dr Frasier's nurse was muttering a prayer. Rolling slightly to one side, awkwardly, she crossed herself.

As the ancient T-6 climbed away, the observer shouted excitedly into his mike.

'It is definitely a military vessel! I saw about ten people aboard, and I'm sure some of them were white.'

That was enough for the pilot. Still angered by the ground fire which damaged his plane earlier; eager to repay in kind, he decided the evidence was sufficiently overwhelming. Either they were rebels or mercenaries; he did not care which; it made no matter. His orders were the same, in either case. Easing his stick back and over, he began to turn his aircraft again. Reaching for the transmit button at his throat, he said to his observer,

'I'm going to attack…'

Chapter Twenty-Six

Pat and his men were watching the aircraft closely, as it began to bank, well to their stern. It was Danny, who yelled,

'Bloody hell Pat. They're coming back!'

Pat nodded, as his heart began to race. The boat was hideously exposed from the air. With clear water all around the Victoria, in broad daylight, there was nowhere to hide this time.

It had taken him almost ten minutes to drain the diesel into the bucket as they approach Birundi the previous night. Pat doubted they had more than seconds, if the aircraft was indeed going to attack. Frantically, he yelled again at Julius, then pointed,

'Wake the Captain up, and give it full power over to the bank, quickly man!'

Frozen where he stood, Julius was not listening. He looked straight through Pat; his face was masked with pure terror. As the drone of the aircraft's supercharged engine grew louder, Pat was standing beside the loading ramp at the prow. With growing horror, he realised he was too far away to sprint across the open hold, climb up the iron ladder welded to the bulkhead, and reach the cockpit in time. Frantically, he picked up a discarded spanner from the deck, and hurled it at Julius. It flew wide and clanged against one of the exhaust pipes. The loud metallic clatter broke Julius' paralysis. Blinking as if awakening from a bad dream, Julius suddenly began spinning the wheel hard over, as he turned and looked behind him again.

Pat raged,

'The throttles man! *Now, Full power!*'

But it was too late. Its engine screaming, the plane was almost on them. Everything seemed to happen in slow motion, as Pat and his men desperately threw themselves over the civilians. Julius was a statue, staring up at the onrushing plane, unable to tear his eyes from it. Like a mesmerised mouse, frozen before a cobra, his face contorted with a silent scream of terror, as the ground-attack T-6 fired two five-inch rockets at the slowly turning Victoria. They were followed almost instantly with a long raking burst from its wing mounted machine guns.

The noise was deafening as the supersonic bullets smashed into the water, hammering two vertical lines of spray into the river's surface to either side of the Victoria. One rocket whooshed in and missed; it detonated harmlessly in a massive column of flame and water in midstream. The other exploded directly under the waterline of the landing craft's stern, lifting the back of the craft inches from the water. His hand still holding the wheel, Julius disappeared. Caught close to the heart of the powerful explosion, his body spun smoking through the rising column of water. What was left of him arced through the air, splashing in a bloody spray of froth and foam, thirty yards further upstream.

As the Victoria settled again into the water, Pat was first on his feet. Shaking his head to clear the concussion, he saw the aircraft about to overfly. With a primordial snarl of rage, firing his AK on full auto from his hip, he hosed the entire magazine skywards, as the attack aircraft zoomed at full power, directly overhead.

'*Shit!*' he cursed, as the magazine ran dry. Pat's spirits lifted a moment later, when he was rewarded by a thin trail of black smoke, issuing from somewhere within the guts of the rapidly disappearing aircraft.

Ears still ringing from the explosion, Pat turned and looked at the jumbled heap of his men, and their civilian charges. The worst of the blast had missed; the engine compartment's steel bulkhead had saved them. Despite this, Spike eyes looked glazed, as he disentangled himself from the two women, who he had thrown himself across seconds before the Victoria was hit. Angry black smoke was billowing from the mangled engine compartment at the rear, behind the wreckage of the pulverised cockpit. Danny was sitting on the floor, with his head in his hands, but Charlie was already on his feet, helping the shaken doctor to stand up. Barney Morris sat up ashen faced and silent, then suddenly vomited noisily across the landing craft's steel floor.

Krutz had hauled himself up, and was kneeling with his head down, besides Jan. The big Swede was lying motionless, on his back. A vivid red stain was spreading across the Swede's white tee-shirt. Pat saw the cause instantly. A fat, jagged piece of iron was lodged deep in Jan's broad chest. The Boer Colonel tore his eyes from the body of the last of his men, who he had led so confidently from the Skeleton Coast. This was one too many battle; something broke inside him. He looked up at Pat; there were tears running down his dirt-streaked cheeks. Eyes glazed, his voice a whisper; he shook his head slowly and said,

'He's dead…They are all gone now!'

Pat nodded grimly. There was nothing he could do. His duty was to the living. He looked around, then turned to Charlie,

'Where is O'Rourke?'

Charlie shrugged, and nodded towards what was left of the stern,

'He was still asleep up there in the cockpit, I think.' Reluctantly, he added, 'Do you want me to take a look?'

Pat shook his head. As leader, it was a job he had to do. In their hearts, both already knew what his search would uncover.

'No thanks, I will see to it,' Pat said coldly, as he turned and began to climb up the ladder. He picked his way across the tangled wreckage of the vessel's aft section. Pat swung himself clear of the black smoke billowing from the burning diesel, which surrounded the engines below. What he saw made his mouth suddenly dry, and his stomach tighten. Vivid memories of another time and place flashed back to him. The ruined bar, the bloody remains of partygoers, shattered by an IRA bomb...Pat stopped abruptly. With the stink of fresh blood filling his nostrils, he closed his eyes for a moment. Once had been enough, but now, he must see it all again. Swallowing hard, he turned. His foot scuffed something on the deck. Pat bent down and picked up what was left of O'Rourke's hip flask. The massive force unleashed by the explosion had folded it in half. He slowly clambered back into the hold, and tossed the remains of the flask to Charlie. The trooper stared at it for a moment. Now, his face was as grim as Pat felt,

'Dead?'

Pat nodded,

'He must have taken the full force.' Pat shook his head sadly at such pointless waste.

Charlie nodded. As he turned away, fearing he might not heed the unspoken warning, Pat caught his elbow,

'Trust me Charlie. Tell the boys, there's nothing up there any of you want to see…'

Charlie stared at his sergeant for a moment. He saw both sadness and pain in Pat's eyes. He nodded his understanding,

'Well,' he said, trying to make things better, 'at least it was quick.'

Drifting helpless now, with the awning torn and hanging over its steel side, the Victoria was suddenly shrouded by shadow. Masked beneath a lattice of overhanging branches, the burning vessel drifted into the bank. There was a grating bump, which reverberated through the shattered hulk. Pat looked up again at his trooper. He said,

'We're aground Charlie. Do you feel up to climbing over the side with me, and making us fast?'

Charlie nodded.

'Sure Pat,' he said with a sigh, 'no problem.'

As the Irish nurse moved from one survivor to another, cleaning and dressing a mixture of cuts and minor wounds, Dr Frasier lent against one the gnarled trees which lined the riverbank, a little way downstream from the others. Pat was with him; he needed the doctor's medical opinion before making a new plan, and taking the next step. What he heard concerned him.

'I'm telling you Farrell, you cannot move them yet. Apart from minor injuries, every one of them is mentally and physically exhausted…they desperately need to rest.' He looked back at the others for a moment, and then fixed Pat with a stare. 'The poor girl with Morris is on the verge of mental collapse, and Morris is not in much better shape. Krutz is in deep shock. I feel like crap and the rest of you, frankly, look pretty beaten-up, too.'

Pat nodded. The doctor was right, of course. All of them needed to be evacuated to the sanctuary of a cool hospital, but that, Pat knew, was not an option currently on the table. He stared for a moment at the burning hulk of the Victoria, and the tell-tale column of black smoke, which continued to mushroom high into the sky.

When he civilians were safely helped onto the riverbank, and their possessions unloaded, despite their best efforts to extinguish the fire, the flames had stubbornly refused to go out. Seeing the hopelessness of the task, Pat ordered his men to abandon the attempt. With a sigh, Pat said,

'The problem is Doc; we simply can't stay here.' Jerking his thumb over his shoulder towards the mortally wounded Victoria, he added, 'That smoke will be visible for miles, and is bound to bring rebels here to investigate. We need to put some serious distance on the clock, before they get here.' Pat spread his hands. 'You see, we simply do not have the firepower to withstand another attack.' He pursed his lips, then added, 'the bottom line is; if we do not move straight away, it's simple…we are dead!'

Dr Frasier understood the danger, but despite the threat to all of them, the immediate welfare of his patient's had to come first. With growing frustration, he tried again to convince the hard-faced man standing in front of him,

'Look, you asked for my professional opinion, and you have got it. I simply will not take medical responsibility for them, if you move them away from here, before they are properly rested... Surely you can allow them a few hours, at least?'

Pat shook his head,

'No, I'm sorry Doc. In the battered shape they are in, they will move slowly, even with a few hours rest. We are going to need to use every moment of daylight available, to get as far away from here as possible. We'll stop shortly before it gets dark, if that is of any help?'

With that, Pat's appreciation was over. His mind made up, he turned and walked towards the others. Calling out to his nearest trooper, he said,

'Saddle them up Spike, we're moving out.'

General Ojukwu sat in his headquarters. Like Pat, he was also considering his options. Despite a thorough and extended search of both riverbanks by his soldiers, no boats had been found, which were even remotely usable; his men had found nothing. Without boats, Ojukwu knew it was impossible to follow the escape route along the Mpana, which the white men's vessel had used the previous night. Everything which could float had already been pressed into service by the fleeing Hutu, before the arrival of his Tutsi army.

A national air force plane had flown overhead earlier, but thanks to his magic; it did not attack. Instead, it had turned-tail and simply flown away after some of his men had fired at it. The General was concerned by its presence, however. It must have passed their location back to its headquarters. The reconnaissance flight made it all the more imperative to link up with the rest of his troops at Kabbali, and prepared for a government counter-attack. The general stroked his chin, deep in thought. Shortly after the aircraft had gone, a report had been brought to him. A column of smoke had suddenly appeared, some miles to the south; roughly in line with the path of the Mpana River. It might mean the whites were in trouble, or it might be nothing. The general had sent a strong patrol to investigate, but it would take many hours to reach the source of the smoke on foot, and find out the truth.

It was late afternoon, when, in a fanfare of blaring horns; the Mia-Mai vehicles arrived in convoy back from Kabbali, into the very heart of Burundi. For once, as men and booty were loaded, the general's mood improved. The Mpana River was known. It was plagued with slow, winding twists and turns. If he was lucky, and they remained on the river, he could still get to Kabbali before the whites.

He must send some of his men to ambush the river when his column arrived at the railhead, he decided. There might yet be a chance to retrieve the diamonds, and as a bonus, have his own pleasure with any who survived his men's attack.

His mind focused on the diamonds. They were riches that could buy weapons and fund a full-scale war for years, should it proved necessary. One day, he thought smugly; he would take off his generals C.F.P. uniform, and instead, wear an expensive western-style suit. He preened and smiled to himself. His voices whispered greatness. Clearly, that was his destiny now, to accept his fate, and one day adorn himself in the formal dress of the office of Congolese President.

The officer who had led the vehicles back to Birundi broke his visions of the future. The man strode confidently into the banqueting suite and knelt before his leader,

'Forgive my intrusion, Excellence; all is ready. We await your order to depart for Kabbali.'

Ojukwu nodded, 'Have my orders been carried out? Did your men make an example at the railhead?'

The kneeling Captain looked up. With a savage grin, and a feral gleam in his dark eyes, he said,

'Yes Excellence. We made an example of those, foolish enough to defy you. Kabbali is now a symbol of your power, which will be remembered across Africa forever. Your glorious name will go down in history!'

The sun was setting when Pat finally called a halt beside the Mpana. Their luggage long abandoned beside the wreck of the Victoria, led by Pat and Spike, the civilians had staggered behind them throughout the long, hot afternoon. Pat was not blind to their suffering; blisters, and dehydration from the unrelenting heat were taking their toll. Knowing what might be coming after them, he had pressed on regardless, at a pace that had left them spent, and brought them to the very edge of utter and complete exhaustion.

During the long hours of forced march, the country around them had changed. The dense jungle of canopy, tree trunks and lianas had been consigned to memory. Now, the going was easier, but they were exposed and naked, out on the vast expanse of dry, open savannah. Staying close to water, Antelope grazed around them, their sensitive ears pricking up at the sound of the party's approach. Sniffing the air nervously, small herds of skittish animals suddenly bolted, when they detected the acrid scent of man.

Pat held his hand up. Like his men, he used the moment to ease the weight of his bergan. Surveying the area, he decided this was as good as any to hold up for the night. As long as the light lasted, they could see for miles in all directions, and they had excellent access to the life-giving waters of the river, just a few hundred yards away. Slipping off his bergan, he said,

'OK, folks. This is as far as we go today. Get some rest, while we sort out some food and water for you.'

With a collective groan of relief, feet sore and lips cracked with thirst, the civilians dropped thankfully to their knees. Siobhán had been guiding the cub photographer for some miles. She helped the girl along, supporting her when her knees gave way. Now, she let the exhausted girl slide to the ground, and then sat down beside her.

'There we are now. All finished for the day,' she said reassuringly, as the girl curled into a ball and whimpered miserably next to her. Barney Morris was spread-eagled on his back. Eyes closed, and hipflask long emptied, he would have killed for a chilled lager, or something stronger. Kurtz flopped down. He had not uttered a word since they had left the wreck, and that bothered Pat most of all. When he thought about Krutz a little more, he wasn't sure that the man hadn't been silent, since he had sadly announced Jan's death.

Spike dropped his bergan beside Pat's, sat down on it and unlaced his boot. Shaking out a small pebble, he asked,

'Are we're just going to follow the Mpana all the way to Kabbali then, Pat?'

Pat nodded,

'That is pretty much the plan Spike. The rebels are behind us, as far as we know, so its foot down tomorrow, once this lot have had a good night's rest. With luck, even at the rate the civvies can manage, we should be safe and sound in Kabbali by dusk tomorrow.'

Spike grinned, 'Works for me!'

Pat nodded.

'We'll be all right here. Any enemy patrols following the river should miss us, where we are lying up.' He crouched down and opened one of the side flaps on his bergan. Pat lifted out a water bottle, took a swig and said,

'Pull your bottle out too Spike. We'll share the food we've been carrying, when Danny and Charlie arrive. Drink something now, and then give the rest with the men over there.' He stood up and started walking. Over his shoulder, he added, 'I'll give mine to the women, and we'll refill from the river in half an hour or so, when it's fully dark.'

Danny appeared, quickly followed by Charlie. Danny nodded to Spike and his sergeant,

'All clear behind us Pat. No sign of a follow-up.'

Pat nodded. He had ordered the two troopers to drop back, and follow at a distance, after they had crossed over from the cover of the jungle. Pat wanted plenty of warning; he would need time to shepherd his exhausted charges into cover, if they were followed, and his rear-guard was bumped.

As Danny and Charlie dropped their heavy bergans, Pat told them to drink something. Eying up a patch of nearby thorn bushes, as his two men stretched their tired shoulders, he said,

'Take five boys, and then I want you to cut down all those bushes, and drag them into a tight perimeter around us.' He gazed at the sun dipping on the horizon, and the long shadows spreading across the darkening savannah. The sound of something big, roaring hungrily floated to their ears on the gentle breeze from across the river. 'We need to keep the beasties out tonight, and we can't risk lighting a fire.'

Chapter Twenty-Seven

The night had proven uneventful. Guarded in turn by Pat and his troopers, the civilians had slept fitfully throughout the hours of darkness.

An hour before dawn, under Pat's order, Charlie and Spike, who had pulled the last two-hour period of guard duty, ignoring the grumbles, quietly moved from one to the next, rousing the tired folk who had spent the night behind the safety of the thorn redoubt.

After distributing all the water that remained, Pat sent Charlie and Spike down to the river, to refill everything that would hold spare water for the long walk ahead.

'Is there anything left to eat?' asked Barney Morris hopefully.

Pat shook his head,

'Not really. What we brought with us has almost gone. What is left, I will ration out tonight,' Pat stared at the scowling reported. 'Don't worry, a brisk walk will sharpen your appetite… trust me, it works wonders.'

Morris looked at the dry earth beneath him, and stayed truculently silent.

Pat led the group away from their temporary encampment at a moderate pace. He wanted to loosen stiff muscles, and he'd estimated they had about twelve miles to walk, before they reached the safety of Kabbali. With no sign of pursuit, he was happy to ease off the punishing pace he had set the day before.

Although the sun shone, there was just a hint of dark clouds, forming in the skies ahead.

At midday, Pat was taking his turn in the role of lead scout, about twenty yards ahead of the main party. As he breasted a low ridge, he raised his arm to halt the others behind, which walked in silence, single file behind Charlie. The remaining troopers were following up, at a distance behind them.

To avoid sky-lining himself, Pat dropped to his stomach, and crawled forward into cover, where he could observe, without being seen. Ahead, some two hundred yards away, was a deserted dirt road, which ran directly across their line of march. Beyond it, a dry watercourse cut through the savannah towards Kabbali.

A herd of antelope grazed quietly, close to the track. Slowly bringing them to his eyes, Pat swung his binoculars left and right. All seemed clear. Keeping low, Charlie crawled up beside him.

'What's up, Pat?'

Pat passed him the binos,

'There's a road ahead.' Pat sniffed absently, 'It's deserted, and looks OK, but we might as well rest the civvies, and watch it for ten minutes or so. I don't want to get caught out there in the open, if anything uses it as we cross over.'

Lowering the binoculars, Charlie handed them back and nodded,

'Yeah, all looks peaceful enough. I'll nip back and tell the civvies to grab a quick break.'

Pat watched, but saw nothing in either direction during the next quarter of an hour. It seemed odd that absolutely nothing used the road, but glancing at his watch, he was satisfied the chance of discovery was minimal. He waved at Charlie and the civilians to get up, and follow behind him.

Rifle at the ready, senses alert, he patrolled forward, down the slope towards the road; It may have been an old soldier's instinct, but there was a niggling in the back of Pat's mind. It tickled, and warned him that something was wrong. He kept a sharp lookout, but no movement or unusual sound disturbed the quiet of the sweeping savannah around him. Pat thought about turning around, but decided against it. Time was pressing, and he wanted to get to Kabbali, before the storm which threatened on the horizon, broke over them. Pat licked his cracked lips, and pressed forward regardless through the tall dry grass, which whispered gently in the breeze...

Pat froze. Something moved ahead, crashing unseen through the waist-high grass which surrounded him. Pat jerked his AK into his shoulder, and drew a bead on the sound. Focusing one eye along the sights of his weapon, Pat silently pressed the safety catch into semi-automatic mode. His heart beat faster as he applied more pressure to his trigger. Whatever it was; it was big, sounded really pissed off, and was coming straight at him.

Suddenly, the biggest, ugliest warthog Pat had ever seen outside a BBC wildlife documentary burst through the tall grass, and stopped abruptly, when it saw him standing less than fifteen feet in front of it. Snorting, it glared balefully at Pat with its little piggy eyes. The heavy animal snuffled noisily, as it swept its sharp tusks through the air, and threatened to charge. Pat held both his nerve, and his bead between its flashing eyes. He remained perfectly still. Abruptly deciding the strange creature in front of it posed no threat; the warthog turned, skinny tail erect, and bounded back into cover. Disappearing from view, its tail was all he could see, as it dashed chaotically back towards the road.

Pat breathed deeply and smiled with relief. He watched the animal's tail zig-zagging a path, as it bulldozed its way through the long grass. He was just about to signal the all clear, when there was a sudden brilliant flash, and the deafening boom of an explosion. With an agonised, dying squeal, the warthog's bloody body spun through the air momentarily, then fell back into the long grass with a loud thump.

Pat ducked involuntarily at the blast. Straightening, he knew instantly what had happened. Even second precious, he spun around and bellowed at the party advancing slowly towards him, and yelled.

'Freeze everybody! We're in a bloody minefield.'

After two barbaric civil wars, according to a highly detailed report commissioned by the United Nations, the use of landmines had been common in the region. All sides were guilty of utilizing them, during both long and bloody wars. The landmines left a deadly legacy across the northern reaches of the Congo, for the survivors who continued to live there. In many cases, minefields were completely unmarked, or had been poorly recorded, with all records now lost. Most mines simply remained where they had been laid; long since abandoned by the warring combatants, who had deployed them.

Sweat dripping down his face, Pat remained perfectly still. High above, a soaring eagle screeched out across the heavens, but as the cry echoed into nothingness, apart from the wind rustling the grass, silence surrounded him once again. Pat made a careful visual survey of the ground around him. He was looking for the slightest sign; a subtle disturbance of the surface; the merest hint of something which did not look natural or belong. As Pat scanned the immediate area around his feet, he guessed why no-one had used the road. The locals that lived and worked within the area, toiling on farms and engaged in herding livestock to fresh pastures, knew this particular area was heavily mined, so naturally, avoided it like the plague.

Just a few feet ahead in the grass, Pat spotted something. It looked at first, like the edge of a rusted shoe polish tin. His mouth dry, Pat licked his lips, as he decided. Taking a deep breath, he knelt down and laid his rifle gently beside him. He carefully scooped away the sandy soil which surrounded the broad tin. What he uncovered, confirmed his worst fears. It was the unmistakably shape of an anti-personnel mine. One thing was clear to Pat. Where one lay, there would be hundreds more.

It was down to pure, dumb luck, no-one had stepped on a mine so far, and Pat had no idea how far into the deadly minefield he had inadvertently led them. The road was now only twenty feet in front of him. He had to assume that he and the party behind him were well inside the deadly field. If he brought the others to him in single file, using the track, he had unavoidably left through the grass; he might be able to get them out of danger, by moving forward, and clearing a new narrow path to the road. They could all back-track, but that would mean, perhaps triggering a buried device, or miles of detour to find safe passage around the minefield. The dry watercourse over the road should be a safe enough bet, he reasoned; and free of booby-traps. In years of flash floods, anything buried in there had long since have been swept away, Pat hoped to himself.

There was only one choice that made sense. He stood up and called over his shoulder to Charlie and the others, who were nervously staring at the ground surrounding them. In such a highly charged situation, he must, at all costs, avoid panicking any of them. They must stay still, or they would die.

'Right then,' he started confidently, 'the safest option is to follow in my tracks and come up to me.' He explained his plan, and then beckoned them towards him. 'Watch where you put your feet, and do not rush... take it nice and slowly and stay glued to where I have already walked. If I find anything, I will mark it clearly with a sheet of paper.' Seeing Charlie raise his hand in acknowledgement, Pat added, 'Charlie...Make sure Spike and Danny know what is happening, and tell them to close up with the rest of you. I want the last man to lift the markers, and everyone over the road, safe in the watercourse, before we shove off again, clear?'

Charlie raised his thumb. Pat turned and took a notebook out of his back pocket. Ripping a blank page from it, he crouched down again beside the mine he had uncovered. With a detonation pressure of just 8-10lbs, he did not dare to touch or move it, but instead, placed the white paper sheet beside the mine, and then put a stone on the paper, to keep it safely in place.

Wiping fresh sweat from his brow, Pat carefully stepped over the mine and immediately crouched down again. Drawing a knife from its sheath, which was firmly taped to his bergan's shoulder strap, Pat began to slowly and carefully probe and gently prod the ground ahead.

Although only minutes had passed, Pat felt he had been in the minefield for a lifetime. Although his mind was totally focused, his mouth was so dry; he felt he could drink a river. He could not remember ever being as thirsty as he was now. But then, apart from several lectures over the years, and training once, long ago in a practice field, he'd never had the misfortune to cross a live minefield before. First time for everything, he thought ruefully, as he slid the silver blade under the surface for the hundredth time. Concentrating on the task, Pat tried desperately to remember every last nugget of information the Royal Engineers had taught him, concerning the almost suicidal task, of breaching a fully armed minefield.

It had taken Pat almost ten nerve-wracking minutes to cover fifteen feet.

Inch by inch, his blade slid smoothly through the soil. Pat let out a sharp exhale each time he withdrew the silver blade. He shook his head, to clear the sweat which kept running into his eyes. Despite the danger of the rebels who might be following behind them, he had to put the threat out of his mind, take his time, and painstakingly clear an area wide enough for the frightened civilians to follow in safety. One thing was for certain; he must probe every inch; he could not afford to miss anything within an arm's length, or directly beneath his current path.

Easing his blade forward again, the point disappeared into the dirt. Pat felt something, as its metal tip grated against, what? Pat froze. It might be another rock, but he could not leave it to chance. It was not the first false alarm; the area around them was littered with stones, but he had to make sure, and see for himself. Drawing in a deep breath, he gently swept away the sandy soil. He touched something. It was smooth and metallic, laying at the bottom of the depression his fingers had made. Pat's eyes narrowed. He didn't need to know more. Taking out the notebook again, he marked the mine, mouthed a sulphurous curse at it, and pushed grimly on.

His shirt drenched with sweat, Pat reached the road. Heart still pounding, he gratefully stepped onto the compacted earth, with a sigh of relief. There was always a chance the road beneath his feet was mined. He would check it, of course, but Pat doubted there was any real danger. If whoever had planted the anti-personnel minefield beside it, had also wished to mine the road, training and cold military logic dictated that they would most likely have used big, heavy-duty anti-tank mines for the task. Designed to explode under an unsuspecting vehicle, and constructed to avoid being wasted on a foot soldier who inadvertently stepped on one, the valuable anti-tank mines required hundreds of pounds of pressure, applied directly on top of them, to explode.

As he slipped off his bergan and replaced the knife, Pat pulled out his water bottle and drank deeply. The water tasted sweet, and wonderful.

The civilians were not far behind. As Pat had probed and crawled forward, they advanced steadily behind him, taking one careful step at a time. Charlie was playing his part well, as he talked softly to each of them. His calm words were reassuring them, at every nervous step they took. As his eyes flicked from one ashen face to the next, each of them looked tired and haggard, but then, it was hardly surprising. They all knew oblivion awaited just one careless step away, as they tip-toed painfully slowly towards him. Eyes wide, Barney Morris grumbled silently. He was white as a sheet, but then, Pat noticed, so were all the others. The Doctor and both women walked with arms outstretched, to maintain their balance. Krutz wandered close behind, carefully guided by Danny, with his hands placed firmly on each of the Boer's broad shoulders.

As Charlie finally reached the road, he stepped onto the hard surface gingerly, blowing out his cheeks, as he did so.

Before the Doctor reached him, he whispered,

'J..j..jesus P..p..pat! I've n..n..never been so s..s..scared in all my l..l..life!'

Pat couldn't resist the grin, which spread instantly across his face. Victory was his, and black humour returned. 'You are a Special Forces hero, Charlie...get used to it mate, it goes with the badge!'

Chapter Twenty-Eight

Pat allowed the civilians ten minutes rest, as they lay silent and recovering from their terror. They were concealed inside the dry watercourse, and their shaking had gradually stopped.

Spike handed Pat four pieces of paper, which, as last man through, he had gathered up as he passed through the minefield.

'Worried about litter?' he asked with a grin.

Pat shook his head. His eyes glittered for a moment. Somehow, they seemed to bore straight through him.

'No, not at all. If we are being followed, the rebels will follow our tracks straight into the minefield...They will take casualties without the markers; it will buy us valuable time.'

Spike's grin faded suddenly. He had seen the same look on Pat's face before. There was something cold and murderous in his sergeant's expression, which brooked no further the conversation on the subject. Rubbing at a cramped thigh muscle, Pat said,

'Better get them moving again in a minute. We'll stay in the watercourse for a while, and make sure we are well clear of any more mines before we break out.' Pat looked back towards the road, and then up at the dry earth walls on either side of them. He said firmly, 'There's good cover in here; we'll be out of sight, and should make up some of the time we have lost.' Pat stood up, and stared towards Kabbali. The distant clouds had not moved. He looked down at Spike. 'Get them on their feet will you?...it's time to go...'

As Pat and the others approached Kabbali, they realised it was not rainclouds heralding a storm above the railhead, instead, it was sombre clouds of dense oily smoke. The wind had changed direction when they were within a couple of kilometres; the smell of fire and destruction became oppressive. As they got closer still, another smell assailed their nostrils. It was a heavy smell which seemed to hang around them; it was a sweet clinging smell which could never be forgotten. Pat recognised it instantly, if the other did not. He had smelt it once before in Iraq, when his regular SAS patrol, during the first Gulf war, had discovered a partially covered mass grave of hundreds of slaughtered Iraqi civilians. Suspecting disloyalty, it was Saddam Hussein's men who had committed the massacre, as they prepared to run from the approaching Allies. It was a foul smell which once experienced, was unmistakable and unforgettable; it was the sickly-sweet stench of death.

Pat called a halt, and then led the survivors into a derelict farmhouse, on the very edge of the railhead township. The look on his face did not bode well. Trying his best to hide his disappointment, he said,

'Looks pretty obvious the Mai-Mai have beaten us to Kabbali. We'll have to wait until dark, then I will take one of my boys with me. We'll go and take a closer look, and see what is happening in there.'

Angrily, Barney Morris blurted out,

'But…but you said we would be OK, once we got here!'

Pat shrugged; like the others, he was getting tired of the reporter's constant snipes.

'Look, we are caught in the middle of a real war. I'm afraid it is a fluid situation. Front lines move, and change all the time.' Pat stared around at the worried faces of the civilians. They needed reassurance, so he quickly added, 'don't think of giving up though. We have a number of solid advantages. We're still free, the rebels do not know we are here, and this must be the front line as it stands right now. Once we can get past it, we are in really good shape, and should be in the clear.'

Morris was not satisfied. Sarcastically, he demanded, 'And how exactly are we going to get away, then?'
Pat stared at him coldly.
'Leave that to me!'

Like phantoms, Pat and Spike slipped through the darkness, into the shattered township of Kabbali. Even at its edge, gangs of drunken rebels staggered through the streets by the light of the fires that still burned, laughing and shouting to each other. A powerful smell of marijuana wafted through deserted streets, and mixed with the smell of fire and death.

It was a vision of hell in the darkened township. Caught unawares by their rapid sweep south, the inhabitants of Kabbali did not stand a chance. The rebels suddenly appeared, and disgorged from a long convoy of trucks. They quickly fanned out and swept through the town, slaughtering all before them. The bodies of men, women and children, some mutilated, some horribly burned, were scattered everywhere. Half-way down the street, drifting in and out of the flickering half-light, dogs snarled and growled at each other, as they feasted on the remains of one hapless victim. Broken glass lay strewn and glittering across the dusty street, mixed with the debris of smashed furniture and fittings, thrown from surrounding buildings, during an orgy of looting, destruction, rape and killing.

With its headlight shining, two rebels weaved drunkenly along the street on a motorbike. In the red glow of its back light, Pat and Spike could see they were towing a headless body, to the delighted cheers of each gang of rebels they passed.

From the shadows, the two SAS men heard a terrible, anguished cry of a woman, somewhere deep inside the township, followed by shouts and the raucous guttural laughter of her tormentors. The shrill screaming stopped abruptly. Pat whispered into Danny's ear,

'There's no point going further in, there's nothing here for us. We'll pull back and skirt around to the railway. Maybe something there which will be of use?'

Spike nodded in silence. His stomach was churning. He had no words for what he had already seen, and was relieved to be moving away from the terrible carnage, and the horrifying madness which stalked around them in the night. For Spike, it could not be soon enough.

Keeping close together, faces and arms blackened, the two men crept through the darkness; a door suddenly banged open, spilling light into the street ahead of them.

Pat and Spike ducked. There were furious shouts from inside. Two men staggered from the building, dragging a naked wretch out into the night. Others followed them outside, semi-naked, laughing and jabbering boastfully to each other. Their leader shouted to the two who held their bloody captive upright. He waved them aside. Dropping the young woman, both men stepped back. Even at a distance, the two SAS men heard her groan as she fell forward and her head hit the hard ground. The leader of the group of rebels held his hand to his crutch, winced with pain and snarled something down at the girl. Drawing a pistol, he spat on her and fired a single shot into her head, killing her instantly. Waving the smoking pistol through the air in celebration, he shouted something unintelligible to his men, threw back his head, and roared like a beast into the night. Satisfied with his revenge was complete, the rebel Captain followed them back to the laughing and drinking, which had continued unabated inside, as he had coldly murdered the girl.

Spike stared at the still body lying abandoned on the ground; his blazing eyes betrayed the massive surge of anger, which engulfed him. He took a half step forward and hissed,

'Fucking animals!'

Pat remained silent. Holding him back with a clenched fist against Spike's heaving chest, Pat put a finger to his lips. With a jerk of his thumb, he motioned Spike deeper into the shadows, to a space where they wouldn't be overheard. Keeping his voice just audible, Pat hissed angrily,

'*Get a grip on yourself, Spike!*' Pat's tone changed after his rebuke; it eased away from anger. He understood how the young man felt. 'We have already seen plenty in here to turn our stomachs, but we have got to ignore it and stay focused. There are some very frightened people out there, who are relying on us to save them... You're right though, they *are* fucking animals, but we've got a recce to do,' he tapped Spike's heaving chest, and said gently, 'so let's get on with it, OK?'

In the gloom of the shadows, there was silence between them for a moment. Swallowing hard, Spike fought to control the murderous tsunami of anger, which had surged through him when the girl was murdered. With a forced sigh, he whispered,

'Sorry Pat. I nearly lost it... I'm OK now though.'

Pat nodded; he whispered,

'Good lad. Now let's get on with it...'

Using every scrap of cover the night offered, Pat and Spike moved silently towards the marshalling area beside the railhead. There were sentries, but so far, they had all been drunk, or sound asleep. There was a train, standing silently beside the platform of the main terminus building. Stepping carefully over several sets of rails, Pat and Spike crept forward. The smell of death was strong here. As they approached closer, they saw why. Piled neatly beside each carriage, were bodies, dozens of them, stacked like cordwood, ready for a party bonfire.

Pat ignored the piles of neatly stacked corpses, and indicated they should climb aboard and take a look. Gagging at the smell, they hauled themselves up onto one of the narrow wrought-iron platforms, guarded by railings and mounted above the couplings. Pat cautiously opened the carriage door, and quickly recoiled at the stench. Pat stared at Spike, and shook his head in silence. He pointed towards the platform.

It was the same, but different on the other side of the train; more brutal evidence of the rebel's barbarity was waiting for them. Along the length of the platform was a line of passengers, silently kneeling headfirst against the waiting room wall. A dark splatter above each body stained the whitewashed wall. Even in the dark, it was clear to both men what must have happened. Forced from the train at gunpoint, and made to kneel against the wall, some merciless rebel had walked down the line on terrified prisoners, methodically shooting each one, with a single bullet to the back of the head.

It was Pat's turn to snarl a whisper…

Bastards!

The reconnaissance was almost complete. The two SAS men had discovered that rebels had begun to fortify the tracks just beyond the station, presumably to defend against the sudden arrival of a troop train full of soldiers, loyal to the government.

Pat was deeply concerned that he and Spike had found not a single vehicle in working order during their sweep. There were certainly plenty of burnt-out hulks scattered here and there, but nothing even remotely serviceable which they could hot-wire, and use to make their escape. Pat reasoned that there must be working vehicles somewhere in Kabbali, but given the high concentration of rebels, and the glass and sharp debris scattered across every street they had searched; Pat doubted they could steal a rebel vehicle, even if they could find one, without blowing a tyre in the dark, when he and Spike attempted to smuggle it out of Kabbali.

The two men had quietly swept the railhead complex. The engine sheds; station office and main signal box were ransacked. The rails seemed to be sound enough, but each building bore silent witness to a whirlwind of wonton destruction. There were three more buildings, some distance from the main complex to search, and then they must return to the others, empty handed. Pat called a halt, and they both slipped quietly into the dark shadows. Satisfied there were no rebels close by, Pat whispered,

'It's not looking too good, Spike. We've found nothing we can use to get away. What worries me, is in the shape they're in, I don't reckon the civvies are up to a two hundred-mile trek out of here on foot.'

Spike nodded. He had seen the dark circles under their eyes, and the exhaustion on their faces.

'Yeah, they ain't going to make it Pat,' he breathed.

As Pat took a swig from his water bottle, he stared at the dark outline of the buildings ahead. With a heart heavy with their situation, which was getting worse by the minute, he said,

'We'll finish off and check those building, and then I guess we'd better head back, and give the others the bad news…'

Chapter Twenty-Nine

The first two buildings were empty, but even in the darkness, they appeared untouched. One was an office of some kind, lined inside with metal filing cabinets; piles of dusty record folders piled chest high in one corner, and a wooden table and chairs in the centre of the room. The other structure turned out to be an engine workshop. As Pat and Spike eased the door open, and crept through its darkened interior, the welcome smell of oil and heavy machinery replaced the stench of death, which hung like a shroud over the rest of Kabbali. When their sweep of the shed was complete, it was clear that rebel hands had not yet touched this section of the railhead. Confused, Spike whispered,

'Two out of three, all clear, Pat. I wonder why they haven't smashed these up too.'

Pat shrugged in the darkness,

'Dopey bastards might just have missed them…truth is Spike, I honestly don't know.'

Pat glanced at the luminous dial of his watch,

'It's almost two o'clock. We might as well check out that last building, then head back.'

Spike whispered softly,

'So what do we do then, Pat?'

His sergeant tried his best to stifle a sigh,

'There's nothing else for it, Spike. We start walking…'

When the two SAS men left the third building, trying to contain his excitement, Spike breathed softly,

'Bloody hell, Pat! Do you really think we can get away with it?'

Pat checked himself, before he whispered his reply. Spike could not see it in the shadows, but there was now hope, and the faintest glimmer of a smile spreading across his sergeant's face. What they had discovered maybe, just maybe, gave them a fighting chance, he thought. The smile faded into reality. It was certainly about time they had some luck he thought sourly, because ever since they had arrived in the Congo, the Gods of good fortune had clearly abandoned them. It might be a ridiculous plan, but at least now, Pat thought, he had something…. He whispered,

'Time you started believing what it says on your cap badge, Spike.' Pat sniffed. 'Now, come on, let's bugger off and bring the others back here, and then find out just how good that mate of yours; young Danny, really is...'

Pat led Danny into the last building they had searched. The others were safely stashed in a stand of trees, less than a hundred yards away, under Spike and Charlie's armed guard. It was now three o'clock in the morning.

Danny stood in the gloom, with his mouth open. He shook his head in utter disbelief and laughed silently,

'I do not believe it!'

Pat grinned,

'Well...what do you think?'

Danny shrugged,

'Well... it's an old steam shunting engine, by the look of it, with a flat-bed truck attached to the front of it.'

Pat nodded; he had noticed that much. The wagon in front was empty, save for some iron pipes chained to one side of its wooden floor.

'Question is Danny...will the engine work?'

Danny turned to his sergeant. There was a gleam in his eye. He was a legend in the Squadron with anything mechanical, but his favourite toys were engines, however they were powered. Licking his lips with anticipation, Danny replied,

'I'll have to check it over of course, but first impression is that they have been using it recently. I'll need to make a quick inspection of the steam chests and drive valves, to make sure they're sound.'

As Danny pondered his next move, Pat's heart rate increased in his chest. He could not put it off any longer. He had to ask the big one,

'If it all checks out, question is, Danny… can you make it go?'

There was silence for a moment, while Danny considered the question. Absently, he kicked one of the engine's huge driving wheels. He turned to Pat and whispered.

'If the pipes and boiler are sound, none of the valves leak, and the two steam chests down the front are OK, I reckon, if I can get the boiler lit, it will take about an hour, maybe a bit more to get steam up….Will that do?'

Pat breathed a sigh of relief. Danny had a magic touch with engines; there was still a chance. He said quietly,

'Yes… that will do just nicely.'

Danny nodded, but there was concern still in his voice,

'I'm afraid it's 'gonna make some noise, Pat, if I can get everything fired up. We'll need to cover the windows too. When the fire's burning, it will throw out quite a bit of light every time we open the firebox.'

Pat though for a moment.

'OK, we can put something over the windows to block the light. How long before it gets really noisy?'

Danny shook his head and shrugged.

'A few minutes before we are ready to go, I expect. I will do my best to keep things quiet, but with the state it's in, I can't promise anything.'

'Fair enough. Do your checks, and let me know how much fuel and water you can find, while I sort out the windows.'

Pat turned away. One thing was certain; he needed more manpower. Apart from sorting the light emissions, the track outside needed to be checked, and the exterior of the engine shed needed a guard. When the time came to make their escape, Pat knew it would most likely be a hot extraction, under fire. If the track ahead of the engine was blocked, or the points were incorrectly set when they made their dash, they would be in big trouble. There was only one answer; he would have to bring his other troopers in, to help. He daren't leave the civvies alone, so he decided to move them all to the shed, where he could keep them as safe and protected as he could.

Danny was busy making his all-important checks, so Pat went and got the others. As he approached in the darkness, he was challenged with a whispered '*SIX!*' He hissed the return password as he approached the spot where he had left the civvies. As long as his answer added up to the total password number of nine, he would be OK.

'*THREE!*'

Charlie crept off into the night. He was going to check their escape route along the railway track, which ran out of the engine shed. Spike had secreted himself outside, where he could watch the rest of the station in concealment. Pat busied himself securing some old sacking across the windows, which faced the station. The civvies sat fearfully at the back of the shed behind the engine, beside an elderly steel sided ore wagon.

Danny's initial report was encouraging. The big jacketed water tanks, which covered either side of most of the engine's body, were almost full. They were vital, he said, to provide the water which, once lit; the boiler would turn into super-heated, high-pressure steam that provided the power to drive the engine forward. The old shunting engine was designed to burn local wood under the boiler, and the fuel bunker was nearly half full. Danny was happy with that. He was convinced there was enough to get them many miles away from Kabbali, before they needed to cut more wood, or take on more water.

Danny quietly liberated a bundle of old paper records from the adjacent office. Pat had followed him back to the engine shed, carrying the chairs which he quietly broke up for kindling. Once the cavernous firebox was liberally stuffed with paper, Pat added the remains of the chairs, and some other scrap wood he had found. Placing logs from the bunker on top of the pyre, Danny whispered,

'All set Pat, just got to add a match.'

Because the windows were covered, with Pat's permission, Danny switched on a small torch. He shone the pencil beam for a moment on a large brass pressure gauge mounted at head height inside the engine's cabin, and said quietly,

'When the water inside boils and the needle reaches the first red like; we have got the correct pressure.' He swung the beam a little higher, to some levers growing out of the roof of the drivers' cabin, 'the left one releases the brake, and the right one, once I have opened the regulator valve, will send the train forward. Reverse is the opposite direction…all dead simple, really.'

Pat was impressed; he said,

'All right, Casey Jones...light it!'

As the needle began to flicker, pressure began to build in the boiler. Pat was looking over the ore wagon. Danny stood beside him.

'We need this wagon to carry the civvies Danny. I want it coupled to the engine, before we are ready to go.'

Danny heard what his sergeant said, but there was a problem,

'I can't shunt the engine backwards Pat, to get it coupled. I don't have enough steam yet, and when I do, even the rebels on the far side of Kabbali will hear us.'

It made sense to Pat. When they were ready to go, with the engine hissing like an old kettle, there would only be one chance to make their escape. Pat considered the problem for a moment, then said,

'OK, so we'll have to shift it by hand. If we pack some sacking over the engine's buffers, to muffle the sound when they collide with the wagon, we can get the two coupled together...yes?'

'Sure, Pat. But that wagon must weigh at least five tons, maybe more.'

Pat grinned. With more than a hint of sarcasm, he said slowly,

'I didn't say it was going to be easy, did I?'

Charlie had been gone for nearly forty minutes. When he returned, he was struggling under the weight of something heavy. He found Pat in the gloom, and, kicking at one of the rails beside his foot, he whispered his report.

'I went down to where this maintenance spur joins the main line out of Kabbali. Just as well I did, because I had to reset the points. It made a bit of noise, but I didn't see anyone around there while I was doing it. Luckily, the lever was still in place, so I threw the switch and changed them over as quietly as I could.'

Pat nodded,

'Good. Anything else...what's that you've got?'

Charlie chuckled,

'Well, I got to thinking. If I was them, I would have booby-trapped the line, in case their government sent a train up here. I checked about two hundred yards further along the track, and found this wedged under a rail.' With a grunt, lifting it up level to his chest using both hands, Charlie triumphantly showed Pat his prize.

'Jesus! Is that what I think it is?' gasped Pat.

'Yeah! It's a bloody great anti-tank mine. Chinese, I think. Little wonder they aren't too bothered about guarding the track. I bet they are relying on this to give them plenty of warning.'

Pat took a step back. He'd had quite enough of mines recently. Sensing his discomfort, Charlie chuckled again.

'Don't worry Pat, I've made it safe. Just needed a nail shoved into the arming mechanism, where the safety pin usually goes...' He gave it a thump with his fist. 'All good, and safe as houses...'

Pat had everyone behind the wagon. Although it would roll freely along the fifteen feet of steel rails which separated it from the engine, it would take every ounce of strength they had between them, to get the big wagon moving. Only Spike was missing, he remained outside, prowling the shadows on guard.

'Right then,' said Pat, 'Danny's released the wagon's brake. When I say push, I want you to give it everything you have got.' He paused for a moment in the darkness. In earnest, he said, 'This wagon is the difference between life and death to you all. There isn't room for everyone in the driving cab, so we have to attach this bloody thing to the engine, to get you all out of here safely, and we are running out of time. Right, put your shoulders against the buffer bar…Get ready…Now…*Push!*'

Straining against the solid weight of the ore wagon, the survivors from the wrecked Victoria heaved against the broad steel plate, which separated the two rear buffers. For the first muscle tearing moments, the ore wagon refused to budge, but then, suddenly, with the slightest shudder, each of them felt it give, just a fraction. Pat hissed between clenched teeth,

'Keep going…yes!…it's moving.'

Grunting with effort, civilians and troopers alike strained and pushed at the wagon until it began to roll, painfully slowly, towards the engine. The steel wheels squeaked, and the wagon rumbled as it moved, but in two minutes of exhausting, back-breaking effort, the survivors were rewarded with a reassuring thump, as the muffled buffers collided together.

Panting with effort, his shirt drenched with sweat, Pat lent against the buffer bar for a moment, seeking relief for his burning muscles. He said, between gasps,

'That's it! …well done …everybody… Danny …Charlie… get the couplings… sorted.'

As Charlie and Pat lifted the last bergan aboard, having helped each of the civilians to clamber over the ore wagon's steel sides, Pat glanced at the glowing figures of his watch. He was growing increasingly concerned as the minutes ticked by. They had, at last, enjoyed a huge slice of luck, but the veteran SAS sergeant knew it could not last forever. The muted cacophony of super-heated steam escaping from worn valves and rusting pipework was increasing all the time. By now, the hissing must have been detected by the rebels. The others aboard the wagon could also hear the growing noise. They heard too, the urgency and strain in Pat's voice, as he called softly from the edge of the ore wagon to Danny,

'How are we doing? Is there enough steam yet?'

Using his torch to illuminate the gauge for a second, Danny replied,

'Almost. Another ten minutes or so, Pat; that should do it.'

Hope and rising spirits inside the ore wagon were dashed suddenly, when Spike rushed in. Urgently, he hissed towards the dark outline of the train,

'Pat, we're out of time. Patrol coming!'

Chapter Thirty

His face illuminated by the glow of his computer screen, Cornelius reached for the half-empty cup beside his keyboard. He winced, as he absently sipped its lukewarm contents.

The analyst's attention was riveted to the glowing screen. He had spent hours, totally focused, trawling their African Desk intelligence records. He was sitting deep inside the bowels of MI6's ugly HQ building beside the Thames. He had spent the long hours of the night searching for anything, which might help his distant friends.

At last, he had found something interesting, after filtering through vast numbers of computer files comprising dull, geo-political analysis reports; grain harvests, GDP financial projections and the Congo's political stability reports. He also checked a seemingly unending stream of other information, which at first appeared mere trivia. He knew the collective value of such information, however. Individual, routine reports were, in themselves, normally quite useless, but all together; they provided pieces to the jigsaw which created an overall picture of the state of the Congo. When analysed, they gave critical insight to the Ministers who formulated overseas policy, within Her Majesty's government.

Lacking the necessary clearance, and unable to access policy files direct from the Foreign Office, Cornelius was reduced to sifting through thousands of reports, going back five years or more, which had been sent on from Vauxhall, to Whitehall.

Still staring at the screen, he took off his reading glasses, and slowly polished the lenses with his handkerchief. It was peaceful and quiet where he sat. Only Duty Officers and security staff prowled the darkened corridors during the night. That suited Cornelius.

His long search had finally taken him back to the beginning of 2008, when he stumbled across an old telex message from the Pan Global Corporation. As first glance, it was just an internal memo, but Cornelius' instincts were aroused, when the routine report, according to the MI6 classification at its beginning, carried a Level Five (Commercial) Encryption. That was equivalent to military-grade or better, which seemed to Cornelius, too much security for something apparently trivial. Intercepted by GCHQ in Cheltenham as a matter of routine, they ran it through their fabulously powerful array of Cray super computers. Using their highly advanced mathematical algorithms, the encryption was broken within hours, and the contents passed, via the Congo desk upstairs on the fourth floor, to the Foreign Office.

What he had discovered was beyond even his security clearance, and way above his pay grade. Sometimes, he thought sadly, things were better left alone. The information was of no use in saving his friends, and could land him in very serious trouble, now he had inadvertently tapped into the murky world of H.M. governmental foreign policy.

Cornelius whistled softly. A blind man could see the connection he thought, as he finished reading the intercepted telex. Given the current situation in the northern Congo, he finally understood why the Pan Global directors had been part of the Minister's emergency meeting, the previous morning. If they were successful, their corporate dabbling in the Congo could, like the vast reserves of oil recently discovered beneath the wild south Atlantic waters around the Falklands, be worth billions of pounds in the future, to the UK's economy. Right or wrong, this was H.M. Government sponsored regime change, pure and simple. Pan Global, Minister of the Crown David Benchley and the Foreign Office, were all up to their grubby little necks in it...

It was time to go. Pat yelled,

'Jump aboard, Spike.' As Spike scrambled into the ore wagon, Pat turned and shouted to Danny. 'We are out of time. Go with what steam you've got. For Christ's sake Danny, get us out of here!'

Danny heard Spike's desperate warning, and was ready for Pat's order. He tried not to look at the flickering gauge, which was still dangerously short of optimum pressure. Offering up a silent prayer, Danny released the brake handle, threw the forward gear lever into position and spun the steam regulator until it was wide open.

With a roaring chuff from the smoke stack, and a deafening hiss of escaping steam, the ancient engine shuddered, and began to roll forward. Clouds of black smoke and jets of swirling, whooshing steam filled the interior of the engine shed. Coughing, the civilians clasped their hands to their ears, to protect themselves from the terrible din.

Danny had covered the rails inside the shed with sand, to give vital grip between the steel wheels and rails. To his relief, it appeared to be working. The massive drive wheels spun for a second, and then gripped the sand. They slowly began to turn on the polished silver surface of the rusting rails.

Like a steel leviathan, the train rolled closer to the shed's closed doors. Pat had ordered that they remain shut and securely fastened, to hide the light of the firebox, and help deaden the sounds of the escaping steam. There was no time now to jump from the train and open them. Danny and the others could see the looming doors, and ducked.

With an ear-splitting crash, the flat car in front of the engine hit the termite ridden doors, and blasted them apart. The two doors disintegrated in a shower of dust and splinters. Still gathering speed, the engine and ore wagon followed the flatcar, and suddenly the fugitives were clear of the smoke and fumes, and out into the sweet smelling, star-studded night.

There were guttural shouts of surprise and anger from the maim terminus buildings. Two hundred yards behind them, a rebel machine gun suddenly opened fire. It chattered, hosing glittering green tracer towards the fleeing train. It was accompanied by more yelling and a fusillade of rifle fire. Even in the darkness, the guerrillas' target was huge. Bullets cracked like bullwhips overhead, and careened off the steel side and back of the ore wagon. Pat was up in an instant. Fearing an RPG strike; he roared,

'Suppressive fire, lads. Everything you've got ..*NOW!*'

Coughing out clouds of smoke, timed to the growing tempo of the chuffing engine, three AKs opened fire in a deafening crescendo of noise, from the back and sides of the ore wagon, shooting towards the rebel gun flashes, with long raking bursts of automatic fire. Danny snatched up his weapon, and added to the firing as he crouched on the footplate, behind the steel guard at the side of the engine's driving cab.

Releasing an empty magazine from his smoking assault-rifle, it clattered to the floor. Pat slammed another home and, like the others, continued to pour deadly fire onto the chaotic patrol in the growing distance behind them. Danny emptied his full magazine of 30 7.62mm rounds, and then ceased fire. He had only a window of seconds; he must watch the tracks, and look out for their junction with the main line. Charlie had reported there were points somewhere ahead in the darkness. Danny mustn't hit them too fast, or the entire train would tip over, and de-rail.

Hoping he wasn't hit, Pat quickly realised why covering fire had stopped from the driver's cab; Danny had a train to drive. Desperately, with tracer fire flashing past all around him, Pat turned and yelled at Krutz, who was sheltering with the civilians at the bottom of the wagon,

'Get up here, you bastard! We need more firepower!'

Krutz started. The sounds of his name and the battle which raged around them suddenly galvanised him. Like a slap in the face, old disciplines returned; shaking him abruptly from the lonely world of misery and depression to which his mind had retreated. Drawing his pistol, he stood up and glared at Pat. Without a word, grim faced, he cocked his pistol, took aim at the guerrillas and opened fire.

From within the dark shapes of the main engine sheds, there was a sudden flash, and almost instantly, the familiar whoosh of an RPG rocket. It screamed past them and exploded in the darkness beside the fleeing train moments later, with a brilliant orange flash and a deafening roar of thunder.

Under the screamed orders of his officer, the teenaged RPG gunner reluctantly rose up in the darkness, from behind a pile of old railway sleepers. With the fugitives' bullets hammering into the long wooden blocks he had been sheltering behind, and cracking all about him; he quickly took aim, but jerked the RPG's trigger. As a result, he fired his deadly anti-tank rocket wide of the target, before rapidly ducking back behind the stout protection offered by the thick wooden sleepers.

The floor of the ore wagon was littered with spent cartridge cases. Ammunition was running low, but Pat's suppressive fire was working.

'Keep firing!'

Danny was ignoring the fire-fight; his eyes were glued to the smooth lines of the steel rails ahead. Suddenly, the silver lines were interrupted by a spaghetti junction of new rails and points. If Charlie had got it right, they would guide the train onto the main line, and away from the hell of Kabbali. Danny snatched up an oily rag. Using it to cover the hot iron wheel of the steam regulator, he quickly turned it until it was half closed. He stood on the rocking footplate, one eye on the needle within the pressure gauge, with his hand clutching the brake, waiting for the right moment. He was not really sure what would happen, if he applied the brakes too hard. Ever since he was a kid, Danny had always wanted to drive a train. The theory was simple enough, but doing it for the first time, under rebel fire was, in his opinion, pushing it a bit. Dismissing the thought, Danny refocused; now was the time. Trusting to luck, Danny pulled the lever back, but only partially applied the brakes. The whole engine shuddered alarmingly.

To his relief, the combination of reduced steam and brakes worked, and the rhythm of the train changed, as it began to slow. The flatcar hit the points first, with a juddering clatter. Clinging to the cab's hand rail, to Danny's profound relief, it remained upright, and in firm contact with the mainline's rails. The engine followed moments later, and then the ore wagon clattered and vibrated, as its squeaking wheels also rattled over the points.

Pat called a cease fire, and his men's firing stopped.

Clear of imminent derailment, Danny wiped the sweat and grime from his brow, as he offered a silent *thank you* to the Gods of war. Taking a deep breath, he released the brake and opened the steam regulator once again. The nerve jangling squeal beneath the engine disappeared; the tempo of the chuffing engine changed instantly. In hissing clouds of smoke and steam, the old shunting engine began to accelerate slowly into the enveloping darkness. Among its weary defenders, a half-hearted, exhausted cheer of victory rose, as the train began to gather speed.

Settling down to a series of deep rhythmic chuffs, smoke billowing from its stack, the engine and its trucks rattled along the mainline, beneath a peaceful starry sky. Pounding hearts began to slow; every moment took the fugitives further away from the reeking stink of Kabbali, and the horror and madness which roamed within it…

Chapter Thirty-One

As dawn broke in the Congo, Cornelius still sat alone in his office, inside the Ministry of Defence. Without a single word of his friends' fate, or a plan to help them if they still lived, he felt tired to the bone, and utterly useless.

The latest news from the Congo was bad. The Attaché from Kinshasa, having arrived in Katinga province, reported that the Mai-Mai had swept south beyond Birundi, and were now consolidated around Kabbali. Their front was broad; rumours abounded, his report added that so far unchallenged by government forces, they had been holding their front line, and gradually spreading west, towards the Congo's border with Cameroun.

In times gone by, Cornelius would have reached for the bottle to drown his feelings of frustration and despair, but now, with Pat's recent intervention, he was dry, and determined to stay that way. Jennifer had taken him back; his job and reputation were secure, and his life was firmly back on track. He owed so much to the tough, unflinching SAS man who had slipped into his world, and saved him from slithering into self-inflicted destruction. Trapped against a wall of secrecy and Foreign Office plots, he knew there was nothing he could do.

With a sigh, he switched off the glowing monitor, and stood up. He stretched, and rubbed his hand over tired eyes. Cornelius owed so much to the man, who for all he knew might very well be dead. The analyst helped himself to more black coffee. It tasted bitter; he shuddered. At least, he thought, he did not need it to wash down any more bitterness from a handful of aspirins. With another sigh, he sat back at his desk and wracked his brains. Surely, there must be something he could do?

In Kabbali, General Ojukwu listened to the officer, as he reported the incident with the train. Angry and frustrated, the general knew it must be the whites, when the officer reported eight dead, and eleven wounded from the deadly accurate fire, which had erupted from the train, when his men discovered it. The general doubted it had been local inhabitants fleeing on the train. All weapons and ammunition belonging to the national army's small garrison, based just outside the railhead town had been seized by his men, days earlier. The patrol sent in search of the landing craft had found its burnt-out hulk on the banks of the Mpana, less than fifteen miles from Kabbali. There had been bodies, but not enough, which led the general to only one conclusion. The white men and the diamonds were still out there somewhere, but perhaps still remained within his grasp. The fools knew nothing of his intimate knowledge of the railway system in the province. They were flies, who he would trap in his ever expanding web. Smiling with satisfaction at this fresh opportunity, and impressed by his own cunning, he turned to one of his officers and rumbled,

'Have my orders been carried out on the Zamba bridge?'

The Captain lowered his eyes and bowed slightly. Nervously, he replied,

'Yes excellency. Everything was done yesterday before sunset. It is exactly as you instructed…'

The general nodded. A cruel smile of anticipation spread across his face.

'With the bridge already destroyed, there is only one place they can go, and we will be waiting for them....'

After dawn, and now more than thirty miles from Kabbali, Danny noticed something was wrong as the engine's rhythm changed, and it began to slow.

The steam pressure gauge was falling rapidly, despite his best efforts to keep the firebox burning brightly. If something was damaged during the fire-fight, he had to find the problem, and fix it quickly, or they might find themselves permanently stuck out here, in this vast, empty tract of wilderness. He yelled back to Spike, who was on guard, watching the skies in case of another air attack,

'*Spike!* Tell Pat we have got to stop... something's wrong with the engine.' To reinforce his news, Danny drew the flattened edge of his hand across his throat.

Spike raised his eyes to the sky, paused, and then nodded with resignation before ducking down to pass on the message. Danny turned his attention back to his controls, busying himself with closing off the steam regulator, and gently applying the brake.

With a final squeal and loud hiss of steam, the old shunting engine rolled to a stop. Danny fully applied the brake, and then climbed from the driver's cabin onto the dry earth beside the engine, as Pat jumped down from the ore wagon. As he walked towards Danny, Pat lifted his hand to shield his eyes; they narrowed as he surveyed the vast brown savannah which danced in the mornings growing heat around them. Satisfied that although open and exposed, they remained undetected, Pat turned his attention back to Danny,

'*What's up?*'

Danny blew out his cheeks, and pointed up to the left-hand saddle, which held half the engine's precious water. The reservoir's thin steel side plating was riddled with bullet holes. The saddle's outer skin was stained with rust and water, which had gradually escaped, but not yet fully evaporated.

'That is the problem, Pat. We've lost nearly half our water, and the steam pressure has dropped accordingly.

Pat stared at the bullet-riddled side of the water tank. Angered by this latest twist, he spat,

'*Damn!*...Can you fix it?'

Barney Morris suddenly lent over the side of the Ore wagon, and angrily demanded,

'What now, for God's sake?'

The two SAS men ignored him. Danny shrugged,

'I can probably plug the holes with rags. The water is not under pressure in the tanks thankfully; the system is gravity fed. The other side's tank looks fine, but we'll need to take on water more often, as I doubt the patches will be fully watertight.'

Pat nodded and said grimly,

'OK Danny. Do as much as you can, as quickly as you can. I'll get the others to climb down and help you. Once that's done, can you switch to the other tank for now?'

Danny grinned, as Morris yelled again,

'*Oi!* Are you both deaf? Why have we stopped?'

The two SAS men turned, and glared the reporter into an embarrassed silence. Danny turned back to Pat and said,

'Shouldn't be a problem,' he shrugged, and stared across the arid land around them, which stretched in all directions to the distant horizon, 'Trouble is, Pat, I don't know what range we've got now, with the water that is left in the one good tank.'

Pat shrugged. He knew there was nothing for it, and said,

'Well, we have got at least a couple of hours' worth of water in the other tank, and we certainly can't stay here, Danny. I don't see we have a choice. When you've switched tanks, and got some more steam up, we'll just have to push on, and find some water up ahead.'

'And keep our fingers crossed, sergeant?' said Danny with feigned innocence.

Pat nodded. With an exasperated and humourless snort, he replied,

'Yeah, pretty much same as always mate, ever since we got here...'

Pat rode on the engine's footplate for the rest of the morning. The holes were patched, but the damaged tank remained empty. They crossed plenty of water courses cut into the iron-hard ground, but they were bone dry. Danny had stopped the train twice, and banged the side of the good saddle tank, to gauge the remaining supply of water. When he returned to the footplate for the second time, he did not look too impressed, and said,

'We are getting a bit short, Pat. I reckon we have got about another hour before we run dry.' He pounded the saddle with his fist, 'This old girl was never designed with long trips in mind.'

Pat glanced towards the open fuel bunker at the back of the driver's cab. It was also getting ominously low. Pat stared ahead, at the mountains which now cleaved the horizon.

'If we can make it another fifteen miles or so, and get to those hills ahead, we should be able to find a stream running off them to refill both tanks…can you make it that far?'

Danny pulled a face; only one answer seemed appropriate,

'I'll bleeding have to, won't I?'

The train clattered over a set of points. The spur which spliced to the main line looked overgrown and pitted with weeds. The rusting rails swung away after a few hundred yards and disappeared into the foothills which now surrounded the fugitives. The terrain had changed again; no longer surrounded by dry, open savannah, they rode through lush forest for the last ten minutes, which softly clothed the rolling hills around them.

As the train limped slowly around a steep curve, Pat saw the dark shape of a huddle of single storey buildings, a little more than a few hundred yards ahead, surmounted by the distinctive shape of a water tower, close beside the tracks.

His caution aroused, Pat said,

'Better stop, Danny, while we take a look.'

Danny nodded, and began to slow the train. Pat turned, and whistled. Spike looked towards the engine, and his sergeant. Above the noise of the hissing engine, Pat pointed to Spike, and then placed his flat hand on his head. Pat pointed to his eye, and then the buildings ahead.

The signals were as clear as the spoken word to the trooper. Pat wanted him to accompany him on a recce. Spike nodded his understanding. Checking the magazine was full, and his AK's safety catch was on, Spike climbed down from the wagon, and joined Pat beside the track. Pat was sweeping the area around the buildings with his binoculars. Satisfied that no obvious threat existed, he lowered them and said,

'We'll go and check out the buildings on foot, Spike. It looks peaceful enough, but I would rather eyeball the place and make sure, before we bring the train in and fill the tanks from the water tower,'

Pat looked up at the ore wagon, at Charlie, who was staring down at them,

'Charlie, keep your eyes open, and give us covering fire if we need it. Spike and I are going ahead to take a quick look around... Tell Danny, I will wave you forward when I'm happy, clear?'

Charlie nodded silently. Pat turned back to Spike, and said,

'Come on then. You take the right-hand side of the track, and I will go left... Let's go.'

Sense's alert, and rifles held ready; the two men moved cautiously towards the way station. They swept the surrounding forest as they approached, but just distant, unseen animal calls and the occasional shrill cry of some exotic bird, hidden high in the forest's canopy, drew their attention. The only other noise they heard was the sound of their boots crunching on the dry ballast underfoot.

When they reached the first shed, Pat raised his arm. Spike saw the signal, and stopped. He waved Spike towards the nearest hut. Spike glanced in through the grimy window, then, to show no-one was home, shook his head towards Pat. Spike tried the door handle; it was unlocked.

They searched the shed, but found only a collection of rusting track laying equipment and an array of discarded tools. The next shed contained half a dozen soiled mattresses on the floor. On a shelf were some chipped cooking pots. An old gas ring, on an equally ancient wooden table, stood beneath them.

The small office yielded little; a faded timetable pinned to the wall. Next to it, hung a map of the region, displaying details of the mainline, and the spur they passed minutes earlier. It showed something else; the position of the bridge over the Zamba River. The bridge stood just a couple of miles further ahead on the main line. There was one more thing in the room, which caught Pat's attention. Mounted on the wall, in a gloomy corner, was a telephone.

Pat stared at it for a moment without expectation, and then nodded into the gloom.

'We might as well finish the sweep in here, by checking that out, Spike.'

Spike nodded, and walked over to the telephone. Quickly checking for booby-traps, Spike licked his lips, and snatched up the receiver. The line was as dead as mutton. Attached to the box below the telephone's cradle was a pitted brass crank handle. Keeping the receiver against his ear, he turned to Pat and said,

'Give it a go?'

Pat nodded,

'Why not,' he said absently with a shrug, 'nothing to lose…'

Spike grasped the crank handle, and turned it vigorously. The telephone jangled as he spun it. Unfortunately, he heard only silence. Disappointed, Spike looked at his sergeant, and shook his head. Not expecting anything to come of it, Pat shrugged again and turned towards the door. Spike glared at the device, and spun the crank again, this time even more vigorously. The gesture was part hope, but more, forged in frustration. He was about to hang up, when there was a sudden hollow click from the bakelite earpiece, and a crackling burst of static. Spike's eyes opened wide with shock, when a distant, heavily accented female voice suddenly answered,

'*Hallo?...*'

It took heart-stopping minutes to connect via the international exchange in Kinshasa, with the London emergency number he had memorised, before Pat and the others had left Kenya. When the collect call was finally established, the duty officer he spoke to at the Foreign Office, was suspicious at first, believing it was just some elaborate crank call. It was only when Pat mentioned him by name, and demanded to be put through to Cornelius' extension in the basement of the Ministry of Defence, that the duty officer realised the call was genuine...

After he had finished speaking, Pat hung up and stroked his chin. Bursting with excitement, Spike eagerly asked,

'What do you think then, Pat, what did Cornelius say?'

Swatting at a fly which buzzed about his head, Pat calmly answered,

'Cornelius says the latest intelligence is that the bridge ahead has been blown, so we can't get out that way. He suggested we try the spur, back a couple of miles along the main line. Apparently, it serves an old iron-ore mine. Cornelius said the spur was originally built by the Belgians for direct export, and runs in a wide loop through the hills, straight down to the border with Cameroun.

Spike's face clouded, as his stomach tightened,

'Is it still in use then?'

Pat shook his head.

'Cornelius didn't know for sure, he'd pulled out a satellite picture while we were talking. He could not vouch for its serviceability, so I think we'll have to take it pretty slowly.'

Something more serious was worrying Spike,

'But doesn't that mean swinging back into enemy held territory, Pat?

Pat nodded,

'Yes, I'm afraid, according to what Cornelius told me, that is exactly what it means. Trouble is, it is the only option left to us, Spike. We have no other choice, and nowhere else to go; so we have got to risk it.'

With resignation oozing from every pore in his face, Spike sighed. How many more times would salvation be snatched from them, he wondered, just when they thought they had finally escaped? His voice lacked its usual enthusiasm, and sounded bitter as he said,

'What about this place then, Pat? Can we risk staying here while we refuel?'

Pat nodded, 'I reckon this must be some sort of track repair station, but the gang that works the area probably heard the bang from the bridge, and legged it. We can't stay for long, but judging from the lack of damage, the rebels have not been here yet, or just haven't bothered to trash the place, or cut the telephone wires.'

Deciding on balance it was safe, Pat added, 'See if you can find any food Spike, while I go and call the train in.'

Pat stepped outside. Standing beside a pile of logs, he waved his arm, and beckoned the train towards the deserted track depot.

Once the water had been replenished, and the engine's bunker filled with split logs, Pat spread out the map he had found in the office, and held a quick briefing to the whole party. Using a stick, he pointed to the spot in the middle of the map, and said,

'We are here folks,' tracing the marked route of the railway, he continued, 'the bridge ahead is gone, so we are going to back-track a couple of miles, and use the spur we passed to reach safety over the border in Cameroun. As I have already mentioned, our people in London will arrange safe passage for all of us, once we cross the border. With the water and fuel we have taken on board, if the patches hold, we should be good for at least another hundred miles or so, before we need to stop again.' Pat added a smile of reassurance. 'With luck though, we should be in friendly territory, long before then.'

Barney Morris sneered,

'Oh really, you think?'

Resisting a sudden surge of rage, and the impulse to floor him, Pat gave the slightest shake of his head towards all three troopers, who had angrily taken a half step towards the reporter. Pat noted their loyalty, but now was not the time to deal with Morris. Deliberately ignoring the newsman, Pat said brightly,

'Right then, we're pretty much set, so we go in five…'

Sitting high on an adjacent hill, beneath the cool shade of a tall tree, the Mai-Mai officer, whose men had destroyed the bridge in the twilight of the previous evening, lowered his binoculars. He stubbed out his cigarette on the ground beside him, and exhaled the last of the tobacco smoke in his lungs. Lazily, he reached for the handset of his Russian-made radio as the little train began to puff clouds of smoke across the narrow floor of the valley below, as it reversed slowly back down the gradient. He shivered involuntarily, in awe of his general's powerful spell, which was leading them into a trap. With a cruel smile, the rebel pressed the radio's send switch...

'Allo Almighty... 'allo Almighty....Eagle one is here...over.'

Chapter Thirty-Two

It took all three troopers to throw the rusted lever. The mechanism had screeched and squealed in loud protest before reluctantly swinging the points into place. Unlike the main lines shinny upper surface, which was polished by regular use; the entire surface of the spur's rails was covered in dull rust, with a profusion of plants growing in the ballast between them. The wooden sleepers supporting the rails looked pitted and rotten; they were stained and marked with a decade or more of neglect.

As the hissing train slowly rumbled over the spur line's points, Pat leant out of the driver's cab, and eyed the overgrown rails in front of the rumbling flat car, with growing concern. The tracks ahead looked almost derelict, as if they hadn't been used in years.

Pat had seen enough. He heaved himself back into the cab,

'Better keep the speed right down, Danny. It doesn't look like this line has had any traffic on it for years.' Danny agreed,

'It might be worth putting someone out on foot, to walk the track ahead of the train, Pat. I can easily keep the speed down to walking pace, until we're sure the tracks are safe.'

Pat nodded,

'Agreed Danny; that makes good sense. Stop the engine for a minute, and I'll sort out a volunteer.'

'There's no problem. I need someone to walk ahead of the train, and check the track.'

Before anyone else could speak, Krutz said quickly,

'I'll do it!'

Pat shrugged, and said,

'Sure, OK. As long as you feel up to it?'

Krutz scowled at Pat, as he climbed down. When he was safely beside Pat, and away from the others, he whispered almost apologetically,

'Look man, losing my men hit me really hard…we are still in danger, and I need to start pulling my weight again, OK?'

Pat understood. He had lost friends in the past, and knew the bitter pain Krutz was enduring. He said,

'Fair enough. I'll spell you after an hour, and put one of my boys on it.' As Krutz turned to go, Pat added, 'you don't need to carry your pack with you, you know. Throw it into the wagon, it will be safe enough there.'

Krutz shook his head. The pack and its contents were all he had left, all he could salvage from the whole disastrous mission. His eyes narrowed. Suddenly, his face flushed and he flared at Pat,

'*No!*...It stays with me. Nobody touches it...*understand?*'

Surprised by the Boer's angry reaction, Pat held his hands up and said,

'Fine, it's your call mate...We'll follow about fifty yards behind you. If you want us to stop, just raise your arm.' As Krutz turned to go, Pad added, 'And stay in sight of the train, so we can cover you...'

At walking pace, progress was painfully slow. Several miles along the winding spur, Krutz suddenly raised his arm. Pat ordered the train stopped. He dismounted and jogged up to Krutz. What he saw left him instantly dismayed. Twenty yards ahead, an ancient iron bridge spanned a deep gully cut into the hillside by a stream, which splashed and foamed through the jagged boulders, which lay more than fifty feet below it. The damage was instantly obvious. One of the bridge supports was gone; its foundation washed away in the catechism of some past storm. The track still looked sound enough, but in its damaged condition, Pat wondered, could the bridge take the train's weight?

Staring at the damage, Krutz growled,

'Well, what do you think?'

Pat stared at the bridge for a moment. It had been designed and built to carry heavy engines and fully loaded ore wagons. With just a couple of empty wagons, and a small shunting engine, the odds seemed at least fair that they could make it safely across. Pat chewed on it for a moment longer, and then said,

'We'll have to risk it,' to reinforce the point, he shook his head, 'we can't go back. We're inside enemy territory again, and still a long way from the border. It will be dark in a couple of hours, and I don't want to spend the night trapped here, with no way forward if we get bumped.' Pat nodded back towards the engine and wagons, 'it's a relatively light train, so we'll get the civilians off, and take it over, really slowly.'

Krutz scowled,

'I think it would be better to take a run at it, and get across quickly.'

Pat shook his head,

'No. The sudden pounding and vibrations might cause more damage, and bring the whole lot down before we can get the train even half-way.'

His decision made, Pat turned, and waved the train forward. With a fresh hiss of steam, Danny released the brake, and the train began to rumble along the track.

With everyone off the train and gathered around him, Pat briefly explained the situation, and his plan,

'Right then, this is what we're going to do. We need to get past this obstacle before it gets dark. Spike and Charlie will lead you over to the other side of the bridge on foot, in a minute or two. When you're all safe, Danny and I will bring the train over, nice and slowly…

Once we're over, we'll get you all back on-board, and push on to the border until it gets dark. Questions?'

For once, to Pat's relief, Barney Morris remained silent. Everyone realised the danger, but what other options were there? The men sent from the High Commission in Nairobi, had got them this far, and none of the civilians had anything useful to contribute. Krutz said,

'I'll go over first.'

Pat nodded,

'Fair enough.'

With the civilians waiting safely on the far side, standing on the driver's footplate, Pat turned to Danny,

'OK, you know the drill. We'll ease the train over, as slowly as we can. I'll hang out and watch the bridge as we cross. If we need to gun the power, I'll yell,' with a reassuring wink, he added, 'Don't worry, we'll make it....you ready?'

Danny nodded. He had his reservations, but showing fear wasn't done. Pat walked to the side of the footplate. Turning at the edge, Pat grasped the handrails and lent backwards. With a sniff, grim faced, he shouted above the hissing steam,

'Right Danny, let's do it!'

Danny swallowed hard, and released the brake. He reached up and carefully opened the steam valve just a little, until he was rewarded, as the hissing engine began to roll slowly forward.

The flat wagon reached the edge of the bridge first. Hanging precariously over the side, Pat stared intently at the iron supports beneath. So far, he saw nothing new to concern him. The engine chugged slowly forward, until it too began to cross. As the last drive wheels bore down onto the bridge, there was a grinding squeal of metal somewhere underneath, and almost imperceptibly at first, the engine began to tip over to one side. Something supporting the engine was buckling under the weight, Pat realised with horror. He knew there was no time to stop and make another inspection. It was a balls to the wall moment. Still staring down at the buckled supports, he yelled desperately,

'It's OK, Danny, keep going…nice and steady!'

The sound of groaning metal was getting louder, overcoming even the hissing of the engine. Suddenly, something fell from the bridge. A rusted iron girder, torn from its mountings, splashed into the water as it crashed and clanged against the jagged rocks below. The engine continued forward, but tipped even more, as the rail and track bed beneath it began to ominously sag to one side.

The two women watching from the far side threw their hands to their mouths in horror, as the engine suddenly yawed drunkenly. One screamed her anguish, as another piece of metal tore loose from its crumbling brick supports, and crashed into the foaming water below. Thinking his two friends were about to die, helplessly, Spike whispered,

'Oh, Jesus!'

Ancient rivets popped and sheared beneath the train's crushing weight, as it continued inexorably on its perilous journey, and continued to rumble across the empty void below.

Pat still hung precariously from the engine. He yelled to Danny,

'Almost there!...keep it steady...'

With nothing to do, white faced; Danny didn't move. Sweat ran down his forehead, washing the smuts and sooty grime from his cheeks. He felt the engine begin to tip through his boots on the footplate. Grimly, he braced himself and hung onto a handrail, ready to open the steam valve, the moment Pat demanded it.

Pat watched as the flat car's wheels reached the middle of the bridge. If he was right, the other half of the bridge was sound; the central column and the intricate lattice of supports beyond seemed in good shape, when he had inspected both sides, before bringing the train over.

Slowly, the flat car began to straighten and level on the track. The engine followed, and straightened as it reached the central support column. Pat heaved himself back into the cab. He saw Danny's ashen face. With a triumphant grin, his heart thumping, Pat couldn't resist it,

'Having fun yet?'

Back on firm ground, clear of the bridge, Pat ordered Danny to stop the train. With his heart still hammering fast enough to burst through his chest, Danny closed the valve. Shutting his eyes, he gratefully slumped backwards against the steel wall of the wood bunker, and slid slowly to the floor.

Pat watched Danny for a moment in silence. He knew the massive rush Danny was dealing with. The mixture of abject terror and an overdose of pure adrenaline, pumped into his bloodstream by a pounding heart and overworked adrenal glands, was a powerful, heady brew. Danny would be fine, but needed a minute to get over it. Pat felt the same way, but this was why he had come back to the Regiment. A dull, flat civilian existence, dealing with the mundane, routine chores of living in society just hadn't cut it for Pat. After the constant excitement and rigours of life in the regular SAS, he'd fallen into the miserable black hole of civilian routine. Comradeship, adrenaline, and moments like this, he knew, were the real motivations to his enlistment into the SAS reserve...

Life, Pat knew, was never more precious and exhilarating, than when it hung by the slenderest of threads...

Chapter Thirty-Three

David Benchley replaced the telephone receiver, and looked smugly towards the concerned faces of the other two men sitting in on his latest briefing. After the unexpected news from the Congo, quickly passed back to the Foreign Office by Cornelius, his telephone call had just gone well. The French Red Cross had agreed to send in a small team to the crossing at Mongoumbe, between the Congo and Cameroun border. Their mission, under the protection of the U.N., was to receive the train, and the refugees it contained. Once they were on Cameroun soil, the Red Cross would arrange their safe repatriation back to the United Kingdom.

Benchley had noted that the Pan Global directors had shown little reaction or emotion when he reported a number of their employees had been murdered, but did show considerable interest, almost excitement, when he told them that one, Otto Krutz, remained alive. The Minister dismissed the thought; there were more important issues to discuss. He said,

'It would appear that General Ojukwu has become the major player in northern Congo, gentlemen. Tell me, under the umbrella of Condor, what exactly are you planning to do about your own Corporation's involvement there?'

Franz De Keizer shuffled in his seat uncomfortably for a moment. Realising that prevarication was futile, he came straight to the point. He said,

'Well Minister, it's simple really. Our Chairman thinks that circumstances have changed dramatically, and we have inadvertently backed the wrong horse. Having already committed to so much planning, effort and resources into Condor, he believes that given Ojukwu's recent success, it is time to drop the Tutsi guerrillas, switch sides, and support Ojukwu's Congo Freedom Party.'

Benchley nodded,

'Go on…'

'Minister, we will not move without the agreement of your Ministry of course, but we are ready to begin negotiations with Ojukwu, once we have your quiet nod of agreement.'

The Minister clasped his fingers together, and rested his hands on his desk. Perhaps, he thought, something might yet be salvaged. He turned to De Keizer's companion,

'Do you have anything to add, Mr Campbell?'

Archie Campbell cleared his throat, which did nothing to remove the scowl from his face. His conscience pricked him, despite his involvement. He had a reputation in the city for being blunt. Looking sternly at the blotter in front of him, he said icily,

'I think it is a perfectly sound manoeuvre from a business point of view, but frankly, it sticks in my craw to even contemplate dealing with a bloody murderer like Ojukwu.'

David Benchley smiled. He held up his hand in acknowledgement. A resigned, almost condescending sigh escaped him, as he replied,

'Mr Campbell, as a matter of course, my Ministry deals on a day to day basis with a number of dictators in Africa, all of whom has plenty of innocent blood on their hands. Every single one of them are vile, corrupt despots, who steal British taxpayer's aid money, and food we send from their own starving people, and pocket the proceeds in offshore accounts around the world. They strictly control their state-run press and judiciary, and enforce their power using a secret police force, which routinely use torture and brutality on their own citizens, without the slightest redress. The only difference between them and

Ojukwu is that they currently hold the reins of power, and the office of their nation's Presidency.'

Archie Campbell nodded in silence; he was Pan Global's African Operations Director, and knew the cruel truth in the Minister's words. Frowning, he said,

'Aye, I know, but it's still a bitter pill to swallow.'

The Minister nodded,

'Yes it is, Mr Campbell, but that is how international politics works; I'm afraid. We are a trading nation, and must do deals, and find markets for our services and products where we can. When, for example, considering exports licences, the Foreign Office must regularly turn a blind eye, whatever the circumstances or internal actions of any particular overseas government.' He turned back to De Keizer. 'I think we should drop the moral angle of this discussion. It is pointless to pursue it any further.'

The clock chimed ten behind the two directors. The Minister continued.

'If we drill down to the bedrock of this situation, we have a simply dilemma, gentlemen. Given the new circumstances; either we agree to back Ojukwu, or both Her Majesty's government, and Pan Global will, in the next few years, come out of this mess as losers.'

Both directors nodded reluctantly. Seeing their tacit agreement, David Benchley delivered his decision,

'In principle, we are in agreement then, but I suggest you hedge yours bets and leave, at least in morale terms, your support for the Tutsi rebels in place, for the time being, anyway, until you have successfully concluded firm agreement with the C.F.P..' With a formal nod which safeguarded Pan Global's future, the Minister said,

'You may, gentlemen, begin negotiations with Ojukwu, with my Ministry's…ah?… unofficial blessings…'

Their meeting concluded, the two directors nodded their thanks, and stood up to leave. David Benchley rose with them. An aide rapped softly on the door, and stepped into his office. She handed the Minister a memo, and withdrew. After quickly scanning it, David Benchley removed his reading glasses and sat down heavily. Lifting the paper, he said gravely,

'There has been yet another twist to the situation in the Congo, gentlemen. I'm sorry to tell you, that according to this message intercepted by GCHQ, the border crossing at Mongoumbe fell to the rebels, yesterday morning… Unfortunately, we have no way of warning our people, who now, given our change in circumstances, have become an embarrassment to our respective future dealings with the C.F.P. We will simply have to hope the Brigadier's men realise the checkpoint is in rebel hands,' Benchley shrugged, '… and they don't end up dying in sight of it.'

The night was uneventful for the fugitives. They had made good progress for the rest of the previous day, after the incident at the bridge. Reluctantly, Pat had ordered the train stopped, as the sun disappeared behind the horizon. Unable to see the track clearly anymore, he judged it safer to stop, and give his charges a much-needed rest, rather than risk derailing on a stretch of damaged track, or perhaps even bump an enemy patrol, in the darkness.

Shaken awake by Charlie, who had drawn the last guard duty, Danny rose an hour before dawn to raise fresh steam, and check his temporary repairs to the water jacket were still in place. As he packed the smouldering firebox with timber, yawning, Pat joined him on the footplate,

'How much water have we got left, Danny?'

'We've used about half, Pat.'

Pat nodded. Pulling out the map he had taken from the way station, he jammed himself into a sheltered corner of the driver's cab. His pencil torch flicked on, as he studied the map for several minutes, judging time and distance of the miles they had travelled so far. Satisfied that he knew where they currently were, he flicked off the torch and stood up,

'I reckon we still have about fifteen miles to go before we reach the border Danny. At the rate we travelled yesterday, that should put us very near by late afternoon.' Pat thought for a moment, 'I'm not happy with the speed the rebels seem to be able to travel across the province, so I want to do a full target recce on the border, before we try to cross. We're so close; I'd hate to blow it now, and get us all killed, by not knowing exactly what's in front of us, when we get there. We'll stop and lay up a few miles short, while I take one of the boys with me, and go and have a good long look at what's happening there, yes?'

Danny could see the sense of Pat's plan. Intelligence gathering and reconnaissance were fundamental to the SAS, and like the other troopers, he trusted Pat's judgement one hundred per cent. Pat scratched the stubble on his chin and said wistfully,

'Shame our supplies have all gone…I could murder a brew!'

The train passed the deserted ore mine just after midday. The derelict facility was an obvious causality to the ravages of neglect, weather and the surrounding jungle, which was slowly encroaching, and reclaiming it. Ignoring the temptation to stop, Pat wanted to push on, so they continued their slow meandering journey through the jungle covered hills, towards the unseen border. In the early afternoon, Pat checked his map and ordered Danny to stop the train, concealed within a deep valley, besides a fast-flowing river. Checking the prismatic compass he habitually carried, Pat climbed into the ore wagon, and briefed the passengers,

'We'll stop here, while Spike and I go forward to take a look at the border. According to the map, it will take us a good couple of hours on foot if we follow the track, so we're going to take a shortcut across the hills. It will be a stiff climb, but will save us at least an hour both ways. Staying away from the tracks also avoids the two of us running into an ambush. We should to be back around dark, with a clearer picture of what is going on at the crossing…if its all clear, we'll go straight across the border into Cameroun, tonight.'

It was Morris again, who voiced the question on everyone's mind,

'But what if it's not all clear?'

Pat's eyes glittered dangerously. He had tried hard to find something he liked about the man, but had come up short, every time. Matching the reporter's sarcastic tone, he replied,

'Well, I'll have to think of something else then, won't I?'

The two SAS men had long recovered from the difficult approach to the border. It had been a demanding forced march through hot, virgin jungle. When they had slipped over the last ridge, Pat spent precious time searching for the ideal lying-up point, to fulfil their reconnaissance mission. Moving cautiously, both slid on their bellies into the observation point Pat had chosen. It was shaded, and well camouflaged with natural foliage. The concealed observation point provided an excellent panoramic view of the valley below. It also fulfilled the last vital criteria Pat sought. The OP offered a concealed exit route, if they found themselves in danger of discovery, and need to bug out in a real hurry.

Surrounded by the buzz of unseen insects, their faces and arms smeared with dark soil, Pat and Spike lay sweating, concealed in deep cover, just below the top of the ridge line. Below and to the right of their position, the single track appeared abruptly from the jungle, running straight down a long sloping gradient, framed on both sides by dense bush. Less than half a mile from where they lay, the silver tracks ran up to a clearing, and then disappeared beyond a closed red and white gate. Either side of the swing-arm barrier, were high parallel chain-link fences, separated by fifty feet of ploughed earth. The two fences appeared to merge into one, as they ran away into the shimmering distance. Spike handed the binoculars back to his sergeant and said softly,

'Jesus Pat... We're stuffed!'

Remaining silent, Pat raised the binos to his eyes once again; he slowly swept them over the crossing. Spike was right.

Two bodies dressed in the green uniforms of the national army of the Congo, hung limply from a telegraph pole in the airless atmosphere of the valley floor. Beside the hanged border guards, close to the barrier, was a dilapidated single-story office building. Ignoring the bodies, Pat made another sweep, as he tallied a rough count. By his reckoning, he estimated there must be at least two hundred armed guerrillas swarming around the barrier, on the Congo side of the border.

Many of the rebels were toiling in the relentless heat of the afternoon. Several groups were setting up heavy machine guns on either side of the crossing. Others were busy siting a mortar. Close to the barrier, more rebels were working in pairs. Swarming around the track, they were building a barricade. Stripped to the waist, the rebels were laying heavy wooden railway sleepers across the track; bracing them with vertical timbers driven into the ground. The two SAS men couldn't hear the barked orders, but could see what must be officers waving their arms and directing the tasks, as they urged their men to work harder.

Pat adjusted the focus of the binos, and swept beyond the fences. Given the distance, he couldn't see any real detail, but there were several figures wearing the unmistakable light blue helmets of the United Nations, observing the guerrillas' activity from the other side of the border. Pat cursed softly. Salvation was tantalisingly close, but might as well be a million miles away.

Under the distant gaze of Pat and Spike, after almost half an hour of heavy work; their bodies glistening with sweat, the rebels were finished. The completed barrier looked ominously solid. It was several sleepers thick, spanned the single track comfortably, and stood at least twelve feet high. Spike whistled softly,

'Hell fire, Pat. Looks like that bloody barricade could easily de-rail the train.' He chewed on his lip anxiously and his brow furrowed, 'What on earth are we going to do now?'

Pat lowered his binoculars. He turned his head slowly towards the trooper. Sternly, he replied,

'We'll do exactly what we've been trained to do, Spike.'

Taking his notepad from his back pocket, Pat began to draw a detailed sketch map of the border crossing, marking in the heavy weapon positions, structures and general layout of the clearing. When he had finished, he checked it carefully for detail, then marked in the geographical features which surrounded the border post. He finished by putting a question mark between the thin lines he had drawn, depicting the double border fence, Satisfied, he turned the map over, and began noting weapon types, vehicle locations, enemy numbers and anything else, which seemed relevant, which might help him later. Finally, below his notes, he made a detailed sketch of the barrier the rebels had built.

When he had finished mapping, he snapped the notebook shut. Keeping his narrowed eyes on the crossing, he said thoughtfully,

'Right, I've got enough.' Pat turned his head towards Spike, 'come on, let's get back to the others... I've got some serious planning to do.'

Chapter Thirty-Four

As the light began to fade, to the obvious relief of everyone who had remained behind, Pat and Spike returned to the train.

Pat called his men together first; he wanted to informally update Danny and Charlie on the new developments on the border, which he and Spike had discovered. Briefing like this was a common feature of the SAS. Fondly known within the Regiment as *Chinese Parliaments*, everyone had an equal chance of offering ideas based on their own skill sets, and injecting whatever useful input they thought might help. Pat started the briefing,

'Right lads, here's the situation. The rebels must have guessed we're coming, and have blocked the rail line crossing into Cameroun. There are several hundred of the buggers over there, and they've got the place pretty well sown up.' Pat opened his notebook, and showed them the sketches he had made. He pointed to the border fence lines first, and the question mark between them. 'I reckon the area sandwiched between the fences was most likely mined by the government, whenever they built the crossing.' Pat looked up from his sketch, and stared at his troopers in turn, 'it won't be like the one we crossed before at Kabbali; it will most likely be properly laid, with a much higher concentration of underground pressure mines, and probably guarded by surface trip-wire mines. Frankly, we got lucky outside Kabbali, but I wouldn't fancy our chances crossing this one, especially with the civvies in tow.'

All three troopers nodded without reservation; clearly, the experience of breaching one minefield was enough to convince each of them that their sergeant was right. Pat continued,

'I've no idea how far the minefield stretches in either direction, so I'm not even going to consider the option of trying to cross it anymore.' Pat turned the map over, and pointed to the sketch of the barricade. 'We can't slip past the border crossing on foot. It's too heavily guarded, which means our only option… is to use the train.'

Danny interrupted, with his eyes fixed on the sketch. With a frown, he shook his head and said, almost apologetically,

'I can't possibly ram that barricade with the train, Pat. It will de-rail the whole lot if I hit it at flank speed.'

Pat nodded. Calmly, he said,

'Yes, I know that Danny, and there lays the problem. If we hit it too hard, the train will de-rail. If we try to hit it slowly, and shunt the barricade aside, the rebels will swarm all over us. We'll do an ammunition check in a minute, but with what we've already used; we simply won't have the firepower to keep them off our backs for more than a few seconds.'

There was a gloomy silence between them for a few moments. Pat had said enough; they all knew the situation now. He said,

'Right, get away and have a think about what I've told you. Unload your begans from the wagon, and then bring them over here. We'll do a thorough inventory of everything we've got left that might come in handy, before I work out what we're going to do. Get everything laid neatly so I can see it, while I go and have a quick chat with the civvies, and bring them up to date.'

As his men sauntered back to the train, Pat watched in silence as they walked away. He'd faced life-and-death situations before, during a long career with the regular, and now, reserve SAS Regiments. This time, however, the situation was a real mess. The truth, he thought grimly, was that their current situation was nothing short of bloody awful...

Pat's equipment check made bleak viewing. Danny had laid a full thirty round AK magazine on the ground in front of his bergan, and a half-full 9mm pistol mag. Spike had only fifteen rounds left for his AK, and nine pistol bullets. He also placed the bullet-holed radio on the ground. Pat hoped for more spare ammunition, but they'd come into the Congo travelling light, and he knew the two suppressive fire-fights his men fought, simply ate up their ammunition at a hideous rate.

So far, the inspection offered Pat no inspiration. He turned to Charlie, who had covered his offerings with a towel. To his surprise, Charlie was wearing a smug grin on his face. Pat was not in the mood. He glowered at Charlie,

'What are you smirking about?'

Charlie's grin stayed where it was. He said,

'I've only got twelve rounds left for my AK, Pat, but I've also been lugging this lot across Africa in my bergan, for the last few days...'

With a flourish, he pulled the towel aside. Pat's face registered his surprise. He'd assumed Charlie had left his inventory on the plane, along with the RPG. Pat's mouth fell open for a split-second, as he whispered,

'Bloody hell!'

Laid out neatly on the ground, were two directional claymore mines. Inside their plastic bodies, were six hundred tightly packed and extremely lethal ball-bearings. When the claymores exploded, the ball-bearings were projected into an instant, expanding cloud of deadly shrapnel. Little bigger than a box of chocolates, to ensure the projectiles were sent on the right direction, the American manufacturers had stamped an idiot's guide on the front of the mine; it said simply, *'Point towards enemy'*

Beside the mines lay some eight-ounce sticks of plastic explosive, a roll of det cord and a small metal box, which Pat assumed contained detonators. Pat licked his lips and looked up at Charlie, but Charlie was in his element, and wore a devilish sparkle in his eye. He hadn't finished yet. Triumphantly, he said,

'I've got something else Pat, which I couldn't bear to leave behind.' Charlie bent forward, and slowly lifted his bergan. Pat felt his heart thump in his chest. He laughed out loud with surprise. Lying there in front of him was the heavy anti-tank mine Charlie had lifted from under the track in Kabbali. Embarrassed, Charlie inspected his boots and said,

'Sorry Pat, I know I should have left it behind, but it's quite safe,' he shrugged and pointed towards the mine at his feet, 'there's at least thirty-five pounds of really powerful high-explosive packed inside that thing. You did say we should replenish our stocks when we could...'

But his sergeant wasn't listening. The first glimmer of a plan flashed into Pat's head, as he stared unblinking at the Chinese anti-tank mine, and the small pile of explosives in front of it. A sudden surge of relief flowed through him, as things rapidly started falling into place. Nodding his head with satisfaction, Pat looked up. Triumphantly, he said,

'Charlie laddie; I take back everything bad I've ever said about you....you are a genuine, one hundred per cent, genius!'

Charlie had half-expected a balling out. He stepped back in mock surprise and said,

'I am? Oh,... thank you very much!'

The other two troopers grinned at Charlie's apparent confusion. After working closely with him for almost a year now, they both recognised the sudden, devious look on their sergeant's face, and sensed Pat was onto something. Filled with growing encouragement and anticipation, Spike said eagerly,

'So what's the plan then, Pat? What exactly are we going to do?'

As Spike and Danny unloaded the iron pipes from the flat car, and busied themselves under Charlie's direction at the front of the train, Pat put the finishing touches to the rough model he had laid out on the ground, to brief everyone before they set off. He used string to show the border fences; an empty tin represented the office building, and a sling taken from an AK was the railway track. Pat referred constantly to his sketch map; he used stones to show where the machine guns and mortar were located. He finished the layout by scattering leaves to represent the surrounding jungle, and placing a fat twig across the sling, to display the barrier the rebels had erected. Making a last reference to the sketch, fully satisfied with his efforts, Pat walked away from the model to check on his trooper's progress.

Danny and Spike were working at the front of the train. Charlie laboured alone. Lost in concentration, Pat found him kneeling on the wooden floor of the flat-bed, busy unrolling his spool of det cord. It was standard issue, and useful stuff to anyone trained in demolition. It always reminded Pat of washing line; however, looks could be deceiving. In fact, the det cord's unassuming plastic-coated outer wrap was filled with powdered PETN high-explosive, which when linked to separate charges, once detonated; the blast wave would travel through the det cord, and explode everything together, virtually simultaneously. Charlie was feeding the det cord towards the other two troopers standing at the front of the flat-bed wagon. Startled out of concentration by Pat's hail, he looked up from his task, and said.

'*Yeah*... it's all going very well.'

Pat nodded and enquired,

'How long before you're finished?'

Charlie thought for a moment,

'Oh, another five minutes or so tops. Most of the work is already done...I've just got to remount the pipes, connect everything together with det cord, and run a final check.'

Eying the fast disappearing sun, Pat said,

'Right, crack on then. As soon as you've finished, grab the others and come over for the final briefing as quick as you can, before it's too dark to see the model....'

'Sorted Pat; all ready, everything's done.'

Pat acknowledged Charlie's news, as his three troopers arrived. Despite their own fatigue, their spirits appeared high, but then, Pat thought; they knew what he had planned for the rebels waiting just a few miles away, at the border crossing.

Pat turned and stared at the civilians, who had obediently gathered in silence beside his model. Exhaustion and anxiety showed clearly on their drawn and haggard faces. The last four days and nights had taken their toll on each of them. They were all hungry, but it was lack of sleep, which was the problem. To untrained civilians, snatched cat-naps just weren't enough during the adrenaline fuelled last few days; he thought. Even Siobhán had lost her sparkle; she looked utterly spent, but Pat wasn't surprised. Although he was impressed with her efforts, he knew that like everyone else, she had been almost constantly awake, reassuring and supporting Morris' young photographer, who seemed to be surviving on the edge of physical and mental collapse. Morris looked equally drawn and ragged, and as surely as ever. The young doctor, judging by the dark circles under his eyes, needed safety, a hot meal and 24 hours of solid, uninterrupted sleep before Pat trusted him to prescribe anything stronger than an aspirin.

Like his own SAS troopers, Krutz was drawing heavily on his tough commando training, and used years of experience and hardship in the African bush as a bulwark to stay sharp. His alert posture showed he continued to successfully fight off the ravages of hunger and sleep deprivation. Despite the privations and horror, Krutz alone still stood tall among the civilians. Pat stared at the powerfully built man for a moment. He wondered how many times in the past, had Krutz given a final twilight briefing like this, before he had sent his own men into harm's way?

Now that they were all assembled, Pat picked up the long stick he had torn from a tree earlier. He pointed it towards his model, and began the introduction to his daring plan,

'Ladies and gentlemen; I know you are all extremely tired and hungry, but I want you to stay focused, and do your best to concentrate for the next few minutes on what I'm saying….' Pat's eyes flicked from one civilian to their neighbour, to make sure he had their full attention. Satisfied they were all listening; he said in a matter of fact voice, with a usual casual sniff,

'Right then folks, this is what we're going to do…'

Chapter Thirty-Five

Danny and Pat watched from the footplate, as the civilians climbed wearily over the steel sides and down into the ore wagon. It was almost dark, as the four wretched men and women sat down on the steel floor of the wagon. Krutz was with them, but still wearing his knapsack, he remained standing while he looked towards Pat and his driver.

Charlie and Spike were out of sight, crouched at the front of the engine. On a nod from Spike, they heaved upwards and unhooked the massive chains which held the train together, as they uncoupled the flat-bed wagon from the engine. Pat's plan to escape the Mai-Mai rebels hinged on it being free, and rolling away unfettered, when the time came.

Their task complete, Charlie and Spike ducked under the touching buffers and straightening, stepped out onto the ballast beside the waiting train. Hot steam escaped from the steam chests as they parted company. Spike headed back to his assigned position in the ore wagon, while Charlie walked around to the front of the flat-bed. Stepping over the rail, Charlie positioned himself squarely in front of the anti-tank mine, which his two friends had securely hung earlier against one of the front buffers. Checking the knotted end of the line of det cord he had prepared earlier was still held firmly in place; it was rammed in and taped securely into the anti-handling well on the side of the mine. Charlie licked his lips. He reached up and carefully removed the nail he had used as an improvised safety pin. Satisfied the device was now fully live; he stood back in the growing gloom and admired his handiwork. When the mine hit the rebel barricade, the enormous blast would hopefully destroy the obstruction, but also instantly run back up the det cord, and detonate the lethal array of explosives packed on the top and sides of the wagon's flat bed. Pat's idea to turn it into a rolling bomb was spectacular, Charlie thought. It was as simple, as it was deadly. Provided he'd followed Pat's instructions, and had done his job properly, the devices he connected together would destroy both the barricade, and any living thing within several hundred feet of the explosions.

When Pat had discussed his idea with Charlie earlier, Pat had stressed the importance of most of the mine's blast going forward into the barricade, rather than down into the rails and track bed. Designed normally to lay flat and focus the explosion upwards, Charlie was convinced that sideways-on, the powerful blast would go forward from the hanging mine, rather than downwards.

Charlie had fixed a claymore on each side of the flatcar, and packed his small supply of plastic explosive into the middle of six of the iron pipes. Spike and Danny had watched his efforts, and then stuffed each iron tube with pieces of stone ballast, taken from underneath the train. Their efforts formed a series of fat, double-ended shotgun barrels. Because everything was directional, having sited them carefully, Charlie was happy that the duel blasts and improvised shrapnel would fly forward and out to the sides of the exploding wagon, not backwards towards the engine and ore wagon.

Patting the anti-tank mine for luck, Charlie stepped back over the steel rail, and walked through the hissing steam. He gave Pat a thumbs-up, to signal all was ready as he passed by. As Charlie climbed up in the wagon behind him, Danny opened the fire box. Ignoring the cherry glow, and the intense blast of heat, he threw in more logs and quickly closed the small iron door with his boot. Looking up, he tapped the pressure gauge. The needle flickered on the red line. Turning to Pat, he said,

'The old girl's all steamed up, Pat, and about as ready as I can make her.'

Pat nodded. There was nothing to keep them here anymore. The remaining ammunition was equally redistributed; Krutz sat with Danny's AK across his knees, in his allotted corner of the ore wagon, and the flat car was primed and ready. Pat had two pistols tucked in his belt, and all the spare pistol magazines from the others. He rubbed his hands together and taking a last look outside, beyond the steam swirling from the loudly hissing engine. It was time to leave their final safe haven and take their chances; he said,

'OK, Danny, better open her up then. Come on mate... *let's go!*'

Danny nodded and reached for his controls. With a loud chug and hissing whoosh of steam, the old engine shuddered and began to roll forward. Above the growing din in the cabin, Pat shouted into Danny's ear,

'Keep it nice and steady Spike. We'll build up our speed gradually as we get closer to the border.'

Danny nodded. Apart from the bridge earlier, the track had proven to be in surprisingly good condition but then, Danny thought, it hadn't been used for over a decade.

In the ore wagon, no-one spoke at first. Krutz and the three troopers were sitting in each corner, with their backs jarring against the rusting steel walls. According to their leader, as he allocated tasks, their only job was to defend the civilians if things went wrong. With less than a full magazine of bullets each, it would be a short defence, Barney Morris thought miserably. He looked across the wagon to the nearest man, who he had first seen down the barrel of a gun in the hotel. His tired mind tried to remember; was it three, or four days ago?

'So who are you then, really,... SAS?'

Spike remained silent, and replied by returning nothing more than a cold stare. Krutz and the two women heard the reporter's question. Krutz noted the lack of response and smiled to himself. He had spent too long with the South African Special Forces before retirement, and what he had expected to be a quiet life heading up security on the Skeleton Coast, to doubt the truth of it for a second. Discussing membership of the elite wasn't done in public, especially with the press around, but he hoped he would have the chance for at least one beer with these very useful boys, before they went their separate ways. Provided of course, he thought ruefully, they managed to escape the clutches of the Ojukwu, and his murdering cut-throats. Krutz glanced over at the civilians. Strange how it had turned out, he thought. His specific orders from

London had been to abandon them to their own devices, but now, his own men were gone, and their fate had become inexorably bound to his own. Under a starry sky, within the claustrophobic confines of a dirty, ancient piece of rolling stock, which in most civilised countries would have long since been consigned to the scrap yard, each of their lives and futures would be decided within the next hour.

Danny was sitting opposite the two women. The nurse had her eyes closed. He caught Patti's half-open eye, and gave her a reassuring wink. Poor little cow, he thought. She looked vacant and utterly lost; clearly frightened out of her wits, and at the extreme end of her tether. Hardly surprising Danny though, after the trauma and horrors she had been exposed to since the arrival of the Mai-Mai.

Danny had taken life during Operation Windmill; experience had taught the whole of Two Troop the grim lesson, that it was the soldier's lot to face the inevitable choice; kill or be killed. Terrorists in London had forced them all to stare into death's ugly face, but never on the unimaginable scale of this God-forsaken, backwater wilderness. Spike bitterly told of the stomach-churning scenes he had witnessed in Kabbali. Charlie was struggling to get his head around the unbelievable brutality of this mindless, inter-tribal hatred. This was the twenty-first century; he reminded himself with growing disbelief, but right now, it felt like he was a player, living through some dark and terrible tragedy from ancient times.

Spike was trying not to think of the coming battle. He tried his best to cloud his mind with thoughts of girls, Tottenham football club and his civilian job working for BT. Despite his best efforts however, to the rhythmic chuff of the engine and the powerful reek of wood smoke, lulled by the constant click-clack of the wheels beneath the wagon; his mind kept returning to recent horrors, and the short, sharp engagement that awaited them soon.

Earlier, eyes narrowing, Spike had listened to Pat's private briefing with mounting satisfaction, as his sergeant's plan was laid before him, and his mates. Allowing another quick Chinese parliament at the end, Pat had asked for comments from his men, in case he had missed or forgotten something. Combat changes men in different ways. Vivid memories flashed through Spike's mind; of patrolling silently through Kabbali, the motorbike and the stark image of the dead girl. With an involuntary shudder, his voice filled with pure hatred. Brimming over with uncharacteristic malevolence, he snarled,

'Yeah, let's just hope we kill every one of those murdering, gutless fuckers....'

Sitting on one side of the rocking floor of the driver's cabin, Pat's eyes flicked from the glowing dial of his watch, to the map spread across his lap. If his sums were right, they were getting dangerously close to the border crossing. As he always did before an operation, he had spent the last thirty minutes, since they began the final leg of their journey, running the plan over and over in his mind, seeking the slightest weakness in it. Soon, they would be committed, and it would be too late to make any last-minute adjustments. As satisfied as he could be, Pat stood up and folded the map away. Stepping forward, he stood beside Danny, who kept his eyes glued on what he could see of the track ahead,

'I reckon the border is about a mile away, Danny. Start opening her up, a little at a time. I want full power when we reach the last downhill gradient.'

Keeping his eyes ahead, Danny nodded and opened the steam valve a little. Over his shoulder, he said,

'OK, Pat...understood.'

The rhythm of the engine changed. The tempo of the chuffs of smoke spewing from the shunting engine's soot blackened chimney increased slightly, as the train's speed began to increase. The others in the wagon behind Pat and Danny felt the vibrations change. Fingers gripped the pitted stocks of Russian-made assault-rifles tighter, as the civilians' defenders began to stir and stand up. Charlie looked towards the engine, and saw Pat hold up his hand, with his fingers extended. Nodding his understanding, Charlie turned and hissed,

'Get ready everybody.' He copied Pat's gesture. Hand up, all fingers extended, Charlie did his best to keep the tension he felt pounding in his temples out of his voice. He said quietly,

'Five minutes…

Chapter Thirty-Six

Bathed in pale moonlight, the General stared up at the temporary gallows, and his two gently swaying victims. He smiled to himself with satisfaction. It was a stark demonstration of his power over life-and-death in the region, to the U.N. soldiers who had looked on helplessly close by, as his men had hanged the screaming border guards earlier in the day. His brave warriors had whooped and danced with the pleasure of it. They jostled and crowded around the tall pole, yelling with delight and brandishing their weapons as their victims, securely bound, had kicked and danced while the life-force was choked from their writhing bodies. His gaze moved beyond the red and white barrier, and the high fences which marked the border. He had laughed aloud when he saw the shock and horror which registered on the anguished faces of the young Danish soldiers who wore blue helmets. Although only a handful, they would report his ruthless demonstration to the rest of the world; it would send a clear message to men who mattered, that he was not a leader to be trifled with. If he did not immediately earn the respect of other leaders, he would settle for their fear. Ojukwu spat contemptuously towards the Danes. The white men from far away were impotent, and stood powerless before him.

The cruel smile lingered on his face, as he returned his gaze to his own side of the border, and the ten posts which stood tall, and cast long shadows in the moonlight. He had ordered them erected close to the office building, before the sun set. The young white soldiers of the U.N. would see a much greater display of his awesome magical power, when the sun rose and gilded the distant mountains tomorrow. The General chuckled softly into the darkness. That of course, would happen only after the diamonds were safely recovered, and the white fugitives were in his custody. Calling to one of his immediate staff, he rumbled,

'Have my orders been passed to your men, Captain?'

The Mai-Mai officer replied respectfully,

'They have, Excellency. They are waiting beside the tracks, and will attack as soon as the train stops.'

The general's eyes narrowed,

'They understand that I want the whites alive; they are not to be harmed?' he growled.

Before he answered, the officer lifted his hand in the moonlight and touched the small ampoule of magic water, which hung around his neck. The phials had been distributed to him and his men by their mighty General, before the sun went down. The mystical charm was a powerful piece of their leader's witchcraft, which would protect his most loyal followers from enemy bullets. The magic of course was invisible; hidden somewhere in the muddy river water the phials contained. The charm would make him and his warriors invulnerable, when their time came to attack.

'Yes Excellency. I have ordered more than a hundred of my best men, to leave their guns behind and storm the train when it arrives.' With a knowing grin, he added, 'every single man knows you want the whites alive.'

Ojukwu nodded. Trifling pawns, he cared nothing for the lives of this man, or the Mai-Mai who would be sacrificed in the attack. The charms would protect some, and those they didn't could easily be replaced. He needed live prisoners for the ceremony at dawn. That was when he would take the hideous revenge, he has forsworn, against those who had defied him in front of his men, on the banks of the Mpana River. When he had planned the train's capture, he certainly didn't want the train blasted with RPGs, in case most of the whites were killed, and the diamonds scattered and lost. Some, perhaps many of his men would die, that much was certain, he mused, but with overwhelming numbers, he thought imperiously, it was inevitable that his men would sweep over the train like an unstoppable tidal wave.

Satisfied that everything was in order, General Ojukwu let out a sigh of contentment. Soon, he thought; with a new fortune to fund his war, the entire Congo would begin to tremble.

Aboard the train, Patti began to cry softly as the civilians lay down on the floor of the wagon. Barney Morris looked on and trembled with fear. He did as that arrogant bastard; the leader of the rescue party had told them all to do in the last briefing. Morris stuffed his fat fingers in his ears and left his mouth open. Farrell had warned them all of the dangers of explosive concussion, and protecting their delicate eardrums with their fingers was the best safeguard available. With his mouth open, Morris remembered, Farrell had said his lungs would not burst when the massive wave of overpressure hit them.

Under the shining moon, Pat and Danny were watching the track, and the slowly rising gradient ahead. The duel lines of rusted steel rails disappeared only a few hundred yards ahead. Beyond was the top of the ridge, and a dark, star-filled sky. Pat took a deep breath,

'That's it Danny! Once we crest the ridge, we go straight down towards the border.'

Danny swallowed and nodded. Pat slapped him hard on the shoulder,

'You know what to do?'

Pat noticed how pale his driver looked, as Danny nodded again,

'Right then, time to open the throttle wide.'

Licking his lips, Danny reached up to the steam valve, and cranked it open as far as it would turn.

The puffing engine responded immediately. Its rhythm changed, and the tempo of the vibrating train surged. Internal pressures escalated, as more steam flooded into the front drive pistons, hissing angrily in breaths of white steam as it was expelled like dragon's breath. Fresh clouds of dense black smoke poured from the little engine's chimney, and the rattling of wheels against rails increased along the length of the speeding train, with the sudden surge of extra speed.

Pat's eyes were glued to the fast-approaching ridge line.

'Fifty yards…forty yards…thirty. He yelled, *'get ready, Danny…almost there!'*

Suddenly, the train crested the ridge, and both men felt, through the floor of the driver's cabin, almost imperceptibly at first, the engine began to tilt forward. In a heartbeat, the train was rattling down the long gradient towards the border crossing.

In the clearing, the Mai-Mai tensed when they heard. Among them stood many brutal murderers, rapists and child killers, but as usual, all were liberally drugged with cocaine and hashish. The drugs made them eager to carry out their general's orders. Protected by the powerful magic of their suspended charms, they felt supreme and invincible. Every one of them eagerly awaited their officers' orders to storm the train, when it slowed in front of the barricade.

The train had almost reached the half-way point. It had picked up speed as it chugged and rattled down the gradient. In the moon's pale light, Pat could just make out the clearing ahead. With each turn of the wheels, the crossing became clearer. Pat's brow suddenly furrowed. There seemed to be a dark, seething mass of shadows on either side of the tracks ahead. With growing horror, Pat cursed; he realised what the shadows were massed ranks of Mai-Mai, silently waiting for them. Pushing the thought from his mind, Pat turned his head from the open window and yelled,

'NOW! Danny.'

Danny was ready. His hands moved in a blur, as he shut the steam valve and slammed the engine into reverse. In a shower of cherry red sparks, there was a sudden and deafening squeal from the rails and wheels underneath, as the engine and ore wagon juddered violently, and began to slow in clouds of swirling steam.

Still travelling at almost forty miles per hour, the unfettered flat-bed, loaded with its deadly cargo continued forward unchecked. As the train continued to slow behind it, the gap widened as it thundered down the gentle incline under its own momentum, gathering speed as it hurtled towards its target. The gap continued to widen; the flat-bed wagon was almost seventy yards ahead. Pat shouted again.

'OK, Danny, set her forward again... but not too fast!'

As the engine and ore wagon began to roll towards the crossing once again, the Mai-Mai ahead could hear the flat-bed, as it rumbled and roared towards them. When they stepped closer to the tracks in grinning anticipation, their arrogant confidence suddenly evaporated, as the closest of them realised something was terribly wrong. Confused, some rebels turned to shout a desperate warning, but they were too late.

The flat wagon thundered past them and rammed into the barricade with a blinding flash, and thunderous, ear shattering explosion. In a single moment, the barricade disintegrated into a swirling mass of smoke, splinters and smashed timbers, as the claymores detonated simultaneously with Charlie's improvised shotgun barrels. Stones, iron shrapnel and a lethal cloud of ball-bearings hissed through the air on both sides of the shattered barricade, smashing into the Mai-Mai, at point-blank range. They were cut down like wheat before the scythe. Torn, shredded bodies were hurled backwards into the air on either side of the flat-bed. Four tons of mangled flat-bed wagon spun through the air, and landed with a deafening crash beside the track, on a group of rebel officers who were blown off their feet by the enormous blast. One of the crushed bodies wore the stars of a General…

As the powerful echoes of the explosion began to fade, the distant reverberations were replaced by the groans of the dying and severely wounded. The ground beside the tracks, where the solid barricade had stood until only moments before, was stained with a blackened carpet of torn limbs, and flowed with rebel blood.

After the concussion, as the train approached the crossing, the men in the ore wagon leapt to their feet, expecting in seconds, to be fighting for their lives. In the moonlight, they paused, and breathlessly lowered their guns. All they could see in the eerie calm, under the haunted moonlight was shattered bodies, laying scattered everywhere. Charlie stared at the carnage caused by his handiwork with his mouth open. He knew his explosive skills had saved them all, but dear God, he thought, at a terrible cost.

His friend stood scowling beside him. Spike stared at the slain rebel with distain, as the train trundled slowly passed them. Like Pat and the others, he had no truck with political correctness, or the killing of so many murdering Mai-Mai scum. Realising they were safe, and remembering the horrors he had witnessed, he balled his fist. Pulling it smartly towards his chest, a single word escaped his lips,

"Yes!"

Pat and Danny had ducked; a moment before the barricade exploded. After shaking his head to clear the ringing concussion in his ears, Danny stood up and tended his controls; Pat snatched out both pistols; ready to defend the train and his charges with his last breath and bullet. Seeing the destruction, he relaxed a little. His plan had killed a lot of men, but he knew they were intent on killing him. It was the balance between life and death, and he sniffed dismissively. He stared with cold eyes at the carnage. Even to the battle-hardened veteran, it was unfortunate that the cost was so high; but for this successful mission, it's high price ultimately was paid in rebel blood.

Krutz was helping the two weeping women to their feet. Their cheeks stained with tears, both looked dishevelled and profoundly shaken, but at least they were alive. He turned and slid his knapsack onto his broad shoulders, and tightened the straps. The last few days decided his future for him. This would be his last adventure; he'd hand the diamonds to their rightful owners when the time came, resign from the Corporation, and head back to a quiet life on his farm in the Transvaal. Somehow, he thought, retirement suddenly looked like his only option.

Trembling, Barney Morris heaved himself up from the cold steel floor. Ignoring the other occupants, he stared in silence at the sea of bodies around them. He licked his lips. What an ending it would make, he thought, to the book he was going to get out of this mess.

As the train rumbled over the border, it squealed to a halt beside the waiting men wearing blue helmets. A powerful memory occurred to Pat Farrell, which made him find a faint smile, even after raining down so much death and destruction on Ojukwu, and his feral killers.

Years previously, when Pat joined the regular SAS, he had been about to depart on his first covert mission; parachuting into a dangerous hot-spot in the Middle East. His veteran patrol commander had surprised him, by giving the new boy some very sound advice, which Pat had never forgotten. It was how he dealt with missions, and helped at times like this; and afterwards, when he had to deal with the dark memories he knew would come later.

Rocky Blain had taken Pat aside; as they stood together in the darkness, on a cold and rainy RAF apron, waiting for the loadmaster's immanent order to board the aircraft. As Rocky tightened the last strap on his free-fall harness, he fixed Pat with steely eyes and whispered gruffly,

'Remember son; there's no glory in dying for your country…' with a knowing nod, as the order was given to board, he added over his shoulder.... 'It's definitely a much better idea to make your enemy die for his...'

THE END

Also by David Black

Playing for England

What makes a man even want to join the reserve SAS? - The famous British Special Forces Regiment whose selection process boasts more than a 90% failure rate.

In the Shadow Squadron series, Pat Farrell is David's fictional hero. But what of the men Pat leads?

David Black's book - **Playing for England** gives the reader a fascinating first-hand insight into the rigours of the selection and training process of those few men who earn the privilege of wearing the SAS Regiment's sandy beret and winged dagger cap badge.

Published on Amazon in Kindle Format & Paperback.

http://www.david-black.co.uk

Also by David Black

EAGLES of the DAMNED

It was autumn in the year AD 9. The summer campaigning season was over. Centurion Rufus and his battle-hardened century were part of three mighty Roman Legions returning to the safety of their winter quarters beside the River Rhine. Like their commanding General, the Centurion and his men suspected nothing.

Little did they know, but the entire Germania province was about to explode...

Lured into a cunning trap, three of Rome's mighty Legions were systematically and ruthlessly annihilated, during seventy-two hours of unimaginable terror and unrelenting butchery. They were mercilessly slaughtered within the Teutoburg, a vast tract of dark and forbidding forest on the northernmost rim of the Roman Empire.

Little could they have imagined, before they were brutally cut down, their fate had been irrevocably sealed, years earlier, by their own flawed system of provincial governance, and a rabid traitor's overwhelming thirst for vengeance. But how could such a military catastrophe have ever happened to such a well trained and superbly equipped army? This is their story...

http://www.david-black.co.uk

Also by David Black

THE GREAT SATAN

Shadow Squadron #1

In The Great Satan, the first of his compelling new Shadow Squadron series, author David Black has produced his own fictional nightmare scenario: What if the Iraqi weapons that were said to be dismantled in the late 1990s included the ultimate WMD? And what if the deposing of Saddam Hussein left one of his most ruthless military leaders still at large, and actively seeking a customer for Iraq's only nuclear bomb? . . .

Introducing Sgt Pat Farrell – Hard as nails ex-regular SAS, now leading the elite SAS reserve - Shadow Squadron.

Published on Amazon in Kindle Format & Paperback.

http://www.david-black.co.uk

COMING SOON!

Also by David Black

The Devil's Web

Shadow Squadron #3

Al Qaeda have been quietly potting their revenge, after the death of their Saudi-born, spiritual leader, Osama Bin-Laden. A simple bombing or assassination won't do in the eyes of Zahira Khan, Pakistan's sinister chief Al Qaeda facilitator and planner. Hate-filled and utterly ruthless, he has devised something terrible – Al-Amin (the faithful), which will rival or perhaps even surpass the 'Spectacular' 9/11 attack on New York's Twin Towers.

Can Sgt Pat Farrell and his reserve SAS Troop do the impossible, and thwart this diabolical plot, before acts of unspeakable horror are committed by men who welcome death?

The Devil's Web – Exclusive to Amazon and CreateSpace .

To be released soon!

http://www.david-black.co.uk

Also by David Black

Siege of Faith

The Chronicles of Sir Richard Starkey #1

Far to the East across the sparkling waters of the great Mediterranean Sea, the formidable Ottoman Empire was secretly planning to add to centuries of expansion. Soon, they would begin the invasion and conquest of Christian Europe.

But first, their all-powerful Sultan, Suleiman the Magnificent knew he must destroy the last Christian bastion which stood in the way of his glorious destiny of conquest. The Maltese stronghold... garrisoned and defended by the noble and devout warrior monks of the Knights of St. John of Jerusalem...

A powerful story of heroism, love and betrayal set against the backdrop of the cruel and terrible siege of Malta which raged through the long hot summer of 1565. The great Caliph unleashed a massive invasion force of 40,000 fanatical Muslim troops, intent on conquering Malta before invading poorly defended Christian Europe. A heretic English Knight - Sir Richard Starkey becomes embroiled in the bloody five month siege which ensued; Europe's elite nobility cast chivalry aside, no quarter asked or mercy given as rivers of Muslim and Christian blood flowed...

http://www.david-black.co.uk

Also by David Black

Inca Sun

Chronicles of Sir Richard Starkey #2

Sir Richard and his giant servant Quinn begin their next great adventure, aboard the Privateer 'The Intrepid', in the treacherous waters off the Caribbean and South America coastline. Their heretic English Queen Elizabeth I has secretly commanded Sir Richard to prowl the high seas in search of King Phillip II of Spain's fabulously wealthy treasure convoys. They sail from the New World for Spain laden with gold and silver ripped from the Conquistador's mines in Peru and Mexico; dug from the dark earth by their cruelly treated Inca and Mayan slaves.

What Richard doesn't know, when he accepts his latest Royal commission, is that his arch nemesis - Don Rodrigo Salvador Torrez has become Governor of King Phillip's Mexican province of Veracruz.

One thing is certain, mere gold cannot pay the debt of honour that exists between the two men, since their first encounter on Malta during the great siege. The only currency which will settle the terrible debt will be the loser's noble lifeblood....

http://www.david-black.co.uk

Published on Amazon in Kindle Format & Paperback.

Printed in Great Britain
by Amazon